FIELDS OF GLORY

Also by Michael Jecks

The Last Templar
The Merchant's Partner
A Moorland Hanging
The Crediton Killings
The Abbot's Gibbet
The Leper's Return
Squire Throwleigh's Heir
Belladonna at Belstone
The Traitor of St Giles
The Boy Bishop's Glovemaker
The Tournament of Blood
The Sticklepath Strangler
The Devil's Acolyte
The Mad Monk of Gidleigh
The Templar's Penance
The Outlaws of Ennor
The Tolls of Death
The Chapel of Bones
The Butcher of St Peter's
A Friar's Bloodfeud
The Death Ship of Dartmouth
The Malice of Unnatural Death
Dispensation of Death
The Templar, the Queen and Her Lover
The Prophecy of Death
The King of Thieves
The Bishop Must Die
The Oath
King's Gold
City of Fiends

MICHAEL JECKS

Fields of Glory

**SIMON &
SCHUSTER**

London · New York · Sydney · Toronto · New Delhi

A CBS COMPANY

First published in Great Britain by Simon & Schuster UK Ltd, 2014
A CBS COMPANY
Copyright © Michael Jecks 2014

1 3 5 7 9 10 8 6 4 2

Simon & Schuster UK Ltd
1st Floor
222 Gray's Inn Road
London WC1X 8HB

www.simonandschuster.co.uk

Simon & Schuster Australia, Sydney
Simon & Schuster India, New Delhi

A CIP catalogue record for this book is available from the British Library

HB ISBN: 978-1-47111-106-8
TPB ISBN: 978-1-47111-107-5
EBOOK ISBN: 978-1-47111-109-9

Typeset by Hewer Text UK Ltd, Edinburgh
Printed and bound in Great Britain by CPI (UK) Ltd, Croydon CR0 4YY

For my parents, Beryl and Peter,
with much love.
A new direction . . .

And

For Andy and Mandy
in the hope this may distract you both from
the events of the last horrible couple of years.
Lots of love.

CAST OF CHARACTERS

Sir John de Sully	Knight Banneret from Devon
Richard Bakere	Esquire to Sir John
Grandarse	under Sir John, the Centener: leader of a hundred men
Berenger Fripper	the leader of one vintaine of twenty men under Grandarse

Members of Berenger's vintaine:
Clip
Eliot
Jack Fletcher
Jon Furrier
Gilbert 'Gil'
Luke
Matt
Geoff atte Mill
Oliver
Walt
Will 'The Wisp'

Ed 'The Donkey'	orphan found by the vintaine in Portsmouth
Roger	vintener of the second vintaine
Mark Tyler/Mark of London	Roger's most recent recruit
Archibald Tanner	a 'gynour' trained in gunpowder and cannon
Erbin	leader of a party of Welsh fighters
Dewi and **Owain**	Welshmen under Erbin
King Edward III	King of England
King Edward II	the King's predecessor, rumoured to have died in Berkeley Castle
King Philippe VI	King of France
Edward of Woodstock	son of Edward III, later known as 'the Black Prince'
Earl Thomas of Warwick	a noted peer of the realm and Marshal of England
Béatrice Pouillet	daughter of a gunpowder merchant in France

AUTHOR'S NOTE

In those far-off days when I was still at school, I was a member of a book club that was devoted to non-fiction books on warfare, and bought vast numbers from them. They remain on my book-shelves, the greater part of them very well-thumbed and yellowed, but all offering a haven of peace whenever I need it. Lyn MacDonald's *They Called It Passchendaele* (which I read when only eleven), books on the Somme, Max Hastings' *The Korean War*, and books about the Das Reich Panzer Division and Bomber Command – they are still there in front of me as I type this.

But one in particular, sadly, is missing. It was a title I enjoyed so much that I kept offering it to other people to read. One of them took it – and lost it. I have mourned the loss of that book for many years. It was *The Hundred Years War* by Desmond Seward, first published by Constable in 1978. I must have bought my copy in about 1983 or so, and I read it twice, back to back, in my cottage in Oxted, Surrey.

The book is a gem of concise, undramatic but enthralling writing. So much so that I was forced to buy a new copy as soon as I was able to do so. Of course, it's not the only book on the Hundred Years War, and, if I'm brutally honest, it's probably not the best. There are many other titles, from Jonathan Sumption's superb studies of the same subject to books by experts like Terry Jones (I have sung his praises many times before, but I'll do it again: if you haven't read *Chaucer's Knight: Portrait of a Medieval Mercenary* it is high time you did) – but it was Seward's book that fired my imagination in the first place. It was his book that persuaded me to find out more about this terrible time, and his book that inspired me to write about the Battle of Crécy.

It is difficult to write a book that includes the lives of real people.

In Medieval Murderers, the performance group I founded more than a decade ago, we have had many debates about whether or not to use real characters from history. When I set out to create my medieval world, I was determined not to look at matters from the point of view of real characters, because I had a secret dread of someone doing that to me. I could all too easily envisage a time when someone read an article on their . . . what will it be in a few hundred years? On their wall? In their retina? Well, no matter where they would see it, they would read about this fellow Jecks who was alive in the early twenty-first century, and might want to write about him. They would have him as a witty, clever fellow, no doubt. Fair enough. And a criminal investigator. And they would state that I was vegan, teetotal, a cat-loving, anti-hunting, football-supporting campaigner for the European Union. In short, I would have to give up my proud disdain for all things psychic and take up haunting the foul blighter for his or her calumnies.

You can see why I did not want to take a real person and infuse them with my own feelings, beliefs and prejudices. It just wouldn't be fair. A kind of 'post-mortem slander'. That is why, in my earlier books, although I make some use of characters like Walter Stapledon, I don't look at the world through his eyes. He is simply included because he was there, in Exeter, at the time. I couldn't ignore him.

However, over time my attitude has changed. There are some situations which do need the perspective of key players. And for this book, I chose a man who has fascinated me for many years: Sir John de Sully.

If you look him up on the internet, you will find his life documented at the website for the *Collegiate Church of the Holy Cross and the Mother of Him Who Hung Thereon* in Crediton (*http://www.creditonparishchurch.org.uk/Sully.html*).

An extraordinary man, Sir John was questioned in his one hundred and sixth year, because of a dispute between two other knights about the arms they were allowed to display. He died, apparently, the following year. But in his long life, he had survived battles all through the Edwardian period, from (probably) Bannockburn through to Najera. That means that the last time he went to war in armour, he was some eighty-six years old.

His character can only be guessed at. In reality, of course, he was probably a hugely aggressive man, arrogant, proud and independent: a terrible enemy. But he came from Devon, too, and I have deliberately made him a more complex fellow and not a mere brute.

Above all, this is the story of a vintaine. A small group of Englishmen in a foreign land, fighting and killing and dying for a cause which they only dimly understood. But they knew that there was money to be looted, that there were women, and there was wine. They were not saints. Soldiers rarely are. But what they achieved was astonishing, and for that, if nothing else, they deserve admiration.

The Battle of Crécy has always been a source of argument. Firstly because most historians find it inconceivable that the commander of such a relatively small force could have deliberately sought to meet the full might of the massive French army in battle; secondly because there has been hot debate over the precise battle-formation used by the English during that battle.

I do not presume to argue the cases either way. You can find the arguments marvellously summarised in *War Cruel and Sharp* by Clifford J. Rogers, Boydell Press, 2000. In Chapter 10 'Invasion of 1346: Strategic Options and Historiography', he goes through them on both sides in some detail. However, it seems clear to me that the English King Edward III would have known that he ran the significant risk of battle by taking war to the north of France. He had tweaked the French King's tail too often already to think he would escape unhindered once more. The prestige of Philippe VI was at stake.

For my story, I have assumed that the argument from Rogers's book is correct: that the English King *knew* he would force the French to battle and was confident nonetheless, convinced that his massed archers would be so overwhelming that the French must be crushed. He suffered setbacks, true, especially on the long march to the Somme, but I believe he had a strategic ambition to draw the French to him on well-prepared ground in a planned manner.

The second issue has given me a great deal more heartache than the simple question of whether the English intended to fight. *How did King Edward dispose his troops?*

I have resorted to many books in researching the battle, from Jonathan Sumption's superb *Trial By Battle*, Rogers's *War Cruel and Sharp* mentioned above, J.F. Verbruggen's *The Art of Warfare in Western Europe*, Maurice Keen's *Medieval Warfare*, Kelly DeVries's *Infantry Warfare in the Early Fourteenth Century . . .* all the way to Ian Mortimer's *The Perfect King: The Life of King Edward III*, with stop-offs at Froissart and other chroniclers.

Some think that there were three battles (groups of fighting men, in modern terms 'Battalions' is the nearest word), with English soldiers spread side-by-side over the top of the hill, with groups of archers between these groups of men, and more archers at either side. I disagree, and side with those who consider the next scenario more likely: that the English had the three battles one placed before the other, and with two large groups of archers at either flank with cannon, so as to keep up a withering fire both on the killing ground before them on the plains, and, as the enemy grew nearer, launching their weapons and missiles directly into the flanks of the French advance. Not only is this the most likely formation to have achieved the victory won at such low cost to the English – but also it was the formation practised and rehearsed in so many prior battles.

But after all my research, there is still a margin for error. I have occasionally guessed at mysteries such as, where precisely was Sir John in the battle-line? – and where my guesses have missed their mark, I can only apologise. Any errors are my own.

This story, then, is the story of soldiers through the centuries, and I have unashamedly used scenes as described by George MacDonald Fraser in his magnificent autobiography *Quartered Safe Out Here*, as well as many contemporary accounts. The story of fighting men, and their experiences in battle, has not changed all that much. Their lives are full of fear, boredom, misery and sudden horror. But they also enjoy making jokes at each others' expense, and gradually they learn to trust and rely on one another.

Finally, I should say that when I was writing this, I had in my mind the young men and women who are fighting with the British Army in Afghanistan.

May they all return safe and well.

Michael Jecks
North Dartmoor
January 2013

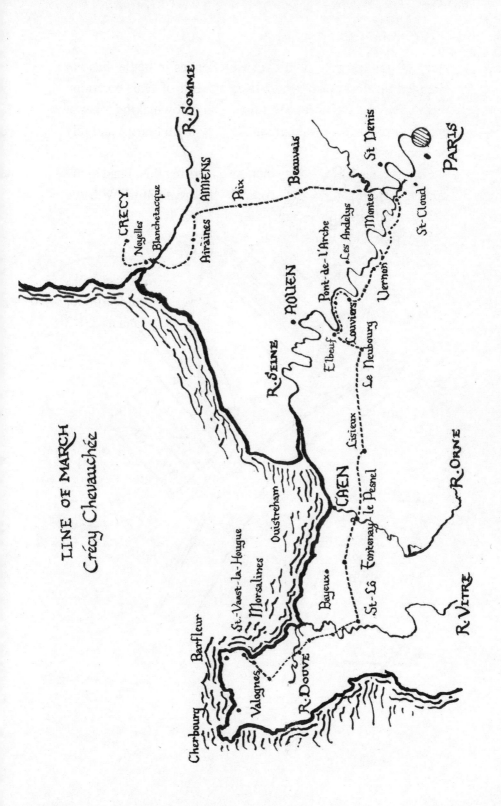

LINE OF MARCH
Crécy Chevauchée

R. SOMME

CRÉCY
Noyelles
Blanchetacque
Amiens
Airaines
Poix
Beauvais
St Denis
PARIS
St-Cloud
Mantes
Vernon
Les Andelys
Pont-de-l'Arche
Louviers
ROUEN
R. SEINE
Elbeuf
Le Neubourg
Lisieux
CAEN
Fontenay-le-Pesnel
Ouistreham
Bayeux
St-Lô
Morsalines
St-Vaast-la-Hougue
Valognes
R. DOUVE
Barfleur
Cherbourg
R. ORNE
R. VITRE

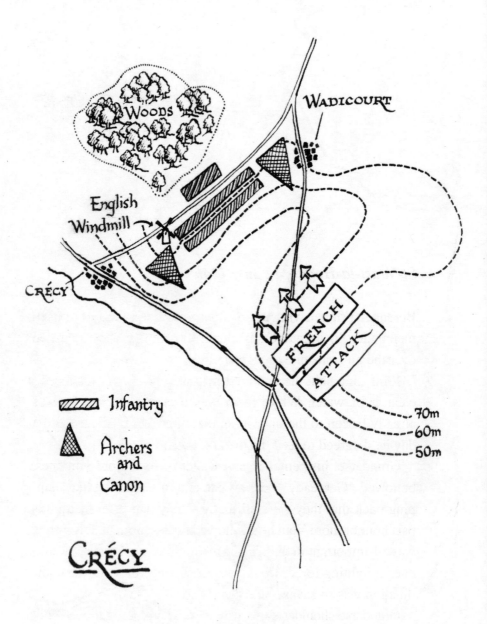

Woods

WADICOURT

English
Windmill

CRÉCY

FRENCH ATTACK

70m
60m
50m

▨ Infantry

▲ Archers
and
Canon

CRÉCY

CHAPTER ONE

St-Vaast-la-Hogue, 12 July 1346

Berenger Fripper, vintener of this pox-ridden mob of sixteen men under Sir John de Sully, ducked as another wave splashed over the gunwale and drenched him.

'Shit, shit, shit,' he muttered, wiping a hand over his face to clear it of water. White foam was everywhere, and he was already frozen to the marrow in the bitter wind. He cursed the day he'd agreed to lead the men on this raid.

Grandarse, his centener, and leader of four more vintaines, bellowed, 'Get ready!' near his ear, and Berenger felt like snapping back that they *were* all ready – they had been ready this past hour or more – but he swallowed his resentment. Discipline was all-important in the army. Any diminution of respect weakened a fighting force, which was why punishment for insubordination was so savage, and rightly so.

Grandarse shouldered his way past. The older man was built like a barrel, with a belly that declared his love of ale and food.

His eyes were blue like the sky, his skin leathery from living rough, marching for his King. He was a hard man, used to the ways of war, but the Yorkshireman was honest enough, and kindly to men he trusted. He respected Berenger's men: such fellows were the backbone of the King's army, and Grandarse knew it.

Another big wave, another wipe of his face. Berenger hated ships. This was no way to go to war. The rolling decks and constant spray, the sound of horses whinnying, almost scream-ing in fear belowdecks, the constant taste of sickness in his throat and the smell of vomit all about him . . . it all reminded him of Sluys, two years before. *Christ's ballocks*, that had been a fight! He was an old man now. Already six and thirty, and a fighter for his King for the last eleven years. He knew he shouldn't feel such trepidation at the prospect of battle.

Yet he did.

He shifted the strap of his pack where it had rubbed a sore patch at his collarbone. The salt in the air was making it sting. Another wave crashed at the side of the ship, spume exploding into his face and beard, and he swore viciously.

Beside him, young Ed was kneeling and retching, his belly emptied many long hours before.

'Get up, boy!' Berenger snarled. 'You want to kneel when the French come and beat you all about your bleeding head?'

He hauled on the boy's arm until Ed was up and could lean on the wale himself, his fist clenched in white determination about a rope.

An odd boy. Too young for this kind of fight, Berenger told himself again. The lads had thought he'd make them a good mascot if nothing else.

They had found him lying in the gutter outside a Portsmouth tavern, dazed from the blow that had broken his tooth and bloodied his face. If he was the victim of a robbery, the thief had poor judgement in selecting his victims. A lad that old could have little indeed worth taking. Clip had wanted to see if he had any money, but Geoff shouldered him aside and picked up the pathetic bundle, carrying Ed back to their lodgings with a gentleness that surprised the other men. With luck, Geoff said defensively, the boy'd earn his keep by fetching and carrying. They could do with a lad to bring arrows or water in battle, and bear food on the march.

Well, that was as may be. As far as Berenger was concerned, Ed was a waste of space. He was a boy, and they needed men. Grandarse didn't care: he would get money for the extra head, and that was all *he* cared about; but Berenger felt responsible for the fellow. Just now the boy's head hung low, drool trailing from his chin. How, in God's name, the son of a fisherman could be so useless and pukey on board a ship, he didn't know. The lad was the most cack-handed prick he had ever met. He wouldn't meet Berenger's eyes but stood shivering, staring miserably at the land ahead, as did all the others.

'Not long now,' Berenger said, more kindly.

The others, he thought. They had all survived the sailing, thank the Lord. His glance ran over the vintaine. Although he wouldn't let it show, Berenger felt a flare of pride to be leading them. At least they were all fighting men.

Beside him, Grandarse stood rolling with the deck, hoarsely singing a crude marching song, his enormous belly constrained by his thick leather belt. Behind him stood Geoff, the square-faced, impassive son of a miller from Tewkesbury, flanked by the lanky form of the grey-eyed Jack Fletcher and the shorter, wiry Will the Wisp. Wisp was scrawny and looked always on the verge of toppling over, but he had muscles like steel cords and could have been pegged to the deck.

Behind him, lumbering helplessly from one man to another with every plunge of the ship, and swearing all the while, was Clip, the shortest of them all. Clip had the pinched wizened features of a beggar. This last winter, the scurvy had laid hold of him, and now he had few teeth remaining. His brown eyes were red-tinged, and he tried to cower behind Wisp, keeping his scrawny arse sheltered from the water, but was flung around by the power of the waves like a rag doll.

And then there were the others: Jon Furrier with the dropped shoulder, the always-limping Eliot, Oliver with the squint and fretful chewing of his inner lip, Matt, Walt, Luke and Gilbert and the rest. All waiting, all watching, veterans of battles in France and Scotland. Geoff met Berenger's eyes and nodded, his mouth twisted at one side as usual. They would soon be fighting: the King had promised them. This was to be the chevauchée that proved once and for all that the English King was rightful King of France as well.

Well, so long as there was wine and plunder in it, the men would be content: him too. Berenger narrowed his eyes against the spray. Since his parents' death four and twenty years ago, he had spent his life searching for adventure. Now, perhaps, it was time to stop. He could buy a little house, find a woman. Brew ale, make friends, raise children. Aye – *mayhap!* he told himself sardonically.

There was a moment or two of peace. Shipmen were up at the sail, hauling for dear life, and on a series of commands from the shipmaster, the vessel began to wallow, her speed cut as the sails were reefed. Soon they would be at the shore, and the tension amongst the ship's company increased dramatically as they prepared to disembark. Bags and blankets were hefted, personal weapons tested in their sheaths, and men muttered prayers. Two near Berenger were murmuring as the beads of their rosaries slipped through their fingers.

Berenger could see the waves ahead battering at the shallow sands. At least the rocks were over to the west of them now. This shoreline looked safer, with smoothly shelving sands that rose up gently to meet the small houses of the town itself. Berenger caught a glimpse of a steeple, a little row of fishermen's houses, a low breakwater that enclosed a wide port, but then another wave was hurled into his face and blinded him. When he could look again, the beach was much closer.

'*Ready!*' he shouted, and as he looked across at his men one last time, the ship struck.

There was a graunching rasp from deep within the bowels of the vessel, a sound felt through the feet, as though a monster was tearing through the hull. He was thrown onto Ed, the weight of the men behind them crushing them both. The planks of the deck were slick with water and piss and vomit and his boots slipped, but then the vessel lurched once more, and he found his foot struck the hull, and he could stand again.

'*With me!*' Berenger heaved himself onto the wale and stared down at the sea below. Beside him, Ed gaped at the drop before them. Berenger grunted to himself, hauled the lad to the gunwale and pushed him over, before closing his eyes and leaping down himself, grasping his sword's hilt as he went. '*Come on, you sons of whores!*'

It was further than he had realised, a good eight or nine feet, and the sea was five feet deep. His ankle twisted on a rock, but he refused to acknowledge the dull pain. Ed was already halfway to dry land, floundering through the surf, and Berenger made his way after him, splashing water high on each side as he swaggered towards the welcoming sands, sword held up at shoulder height. He'd have to clean and dry the blade, he told himself, and his pack would be soaked through. Ah, God, but it would be good to be on solid ground again! That ship had been an instrument of torture. He would never go aboard a ship again, not if he could avoid it.

The waves sucked at his hosen as though trying to drag him under – but then he was into the shallows and up onto the sand. There was no time to pause here. He had his orders: his vintaine was to run on ahead and keep any enemy away while a bridge-head was established.

His world was yet rolling about him. It was as if the land was still moving like the boat, and he had to fix his stare on the men jumping from the ships and making their way towards him to force his mind to accept that he was at last free from that tub.

'Hoy, Fripper! Get your men up to the dunes there!' Grandarse roared.

Berenger nodded, and urged the men on with him, scrambling up the sand. Soon he and the others were huddled on a hillock from where they could see the land before them, while also watching the ships unloading their cargoes of men and matériel.

'Have they all run away?' Ed asked. He was shivering as he gazed about him. All around, the countryside looked empty. A flat land with thin reedy grasses stretched away into the distance; only a few thick stands of trees distracted his eye. One wood stood a short distance away to their right, while on the left was a village. He could see a church looming high over the huddle of buildings, but to his relief, there was no one about.

'Aye, boy,' Geoff chuckled drily, his face pulling oddly as he smiled. His jaw had been broken years before in a battle and had never properly mended. Ever since, his voice had been sibilant and slurred. 'They heard you were coming, and hared off before you could get to them.'

Berenger grinned to himself. Geoff was built like a bull. His arms thick as sacks of grain, his thighs the size of young oaks, and as strong. If the French were to run from anyone, it would be him. Geoff's shrewd grey eyes were wrinkled in humour now as he glanced at the boy.

'When will they come, then?' Ed wanted to know. He was thirteen or so, a thin-faced boy with pale brown hair cut ragged and eyes that slid away rather than meet another's.

Berenger shrugged. 'When they're ready, boy.'

Their personal gear was piled on the sand, while Clip knelt, muttering under his breath, trying unsuccessfully to strike a spark from flint and dagger to light a fire from the driftwood piled all about.

'Get a move on, Clip. You think those French buggers will wait until you're good and ready for 'em?' Matt joked.

'If ye think ye can light it faster, then you do it!' Clip said with exasperation. 'Come here and demonstrate your wondrous skills. Happen, if you breathe and fart on it, your hot air and wind will light the tinder faster than my flint.'

Clip's constant whine grated, but the others had grown accustomed to it over the years and now they laughed. He had kept up his customary wheedling and complaining through both misery and joy, and was unlikely to change now.

'Just hurry up,' Berenger said, wrapping his arms about his damp torso. 'I need some warmth.'

'We'll be hot enough when the French army arrives,' Jack said, and with that, the vintaine fell silent, stilled as they gazed at the lands all about them. Somewhere, out there, was an army preparing to throw them back in the sea.

CHAPTER TWO

Sir John de Sully took the pewter goblet from his esquire and drank deeply.

At five-and-sixty years old, Sir John was the oldest knight here. His first battle had been that bloody fiasco in Scotland, when the late King Edward II of inglorious memory had seen his men baffled by the traitor Bruce in the boggy wastes beside the Bannockburn. It was not a battle Sir John liked to recall. A knight should remember victories, not shameful disaster.

He grunted and rubbed at his knee. A pain there had come on during the voyage – a tight stabbing whenever he bent his leg. He had massaged the area with goose fat, but it seemed to do little good. He would speak to a leech when he found time.

It was the way of things. He was an old man, and should have been pensioned off like an ancient warhorse by now: he would have been, were it not for the reputation he had gained. Sir John had been present at all the crucial battles since 1314. Sometimes he thought he was brought along because his kings viewed him as a mascot of good fortune. But while he had earned his retirement, there was a restlessness in his soul. His sword and mace had stabbed and crushed many skulls, but as soon as he had learned of this latest adventure, he had jostled for a place in the army.

It was where he belonged.

'Sir, your horse is ready,' Richard Bakere, his esquire, said.

Sir John tossed back his wine. 'And so begins our campaign,' he grunted as he made his way to the ladder at the forecastle.

'Yes, sir,' said Bakere.

Bakere had been his esquire for six years now – a reliable young man, the son of a local baron, and determined to serve. Sir John knew the value of a trustworthy esquire, especially in times like this, when the trumpets blew.

Sir John was lucky, living far from London in his two manors of Rookford and Iddesleigh. There he had been insulated from the King's early years when young Edward III had been under the control of the avaricious Sir Roger Mortimer. But even there, ripples from the political storms had been felt. Afterwards King Edward had been forced to impose his will on the realm, going to the extreme of creating a new chivalric Order. It was enough to make older barons roll their eyes. A knight needed no fripperies of that sort: he only required a sharp sword.

He'd seen enough kings: Edward I, the great warrior; his deplorable son, the second Edward. The barons had finally taken offence at his ridiculous extravagances – and those of Sir Hugh le Despenser, his reviled friend. *There* was a man who deserved his end, Sir John thought: hacked apart by a Hereford butcher.

And now there was this third Edward. A man who believed in his 'destiny', and the prophecies that foretold his future: a 'Boar', like the 'Boar from Cornwall', it was said – King Arthur. He would be a great war-leader, and wear the three crowns of the Holy Roman Empire, and when he died, he would be buried in Cologne with the three Magi, who were also buried there.

'Ballocks!' Sir John muttered.

The King wanted glory, and a glory-seeker was dangerous to all around him. Worse, Sir John was commanded to guard the King's son, young Edward of Woodstock, which was sure to prevent Sir John from winning a good prize. Still, a knight's first duty was *service*, as that of the people was to labour.

Since the King had laid claim to the crown of France, the people could understand the reasons behind his crippling taxes. Nobody liked to give away a tenth of their wealth, but they could see their money going to the purchase of millions of arrows, tens of thousands of bow-staves and strings, supplies for siege engines, for wagons, carts and victuals.

For although their King had come to France with the intention of proving his mettle many times in the last ten years, each time the French had retreated and refused his challenges, no matter how small the English forces. Instead, the French burned the lands all about, starving the English of supplies and forcing them to retreat while their King watched like the snake he was. Wary, cunning and duplicitous, Philippe waited, refusing the English the chance of an honourable settlement. It was shameful.

Well, this time – *this time* – they *would* fight. Young King Edward would force a battle, and then perhaps he'd stop squeezing cash from poor rural knights like Sir John.

Sir John's face twisted in a sardonic grin. Aye, and pigs might sprout wings.

As his ship heeled over, Archibald Tanner, the man nicknamed 'the Serpent' or 'the Gynour', amongst several less complimentary epithets, stared back past the ships waiting their turn to beach themselves, his hand resting on the nearest little barrel. It was coopered with hoops of willow rather than iron, an essential safety requirement – for a careless spark struck from a flint against a steel hoop would see the whole ship blasted to splinters. Those innocuous little barrels were filled with black powder.

Up here, he had a fine view of the water, and *Christ's pains*, it was hard to credit his eyes. He had never imagined that the King could command so many ships. They filled the bay as far as a man could see, bright flags fluttering gaily in the breeze, crimson, gold and blue. And on board, he had heard, there were some fifteen thousand souls – knights, men-at-arms, hobelars archers and infantry – a vast number of men and beasts.

Archibald shook his bald head, his thick, greying beard moving with the wind. He wore his customary leather coif, a kerchief about his throat, and a thick sleeveless leather jack with a linen chemise beneath, all pocked and blackened with scorch-marks. Feeling for his short sword, he patted the cross and grinned. He was going to show the men here that a new age was dawning. Archers and knights belonged to the past. His was the new way of war, for Archibald, the Serpent, was a master of powder: black powder, the Serpentine powder that, when carefully tamped and rested, could hurl a stone ball or metal dart for hundreds of yards. With his little cannons firing balls of two and three inches diameter, he could destroy gates, walls, even men, in an onslaught that would send the King's enemies fleeing in fear.

It would be a hard task, but the gynour was confident. He would be crucial to the King's success. There was no doubt about that.

Rubbing his grimy face, he turned to see two sailors manhandling one of his barrels up a plank, ready to drop it.

His face darkened instantly. 'Hoy, you lurdans, take care with that! It's worth more to the King than you and your entire ship! Damage that or break the barrel, and your head'll be on a spike by evening as a sign to all fools to be more careful!'

He didn't point out that first the executioner would have to find all their body parts. If they carelessly struck a spark from their hobnailed boots and had a keg of his black powder blow up in their hands, a man would be hard put to find any pieces of them bigger than a penny piece.

Sir John de Sully stood impatiently while casks and bales of provisions were laboriously offloaded.

It was vital to get the horses and men off the ships so that the beach-head could be defended. While he stood watching, ship-men began to attack the caulking. The cog had massive doors in the hull to give access to the hold, and from here the horses could be released. Seals formed of thick ropes soaked in tar were pulled away, then the thicker pitch was scraped away with chisels, until the doors were exposed and the horses within could be seen.

They were led one at a time down the ramp, to be saddled by grooms at the water's edge. As Sir John watched, one of them slipped on the ramp, falling with a whinny of pain, plunging and rearing in the water. A hoof caught a groom, who fell instantly, his body bobbing on the water with arms outstretched like a crucifix, the blood swirling about his crushed head and turning the foam pink. The horse was eventually calmed, but the next too slid off the ramp, and this one broke a leg. The beast was brought limping to the shore, where a farrier felt the leg, then stood back and pole-axed it.

Not Sir John's brute, thank the Lord.

His own horse came down next: Aeton. The great destrier was jerking his head up and down to tug his reins from the hands of the swearing shipmen. He was ever a vicious brute: keen to trample a man or bite his hand. In battle, he became almost uncontrollable, even when Sir John sat in the saddle attired in full armour. Aeton was born, and lived, only for battle.

'Here, Aeton. Soon you will have enemies aplenty even for the fire in your belly,' the man said with gruff affection. He took the halter and led Aeton away from the rolling thunder of the waves at the shore, through a milling pack of hounds, and past the horse slain by the farrier. At its side, a man-at-arms stood with tears flowing as he gazed down at the body of his mount. There would soon be many more mourning their horses, but no one mourned the groom dead in the water, Sir John noted. It was natural enough. Every one of the men knew that they were here to fight, and possibly die. A horse could help them win victory, but one dead man was merely a corpse.

Further up the beach, Berenger was past caring about the threat of a French army or even the rigours of command. Just now, all he cared about was Clip's fire-making. After his immersion, he shivered with every breath of wind.

The armada had sailed in absolute secrecy. Only the King and his closest advisers knew their destination. If the ships were separated, each shipmaster had written instructions as to where to rendezvous, but because of the risk of spies their letters were to be kept sealed until needed. To maintain that secrecy, the King had commanded that no ships were to leave English ports for another week after the fleet sailed. He did not want a captured Portsmouth fisherman giving away news of the fleet's destination.

Of course, amongst the sailors and men rumours of their landing-place had abounded, but Berenger was not convinced until he saw the stores being brought aboard. He had spoken to an old shipman, who told him knowledgeably that with all those goods the King must be intending a two-week journey at least.

'There's only one place takes that long,' the old tar said knowingly. 'Guyenne. You'll be out there before long, boy. Burning your balls in the Gascon sun.' He hawked and spat, and his faded blue eyes seemed to stare into the distance, past the grey, overcast sky and the steady rain. 'You lucky bastard.'

'My *arse*,' Berenger muttered to himself.

Geoff heard him and threw him an enquiring glance.

'I thought we were going to the south, to Guyenne,' Berenger explained.

'This isn't?'

'No. This is Normandy,' Berenger said, keeping his eyes fixed on the country ahead. He was sure that any attack would come from either the village or the woods. Both areas would afford concealment to enemy forces gathering to confront them. 'We weren't at sea long enough for Guyenne.'

As Berenger watched, more ships were beached. Four or five had disgorged troops, who had already grabbed their favourite weapons and trotted away towards the fishermen's cottages. Just out to sea were more round-bellied cogs, their masts swaying like storm-tossed tree-tops in a forest. There were more vessels than Berenger could count: hundreds. It would take days to empty them all. He only hoped that their bows and arrows would be brought to them before they were on the receiving end of an attack.

The beach looked frantic. Berenger remembered an evening once, when a fire took hold in a tavern. Drunken men hurtled about, grabbing buckets, pots, even coifs and hats, anything that would hold water to fight the fire.

There was the same urgency here. Men went scurrying, some to establish forward pickets while others brought weapons. Haste was in every man's heart; all were aware of the ever-present risk of attack. Some had tied ropes between two wagons, and soon fifteen horses were tethered there. Before long, a group of men-at-arms were mounted and ordered to scour the countryside for news of the French. A knight with light mail and a helm was commanding the men.

'Who's that?' Ed asked. He had walked to Berenger's side and now stood peering at the beach with him.

'Earl Thomas of Warwick. He has command of the vanguard. Anything goes wrong with us here, it's him you have to look to, to save us,' Berenger said.

It was good to see that Earl Thomas was already organising the men on the beach. If even a small enemy posse were to arrive now, while the majority of the men were still on board and those landed were without their weaponry, the day would go ill for the English. Berenger looked about, but could see no other bowmen yet, and that made him scowl. 'Where are they all?' he muttered.

'Look! A spark! A spark!' Jack Fletcher cried. 'He's managed to get a spark!'

Clip looked up with a scowl. 'If ye think you can do better—' he began again, but before he could finish there came the drumming of hooves. A rider was galloping to the ships, lashing his mount, screaming a warning.

'*Fripper!*' Grandarse roared.

Berenger stared at the woods from which the rider had appeared.

'*Shit*! To arms!'

CHAPTER THREE

Sir John was fretting at the delay and felt the thrill when the call to arms came, spitting into the sand and staring back towards the trees. Suddenly he heard shouting and saw the English scouting party sprinting back towards the ships, a motley group of French men-at-arms at their heels, spearing them as they ran.

'*Arms! To arms!*' he bawled, springing into the saddle. He could feel the excitement rippling through Aeton's frame. 'Come, old fellow,' he muttered, grabbing for the reins.

'Sir John, wait for me! My horse isn't here!' Richard Bakere called, alarmed at the thought his knight might ride off alone.

'Do you think they'll hang around for you?' Sir John snarled.

Richard nodded reluctantly, and passed up Sir John's bascinet. 'Can you not wait until—'

'There is no time, man! If they charge the beach now, we'll be hurled into the sea,' Sir John rasped, shoving the helmet over his head and settling the mail-rings of the tippet about his shoulders. He pointed. 'Lance! Quickly!'

He threw a glance at the approaching French. Their line of horsemen were staring along the beach as though thunderstruck by the number of ships. Behind them was a large force of men on foot.

Richard had run to the rack and passed his lord a long, stout lance.

'Good. Now, remain here and organise a defence. Lances facing the enemies' horses, yes? We will hold them off.'

Already there was a screamed war-cry as another knight pounded up the beach towards their enemy. Sir John recognised the Marshal of England, the Earl of Warwick, lance and shield held aloft. The shield bore a bright red background, with a thick, horizontal gold bar, and three stars above and below.

'Shield!' Sir John shouted, and as soon as he had it, he spurred Aeton into a canter as the Marshal rode on a rounsey, not a charger towards the thickest part of the French forces.

'Be damned to that!' he swore. 'You won't have all the glory, Warwick!'

He raked his spurs along Aeton's flanks. His excitement and enthusiasm was communicated to his great destrier, and Aeton bunched his muscles and launched himself forward, his head low as he stretched out. Sir John felt the wind in his hair and heard its roar in his ears, the drumming of hooves on the sandy soil, felt his cloak tugging at his throat as it snapped in the wind, and sheer exhilaration flamed along his spine. This was the life!

'*FOR SAINT BONIFACE, AND FOR ENGLAND!*' he roared, and with his left hand he snapped his visor down. He couched his lance ready for the first impact and bent lower, while beneath him, Aeton hurled them into battle.

*   *   *

Fortunately, Berenger's men were experienced. As he stood and took stock, they grabbed swords and axes, and Geoff took up a long spear.

Pelting by, the messenger threw sand in all directions, making Wisp swear and spit. Geoff clenched his fist, shaking it impotently, shouting abuse at him: 'You son of a Winchester goose! May your tarse shrivel, may you—'

'Geoff, the enemy's *that* way,' Berenger reminded him, pointing.

'God's cods!' Wisp said hoarsely. The thin scattering of trees had given protection to the Frenchmen who were now making their way into the open ground. 'Look at 'em all!'

Berenger was scowling, assessing the risk. Perhaps four or five hundred men on foot had appeared, and Frenchmen-at-arms on horseback were forming up, ready to charge. It would not take much to push the English back into the sea, if these were trained and warlike enough. They had gathered quickly, just as Berenger had feared, and more were joining them by the minute. Gleams of sunlight flashed on steel.

Geoff belched and wiped at his mouth, demanding, 'Where are our bows?'

Matt was pensively scratching his beard. 'Horse *and* foot? I could do with a lance or bill, me.'

'Our weapons are all on the ship still,' Berenger grated. All they had with them were their personal weapons, swords and daggers. It was enough to make a man howl in despair. He had a hollow feeling in his belly, although it was at least partly explained by hours of throwing up on the ship. Still, it was a sensation he knew only too well. He was always afflicted with this when battle approached. 'How many are there, Geoff?'

'I count two, maybe three hundred men-at-arms on horse, and hundreds on foot. Perhaps a thousand?'

'Aye, well, have ye seen the Frenchies in battle? Mad, the lot of them,' Clip said, and dropped his hone back beneath his shirt, spitting into the sand. 'Bugger it: ye'll all be slaughtered. Me too.'

'Shut it, Clip.' Berenger drew his sword and gave the blade a cursory glance. He ran it along the sleeve of his padded jerkin and pulled a face when he saw it grew wetter than before. Still, he was their leader. 'Come on, lads.'

Grandarse had joined them, and now he shouted orders.

'Berenger, you hold this line: Clip, run to the ship with the boy and bring us spears, bows, arrows – anything you can get your hands on. See if there are any more men who can support us. We'll soon be overrun against a force that size.'

While he strode along the beach bellowing to other captains, Berenger jerked his head at his men. 'Go on, you idle goats, you heard him! And Clip: *hurry*! I don't want to die waiting for you to get back!'

Grandarse had brought a second vintaine with him, and now Berenger cajoled and bullied the men into two lines on the side of the hillock. More men were gathering and he had them join the lines to create a wall of men. There was no time to dig holes to make the enemies' horses stumble, and in the absence of pallisades or hurdles they would have to hold their ground as best they could.

There was no muttering amongst the men. The English were used to fighting and gripped their weapons stoically. Only Grandarse, when he returned, showed any emotion, appearing to take the arrival of the enemy as a personal affront. Berenger eyed his men closely, assessing their temper. Geoff alone looked distracted, seemingly by young Ed as much as the enemy. It made Berenger wonder if Geoff was still boat-sick, or whether there was something else troubling him. He had been quiet before boarding, he recalled.

19

Grandarse loudly deprecated the temerity of the French in arriving before he could have weapons readied and men brought to their support.

'Sons of whores,' he grumbled. 'Look at 'em! Sodding about like they have all the time in the world, just because they caught us out here with our hosen down, the bastards.'

'Yes, lookit them,' Clip moaned. 'Bloody hundreds! We'll all get slaughtered here.'

Matt sniffed. 'Ach, stop your whining, Clip. They've got sod-all discipline, eh?'

Satisfied with his vintaine's mood, Berenger grinned to himself.

There was a series of roared commands from the beach, and Berenger turned to see Sir John, his own captain and the commander of two hundred men, galloping past to join the Earl of Warwick's vanguard. Berenger felt a flare of pride at the sight. So few, yet all were riding to meet a force many times their own size.

Geoff gave a hoarse roar of encouragement, and the rest of the men waved fists or weapons as Warwick gave an incoherent scream, couched his lance and charged. A moment later, the men behind him also thundered into the French, and Berenger saw one Frenchman lifted into the air, spitted on a lance, to be thrown down behind the Earl. There was a clash of weapons, shouts and cries, and Berenger could see little through the dust and sand that was thrown into the air by the impact of the attack.

'*UP!*' Grandarse commanded over the sound of battle. '*FORWARD!*'

'Christ's pain,' Berenger heard Matt mutter, but the vintaine began to walk steadily to the battle.

They possessed few weapons, but the French weren't to know that. Berenger marched forward with his eyes moving about the woods and fields before them, searching for the appearance of new forces, fearing this was a ruse to entrap the English.

As his destrier brought him closer, Sir John de Sully felt his spirits soar: even as the great horse's hooves pounded at the soil, his heart beat faster and faster, and he could have sung with joy to be in battle again. This was life! He felt as though his soul was with the angels!

Old age be damned!

His mind was completely focused. It was ever the way for him that, as he approached the enemy, he saw only that which was directly before him. Now two Frenchmen were in his sight-line, one with a steel helm, one with a leather cap, and neither of any importance. He set himself at them, his lance-point wavering, but as he closed he chose steel-cap, and his lance-point fixed on his target. Nearer, nearer . . . and he saw the dark eyes narrow in shock, then the man tried to draw aside, but too late, and Sir John's lance trembled in his fist as the point buried itself in the man's breast.

There was a scream, and as Sir John thundered on, his progress so swift that it took only a flick of his wrist and the dying Frenchman, still spitted like a pig, was lifted high overhead to fall behind. His lance freed, reeking of the blood and shit that dripped down the shaft, Sir John set his mount at another man, spurring Aeton onwards. This man wore a steel bascinet and mail, but before he could close with him the fellow had set his own horse at the Earl.

Frustrated, Sir John snarled and searched for another opponent, but then realised that three men were making for him. He couched lance as Aeton reared, and charged again. This time his lance-point struck a shield, and the point became embedded. The shock snapped it away, sprinkling the shield with faeces and blood. Sir John swung the lance's stump at the second man; it slammed into his upper arm, but not force-fully enough to do more than bruise. Sir John threw it at the man's head in disgust and drew his sword. Now the third knight – a heavy-set brute with a thick, bristling beard – was barging forward, shrieking a war cry, his mouth wide open when Sir John's lucky stab caught him full in the face. His smile was turned to blood, and he spat teeth from his ravaged mouth.

Sir John turned to the first man again, who fought with savage determination, although the two-foot splinter sprouting from his shield must have made it horribly unwieldy. Sir John beat at him, keeping him between Aeton and the third man-at-arms, but it seemed nothing he could do would knock him from his mount. Sir John decided to change tactic. He withdrew his horse a little, and then urged Aeton on again, riding for the head of the man's horse. The beast was shoved aside, and Sir John hacked at its rider with two vicious sweeps right, before bring-ing his sword down onto the horse's skull. It collapsed instantly, and Sir John rode over the man on the ground to get back to the last attacker – but he had given up and was riding away, back into the shelter of the trees.

Sir John had to fight to control Aeton, who was raring to continue the battle. At last he managed to soothe the brute, patting his neck until the bloodlust left him, and he stood shiv-ering, whickering as his rage cooled.

Looking down, Sir John saw that one of Aeton's great hooves had landed on the last man's face, and while he seemed to stare back at the knight with his remaining eye, the other side of his face had been mangled and stamped by the brute's horseshoe.

Sir John studied the body dispassionately.

There would be many more dead, he knew, before this campaign was over.

'Stay with me, lads!' Berenger warned while he and the vintaine slowly advanced. 'We're here to guard the landing, not to go chasing off like hounds after a hare. Hold the line!'

Jack gave a chuckle. 'We're well out of it, I reckon. Getting in the middle of a bunch of hairy-arsed horsemen is one sure way to get your skull broken.'

'Aye, and I don't like the thought of running after 'em. If you want a hound, get a hound,' Wisp added.

A few of the French had tried to coordinate their own charges against the English, but as more and more English knights charged up the beach, the Frenchmen despaired. The foot-soldiers had already mostly fled: those who hadn't lay dead or injured. When only twenty-odd men on horseback remained to contest the landing, it was obvious that the English must prevail. The French faltered, and then, as one body, galloped away.

Two men-at-arms clapped spurs to their beasts to chase after the fleeing enemy, but the Earl ordered them at the top of his voice, *'No! Stay here with the army!'* Then, seeing Grandarse, he indicated the bodies. 'Make sure all are dead, and keep a close eye on those trees.'

Grandarse looked at Berenger, who nodded and pulled out his knife. 'Come, boys. We have work to do.'

CHAPTER FOUR

Ed and Clip rejoined the vintaine as the men were wiping their weapons clean of enemy blood. Berenger watched them approach and snarled, 'You took your time.'

'Scared we'd leave you, Frip?' Clip grinned. 'Wouldn't do that to him, would we, boy? You know you can trust me.'

For a moment Berenger was gripped by the urge to grab Clip by the throat and punch him – but it passed. It was the reaction. He hated slaying the injured. Some were so badly hurt that they barely moved as his knife sliced across their throats, or into their hearts or brains – but there had been two today who had looked up with eyes like puppies' as he delivered them from their pain.

It reminded him of helping the warrener when he was a boy: catching rabbits and killing them swiftly, releasing them from pain. Except here, the men were surrounded by the odours of battle: the metallic smell of blood, the midden-smell of opened bowels. Having to step through and kneel in the stinking puddles where men had pissed and shat themselves, getting filth on his fists and legs . . . he hated that part of a battle: the final butchery.

And Clip hadn't deserted them. He *had* come back – if slowly.

Clip's levity faded as he cast a look behind Berenger and understood. 'Sorry, Frip. We were as fast as possible.'

'Next time, get a move on. If you don't, I'll throw you to the enemy myself.' The vintener looked over them. 'Where are the weapons?'

'Right there,' Clip said, pointing with his chin. On the hillock where they had been standing, Berenger could see a low handcart with a stack of bowstaves and arrows on it.

'Good. Light the fire.'

Clip smiled thinly. 'Maybe Ed would be better? He's quick with his tinder.'

'Do as you're told,' Berenger snapped.

Clip shrugged and went on, his usual whine forgotten: 'Ed here makes a good sumpter. He brought most of them. He was in a hurry to get here and see the bodies.'

Berenger cast an eye over the boy as he wiped blood from his hand. 'Why, lad? Haven't you seen enough dead men already?'

No one could get to the age of twelve without seeing a dead man: a grandparent, a friend, a felon – death was all too common. But Ed wasn't listening. His gaze moved intently over the figures.

'You all right there, Ed?' Berenger said.

Ed wore an expression of such savagery that Berenger was shocked. He had never before seen a look like that in one so young. He shot a glance over at Grandarse, but the centener was bellowing at Geoff and two others to get their fingers out and didn't notice.

'Ed – what is it?' Berenger said more forcefully.

'Nothing,' Ed replied with a little sigh. He turned and strode away, but now he was no anxious young boy with a head permanently bowed in submission. He looked more like a man.

A killer.

It was dark already when Béatrice Pouillet shut the door to the henhouse behind the cottage. The foolish creatures were making a din as they bickered on their perches. She could imagine them pushing at each other, the lowest in the pecking order forced against the walls, the matronly leader waggling her tail feathers and making herself comfortable.

Once, only a short time ago, Béatrice would have grinned at the thought, but not now. There was no place for humour in her life any more. Not since her father's arrest and execution.

Execution: a word that struck the heart with terror. Béatrice knew how men who had incurred the King's displeasure were made to suffer the most savage punishments before death. It was appalling to think that her own father could have endured such horrors. Friends had betrayed him. A respected specialist, valued by all who knew him and his work, and yet his life had been snuffed out like a candle so that no memory remained except in her.

Afterwards she had fled to her uncle's house at Barfleur, some two days' journey north. There she had hoped to be safe, but in the little port, stories about her father's crime were soon bruited about, and all too many assumed the worst. Even her uncle, a decent, law-abiding merchant, was accused of being a spy or murderer. Leaving the house one morning, she was set upon by a gang of urchins, who taunted her and pelted her with stones and ordure. Bloody and bruised, she was left to crawl away.

For her own safety, her uncle had sent her here. The woman, Hélène, was the widow of a former servant of his. She lived on a small pension provided by Béatrice's uncle, but for the last few days she had been unwell. Béatrice was fearful that she too was going to die, and once more she would be all alone; here, further than ever from home. It was no good dwelling on her family – she had no idea where her mother was.

At least the local priest was kind. He had offered to come and help her with the old woman.

At that moment, there was a snap of twigs, footsteps, and she went to peer round the side of the cottage.

'I am glad to see you, Father,' she said now as she saw the priest walking slowly up the path to the door.

'And I to see you, child.'

He was a young man for the job. Only three- or four-and-twenty, short, dark-skinned and with large, liquid brown eyes that smiled all the while as though he could see a joke that was hidden to others. He smiled now, his eyes taking in her clothing. 'You look tired, maid.'

'I am weary,' she admitted.

'How is Hélène?'

'She grows weaker, Father. I have fed her on warm pottage and an egg, but it does her no good.'

'Let us pray for her.'

Béatrice made to go inside, but he stopped her. 'No, we can honour God out here in the world He made.'

'I'd rather go inside, Father. I don't like to leave her alone for long.'

'Come here, maid. Hold my hands.'

She did as she was asked. What else should a woman do when commanded by a priest? But he had different ideas. He took her hands and gently put them on his waist, pulling her nearer. 'Hold me, maid, and we can pray together.'

Béatrice tried to pull away. His voice was grown harsh and hoarse, and when he thrust his groin at her, she felt his tarse poking at her through his habit. She froze. It felt as though her heart stopped beating. 'Father, let me go!'

'Child, do not disobey your priest! I am not evil. Just lie with me, and let me show you how—'

'No, Father!' she blurted, and snatched her hands away.

His voice took on a sly tone. 'You will do everything I say, because if you don't, I will accuse you of being a witch. Would you like that? People already mutter about you here. They say you have a black cat, that you are killing the old woman here in the cottage. They will believe me rather than you. What are you, after all, but a slut who came here because your father was a despised traitor.'

'He wasn't! Leave! Go away,' she whispered. No one could think she was a witch, surely? She felt suddenly weak, as if she was about to faint. And she thought she might vomit.

His tone changed again, became wheedling. 'I love you, can't you see that? Let me have you, Béatrice. I burn for you!'

'Get away from me! We'll both burn if you force me!'

The young man lost patience. 'You are no better than your father. He was a traitor, but *you* are a witch. You give the appearance of holiness, Béatrice, but you despise priests like me. Devil's whore!'

She recoiled from him and from his words. 'Please – have pity on me,' she begged.

'If you don't do as I ask, I will denounce you, *witch*. It is said you are privy to secrets no woman should know.'

'Go *away*!'

Afterwards, there was no memory. She saw him at that moment, his hands reaching for her breasts, a look of pure lust and devilry in his eyes, and then . . . then she was back inside the cottage and kneeling at Hélène's bedside. As she bathed the old woman's forehead to cool her, she was surprised to see the water in the bowl turn red as she put her hands in it.

Later, Hélène died, very peacefully – and when Béatrice went out to throw away the dirty water, she stumbled over the priest's body.

She screamed with shock. She vaguely remembered slapping at him with her hands, but she hadn't realised that she had been holding her little knife.

'Well?' Grandarse was sitting with his back to a tree close by the wood from which the attack had been launched. Flames from the fire were flickering over his bearded features, giving them a devilish tint.

Berenger chuckled. 'I thought your eyes were shut?'

'Aye, even when they are, I'm alert,' Grandarse said smugly.

Berenger grinned as he reported to his centener about the men, his sentries, how he had stored their provisions.

'The men know what they're doing,' Grandarse noted. 'Most have campaigned with the King before, and any man grows easier in spirit, the more there are with him. No man likes to be at the foremost point of a King's spear, to be the first man landed on a hostile shore, but when he is one of hundreds or thousands, his courage is rekindled.'

'True enough,' Berenger agreed.

'You still think he's no good, eh?' Grandarse said shrewdly. 'That boy?'

Berenger squatted beside the fire. 'He's too young to stand in the line; he can't draw a bow – he's a wasted mouth. What will you pay him?'

'Pay? I get a shilling a day, like an esquire; you get sixpence; the men get thruppence; a Welshman tuppence. He's worth a penny, I suppose, if he can carry our stores. He can forage, and he can fetch supplies in battle, can't he? He'll earn it. You saw him today. Was there any sign he would break?'

'No,' Berenger admitted. 'He obeyed orders.'

'He didn't puke at the sight of bodies, did he?'

'No.'

'Then stop worrying! He'll work his way until he's a man. Same as some of us did. Like I did.'

'Yes,' Berenger nodded, staring into the fire. Grandarse rarely tired of telling how he had joined the King's host when he was an orphan scarcely eleven, and had never looked back.

Grandarse hawked and spat, eyeing him keenly. 'Well, Frip? What is it?'

'I don't know. There's something about him that doesn't feel right. I've had boys join before, you know that, and they start out nervous and fretful. But when they have fought some battles and killed a few men, they begin to grow. Soon they're men. But when they see their first fight, see the bodies strewn about, they have a sympathy for them. They realise that these were only men. This lad's different. He was pathetically worried before, but when he saw the bodies of the French, he had a sort of feral enthusiasm for them. There was no pity or concern, only . . . excitement.'

'We've seen enough men like that before,' Grandarse observed slowly, prodding at the fire with a stick. He paused. 'D'you think he's bad luck?'

'I don't know,' Berenger said shortly.

'Keep your eyes on him, then.'

'I will.'

CHAPTER FIVE

Ed felt a part of the vintaine already.

As he sat, nursing a wooden bowl filled with meaty soup and a handful of leaves gathered from the fields, he felt as close to these men as he had to any. It was just like having a family at last, and he relished the sense of belonging.

A man passed by and a hand ruffled his hair, and although he snatched his head away automatically, scowling, he treasured the rough affection.

He averted his eyes when he saw Geoff watching him. Ed felt sure the man meant him no harm, but he was another like Fripper, who seemed to be able to read his thoughts. They both made him nervous.

The others were all kindly though: Jack, who held a senior position along with Geoff; Oliver, who had a horrible squint that made him seem to be leering the whole time; Matt, the square-faced, black-haired man who was proud of his reputation as a womaniser; Walter, the one over at the far side of the fire, with the bright blue eyes and fair hair, who had a thin, sensitive face and puckered lips; Gil with the gingerish hair and the perpetual scowl sitting next to Luke, the man with the round face and air of affable confusion, no matter what he did.

Luke was addressing Ed now.

'So, master, you belong to our vintaine now. The only remaining question is, what shall we call you?'

'My name is Ed.'

'No, master, that will not do,' Luke sat back and belched gently. 'I think you are more of a packhorse. You lumber as you go. Perhaps we should call you "Sumpter".'

'Too long,' Oliver commented. '"Pack" would be better.'

'Whoever heard of a man called "Pack"?' Luke protested. 'Every time we left a camp, the poor boy would think we were calling him as the orders flew around his head. No, we couldn't call him that.'

'How about "Goat"? He smells like one,' Walter said disdainfully.

'Now, Walt, there's no need to be offensive.' Luke stretched and yawned. 'I think my idea was best.'

'What's wrong with my real name?' Ed demanded, colouring.

'It's too cheeky, for one thing. What if we call to you, and the King is nearby and thinks we are insulting him or his son? It is a most *common* name, after all. No, it won't do. Perhaps "Cart"? We shall be using you to carry all our belongings.'

'Call him "Pony" and be done,' was Matt's contribution. 'I just wish we could go to a town. This sand is getting every-where. I swear it's in my cods already.'

'Then it's lucky there are no women for you to sheath your dagger of love, matey,' Gil said with a chuckle. 'No wench would want you near her with a rough edge like that!'

Matt muttered a foul rejoinder, but Luke wouldn't let it drop.

'The boy must have a name,' he insisted. 'Come, shall we have a vote for the most popular?'

'Call him "Boy"!' Gil called out.

'"Mule?"' Jack offered. 'He has the temperament of one.'

'Piss on you, Matt!' Eliot called. He was a short man with greying hair and a ready smile. 'The lad's still new. Give him a week, and he'll be standing us a round of ales in a tavern.'

Ed knew that they were all mocking him, but he didn't care. He felt as though he was being accepted.

'I know,' Luke said into the general mirth. 'He will fetch and carry, and he isn't a Pony, while Mule is potentially offensive. Boy, from here on, you will be known as "Donkey".'

'Why?'

'Because it suits you, but more, because it suits *me*,' Luke said comfortably. He settled back, pulling his dirty old felt cap over his eyes. 'You will learn, Donkey, as you grow older (if you do) that there is more to life than a Christian name. Sometimes the name our comrades give us is much more important.'

'So why are you keeping to your given name?'

Luke opened a bright, beady eye like a blackbird's, and peered at him. 'I was named Martin, Donkey.'

It was late when Berenger finally slumped to the ground near Geoff. The others had already rolled themselves in their blankets and cloaks, and there was a muted snoring from Clip, a whiffling wheezing from an older man nearer the fire. Two members of the vintaine sat murmuring at a farther fire, one of them slowly and methodically stroking a stone over his sword's blade like a harvester sharpening his scythe.

Berenger had walked the outer line of the sentries, and wandered out beyond the light from the fires. There he had stealthily crept from one tree to another, his ears alert for any sounds, but he returned reassured. The French were nowhere about. Not yet.

'That lad – Donkey.'

Berenger didn't have to look to know whose voice it was. The sibilance revealed that it came from Geoff. He squatted down near his old comrade and held his hands to the fire. 'What about him?'

'The boy's made enemies of the Welsh already. I saw him fetching water a while back, and a group of knifemen were laughing and making comments. I swear he would have pulled his knife on one who came too close.'

Berenger scowled. 'He tries that again, cuff him round the head. What, did the fool think they were French or something?'

'He knew they were Welsh, but he has no love for them, it seems. The boy's weird, I know, but he'll work out. He just needs a good thrashing every so often, like all lads.'

'That's what Grandarse said.'

'But you aren't sure?'

'I wish I was.' Berenger picked up a twig and shoved it into the fire. The end of his twig glowed, and he withdrew it, blowing on the ember reflectively.

'You never had a son, did you?' Geoff said.

'No. At least you have your wife and children,' Berenger said. He stared at the fire. 'That's my greatest regret. After this war, I will find a wife. I should give up this life.'

'You think you can?' Geoff chuckled mirthlessly. 'It's easier to be said than to be done. A woman can at least be bought easily enough,' he added. 'There are enough camp followers who would make you a good wife for as long as you want.'

Berenger looked at him, hearing a sharp edge to his voice.

Geoff had always spoken with pride of his wife and two sons. Suggesting Berenger might find a 'good wife' from among the camp followers was unsettling. 'Are you all right?'

'Yes. I'm just tired.'

'It's been a long day,' Berenger agreed.

'Don't worry about the boy. I'll look after him,' Geoff said gruffly.

Berenger nodded. With Geoff taking responsibility, he felt reassured.

'Perhaps Ed is here for some reason we cannot guess at,' Geoff yawned. 'God has His plans, and we rarely comprehend them.'

Berenger gave a twisted grin. The smell of thousands of men, along with the latrines, let alone the French corpses piled a short distance away, all made him wonder what plans God might hold for them. Later, when he was preparing for sleep, his head on his bag, he glanced across at Geoff. The fellow was staring up at the black sky still.

'Bugger it,' Berenger heard him mutter, just before he fell into a deep sleep.

They were a rag-bag of soldiers. Even in her shocked state, Béatrice thought how battered they looked, when they passed by her cottage later that night.

Their leader was a tall, well-mannered nobleman with a face marked by pain and fatigue. Grey bruises under his eyes and deep lines at either side of his mouth and at his brow told of the savage beating they had received at the hands of the English invaders.

'Maid, you must leave here,' he said, halting his horse at her gate while his men shuffled past. His head dropped from exhaustion as he surveyed her sadly. 'It is dangerous. The

English are come. No man, woman or child is safe. You know what monsters they are.'

She looked up at him dull. The priest's attempted rape of her, and his death, had affected her deeply. She felt washed out, weary almost to death. This nobleman could have no idea of monsters: her father had been slain by the King! But she nodded nonetheless. She would not show her true feelings.

'They landed very near,' the man went on. 'We did all we could, but they slaughtered my men and we few escaped with these injuries. They're only a matter of hours away. I tell you again: you have to leave this place before they get here.'

'I cannot. My mistress has died and I must see to her.'

'Let the priest deal with her, if he will come,' the knight said.

She nodded, feeling as if the priest's body was screaming to him from the bushes at the back of the house.

Not that he or his men could hear anything other than the clamour of arms. It was in their faces: they were mired in horror. They marched slowly, mere tattered remnants. A few rode horses or ponies, but most were on foot, limping and staggering, some helping comrades with arms about their necks as they hobbled along, others using polearms as makeshift staffs.

'Sir, what happened?'

'We arrived too late,' he said. 'I should have been there sooner, but one man cannot guard a coast so vast as Normandy's. When we arrived, there were already enough ashore to thwart us. Our bowmen from Genoa had already deserted us, claiming they were owed money, so we had no protection – nothing. We did all we could, but this is all that is left of the force I had to defend us all. I must make haste to reach St-Lô or Caen and warn them. The English rats will infest every part of our county until they can be burned out.'

'I must remain to bury my mistress,' Béatrice said, glancing back at the cottage.

'We can carry her to the church, if it will help you,' the knight said.

'I must collect my things. Some money . . .'

'Then be quick!' he snapped, keen to be off. 'We can help you to the church, but after that you must make your own way to safety – if you can find it anywhere in our unhappy kingdom.'

'I thank you,' she said. She ran back into the cottage and gathered a few belongings, and then, as the men brought out the old woman's body, she threw Hélène's palliasse onto the fire. Smoke rose from the hay inside, and she turned and strode from the place.

Outside, the old cat rubbed against her legs, giving a loud purr that seemed almost demented. She stroked his head as she watched the flames through the doorway. The roof gave off a thick, greenish-yellow smoke as the thatch caught. A flash of heat made the animal leap from her.

She called to the cat, but he had hidden himself away. Unbeknownst to her, it was the last time she would see him, for soon, locals would come to accuse her of witchcraft, and they would hang him, in the casually brutal way of superstitious peasants. If she had known, she would have taken him with her.

'Why fire the place?' the knight demanded.

She looked at him and forgot the cat.

'I'll not have her belongings looted by the English,' she said, adding silently to herself, 'nor by the locals.'

CHAPTER SIX

13 July

Berenger rose as the first horns blared through the early morning. 'On your feet!' he shouted to his men, making a dishonest display of enthusiasm for leadership. In truth, he would have much preferred a cup of warm, spiced ale and another hour under his cloak.

It was still dark, yet all around him men were stirring and grumbling, many searching for a bush or tree to piss against, while others packed belongings and adjusted their coats against the chill. Out at sea, ships waited, and more were being beached and unloaded.

'Aye, there'll be a fight before we see home again,' Jack Fletcher said in his heavy Ousham accent, hoicking up his hosen. Berenger had known him longest, and Jack was the man he relied on to give him the mood of the men. 'Those sailor boys have an easy time of it, eh? Buggering off back to port, guzzling the best wine and ale while we march the soles of our boots thin all the way to bloody Paris. The buggers.'

Berenger grinned.

'How do you think the men are doing?' he asked.

Jack shrugged. 'Clip's whining wors'n ever; Wisp's worried, as usual, but he's keeping it quiet. You know what he's like.'

Berenger knew all too well. Will the Wisp was lanky and clumsy and always fretting: would they win a good reward for their effort, would his bag hold for their campaign, would the rains come on and ruin his boots? In Wisp's life there were so many things to worry about.

'The others?' he asked.

'Oliver has toothache; Eliot's upset because his harrier bitch was kicked by a packhorse and she's limping; Matt's on about needing a whore; Gil wants an ale; Jon is hungry; Walt didn't sleep. It's the usual moaning and griping, but they're fine. It's when they stop bleating you need to worry. That's when they're plotting mutiny!'

Berenger pulled the straps tight on his pack. He wanted to ask about the boy, but there was no point. Of all the men under Berenger, Jack was the most loyal. He would protect any man from the vintaine, especially a youngster, to the utmost limit of his strength. 'What of Geoff?'

'He's just missing his wife and boys, as usual.'

Berenger nodded. Geoff was always sombre at the beginning of a campaign. Berenger had seen it before. His protectiveness towards Ed was just his paternal nature coming to the fore.

Clip had relit the fire, and now the men were heating flat stones. Most men did not bother with an early meal, but Berenger insisted that, when possible, each man should have something inside them to sustain them for the day's march. Each had mixed oats with flour and water, some with honey, to make little cakes. It was a trick they had learned from the Scots.

However, during this campaign there was no telling where they would find supplies. Berenger decided he would keep a store. That way, if the French laid waste the farms before them on their march, they would always have some food.

While their cakes cooked, Berenger wandered amongst the other members of his vintaine, stopping and talking to each.

There were too few. Grandarse had been right on that. Berenger was the leader of sixteen men, where there should have been twenty, fifteen excluding Ed – he couldn't add Ed to the complement. Not yet. Not until they'd seen how he would behave in a fight.

Berenger saw a messenger pick his way across to Grandarse. The old man nodded and looked across at Berenger meaningfully. Picking up his hot oatcake, Berenger blew on it, saying, 'Hurry up and eat, boys. It looks like we'll be working for our money today.'

Béatrice walked slowly amidst the throng that day. A solitary young woman, with dank and matted hair beneath a tatty wimple, she attracted little attention. It was how she liked it. For the first time in days she almost felt safe.

She had left the weary men at the little chapel, where they deposited Hélène's body for her. Since then, she had been trailing along with columns of refugees.

Here, the rutted road was a mess of mud, human ordure and abandoned belongings. Men and women trudged along wearily, carrying their possessions on their backs, under their arms, or on small carts. She saw a man with a tottering pile of tightly-bound bales of clothing crammed into an unwieldy barrow suddenly stop as the topmost ones fell into the mud. He stood, distraught, staring at them, as though that was the ruin of his life, while the endless line of people passed by him without comment. No one could spare even a word of sympathy. Not now. Everyone was too scared: too exhausted.

A child of perhaps eight years was darting from one adult to another, snot running from her nose, crying and calling for her mother. One bent old woman, grey of face and hair, meandered from the road and through a collection of nettles, and then slumped to the ground like one who had given up. Béatrice knew she would die there. And nobody would help.

Béatrice herself was too weary.

The whole world seemed on the move: everybody's faces taut with fear, all so sunk in despair that they had no thoughts for others. Ahead, Béatrice saw a priest with his servants, striding with the careful haste of a cockerel sensing a fox in pursuit, avoiding glances to either side in case he might see someone who needed his help. Here, surely, he should have paused, prayed, offered some kind of assistance to these suffering people. It was his job, his God-given *duty*.

Her experience at Hélène's cottage had utterly destroyed her faith in the priesthood. They were *hypocrites*, she thought bitterly, demanding that others should help their fellow men, but then averting their own gaze from those in need. Unless they could pay, of course. Like the priest who had offered to help her – but only if she would become his whore.

But today, the priests themselves were fearful. Peasants, burghers, even the rich were scared – and who could blame them? All were terrified of the English.

The enemy would soon be upon them, and then the terror would start. Everyone knew what it was like to have an army arrive. The countryside would be devastated, fields and pasture would be ravaged, local stores emptied, and the people . . . well, the people would be lucky if they lived. Stories of the depredations of the English were rife, and everyone had heard tell of their behaviour in previous raids. They would ride over a wide front and slay all who stood in their path. If a town or city refused to let them in, they would have to suffer the torments of siege and starvation, and if the place fell, their reward would be wholesale slaughter: men and boys murdered, women raped by whole companies of men, their children spitted on lances for the amusement of the troops.

So Béatrice walked unmolested among the people fleeing the rumour of invasion. Even here, in the lanes near Carentan, no one was interested in one young woman. There were too many others – maids who had fled their masters' houses, women from the farms who had been sent away by tearful parents, those without homes who had nothing to tie them to a town – all were on the road now.

No one hindered her, but no one aided her. She stumbled as she went, but she could survive.

She *would* survive. Her thirst for vengeance would keep her alive.

Sir John returned with Grandarse. The knight wanted to see how the vintaine was shaping up. Long ago, he had served under two commanders, and both had taught him much about handling men: the first by his utter disregard for them and their feelings, the second by his commitment to his archers and men-at-arms. Men, any men, deserved respect. The alternative was mutiny.

'I give you a good day,' he said to the men as they bickered about their fires.

They were an interesting group, he thought. He knew their leader, of course. Grandarse was a cantankerous, foul-mannered and still more foul-spoken, unrepentant old sinner. Sir John had known him for many years. Berenger, too, was someone he recognised. The man's face was familiar, although he couldn't immediately recall where they had met before. No matter. It would come to him.

'All right, you daft churls, listen!' Grandarse said. 'Will, that means you too. We are to march south and west from here, and check the country for more Frenchies. Hoy! Clip, are you listening? I know your brain's in your arse, but this could be important! We are to scout, and if we find strong forces we're not to engage them, but come straight back. Do you understand?'

Sir John eyed the vintaine. They knew their jobs. They must ensure that no French forces could surprise the English while the ships continued to be unloaded.

'*Hoy*! I said: *do you understand*, you thieving scrotes?'

There was a weak chorus of, 'Yes, we heard you,' and, 'Aye, we did.' Jack snorted and pulled out his sword, studying the blade. Others were similarly undemonstrative.

Sir John took a step forward and waited until he had their attention. These were experienced professionals who had fought together for years. They were confident, if undemonstrative. They had nothing to prove. Sir John was aware he could rely on them.

'I am glad you are here with us,' he said clearly. 'The King is determined to bring the French to battle, but to do that will be difficult. We need to fight on ground of *our* choosing, and not see our men frittered away in silly fights. That is why I've picked you, since you are the most reliable vintaine. Do you have any questions?'

'Do we march soon?' Will asked.

Sir John gave a grin that, to Berenger, made him look like a Lyme pirate. 'As soon as the ships are empty, the King will move. You have been on chevauchée with him before. You will all have rich pickings. Other men have made so much money from taking hostages and winning gold that they have been able to build their own manors and live like lords. You can too!' He cleared his throat. 'The King intends this war to bring the French to their knees and accept him as their rightful ruler. To celebrate his arrival, he has knighted his son and many other nobles. Before the end of the campaign, he will give the same honours to others who serve him faithfully, be they ever so young,' he added, looking straight at Ed. 'So serve your King honourably and well, all of you, and you will be richly rewarded!'

He waved a hand, encompassing the landscape.

'Look at this land! It's so verdant and rich, even the peasants have money. Well, we're going to ruin their lives. Our orders are to wage *dampnum*. You all know what that means.'

He looked about and saw the older men nodding grimly. Newer recruits, and the boy, looked baffled.

Berenger summed it up. 'Dampnum means terror: we wage war through the people. Wherever we go, we'll take their food, their money, their silver and plate. Everything else, we burn.'

Sir John nodded approvingly. 'Aye. It means creating such misery that the folk demand that their masters come and protect them, or they will surrender. It means that we shall make this a land of ghosts.'

Grandarse nodded, then thundered to his men: 'And now, you idle buggers, get your fingers out of your arses! We have work to do.'

Béatrice was passing a little tumbledown home when she saw the huddle of old rags. It was already past noon, and at first she scarcely paid it any attention. But her gown was tattered and frayed, her shoes worn, and, struck with hope that there might be a good cloak to keep the night's cold at bay, or shoes, she hurried over to the bundle before someone else in the struggling column could spy them.

It was an old woman.

The old dear lay on her back with her pale eyes staring up at the sky, and Béatrice felt the breath catch in her throat at the sight. Long white hair spread from her head all about her like a halo. She was no rich burgher's wife, with her face lined and sunburned like that.

Her clothing was russet and green, but at her flank the material was stained with blood. Béatrice thought she must be dead. There was no point being sentimental. She moved closer, thinking to take the cloak but, as she did so, the old woman's eyes turned to her. Aware, but dulled.

Béatrice swallowed. 'Who did this?'

'A fool who thought I was rich,' the woman croaked bitterly. Her lip trembled. 'He gained little by his treachery.'

Béatrice moved to her side and knelt in the damp grass. A twig stuck in her knee, but she scarcely felt it as she studied the bloody cloth. There was no hissing from the wound, which she knew was fortunate, but it had bled a great deal. The cloth was sodden.

'Can you rise?'

'What do you think?' the woman said, but she allowed the girl to help her to a sitting posture, the breath sobbing in her throat.

'We must get you out of the roadway for the night,' Béatrice said, looking at the hovel. There was space in there for them both to sleep in the dry.

'Move me in there and I'll die. If I am to die anyway, what is the point?' the old woman grumbled.

'At least I can stay dry while I nurse you in there.'

'That's the trouble with the young. Always thinking of their own comforts,' the woman said tartly, but her eye held a glint of amusement that shone through her pain.

'Come!'

Struggling, Béatrice managed to get her almost to her feet, but then both fell down. The old woman was no lightweight. A second time Béatrice managed to have her rise, only to collapse once more. Before they could try a third time, a housewife hurried over to them, loudly scolding her husband for his tardiness, and took hold of the old woman's arm while her unhappy spouse was commanded to take the other. Between them, they managed to get the woman upright and help her to the door of the cottage. Béatrice opened it and drew her inside.

There was little left in there. A couple of smashed pots lay on the floor, and a single neckerchief beside the hearth showed how urgently the owners had packed and departed, but the fire still held some heat, and while the two helpers set the old woman down on the ground by the wall, Béatrice tended to the coals. When she turned, she was not surprised to see that the two helpers had left. Why should they wait to help someone who was neither relative nor friend?

'Come, let me see your wound,' she said as she rose.

'You go. I can look after myself.'

'You were going to die out there,' Béatrice pointed out. 'Let me see the wound. I have some skill with healing.'

'You have the powers of a saint? No? Then do not bother.'

'Was it a long knife?'

She held her hands four inches apart. 'No, just an eating knife. But it was enough. Ach! It doesn't hurt too much. It's just every so often it feels as though he's stabbing me again!'

'You are bleeding still. I should bind you.'

'He wanted my money,' the woman said, not listening. Her head was resting against the wall, eyes staring into the distance. She put her hand into her chemise and drew out a purse. 'He thought it was in my pack, so he took that. All the food and some clothes, the fool. He didn't get anything else.'

'Outlaws don't think. They rob and run while they can.'

'He wasn't an outlaw. He was my son.'

CHAPTER SEVEN

The vintaine stopped and had a good lunch of looted bread, sweet cheese and wine, sitting on a low hill from which they could see the sea. It sparkled and gleamed like frosted silver, Berenger thought, and he felt a strange tingle in his heart, like the first thrill of lust at the sight of a beautiful woman. Some things were almost too lovely to endure. Near them was the second vintaine, led by Roger, a dark, narrow-featured man with a determination to survive and prosper. He eyed any patch of ground with a caution that in others would be considered cowardly, except Berenger knew him to be courageous, but careful.

Roger and Berenger had not spoken since arriving on French soil, and Berenger took the opportunity to join him.

'Good wine,' he said.

Roger had a goatskin filled with wine from a barrel at the last farm. 'Better than the piss they serve at the Sign of the Boar in Hereford,' he agreed with a chuckle.

'How are your men?'

Roger glanced about at his men. 'All good, I think. While there's vittles and the promise of women, they're content. A fight won't bother them.'

'Mine too.'

'I see you've taken on a youngster. He bearing up all right?' Roger said, watching Ed.

'Well enough.'

'I've a new fellow, too. See him over there? Fustian jerkin, with the faded red hosen, and a beard that would suit your boy rather than a grown man?'

'I see him.'

The man he indicated was a shortish fellow, perhaps five-and-twenty years old, with a long nose and brown eyes, set in a lugubrious face with sallow skin. His hair was straw-coloured, which made his eyes seem startlingly piercing, and they darted about the land before them and back to the men with a swiftness that was quite birdlike.

'He's a curious one. Says he came from London, but his accent's wrong. Calls himself Mark Tyler, or Mark of London. The boys call him "Cook" because if you give him a rabbit or lamb, he can make a feast.'

'Plenty of men will call themselves "of London", if they've been apprenticed there,' Berenger said.

'True enough, but apart from cooking, this one seems to have no skills. Still, he knows how to broach a barrel,' Roger said with a rough laugh. He pulled out his knife to cut off a hunk of bread. 'And that always makes a man welcome in the army!'

'You think he's an abjurer – an outlaw seeking pardon?' Berenger asked more quietly. If so, it would be better that the other men did not hear. Some took a dim view of harbouring felons.

'He's probably just a runaway, but I'll keep watch on him. A new man's always an unknown until his first fight. Inexperience can be a risk.'

Berenger stood and stretched. 'The sooner we're on our way, the better.'

'Aye. And the sooner we are in a real fight, the happier I'll be,' Roger said, glancing over at Mark.

Berenger and Roger walked side-by-side behind Grandarse on the way back as the sun fell, the men straggling along behind them.

'What's that?' Grandarse said suddenly, pointing.

Off on their right was a little stand of trees, and in their midst a small cottage.

'Looks like someone's been here already,' Berenger said.

It might once have been thatched, but now the little building's walls had tumbled, and spars and joists stuck up jagged against the evening sky. There was an air of sadness and decay about it. Soon, many more houses would be laid waste like this, he knew, and he was struck with a sense of gloom.

'Didn't see it on the way out,' Grandarse said. He already had his hand on his sword. 'It'd be a good place for someone to hide.'

'Grandarse, it's a pit. It's been empty since the days of William the Bastard,' Berenger said, but he was an old soldier, and knew the importance of reconnaissance as well as any. He hitched up his belt, muttered a curse under his breath, and called to Geoff and Clip. 'Come on, lads. Let's get it checked out, eh?'

Their path was a foot-wide trampled passage through grass and scrub. Berenger led the way, scowling at the building as shadows began to dominate the land. It seemed to him as though the slower they walked, the nearer the cottage appeared, as though it was approaching them as well, like a predator stalking its hunter. He felt a slither of unease in his belly.

Closer to the cottage, he saw that where a thick thatch must once have lain, now there was only the stench of burned straw. Some greenish clumps remained on the top of one wall, but the rest had been consumed in the conflagration. It was still warm.

'Some of our boys been here already?' Berenger wondered.

'Must have,' Geoff said.

'There'll be nothing in there to take,' Clip noted sadly.

Berenger nodded, and they all stepped silently to the gaping hole where the door had once stood. It was there still, but burned and ruined, lying half in, half out. The doorpost had been scorched to a repellent, twisted black shape, like a snake standing and staring at him. It was enough to make Berenger swallow hard and take a second look. In the dark he could have sworn that the thing had eyes and watched him closely as he came closer.

'What is it, Frip?' Geoff asked, seeing his stare.

'Just a . . . I thought I saw something.'

It was stupid to be superstitious. It was only a peasant's home, one small room, that was all. Yet he was reluctant to enter. He had seen bodies burned to foetal skeletons before now. When he died, he wanted an arrow in the throat, not a burning.

He looked about him warily and then jerked back. 'Sweet Mother of . . .' Dangling from a cord bound to a rafter, swinging slightly in the warm air, he saw a dead cat. 'Shit!'

'What?' Geoff hissed.

'Nothing', Berenger muttered. He crossed himself hurriedly. A black cat was ominous. Everyone knew that.

Geoff glanced at Clip. The two were either side of the doorway now, and at a nod from Geoff, they raced inside, knives out and ready, low enough to gut anyone foolish enough to try to ambush them.

Berenger entered more slowly, averting his eyes from that unsettling doorpost. One wall, which had supported the end of the beam, had collapsed when the fire had taken hold, and the beam had crashed into the room, smashing everything beneath it. Berenger could see a table, two stools, a couple of pots, even a long scrap of blackened material.

'Nothing here,' Geoff said, after wandering about the room. There was nowhere to conceal a body, and he kicked at some rubble, bent and peered under the beam.

Clip stood with his lip curled. 'You're right. Whoever got here before us took everything left unburned.'

Berenger let his hand rest on the beam. It was still warm. 'It was a recent fire,' he noted.

Wisp had walked in after the men, and stood in the doorway, looking slightly green.

'You all right, Wisp?' Berenger asked.

Wisp felt strangely light-headed. Seeing the cat dangling, he had been struck with superstitious terror. He felt as if he was at the top of a tall cliff and peering out to death far below. His head was filled with a curious dizziness, and he sucked in his breath.

'Wisp? Wisp, what is it?'

He could hear Berenger's voice, but it felt like Frip was a long way away. Wisp's heart was thundering like a horse in full gallop, and he had to grasp a timber to keep from toppling.

'I'm fine,' he managed. 'Just a gut-rot.'

Roger's voice came to them from outside. 'Hoy, Fripper, best take a look at this.'

Berenger gave Wisp a clap on the shoulder, then turned and left.

*   *   *

Wisp remained, staring at the cat.

'Cut that thing down,' he gulped.

'What, the cat?'

Wisp nodded.

'You do it,' Clip said. 'You think I'm your esquire?'

'Just cut the bastard thing down,' Wisp said with a sudden venom. He wanted to throw up. 'You see what it is?'

'Yeah – a dead cat. So what?'

'It's a sign that a witch lived here. They killed her cat, because it was her link to the Devil. Christ save us!'

Wisp stumbled from the sad little house and, once outside the door, he fell to his knees and puked.

Berenger had walked out to Grandarse and Roger, who stood near a little spring with the rest of the men. 'What?'

'Looks like someone wasn't too popular,' Roger said with a grin, pointing. On the ground at his feet lay a man in a foetal curve, arms clutched to his belly.

'A priest? Who did it – one of our scouts after the landing?' Berenger said, prodding the body with his foot.The skin was foul already and had dark veins showing.

'Who'd bother to kill a priest?' Roger wondered. 'They don't carry money.'

Grandarse spat. 'Aye, well, priest or sinner, there'll be plenty more like him before long.'

CHAPTER EIGHT

They returned to the camp late in the evening, and Berenger was glad to be able to sit down and warm his hands at a fire.

All the way back they had seen fires in the distance, and now smoke was rising like scars on the sky to south and west. Berenger knew what was happening. English and Welsh opportunists were slaughtering cattle, sheep and people, before the stores of food and fields of wheat were burned. That was why they were here: for wholesale destruction.

But he wasn't thinking about the fires. On the way back, they had passed a group of Welsh knifemen, and one of them called out: 'Glad to see someone took on the brat. Hey, boy, thanks for the ale!'

Berenger turned. The speaker was a thin-featured Welshman with a scar over his left cheek that left a white mark in his sideburn. The top of his ear had been removed with the same slash.

Ed lifted his head, and at the sight of the Welshmen, he seemed to shrink into himself, as though he was petrified. His hand rested on his knife's hilt.

'You know our Donkey? He's a good worker. You should have used him yourself,' Berenger said.

There was some ribald laughter at this, which seemed to hold an edge of contempt.

'What is your name?' he asked.

'I am called Erbin. I am leader of these men,' the man said.

'Know that I am called Berenger. I am in charge of this vintaine under Sir John de Sully.'

'We are under the command of the Prince of Wales,' Erbin said sneeringly. 'That beats a poxed knight.'

Berenger held up his hand when he saw Geoff and Eliot bristling. 'Leave them, lads. You, Erbin, had best watch your tongue. You have the ear of the Prince. I have the ear of his father, so go swyve a goat!'

'You offering me your mother?' Erbin called back.

Berenger felt his jaw tighten. 'If you want, we can test which of us is the stronger.'

'Maybe we should put that to the trial!'

'Carry on,' Grandarse said. 'Enough of this ballocks! Welshman, keep a civil tongue or the Prince will hear of it. Come on, Frip, and the rest of you!'

They carried on, ignoring the mocking laughter behind them, but Berenger threw a curious glance at the Donkey, wondering what was going on in his mind. 'Boy, do you know them?'

'Yes. What of it?' the lad snapped. 'They don't scare me!' But his eyes held an unmistakable fear.

Berenger decided he would find out more when he could. Just now he had other things to think about. Wisp looked as though a carthorse had kicked him in the cods. It was unnerving to see a usually reliable member of their vintaine in such a strange taking.

Jack was standing nearby, whittling a stick into a sharp spike. Berenger called to him.

'Jack, speak to Wisp. Something's upset him. Find out what's wrong, eh? It's not like him.'

Jack nodded and ambled over to Wisp as Berenger returned to his seat at the tree. He had hardly settled when Grandarse came back from reporting their findings to Sir John de Sully.

'Well?' Berenger said, looking up.

'All's well enough,' Grandarse replied, levering his massive bulk onto a log. 'The King's men are at the next town away over there – Morsalleen or somesuch. Suppose they'll all be sleeping in warm cots the night.'

'Knights and nobles always get the better lodgings,' Berenger said.

'Aye. Not that I have to like it though.' Grandarse scowled resentfully up at the trees. 'Did you check for widow-makers?'

'There are no limbs about to fall from this tree,' Berenger said.

'Aye,' Grandarse continued. 'I could just do with a warm bed, a fire roaring on the hearth, and a saucy little French maid to liven my evening.' He sighed hopefully. 'Not that we won't be able to win such soon, with luck.'

'Any news of the French?'

'No sign to east or south. There are Welsh fighters searching, and the King's already in a rage with them.'

'Why?'

In answer, Grandarse jerked a thumb towards the columns of smoke. 'Look! The King made a proclamation: all would be safe if they came into his peace – does it look like the French can trust his word, do you reckon? We're supposed to wage *dampnum* against those who reject our King, but if he offers protection to those who accept his rule and the Welsh still go ahead and slaughter them, the French will support Philippe. The King isn't best pleased.'

The Donkey returned with two water pails and squatted nearby. At Grandarse's words, he stirred. 'The French need to be ruled with an iron fist. They are a wicked people.'

'Oh, aye?' Grandarse threw him a glance of amused interest. 'What, like the English, are they?'

'The English only defend what is theirs.'

'You think we are any better than them?' Geoff put in harshly.

Grandarse ignored him. 'He's right, eh, Frip? *Ballocks*, boy!' he said, giving a broad smile. His hands behind his head, closing his eyes, he muttered dreamily, 'You ought to be back in England if you want to defend things. We're here to take what we want, and I'm going to make the most of it. And then get home and make a wife of the naughtiest little wriggle-arsed wench I can find. Ah! That'll be the life. Ale whenever I want it, a good house, and a bad little wife who'll adore me in my bed each night.'

'So you'll want her blind as well, then?' Berenger asked mildly.

Grandarse opened a bright blue eye and grinned wickedly. 'Wouldn't hurt, Frip. Wouldn't hurt.'

'Why do they call you Fripper?' the Donkey said.

Berenger cast him a look. 'What is a Fripper, boy?'

'A man who sells second-hand clothes.'

'Aye, boy,' Grandarse said, and suddenly opened both eyes, glaring. 'And this dangerous man is known for stripping the dead and selling their clothes after a battle, see? It's not every man's job, but it keeps him in ale.'

Ed stared at him, then at Berenger, who sighed.

'My friends here reckon my clothing is old and worn, Donkey. Listen to Grandarse about fighting and warfare, but

57

not about women, the characters of other men, or the ways of the world.'

'That's what I want: to learn how to fight the French.'

'Aye, well, you've come to the right place to learn,' Grandarse said. He stretched and broke wind flamboyantly, an expression of pained concentration twisting his features. 'Aye, that's better,' he grunted. 'And for now, boy, you can bugger off and fetch us some wine. You see, that's how you support your King: you look after his men, eh?'

Jack beckoned Berenger as Grandarse began to snore. Jack's expression didn't bode well.

'What have you found out?' Berenger asked quietly.

Jack's grey eyes were serious. 'Wisp's convinced himself we're heading for disaster. He reckons the cat was an omen.'

Berenger looked past Jack's shoulder at Wisp, who sat wretchedly plucking at tufts of grass. 'I'll have a word,' he said, and got up and walked over to Wisp, dropping to sit beside him. 'So?'

'I told Jack already. I may as well tell you.'

'Tell me what?'

'This whole enterprise is going to fail. We'll not make it home again. None of us.'

Berenger said gently, 'Look, you're taking this cat business for too seriously, my friend.'

Wisp looked up and met his eyes. 'I've never felt like that before, but I did at that cottage – when I saw that witch's cat hanging. The folks about there knew the woman who'd been inside. They saw that she was evil. It wasn't done by someone who dislikes cats, Frip. It was done by people who hate witches.'

'You don't know any of this for sure, Wisp. You saw a cat.'

'And the dead priest outside?'

'He could have been killed by our scouts. It wasn't magic killed him, I know that much.'

'This chevauchée is going to fail, Frip. We should get away while we can.'

'No one's going to run away from the King's host, lad. You know the penalty for desertion.'

'I know we'll all die. I can see it just as if it's already happened. I'm dead. We all are. I won't see home again, just as you won't.'

Wisp gave a sob. 'The chevauchée is doomed. And so are we.'

CHAPTER NINE

When Sir John de Sully arrived, just before dawn, the men were already standing-to with their weapons.

Berenger had not seen Sir John above a handful of times since landing. The knight had been too busy seeing to the disposition of the archers and men-at-arms under the Prince of Wales. Like the other men, a thick stubble was already forming over his jaw. At his chin it was grey, the colour of old, unpolished pewter, like his hair. His eyes were firm and steady, as befitted a senior warrior of five-and-sixty years who had taken part in every battle his King had fought since Edward II's first wars against Scotland, three-and-thirty years ago.

Grandarse called Roger Bakere and Berenger to join them.

'The King's unhappy,' Sir John said. 'Men are ignoring his proclamation to spare towns and people who wish to come under his protection. You are to look for French militia, but also to search for any plunderers.'

'And what – um – do we do with them if we find them?' Roger asked. He had a lazy drawl that made him sound foolish on occasion, like an inbred peasant with scrambled brains. But there was a shrewd gleam in his eyes. At his side, the man he had spoken of, Mark Tyler, or Mark of London, showed a quick interest.

'Use your imagination,' Grandarse snapped. 'I don't like it any more than you do, but those are our orders, so get used to it.'

It took the men only a short time to grab hot bread from their morning fires to eat on the march and soon they were away. Berenger looked at Mark Tyler thoughtfully. The fellow was too keen by half about the idea of fighting. That was why Roger kept him close, no doubt. Always best to have the least-trusted men to hand where they could be watched; in a fight it was best to keep your friends close, and your enemies closer still.

Béatrice was glad to reach the little inn.

The old woman was dead. She had not lasted the night, and Béatrice wept over her corpse with a feeling of genuine bereavement. Both had suffered much in the last few days, and to lose a friend, even one of such brief duration, was a further blow to Béatrice.

That morning, she took the old woman's shawl and her purse, and set her hands crossed over her breast. There was no guilt at taking her money or belongings. Those items could not help their owner now, but they might serve to help Béatrice.

Setting out, she joined the thinning column of refugees. She had already marched many leagues, trying to put distance between herself and the English, but no matter how far they tramped, the news of murder, slaughter of animals, senseless ruin and rape increased. Riders from the coast with pale faces told of bestial acts by the enemy that were enough to chill the blood of any Frenchman. One shivered so with horror that he could not speak, and merely mouthed his shock when questioned.

The people slogged on, none too certain of their destination, hoping, all of them, that they might reach some sort of refuge. The King must arrive soon, they said, and throw these English swine from the land. But others disagreed: all too many had heard that Philippe had resisted the urge to do battle before. Some doubted that, even now, he would come to protect his people. The reflection did little to raise the spirits of the weary travellers.

This place, therefore, was a welcome sight: a large inn by the side of the road, already packed with people, but not turning any away. It made Béatrice feel a surge of joy, seeing that some people could still offer kindness to strangers, even one weary, dispossessed and desperate.

'What do you want?' The man at the door was short, but broad as the doorway itself. He eyed her truculently.

'I seek a chance to sit by a fire,' she said meekly.

'Where is your money?'

His manner was brusque, and Béatrice didn't understand why – and then she reflected that the poor man must have had hundreds no, thousands, beating at his door.

'I only want to sit at your fire a moment and warm myself,' she said. 'I am very tired. I've been walking since—'

'You want food, you have to pay; drink, you pay; a seat at my fire, you pay. Your money – where is it?'

'I have some here,' she said, gesturing at her hip. The purse was tied to the rope about her waist, under her cloak.

A second man had joined the doorman. He had blue eyes and a shock of dark curls. 'Let her in, my host,' he urged. She is hardly going to cause trouble, is she?' he said as she patted the coins, making them rattle. 'She can speak when she is inside.'

The innkeeper stood aside, and she entered nervously. A woman on her own was always at risk of rape or worse in a rural tavern.

Inside, the smoke rose lazily, choking the throat. There was no chimney, only a fire burning on a tiled hearth in the middle of the hall. Fresh rushes had been set about the floor, but the air reeked of rancid wine, woodsmoke and sweat from all the men and women inside.

Their faces were pale and haunted in the dimness. Some shielded children against their stomachs, standing or sitting in postures of feebleness and exhaustion. There were a few benches, and a couple of trestle tables had been put out, but for the most part it felt like a prison. The people in there were like prisoners in a dungeon of their own making. That thought made her shudder.

'Come, maid, I have a space over here,' the curly-haired man said. He led her to a corner. 'You should keep your money hidden,' he advised. 'It's dangerous in places like this or on the road, if people get to know that you are carrying lots of money.'

'Thank you.'

'Perhaps I should walk with you and protect you?'

'I should be glad of your help,' she gratefully said. 'An old woman gave me her purse. Her son stabbed her and left her for dead, and she gave it to me to save it from the English.'

'Really? How much did she give you?'

'I don't know. I didn't count it.'

'All the more reason for you to need a guard,' he said, and when he smiled, his eyes twinkled. 'I shall be your knight, maid. I will protect you.'

At the sight of that smile, she felt as though all her troubles were almost ended. It was the smile of an angel.

* * *

The nearest town, Barfleur, was a scant two leagues hence. It took them until the sun was a quarter of the way to midday, marching steadily but without urgency. They were in no hurry to reach it. They knew what to expect.

Then Berenger heard a sound – a low moaning. It needed to be investigated – although it might be a trap. He sent Geoff to the right, Clip to the left, and the bulk of his men spread between them. He kept only Jack with him, while Donkey he placed behind the rest. There was no point in seeing the boy hurt before he had learned which end of a sword was safest.

They were approaching a low wall, and the men crouched behind it. To their left, a pair of buildings had been burned, and even now the heat was like a dragon's exhalation. The wall appeared to be the boundary of a small pound, while on their right was a huddle of cottages. A vegetable garden nearby was devastated, with boot-prints visible amongst the flattened salads and beans. A boy's body lay among the remains.

The moaning started again as they reached him. His throat had been cut and the wound gaped. Berenger thought that he could see cartilage inside, but then it moved, and he realised it was flies, gorging themselves. Jack ended the boy's misery with his dagger.

Then, peering over the wall, Berenger was confronted with a scene that would remain with him for a long time.

'Your Royal Highness, my Lords,' Sir John said as he entered the Prince's large tent and bowed.

It was a simple construction a short way inland from the beach. Inside was only the most basic decoration: this was the working tent of a knight, not a gaudy display for a tournament. There was a pair of trestles: one covered with pages weighted with leather-covered stones, two clerks murmuring to each other as they worked through correspondence; the other held meats and cheeses set out on plundered silver plates, and wine in great jugs. Beyond that, the room contained all the essentials for a knight: spare armour, spare weapons and surcoats.

He had heard of foreign potentates who insisted upon their subjects treating them with a fawning reverence more suited to God than a mortal. They dared not gaze at their masters directly for fear of giving insult. Not, thank God, in England. Here, if a man were to avoid his eyes, a monarch would rightly be suspicious.

'Sir John. I am glad to see you,' the Prince said.

Edward of Woodstock, Prince of Wales, was a handsome young man of sixteen. Tall, broad-shouldered, with the neck of a fighting knight, he had trained from an early age with a heavy war helm in jousts and tournaments. His fair hair was long, and he had a thin moustache trimmed back from his mouth. His blue eyes were clear and confident.

Sir John thought much of his confidence was due to his father, but a large part came from the men in the pavilion with him.

Sitting on a stool and chewing on a honeyed lark, Thomas de Beauchamp, Earl of Warwick, was a heavy-set, dark-haired man in his early thirties. Already a war leader of great fame, having led the King's armies against the Scots, he was the Marshal of England, known for his intelligence, his devotion to his King – and his utter ruthlessness.

Behind him, resting against a trestle and toying with a long misericord dagger, was the Earl of Northampton, William de Bohun, a man as famous for his cunning as for his ferocity in battle. He had marched with King Edward from the first, being one of the King's most devoted comrades in the recent battles at Sluys and Morlaix.

'Your Royal Highness,' Sir John began, 'my men have returned from Barfleur. It is as we feared. The town is destroyed.'

Warwick took a bone from his mouth and sucked it noisily. 'None living?'

'No.'

'Then there will be no ships from there to harry the fleet, which is good.'

The young Prince glanced at Sir John. 'What do you say?'

Sir John cast an eye at the two magnates. The Prince had the same direct manner as his father. Against his better judgement, he found himself thinking that perhaps he could like this new Edward.

'Your father did not want men and women attacked if they had accepted the King's Peace.'

Warwick shrugged. 'I'm happy if there are no pirates attacking our army from the sea or cutting off our supplies.'

'So you would ignore my father's orders?' Edward said quietly.

There was no answer. After a moment, the Prince faced Sir John again. 'You say it is destroyed?'

'My men said that it was a scene of utter carnage.'

CHAPTER TEN

Carnage was right. Berenger thought the sights would sicken the Devil himself.

It was one thing to participate in the capture of a town, to rush at the walls of a fortress and clamber up the scaling ladders, expecting at any moment to be slain, knowing that the man beside you had fallen with a shriek, that the man before you had been punched in the chest by an arrow, and to expect that your own life was about to end. Then, when your entire mind was filled with the red mist and bloodlust – the primeval desire to slay all who stood before you and survive – then it was natural to use a sword, lance, axe, mace, club, anything, and lash out at those who dared defy you.

But it was different to walk into a town in cold blood and slaughter all the innocents there.

The place reeked of blood and death. Bodies littered the streets. Near Berenger a woman lay gutted on the threshold of a house, a baby sprawled pathetically beside her, its head crushed. Three men and a boy lay in the road, all beheaded, and opposite were smoking ruins where once had been houses. There was little standing that wasn't blackened by soot.

'Why are we here?' Geoff muttered. 'There's nothing for us to do.'

He spoke for them all. They had been sent to scout for potential threats from an enemy who was nowhere to be seen.

They had guessed that the town would have been attacked, but this was far worse than any of them had anticipated. As they wandered the streets, they came across women raped and discarded with a sword in the belly, men butchered, babies kicked or stamped to death. Blood seeped into the cobbles on all sides.

It was natural that the first men to disembark were sent to scout the lands all around. This was one of the first towns the English had reached, and their arrival had been as unexpected as it was savage. The proof lay all around.

'Come on, boys,' Berenger said. He took the lead and walked warily, the point of an arrowhead of men. Hearing a scurrying, he turned quickly, but it was only a pair of startled crows rising from a body near a chapel.

The whole town seemed to crackle and tick as burned timbers glowed and cob or brick walls cooled in the late-morning air. As he passed one ruined building, the heat from the brick walls licked at Berenger's cheek. It was so hot he thought his hair must blacken and curl.

Wisp was at his side, but he didn't meet anyone's eye. Since the day he had seen the cat in the cottage, he had withdrawn into a world of personal terror. The others were beginning to shun him.

'The Devil's been here,' he said. 'This is *his* work.'

'Shut up, Wisp,' Berenger snapped, nerves on edge.

At first, when they saw Wisp's fear, the others had been support-ive – even Clip had gone to speak with him – but the aura of unre-mitting gloom that now surrounded Wisp had repelled all their efforts. It was affecting the morale and cohesion of the vintaine, and Berenger didn't know how to combat it. Perhaps he should bellow and curse them out of this tension? Grandarse would have done so. If they could loot a barrel of wine, that might help.

He was no leader of men, he thought bitterly. When all went well, he was fine, but given a problem like Wisp, he was lost. A man used to dealing with disobedience would have been more competent: a father, a beadle or sergeant. Berenger was just a solitary soul. No woman, no children, only a life spent serving the interests of others.

'There's no one here. No one alive, anyway,' Geoff said, interrupting his thoughts.

'No, but we carry on,' Berenger said.

'Aye. Get your arses up the road,' Grandarse said. 'We have our orders.'

'Yes, there may be something,' Mark Tyler said.

Berenger and Roger exchanged a look. Tyler was too keen, whether on death or plunder, it was impossible to know; they would continue to watch him.

'Is there any sign of who could have been responsible?' Northampton asked. He had set the point of his dagger on his forefinger and was balancing it there.

'My Lord, the men say that there was no indication who the guilty men were.'

'It is fortunate,' Woodstock said. 'I would not want to have to tell my father that a particular vintaine had run amok. He would be displeased to learn that his own men could seek to ruin his plan.'

'My Lord?' Sir John said.

'Come, Sir John. You must know that the King has planned this in great detail.'

'Your Royal—' Warwick began in a warning growl.

'Peace, Sir Thomas! If I cannot trust a knight with Sir John's experience, whom may I trust? Sir John, I know that my father gave it out that he was keen to launch his war from Guyenne, but that was never in his mind. He always intended to begin in the lands from which William the Bastard attacked our shores all those years ago: Normandy. There is a poetic justice in landing in the same territory from which William embarked. My father has only one aim: to bring the false French King to battle and destroy him. Philippe is reluctant to fight, but we will make him.'

'He has a mighty army.'

'The French are bloated. They are so convinced that their horse will defeat any army, that they fail to study how others fight. Look at us! We innovate, we test new systems, new weapons, and when did we last lose a battle? You know Sir Thomas Dagworth?'

'Of course.'

'Did you hear of Brest last month? He stumbled across the army of Charles de Blois with thousands of battle-hardened Bretons. Dagworth had eighty men-at-arms and a hundred archers. Think of that! It was obviously pointless to fight, so Dagworth offered to surrender for ransom, but de Blois wanted his head. You can imagine it, eh? Dagworth's men hardly had time to put their trust in God.'

'This was over a month ago,' Warwick said. He dipped his fingers in a large bowl brought by an esquire, wiping his hands clean and standing.

'And Dagworth won!' Woodstock said gleefully. 'They held their positions – they were cut about dreadfully, of course – but when it came to nightfall, he and his men had fought the Bretons to a standstill and it was they who withdrew to lick their bloody wounds. Think of it! Sir Thomas and his men fought off an army twenty or thirty times their number, and lived to tell the tale! It's more impressive even than Thermopylae.'

'Wonderful,' Sir John nodded.

'Ah, well, you're so much older, Sir John, you will have seen even more marvellous battles, I am sure,' Edward said happily. 'Were you at Thermopylae yourself? You're old enough!' He laughed boyishly.

'Your Highness, that is well, but now the French must come and attack us. This chevauchée will attract a strong response.'

The Prince's eyes hardened. 'You are right, Sir John. But we are not here to terrorise peasants. We are here to *take* the crown. Philippe knows we can do it. We will force him to meet us, and we will wrest the crown from his head.'

'If he will fight,' Northampton said grimly. He had his dagger balanced perfectly, and he flicked it into the air now and caught it neatly. 'He has slunk away from battle before. He thinks to wait until we have run out of food, and then force us back to our ships, keeping his own knights in check.'

'He will have to fight,' Woodstock said. He took a silver-chased goblet from an esquire and drank deeply.

Warwick glanced at Northampton. 'But we will not have those wishing to enter the King's protection thinking they will be slaughtered if they do.'

'No,' Woodstock agreed, a little of his beaming joy falling away. 'Those who wish to enter the King's Peace must be aided, not robbed and killed.'

'Yes, Your Royal Highness,' Sir John said.

'See to it that your men are well-behaved at all times, then,' Woodstock said. 'I will have all obey the King's proclamation.

Especially my Welshmen. I would not have any of my own men become known for disobedience.'

Archibald the Gynour sat with his back to the wagon and scratched his head through his scorched and stained coif, running through the list of items he had stored.

It had taken time for the sailors to help him offload his equipment. One huge barrel, linen bags full of stones and pieces of iron, and the barrels of coarse black powder. This was to be a new war, he knew. A war of destruction; a war of terror.

He had set all his toys in the bed of this wagon, balancing everything fore and aft as well as side to side. With the weight involved, it would take only a slight misdistribution to break the axle or wheels even of this great wagon.

There was a fire a short distance away, and he cast a jealous eye to it, but he didn't bother to go and speak with the men there. He knew how he would likely be received. A Serpentine – one expert in the use of black powder – was more often than not viewed with alarm and distrust by ordinary soldiers.

It meant that most of his life was spent alone. Other men tended to shun him. He had no companion, no youthful apprentice or servant. His work was his own. He must do all his own preparations, his own cooking.

The fact was, a man who could control a vast gonne like his, a fellow who smelled of rancid grease and brimstone, was not thought to be good company.

Brimstone was the smell of the Devil, after all.

CHAPTER ELEVEN

Berenger and his men had wandered back through Barfleur without speaking. There was nothing to be said.

'It will reflect on us, to our shame, this vile carnage,' Wisp muttered.

'Shut up, Wisp. It's not helping,' Berenger snapped. 'Geoff, take Clip and Matt to the church and see if anyone's hiding up there. Jack, take Eliot and Walt towards the harbour. See what you can find there. The rest of you, come with me.'

The vintener was relieved to see that the Donkey's eyes were wide with shock as he walked amongst the dead. He did not appear to revel in the sights, which was a relief. Perhaps there was something in the boy's heart that might be salvaged.

Suddenly there was a cry. Berenger crouched, his hand in the air already clutching an arrow. The men went quiet and he slowly lowered his arm, nocking the arrow to the string, every sense straining. He held the arrow in place with his forefinger and slowly continued forward, step by cautious step, fingers on the bowstring.

He paused in a doorway, searching for the source of the sounds. There were screams now, although they were diminishing in intensity.

Darting from his cover, he trotted onwards, and was amazed at what he found.

Outside a great building, there was a crowd, perhaps a hundred all told, with thirty armed men holding them back. A trio stood before them, wearing tunics and hosen of brown and green. Two held a man against a board that had been set against a wall, lashing his wrists to the top, his ankles to staples at the bottom. Finished, they stood back and the third man took up a lance, stropping it thoughtfully before holding it to his victim's belly.

At either side Berenger saw more bodies. All had been stabbed many times.

Berenger swore and stood up from his crouch, beckoning his men. 'What is this?' he roared.

The man with the lance stopped and turned to face him. It was Erbin the Welshman.

'You came to join us?' he said.

Berenger motioned to the bound man. 'Who is he?'

'A merchant who's trying to thwart the Prince.'

'He doesn't look dangerous.'

'He has concealed his money and won't tell us where it is,' Erbin said. He rested the tip of the lance on the man's breast and one of his men reached forward and tore his cotte open. Beneath it the man had only a pale, cream chemise, and the Welshman ripped it wide. Erbin allowed the point of the lance to fall to the man's breast. It gleamed wickedly.

'This is looting.'

'No, this is the recovery of the Prince's gold. We've won the town, and the treasure within belongs to our Prince. If a man conceals his wealth, he is setting himself in opposition to our Prince.'

The lance began a slow meander down the man's body. It slid to his left breast, seemingly gently, but the blade was like a razor. A thin trickle of blood appeared from his throat to his nipple. And then Erbin moved and the lance was sent to the other breast.

From the merchant's mouth came a thin, high keening. His eyes were wide, gazing up, away from the hideous weapon, and his head slammed from side to side as though he was trying to knock himself out. In the crowd, women screamed and wailed, and would not stop even when the men holding them back beat at them with the butts of their lances. One man pulled a cudgel from his belt and brought it down on the head of a grieving woman who instantly collapsed and fell silent.

Berenger turned and bellowed to his men. As they rushed forward, he once more faced Erbin, but now he drew his bow. 'Release him!'

Erbin snapped a command and three men turned their lances to Berenger. 'You'll be dead before your arrow's left the bow. Don't be foolish, Englishman. Leave us to do the Prince's work.'

'Prince's work be damned. You're looting! Release him, said!'

'If you insist,' Erbin said. He withdrew his lance, turning and facing Berenger. Then, as Berenger let his arrow-point fall, the bow's tension slackening, Erbin turned and thrust. The lance struck the man below the ribs, and he gasped, his entire body convulsing, eyes popping. 'There, *English*, I've set his soul free.'

Berenger's bow was already rising when two lance-tips touched his belly. He hesitated, the bow partly bent, the arrow ready.

Jack and Geoff were with him now. Geoff took one lance and hauled it aside, while Geoff slammed his bow down on the other, knocking it down and kicking it away, but it was too late.

The merchant was panting like an injured dog, the weight of the pole dragging at his body. He wasn't dead, but the terrible knowledge of his doom was in his eyes as he stared at the weapon, at the blood running down the shaft and pooling on the cobbles.

At last the crowd was silent. The sight held all spellbound in horror.

Berenger handed his bow to Geoff. There were more Welshmen than their vintaine, and to fight them would have been pointless. They were all too close. A man with a lance has a long reach.

'You do not fear the Prince?' Berenger said, approaching Erbin.

'He had nothing, but he attacked us,' Erbin said.

'You are like a boy who enjoys tying a burning bush to a cat's tail, or beating a dog with sticks,' Berenger snarled, and his fist caught Erbin's jaw as he spoke, lunging forward with all the weight of his body behind it. There was a loud click as Erbin's teeth connected, and then he stumbled backwards, spitting blood. Berenger followed him and kicked him in the belly, then punched him as hard as he could, his fist meeting Erbin's skull just over his ear. The man reeled.

Berenger went over to the dying man, pulled the lance free and cast it aside, and as soon as he did, the wound gushed. It smelled rank in that town square.

The man sobbed quietly, staring at the blood pouring so thickly, and then cast him a despairing look.

Berenger drew his dagger and, before the man could speak, plunged it into his heart, both hands gripping the hilt, holding it there while the merchant's mouth stretched wide in a gasp of surprise. He sagged, like a man going to sleep after a long day's hard work, and Berenger saw a spark of gratitude flare before his eyes dimmed forever.

Berenger turned to see Erbin slowly climbing to all fours, where he remained, coughing and shaking his head. When he looked around, there was silence on all sides. The other Welshmen watched him sullenly, impassive – although two fingered their weapons. Berenger's sudden attack had stunned them all into immobility. 'Take that piece of dung away from here,' Berenger grated, pointing at Erbin.

Geoff and Jack began to draw their bows, and the nearer Welshmen stood aside. The people held inside the cordon started to move away, nervously glancing from side to side as they went. Children sheltered from the gaze of the soldiers as their mothers pulled cloaks about them.

Berenger removed his dagger from the dead man's breast. The woman who had been clubbed by the guard had managed to get to her feet. He saw that she was about one or two and thirty, with brown hair that held only a few grey strands. She stood with tears streaming down her face, her hand at her mouth to stifle her despair. Then, slowly, she fell to her knees in the merchant's blood.

As two Welshmen helped Erbin to his feet. Berenger went to him. He grabbed Erbin's shirt and methodically wiped the blood from his blade, staring into Erbin's eyes all the time. While he did so, the woman rose and walked to his side. She took his hand.

'Merci, Monsieur,' she said in a low voice, and then turned to Erbin and studied him a moment before spitting in his face.

*　　*　　*

Béatrice was glad to have met this man in the inn. For the first time in months, she felt safe again, with someone to protect her.

His name, he said, was Alain. He came from a little hamlet not far from Barfleur, and had fled when the first news of the invasion came. Luckily he had no family, so he didn't have to chivvy a wife or children; he could merely pack and leave at once.

'The sights – well, you know. You saw the same,' he said, turning his magnificent blue eyes upon her.

'It was terrifying,' she agreed. 'I spent my time in fear.'

A man walking nearby caught a glimpse of her and made a lewd comment. She pulled her shawl tighter about her, drawing her legs up beneath her.

Alain stood up and smiled at the man. 'You like the lady?' he asked smoothly.

'Yes. She's a pretty wench. I'd like to cuddle with her tonight,' the man said. He was built like a bear, with thick arms and legs, and a belly that would have suited a bishop. Greying hair framed narrow-set eyes.

'I'm afraid that will be impossible,' Alain told him. 'You see, she is with me.'

'What, are you married to that?' the fellow sneered and took a pace forward as if to reach for her.

Alain suddenly whipped a knife from his belt and stood with it touching the other's throat. 'I say she and I are friends. I won't see her hurt. So, unless you want to be leeched of all your blood, I would move away.'

A drop of blood like a tear-drop ruby appeared on the man's skin.

'All right, I get it – she's all yours,' the man said, and returned to his own seat with many a black look over his shoulder. Alain, however, appeared to care nothing for his new enemy. He chattered easily and calmly.

'You will need be wary of him,' Béatrice said quietly a while later.

'Not I,' Alain shrugged. 'We shall leave early in the morning, before the drunken sot awakes.'

It was enough to calm her. For the first time since her father's death she slept easy that night.

The box of communal flour was raided again. There was little enough food for the men when they returned to their camp from Barfleur, and now they were all watching their small oat cakes sizzling by the fire, chatting desultorily. Only Wisp was silent, his eyes filled with a terrible conviction.

Berenger walked over to the Donkey. 'You did well today,' he said as he crouched beside the lad.

'I didn't break down, you mean?'

'You coped with the sights, is what I meant.'

Donkey did not reply but sat staring hungrily at the flames, seemingly entranced by the sparks and glimmers.

'Tell me about it, boy,' Berenger said quietly.

'What?'

'Those Welshmen. What happened to you in Portsmouth before we found you?'

He watched the lad closely. He needed to learn more about him, find out what was concealed in his breast. It was vital that he knew he could trust him. There was no room in his vintaine for someone unreliable.

'What happened to you in Portsmouth?' he repeated.

Ed sighed. 'I heard of the men mustering. I had some coin saved, and I slipped from home and made my way to town. It was scary. There were strangers all about, but no matter who I

79

spoke to, nobody wanted to take me on. Until I met Erbin's men.'

'How so?'

'I was in an alley. They came past me, and I followed them into a tavern.'

'They spoke to you?'

'I asked if I could join them, and they laughed. But I had my purse with me, and I showed them my money. That was when Erbin said if I was to buy them ale, they'd think about it. He said the drinks would seal our pact. So I did, and then, when they were about to go, I asked him about joining them, and he spat at me and said it was a joke; they never meant to have me in their party. I wasn't strong enough to hold a sword in battle, he said, so I could whistle for a position in the army. He didn't even mention my money or my purse.'

'And then?'

'I demanded my money back, and they beat me up and left me there, lying in the kennel, where you found me.'

Berenger had watched him all through his speech. His fingers wound themselves about the loose threads of his tunic, and his eyes were occasionally at Berenger's face, at times playing about the land all about them. His feet fidgeted, his toes tapping at the ground.

'The money is gone, boy. And they probably threw away your purse. Try to forget them. They'll forget you soon enough.'

'How can I?'

'Easily. As you get older, you'll realise that it's not worth holding a grudge. Those Welshmen didn't try to insult you personally. They were in a tavern, you had money, so they took what they wanted. It is what men will do.'

He wasn't explaining himself well, he knew. He had another go. 'When I was younger, I used to want to keep holding grudges. I nursed them well so that they grew strong. And then, one day, I was given a pardon from the man I least expected to forgive me. Since then, I've tried to be worthy of it.'

'A pardon?' Ed looked at him with a frown. 'For what?'

'Helping a good man,' Berenger said shortly. 'So if I can do that, and be forgiven by his son, you can forgive a trick.'

No, the boy wasn't lying. It explained much about the attitude of the Welshmen to the Donkey, their sneering and contempt. It also explained the boy's own helpless anger in the face of their taunts.

But it wasn't the whole story. Berenger was convinced of that.

CHAPTER TWELVE

16 July

Sir John de Sully was in his tent when his esquire scratched at the canvas. 'What is it, Richard?' he called.

'Sir John, Berenger Fripper is here.' Richard Bakere gave a meaningful look down at Sir John's hands. The knight was honing his sword's blade, rasping the soft stone along the edges with that familiar swishing hiss.

'Good. Bring him inside.'

It was not Bakere's fault, Sir John thought, but he did assume that his knight was too superior and elevated to sink to cleaning his own weapons. Damn that! Sir John had cleaned and sharpened and oiled and polished his own weapons for more than thirty years now. When he was too old to see to his own equipment, he would cease riding to war. For him, it was an essential part of a knight's duty, to take care of his weaponry. His life depended on all being in perfect working order.

If he didn't like it, his esquire could damn well seek a new master.

'Fripper, come, take a cup of wine with me,' he said.

'You asked to see me, Sir John?'

'Yes,' Sir John said. While Bakere poured them both wine, Sir John studied the fellow. He saw that Berenger's face was haggard. That was natural. They were all tired, after marching or riding all over the countryside without a proper bed. Although they had not been forced to endure the worst of the weather, marching in the heat was itself exhausting. A man trudged on, thinking wistfully of ale and wine, while the sweat soaked his hat and clothing. Soon, straps for knapsacks would wear away a man's shoulder, and blood would begin to ooze. Necks would be rubbed raw, feet would develop blisters, and a man's temper would fray. It was all too common, and no one was immune.

Still, there was something about this man that was familiar. He recalled that feeling from before, when he had visited Grandarse's centaine.

'I know you, don't I?' he said.

'You and I walked together some years ago,' Berenger said. 'We crossed the sea and made our way on foot to Avignon.'

Sir John was still for a moment, then, 'You were with me then?'

'I was one of the party with the Welshman.'

'In God's name, that was a long time ago,' Sir John breathed.

'Sixteen years, I think.'

'The years have not been kind to you.'

Berenger gave a grin. 'Sir John, do you have a mirror?'

The knight gave a chuckle. 'Aye. Every white hair has been earned.'

They were quiet for a while, both remembering: a long journey, walking to visit the Pope and deliver their charge into his care.

'Do you ever hear from him?' Berenger asked.

Sir John peered into his wine. 'There was never anyone to hear from. The man didn't exist, did he?' he said quietly.

'No.' Berenger knew that their mission that year had been secret. No one could know of their companion, because he was officially dead. To talk of him had, for years, carried the threat of execution.

'But now, I think he is dead. You have heard that our King's son has been created Prince of Wales, like the King's father?'

'The King never took the title for himself, did he?' Berenger said.

'His father never relinquished it,' Sir John said.

Berenger nodded. Edward II had kept the Welsh title for his own. He had always been inordinately proud of his Principality, and the people who remained loyal to him even at the last, when the rest of his realm crumbled and submitted to his adulterous wife and her lover.

Sir John took a deep breath and held up his drink. 'To the health of a man who was already dead when he walked with us to Avignon,' he said. The two toasted the memory, and then Sir John frowned. 'Talking of Welshmen, there are rumours of disharmony between them and your men.'

'Sir?'

'The Welsh say that you've started a feud with them. It will not do.'

'That is untrue.'

'Have you not come to blows with them?'

'You want an answer?'

Sir John eyed him. 'Not really, no. But be wary of them, Fripper. They are dangerous enemies to have. Stronger men have been ruined by them.'

Berenger's face went hard for a moment as he remembered the woman murmuring, 'Merci,' to him in the town's square. 'Yes, sir. I'll try to remember that.'

'Are your men bearing up?'

'Yes. Well enough.'

'We'll see their mettle when we have a real fight.'

'Yes, Sir John.'

'Good. And keep away from the Welsh, if you can.'

'We will try to.'

'That will help. You must remember that the Prince has himself only recently been elevated to Prince of Wales. Like his grandfather, he is proud of his Principality and its people.'

'I understand,' Berenger said. Then he added: 'There is one among them, Erbin, who delights in trouble. At Barfleur he burned the town, killing many.'

'So it *is* true about the feud, then.'

'Not on my part, Sir John, no. But he may have taken it into his head to cause friction whenever he sees me and my men, no matter what we do or say.'

Sir John considered. 'Avoid him, and all will be well.'

'Yes, sir. And do you have any idea when we are likely to find the French?'

Sir John smiled. 'They will try to stop us very soon – before we can turn towards Paris.'

'Paris?' Berenger repeated, shocked. That was a vast city, from all he had heard. It would take more than a few score knights and ten thousand archers to breach her great defences.

'We aren't here on a reconnaissance, Fripper. We're here to establish the King's rights. For that, we need Paris. Or at least, to make a demonstration of our power that will so shock the French and Parisians, that they surrender to us.'

'Yes, Sir John,' Berenger said, but his mind was reeling. *Paris*! He had faith in his men, his army and his King, but to take Paris would be like trying to seize Jerusalem again! It was an appalling idea!

Sir John watched him go, grinning at Berenger's reaction. They could not take Paris, of course. That would need many more men – he knew that perfectly well. But the French didn't, and if the English made a strong enough demonstration in the direction of the capital, they might so raise the fever of terror in Paris that the citizenry would hand over the keys without a fight. If all went well.

Aye. If all went well.

17 July

They were marching at last.

'Christ Jesus, it's a relief to be moving,' Geoff declared.

Wisp just grunted.

They had made their way down to the south of St Vaast-la-Hogue, and now the vintaine was descending a hill on a road that had been built for a peasant's donkeys, rather than wagons.

'You're quiet,' Jack said to Wisp.

Wisp peered up at the sky. How could he explain his despair? The sight of the hanged cat was an evil omen, no matter how a man looked at it. He was sure his premonition of doom was correct. 'I am well enough,' he said.

'Glad I am to hear it,' Jack said. 'These French will mass enough men to trample us into the mire if they can. We need all the fellows we have. Even you.'

'Him?' Clip called from behind them. 'Wisp'd blow away in a breeze, he would. Look at him: hardly enough muscle on him to hold a knife, let alone a bleeding sword.'

'He has fist enough to give you a thump,' Geoff grunted. He was scouting ahead to their left, searching every tree, every bush, for ambush.

'Him? His fists wouldn't pass through a fog on the Avon!'

'Perhaps we'll put wagers on you two, then, eh?' Jack chuckled. 'You can fight when we camp this evening.'

'I'd not want to hurt him,' Clip said righteously. ''Sides, the King wants all of us fit and hearty for the real fight to come.'

'When we find the French at last, you mean,' Jack called.

'When we find the French, aye,' Geoff said.

Clip shook his head, hawked and spat. 'It doesn't matter. We'll all soon be dead. They'll murder us, the French.'

'Yes,' Wisp said quietly. Jack heard, and shot him a look, but made no comment. Instead he allowed his pace to slow a little, so that he dropped back behind Wisp.

'Still bad, is he?' Berenger asked, seeing his face.

'As bad as a man can be. By God's blood, I don't want him near me in a battle. He's already convinced himself he'll die, damn his soul!'

'He'll snap out of it.'

'If he doesn't, I'll snap his neck for him,' Jack said bluntly.

Berenger nodded. A comrade who was convinced that failure lurked around every corner was a dangerous companion. If a man could not trust his neighbour in a shield wall or assault, confidence in the whole army was lost. It took only a brief loss of trust during a battle, a momentary loss of commitment, for an army to fail. Just now, Wisp was the worst threat to their vintaine.

Ach, there was little he could do now. Not while they marched.

He would just have to hope for the best.

*   *   *

Béatrice woke to the sound of snoring several times in the middle of the night, but she didn't feel threatened. There was nowhere else to sleep but on the floor – others with better funds had already taken the benches – and whenever one man moved, three or four others complained. No one could attack her in such a press.

The people slept where they had sat, lying higgledy-piggledy like garbage in a midden, all taking what space they could. Although she had planned to be up early with Alain, Béatrice had not realised how tired she was, and did not waken until the sun was over the surrounding hills.

Alain was already awake when she finally stirred, yawning and blearily rubbing her eyes. 'You slept well,' he greeted her.

She rolled stiff shoulders to ease them. 'I could have slept at the bottom of a well, I was so tired.'

'Well, hurry yourself. We must be off as quickly as we can,' he said, gazing across the room to where the bear-like man from the night before stood studying them grimly.

She nodded. Although she had money enough to buy some food to break their fast, it would be better to use it somewhere else. In a chamber like this, too many men could take it into their heads to rob a maid on the road.

They hefted their packs and were soon on their way, but before they had taken more than a handful of paces, there was a shout from the inn.

'Quickly,' Alain said, forging ahead with long strides. It was hard for her to keep up, he moved so fast.

'Maid, maid, are you weary?' he asked when he realised she was falling behind. 'Come!'

She smiled, but then she saw his eyes go over her shoulder. Turning, she saw their enemy running after them, the innkeeper at his side. She gave a little scream, and hurried on to Alain for safety. There was no thought in her mind other than reaching him. Alain was her guide and protector. He had saved her last night, and now, with his clear blue eyes concentrating on the men following, she felt sure he was equal to defending her again.

'Behind me,' he hissed and shoved her from his path. 'Get your knife out!'

She obeyed him, pulling her little knife from its sheath at her belt. It still had a dark crust marring its blade, she saw, and shivered.

The innkeeper ran first to Alain, but the other had different ideas. He slowed as he neared the two, and while Alain and the innkeeper circled each other warily, he stood before Béatrice. He put a hand to his cods and smiled at her. 'You want to fight first? That's good. I like a girl with a bit of spirit.' And suddenly he darted close, his hands grabbing for her.

Béatrice sprang away, her knife held close before her. She had never been taught how to fight. It hadn't been necessary when she lived with her father. And now, she had the skills and knowledge to take care of herself.

'Come, maid! Be friendly, and you'll soon be on your way,' he said with a chuckle.

She ignored him, distracted by the sight before her: the innkeeper had grasped Alain, and the two were struggling with each other, two daggers flashing in the pale light.

The bearded man tried another lunge at her. This time she swung her own knife as she moved away, and he swore loudly as it sliced the back of his hand. A long red cut opened, and he glared at her as he licked at the wound like a dog. 'If you won't be friendly, you won't leave here on your feet, bitch,' he growled. 'They'll have to carry you away.'

But even as he threatened her, a voice shouted. Other refugees had seen the fight, and now they came running, six men, roaring at them to cease. Béatrice saw her opponent turn and eye the new arrivals, and then he ran at her, pushing her to the ground. He didn't wait to pursue his little victory, but ran off up the road.

Alain and the innkeeper were still locked together, grunting and swearing at each other in their unholy embrace. The newcomers ringed them as if unsure what to do.

'Stop them!' she cried, but no one moved. They were watching the spectacle like men at a cockfight.

Finally, Béatrice took matters into her own hands. She walked over to them and with all her strength, she swung her full purse at the innkeeper's head. It struck with a sound like lead maul hitting a plank. The big man took two paces back, swaying, then fell to his rump.

Alain stood there panting. Then he kicked the innkeeper once, with main force, in the side of the head, and the man collapsed. 'So shall all felons meet their judgement,' he said breathlessly. 'This man tried to rob me and rape my wife. Anyone else want to have a go?'

A few minutes later, the pair were on their way again. Béatrice felt safer as they walked on amongst the other refugees, straggling along ahead and behind, but all the way, she knew that somewhere in the road ahead or in the woods at either side, was their enemy – the man with the beard.

She was as scared of him as she was of the English.

CHAPTER THIRTEEN

The army had split into three sections: the vanguard was under Sir Edward of Woodstock. Berenger had looked askance on hearing that but, to his relief, Warwick and Northampton were with the young Prince to advise him on his way. Behind them came the main part of the King's men, with archers, hobelars and men-at-arms in a straggling column across a wide front, and at the rear came the last men with the wagon train, led by the Earls of Arundel, Suffolk and Huntingdon, as well as the ferocious Bishop of Durham, a prelate who was more fearsome than any knight, in Berenger's view. The man's sword was as notched and chipped as a crusader's, and any man seeking compassion from him during a battle had best look to his defence.

'Where are we going today, Berenger?' Clip called.

'East.'

'Any chance of plunder?'

Berenger grunted. So far that morning, all they had found was ruined and burned little hamlets where scouts and hopeful

English had sought to despoil local farms. It was astonishing to Berenger that they had bothered. There could be nothing of any value, save perhaps a woman or two.

The weather was kind. Not too hot, and the dust of the road was lying low after a brief shower.

They were ahead of the main body of the army and to the right. It was because of their position that they were the first to see the French. Thin woods sprawled on either side, with bushes and clumps of ferns beneath. On their right, the land rose, and a hill stood out clearly.

'Berenger?' Jack called, and pointed ahead. The vintener nodded and slipped forward.

'What?' Ed said. 'What is it?' He was too short to see over the scrubby bushes. But though he could not see, he could sense the tension.

The archers crouched, pulling strings from purses or hats and bending their bows, grabbing arrows and nocking them with an easy familiarity, glancing back towards Berenger when ready.

He was standing still, a hand on a tree-limb and staring ahead intently.

'What do you think?' Geoff said.

'You've got the best eyesight,' Berenger said irritably. 'What do *you* see?'

'Four men-at-arms on horseback. I can see the sun catch on mail and plate. I think that's all – I can't see any more.'

'Are they French?'

'At this distance they could be Teutons for all I know,' Geoff said with asperity.

'How far?'

'At a guess, three bow-shots.'

'Then we go on, but archers, watch your front and flanks. I don't want to walk into a trap.'

Ed was about to step forward when Clip grabbed the shoulder of his jack and jerked him back. For all that Clip looked scrawny as an old cockerel that had fasted for a week, he had a wiry power in his fingers. 'Wait,' he hissed.

Geoff, Eliot, Jon Furrier and Matthew had already moved on, weapons ready, while Berenger spoke quickly to Roger, the vintener of the second vintaine. Roger had already pointed to four of his own men, and Ed saw them melting away amongst the bushes. Berenger gave a quiet command, and the rest of the vintaine began to make their way cautiously through the long grasses.

Ed shrugged away Clip's hand and walked on. The whole vintaine looked on him as a slave, he thought grumpily, just a fetcher-and-carrier, nothing more. They couldn't see his fervent desire to find a Frenchman and cut his throat. He had much to repay—

A sudden grab at his arm, and the air was ejected from his lungs as his back crashed to the hard earth. He could do no more than gasp for breath as Clip sprang lightly over him and thrust his sword into a bush.

There was a shriek, and then, while Ed lay staring wildly about him, men erupted from all directions. They had been concealed in the vegetation, and now fought with desperation. Ed rose to his knees, breathing hard, and was immediately hit on his back by something. When he looked around, he saw a forearm with a dagger gripped in its fist lying in the road. The owner was a few yards away, staring at his bloody stump, and then his head seemed to jerk and a blade appeared in his brow. Berenger had struck him from behind, and almost clove his head in two.

The man fell to his knees, Berenger swearing loudly as he struggled to free his blade. As two more men came running through the undergrowth, Ed dived to the ground, and only at the last moment did he see both men punched backwards as English arrows found their marks.

Ed rose to his feet, shivering, as Berenger placed his boot on the back of the dead Frenchman and jerked his sword sideways like a woodsman freeing his axe from a log. The man's head turned, twisted, gave a crack, and then the blade slid free.

'You all right, Donkey?' Berenger panted.

'Yes. I . . . I think so.'

'He didn't get hit,' Clip said. He was behind Berenger, grinning.

'Battle isn't as easy as you thought, is it, lad?' Berenger said.

Ed looked down at the fist with the dagger still clenched in its grip, and puked.

'Hoy, Frip – over here,' Clip shouted. 'Take a look! We've got a live one.'

Berenger left Ed rocking on his knees and holding his belly, and strode across to join Clip and Geoff.

The badly injured Frenchman at their feet was only young, with barely the stubble to colour his jaw. Dark eyes stared with a wild disbelief at the pain, as his hands clutched his lower belly. Blood pulsed thickly through his fingers.

'Where are you from?' Berenger asked in French.

The man winced. 'I will not say! You will kill all our people!'

'Kings don't murder peasants. Who would do the work, then, lad?' Berenger said gently.

The Frenchman closed his eyes a moment. 'Valognes. I come from Valognes.'

'Is it far?'

'A league. We wanted to divert you.'

'With so few men?'

'We didn't think so many of you were here.'

'Where is the French army?'

'What French army? The Marshal rode through a few days ago, kept on going.'

'Are there other forces about here?'

'There were five hundred Genoese, but they left.'

'Left?' Berenger was aware that Ed had joined them and now stood staring at the blood with horrified fascination.

'Three days before you landed. They hadn't been paid,' the man said hoarsely. His face was grey and screwed up with pain.

'Where did they go?'

'I don't know. They didn't pass our town. Only the Marshal. His men were here to defend us. Look at me! Did they defend *me*?'

His face ran with tears as he looked up at Berenger, and as he squeezed his eyes against the pain, more ran down his cheeks.

Berenger looked at Geoff, who met his glance and shook his head. Both could smell the sewer-stench of faeces – the blow that opened his belly had broken into his bowels, and that meant a slow, hideously painful death.

'You wanted to kill a Frenchman,' Berenger said harshly to Ed. 'Here you are: take your knife. Cut his throat.'

Ed looked up sharply. 'Me?'

'You said you wanted to kill men. Here's your chance.'

'I can't. No!'

Berenger looked at him and nodded. He had not expected the Donkey to be able to do this. It was the hardest job of a soldier, killing for mercy. 'Good.'

'You fought bravely, my friend,' Berenger said, and reached down to pat the Frenchman's shoulder. 'Go with God.'

The Frenchman smiled thinly as Geoff slipped the long, thin dagger in at his neck and down into his heart. He was dead before Geoff pulled the dagger out again.

CHAPTER FOURTEEN

18 July

Grandarse spat into the fire. 'Aye, a grand town, that. Full of the choicest furs, pewter, silver, wine, jewels and women, aye – and here we are. In the sodding *shite* again.'

Sir John had apologised as he ordered Grandarse to the east of Valognes. Now, maybe two miles away, Berenger and the others were camping as best they could in a small wood on a slight hill, but while they had some shelter, a thin rain drove at them, and no one was comfortable.

'As usual, we take all the risks, and those bone-idle sons of whores get the wine and warm beds,' Jack complained, swaddled in his blanket.

'It's not fair!' was Clip's view. 'We should have been in there with the others. Why do we always get the bastard jobs?'

'The Welsh, did you see how they went scurrying in like rats after a dead pig? All over the place they were,' Geoff grumbled.

'At least the town surrendered,' Berenger said. He lay back

and closed his eyes. The rain was an irritation, but he had a waxed cloak, and the damp wouldn't stop his sleep. Nothing ever did. He could go to sleep in the middle of a battle, if folk would promise not to stand on him.

'We should have put them all to the sword,' Ed muttered.

Berenger opened an eye and glanced at Grandarse. He didn't want to say, 'I told you so,' but for a moment the temptation was very strong.

Grandarse leaned over and cuffed Ed over the head. 'Boy, when you've killed your own man, you can say things like that. Until then, keep your trap shut or I'll take a whip to your scrawny hide.'

'That's why we're here, isn't it?' Ed demanded.

'No, Donkey, that's *not* why we're here,' Berenger said, his eyes closed once more. 'We are here because our King, Edward the Third of England – soon to be, by the Grace of God, King of France as well – has commanded us to join him. But while you can take all you can plunder from a town that won't submit willingly, you may *not* assault and murder the people who ask to come into the King's Peace.'

'Why not? They're our enemies!'

'If they surrender to his justice, they are the King's people,' Berenger pointed out.

'Well, I reckon the only good Frenchman is a dead one,' Ed mumbled.

'You have so much experience of them,' Clip said sarcastically.

'I've had enough, yes! They— No matter.' Ed put his arms about his knees and hid his face.

Berenger threw another look to Grandarse. There was more to Ed's hatred of the French than he had guessed. He would have to speak to the lad once again and try to learn what was on his mind.

19 July

Archibald Tanner grunted as he clambered from the rear of his wagon. He saw a boy seeking employment, and soon had him rubbing down the oxen in exchange for an offer of bread and wine. The lad worked in a lackadaisical manner, yawning with an almost devotional dedication, his eyes half-closed with exhaustion. He was too young for this harsh world.

Who wasn't too young? Archibald had enough experience of the world to know that the people who infested it were cruel. Even those who enjoyed the religious life could be as unkind and greedy for power and position as any merchant in a city. All wanted money and control over others. He had learned that while in the monastery.

More, he had realised out here in the world of men that a mild manner and genial attitude would not win friends. While affable in all his dealings, because of his craft he was still looked upon as a worshipper of the Devil or worse. Even now, as he sat and made his camp beside his wagon, he could see the suspicion on the faces of the army men. As soon as he held their gaze, they hurriedly turned away.

It was enough to make a cat laugh. But he had no need of boon companions. He was a self-contained man, happy with his own company. That was one useful thing he had learned from the Church.

'Leave them to their rest now, boy,' he called, and set about lighting a fire some safe distance from his wagon. Soon he had flames leaping from his tinder, and he sat and fed twigs to the fire.

He had some bread, old and hard as the boards of his wagon, which he cut apart with his knife, throwing the fragments into his cook pot. Some leaves he had gathered from the hedgerows, and garlic he had found in a field, along with some salt, formed the basis of a good, warming pottage. The boy knelt close by, gratefully sniffing at the odour.

'That smells good,' a voice said.

Archibald had learned the art of remaining still when surprised. A master of theology had often found him dreaming and would chastise him for it. His head, he was told, was too often in the clouds, when he should have been concentrating on his prayers. He had countered that, saying surely by definition prayer *should* elevate a man's thoughts. Now he said simply, 'For a meal without meat, it serves well enough.'

'There's meat if you want it,' the man said. 'There have been two herds captured, if you wish for a cut of beef.'

'Who are you?' Archibald asked.

'I'm called Mark of London, or Mark Tyler.' The man squatted at Archibald's side. 'I'm with the vintaine over there. An archer.'

'I'm glad to hear it,' Archibald said. He recalled seeing the fellow. Tyler was with one of the vintaines under Grandarse. He rather liked Grandarse: a man after his own heart. This Tyler was different. Archibald didn't like his quick, furtive glances at Archibald's belongings and pottage. 'But while I am glad to have news of any food, this is a Wednesday and I am happy to forgo the pleasures of swine and beef, and partake of more modest fare.'

'Eh?'

'I won't eat meat today,' Archibald translated piously. 'I trained to the religious life, and I will not eat meat on a fast day.'

'Who keeps Wednesday as a fast day?' Tyler scoffed. He was peering at the barrels in the back of the wagon.

'Those trained by Holy Mother Church.'

Tyler gave a twisted grin in which suspicion and disbelief were mingled. 'Even when it's put in front of you? My priest in London didn't worry about fasting on a Wednesday.'

'Perhaps he did not. Do you want something from my wagon, my son?'

'No. Why?'

'You appear unable to remove your eyes from my barrels.'

'I was just wondering what you carry there?'

'My friend, you are too rooted in the secular world. It is better to accept the philosophical life. Throw aside greed and avarice. Enjoy in moderation the good things that God has given you.'

Archibald winked at the boy sitting opposite. He was still yawning fit to unhinge his jaw.

'You were a monk, but now you are here with the men working on bridges and roads?' Tyler said.

'I'm a specialist gynour,' Archibald informed him.

'What does that mean?'

'I work with powder and fire: I bring fire from the heavens and thunder from the clouds, and harness them to hurl at the enemy.'

Tyler regarded him with a confused scowl. 'What?'

'It means, my son, you are a man of little wit and less empathy. It means I don't know you and don't trust you, and have made that clear; yet you still persist in trying to learn what you may about me and my business. I do not like that. Nor do I like you.'

Tyler shrugged and tried to grin, but he could not conceal his annoyance. He rose, offended, saying, 'I see I'm not welcome.'

'There you speak truly,' Archibald said comfortably. He watched as Tyler hitched up his belt and walked away, casting a black scowl over his shoulder as he went.

'That man I would not trust with a broken flint,' Archibald said ruminatively.

The boy stared over his shoulder. 'Him? I didn't understand what you were talking about. He said you were a monk?'

'Aye, I was once,' Archibald replied. He took a small leather pouch from beneath his shirt and crumbled salt into the pottage. 'And while I was there, I was taught much from a master who was devoted to learning and the natural sciences. It was while I was with him that I learned about the powders of thunder. And I fell in love with knowledge and study.'

'But if you were a monk, aren't you still?'

'The religious life was unsuitable for me. For my studies, I needed more freedom.'

'But if you become a monk . . .'

'Some men best serve God in church or monastery. Others, like me, find different routes to Him. I find more of His majesty in my works than I would have discovered in a hundred years with my abbot.'

The lad was still frowning with incomprehension. 'But . . .'

'You have much to learn too, boy. Such as: when to ask questions and when to shut up,' Archibald said genially as he poured the thin soup into bowls. 'Eat.'

Béatrice had almost forgotten the stalking man by the end of that second day. She and Alain had kept to the busier roads, joining the throng that wended its way like an enormous snake of despair, heading in any direction that took them away from the English.

It was in the second evening that he struck. They had been settling for the night with others, when Béatrice went to fetch water from a spring. There was a small shrine next to the spring where it bubbled up from the ground. A cross had been fashioned from stone, and a wooden cup rested on the base so that pilgrims could drink. She was thirsty, and as she bent to pick it up, she saw something move from the corner of her eye.

She froze. There were so many wild creatures: boar, wolf, wild dogs – but before she could think of screaming, a lumbering, crashing sound came, and her hair was gripped in a powerful fist.

'Bitch. Did you think I'd forgotten you?'

She gasped with the pain, grabbing for her knife, but his hand took hers before she could find it. He let go of her hair and put his arm about her neck, squeezing until she could scarcely breathe. With his other hand, he pulled the knife from her sheath and dropped it, before his hand rose to encompass her breast. He rubbed and kneaded her through the thin material of her chemise and tunic, laughing deep in his throat as she struggled, but then his hand moved further down, over the smooth roundness of her belly, and on to her upper thighs. She tried to break away, her breath rasping as she felt the panic rise: the primeval fears of rape and death smothering her every thought, until they encompassed her entire soul. There was nothing but terror: no rational thought, no comprehension of existence beyond the present, no memory of happiness or love, only this utter horror.

His questing hand reached her groin, and he clutched at her, his face reaching round, slobbering and drooling at the line of her jaw, as though he would kiss her on the lips.

For some reason, that was more repellent than the thought of his hands on her, or his sex inside her. She jerked with revulsion – and the suddenness of her movement surprised him. He released her neck, and she tumbled to the ground.

She tried to scramble away, but he grabbed her ankle, and she grasped the first thing to hand to try to drag herself away. A stick. She turned and tried to slam it into his head. He smiled as he caught it in his hand. Yes: he smiled. It was the look of a ravening wolf. His mouth was wide with excitement and anticipation as he pulled the stick from her. She couldn't hold it against his strength.

He put his hand to her tunic's collar, and she slapped at it, squealing with desperation. A nail caught at the scab of his wound, and a flake of black clot was yanked away. He grunted, then bunched his fist and drove it at her chin.

With both on the ground, she could roll and evade the blow, and as she moved, she felt a sharp pain. She had rolled onto her knife, and the point tore a wedge from her rib. As he put his hand back to her breast, squeezing hard, and she gasped with the pain, her fingers found the knife.

When she stabbed the priest, she had no recollection afterwards. This, she would remember for the rest of her life. With the priest she had been scared for her soul, but with this man it was the certainty of death that drove her on. Something snapped in her, a cord in her soul that kept her sane. The death of her father had begun the process, the priest's attempted rape had brought her to a new level of shock, but this man had finally broken the fragile bonds of her gentle feminine upbringing.

Her first wild slash missed his face and buried the blade in his upper arm. She pulled it back and stabbed again, and this time her raking cut caught his nose and cheek, and she saw his flesh opened. There was no space in her heart for compassion, only utter, concentrated loathing. She stabbed and cut, striking time and time again, while he bellowed and roared, punching at her, but always trying to move away from the wicked four inches of steel in her hand. He rose to retreat, but she carried on, coldly, methodically, following him with precision, her blade darting hither and thither, lacerating him as it moved. She kept on even when he tried to surrender, even when he covered his face with his hands. She carried on striking him long after he had ceased to be a threat, and then, while his body jerked and spasmed, she stabbed him again and again.

'Maid, maid, what have you done!' Alain cried.

She stopped, panting, the knife still in her hand. And then, she slipped the knife into his throat, cutting through to his windpipe, and rose. The knife she wiped on his hosen, and replaced it in her sheath. Her hands and face she rinsed in the spring water, turning it crimson. Afterwards, when she looked down, she thought only that the spring was polluted – and that was good. It was marked by death. No more would pilgrims come to celebrate and pray here. For ever more, this would be a place reviled, stained with an evil man's blood.

It was only just.

CHAPTER FIFTEEN

21 July

Berenger saw the movement at the same time as Geoff did. 'What the fuck is *that*?'

They had left Valonges some days before and were close to St-Lô. Since then, life had become a banal routine of carnage. Each day, Berenger rose with the men, they attacked villages and hamlets, destroying all in their path, and made camp and slept, ready to continue the following morning. Now, after a week of fighting and marching, he didn't know, nor did he care, where they were. It was merely the approach to another town.

'Looks to me like men are breaking down the bridge,' Geoff said as scurrying figures attacked it with iron bars and axes.

'Can we get around them?' Berenger wondered.

'How?' Geoff pointed to the line of the river. From here, the river curved back towards them on the left and right, with the bridge at the very tip of the loop before them. 'If there's a ford, I don't see it.'

Grandarse scratched under his arm. 'Someone'll have to go and look, won't they?' he said.

Berenger sighed. 'And as usual, that "someone" will be us poor bastards up at the front, you mean?'

'Come on, eh? You think you're all alone up there at the front? Just think how many friends you have behind you, man. You won't feel lonely with all these lads at your back, will you?'

'At my back, Grandarse, thanks. I hadn't thought of that,' Berenger said drily.

'Go on, you daft beggar. You know you love it. All that plunder will be yours, won't it? You'll be first to claim it all.'

'Oh, like in Carentan? And Valognes and Barfleur and . . .'

Grandarse's tone hardened. 'Enough. Get going, Frip. Watch your flanks, and look out for crossbows. Christ's bones, but I hate those things. See if the bridge is usable, and if it isn't, check for a ford and come back.'

'Yes, Centener.' Berenger set his jaw. 'Come along, boys. We have a short pilgrimage before our supper tonight.'

The first bolt hissed past as they approached the bridge, and Berenger saw a crossbowman bending to span his bow for a second shot. 'See him? Come on, can't one of you get the bastard?'

At the far end of the bridge, a scruffy-looking militia was forming. Men with leather jacks or colourful tunics were standing ready to repel anyone who was foolish enough to try to cross. To the left of the bridge stood a group of crossbowmen, while forty more stood shouting their defiance, waving axes and swords.

Jack already had his bow strung. 'I'm going to get that

bugger,' he vowed, nocking an arrow and drawing. There was a moment's silence, then the dull thrumming of the bowstring, and Berenger leaned in front of Jack so he could watch the flight. From here, he saw the clothyard rise, then stoop and plummet. It missed the crossbowman, but hit another a couple of feet away. He gave a shriek as it found its mark in his hip. The other discharged his crossbow harmlessly into the water as he caught his friend's arm.

'You're shite,' Matt commented.

'You missed him,' Geoff said.

'There's a man over there, Jack, he's bigger. Perhaps you could hit *him*?' Clip enquired genially.

'Shut the fuck up, the lot of you!' Jack said, fitting a fresh arrow. 'He was closer than I thought, that's all. Didn't have me eye in.'

Berenger made his way towards the bridge. For all the bickering, he could also hear the sounds of bows being strung, Clip whining about his arrows being held in a quiver, when, 'Ye all know I like 'em in the ground before me!' and Eliot's muttering about his 'Bloody bow's useless – look at the grain there, eh? Knot big as my left ballock. Whoever the bowyer was who made that, the fuckwit should be strung up with his own string!'

Grinning despite himself, Berenger continued until he reached the bank. Here it was a good yard above the water, and it was clear that they wouldn't be able to cross. The bed of the bridge was broken away; the timbers had dropped into the river and were floating downstream. There was no sign of a ford. The river flowed too quickly for a man or cart to attempt to cross here, especially since it looked deep.

He turned, intending to go back to his men, and it was then that the bolt struck him. The steel point hit the upper part of his shoulder, and flew on just beneath his collar bone. It felt like a horse had kicked him with a red-hot hoof.

'Sweet Jesus!' he gasped, and fell to his knees, staring dumbly at the blood dripping from the bolt's head.

Geoff was the first to see him. He gave a roar of anger so loud, Berenger was sure the ground shook, before drawing his bow and letting the first of many arrows fly straight to the enemy archers. In a moment, Jack and Clip and the others were also drawing and loosing, and in only a short time the crossbowmen fled, leaving two on the grass. The swordsmen retreated, trying to conceal themselves behind balks of timber, but even there the English arrows found their mark.

'Donkey? Don't stand there staring, you lurdan, fetch more arrows, quickly!' Geoff bellowed, his face as red as a beetroot, and Ed went scampering up the road to their cart.

Berenger was still on his knees when Geoff came to him, took him gently by his good arm, and led him away.

That was Ed's first real experience of witnessing the risks of battle, the first time he saw one of the vintaine's men struck, and he didn't enjoy it. Until then, the men had seemed impervious to all dangers. He had hurried to bring fresh missiles or water, but none of the English were injured. Now he could see the dangers at first hand as they carried Berenger away.

He saw the main body of the army arrive as he gathered up sheaves of arrows. Soon he was back with the men. Clip stood with his hand on his hip, his face drawn into his familiar sneer.

'Took your time, boy!' he rasped, and grabbed an arrow, aiming and loosing in one practised movement.

The first men joined the archers shortly afterwards. There were carpenters and joiners, and perhaps five score more archers, chattering and laughing as they came. It was like Sunday at the vill's butts, Ed thought, as they strung their bows and started to nock and loose. There was no thought of volleys, just the irregular, carefully aimed flights, and after many there came a cry or scream from the other side of the river.

More Frenchmen were coming. Grandarse gave a hoarse command, and a hundred arrows sprang into the air to plummet on the advancing men like hawks. Five in the front rank collapsed as the first arrows struck. A single man wearing the arms of a lord stood before them in a red tunic with a white emblem on the breast, but as more and more of the men behind him fell to the ground, his exhortations grew increasingly desperate. His ranks thinned rapidly; some men had been struck by English arrows, while others had fled.

Soon those remaining could see there was no point in this unequal battle, and they retreated, while the English kept up a withering fire until they were out of accurate bowshot.

To Ed's surprise, English carpenters were already crawling over the bridge. Fresh timbers were unloaded at the shore, grabbed and carefully positioned. Grandarse barked an order, and the first hundred archers climbed on the makeshift bridge, shooting their arrows at any French defenders who showed their faces. The way to the town was already clear before the bridge was complete, and English archers stood at either side of it on the St-Lô side to provide cover for the infantry as they crossed. Grandarse and the vintaine stood and eyed the walls and gates of the town speculatively.

Suddenly, fresh shouts and curses startled them. Scouts came running back from the east of the town where they had been seeking weaknesses in the defence. A large number of men-at-arms and knights were sallying forth from a postern. Their appearance had terrified the scouts that they might be caught in the open and slaughtered.

Desperate, the men pelted back to the bridge, at which point Geoff began to laugh. Ed thought he was sent mad by his unholy bloodlust, but then the others began to jeer – and he realised what Geoff had seen. The knights were not attacking: they were riding away, leaving the town to its fate.

'We've won it, Donkey! We've won it!' he exulted. 'They haven't a hope now.'

Béatrice kept up with Alain all those weary miles. He had been shocked by the sight of the body by the spring, and she was not of a mood to allay his fears. If he was worried by her, so much the better. For her part, Béatrice felt she could trust no one. All wanted either her body or her money. No one was honest. No one except perhaps Alain.

The passage of time meant nothing to her by now. They walked by day, and at night they found places to hide and shelter from the weather. When they came to towns, she viewed them with an eye to the strength of the defences. Those with meagre protection were rejected almost immediately. It was only when they reached a town a few miles from Caen that she felt more secure. Caen was huge, she knew.

Alain had been quiet since the death of the man. Whereas in the first days he had been thoughtful and caring, he had grown progressively more withdrawn. She knew that her ferocity that day had struck him dumb.

'When we get to the city,' he said now, 'we should find a good inn.'

He was studying the countryside as he spoke. They had reached the summit of a small hillock, and he stood gazing about him. Some people were walking along the road – a man with a cart laden with goods, two women with baskets slung over their backs, children with fear graven on their faces – but as these passed, there were few enough behind them. Traffic on the roads had thinned out.

'We can find a cheaper bed at a tavern,' she said. There was no point in wasting her money. The old woman's purse was still mostly full, for she had hoarded the coins carefully, but there was no telling how long the money must last. With no father, no Hélène, no family and no means of support, she must eke out her remaining funds.

'We can afford a good chamber – food, wine, everything. We don't have to stint,' he said.

There was a subtle change in his tone as he spoke. She looked at him with a quick suspicion. 'What do you mean?'

He had not tried to grope her or even steal a kiss. She had been sure that she could trust him, and yet there was a distance between them now.

'Your money – you have plenty. The man saw it in the tavern when you showed me. That was his problem. He really wanted to have your money as well as taking you. It left him confused.'

'He wanted to rape me.'

'Yes, that too.'

There was a coolness in his tone. She looked about, and realised that the last stragglers of the latest column of refugees had passed on and were disappearing behind some trees. They were alone.

She took a step away.

'I wanted to take the purse as soon as I saw you with all that money,' he said, facing her again. 'I had thought I would have money, but when I asked my mother for some, she said that she had nothing. I searched, but she wasn't lying. The stupid old hag must have forgotten and left her money behind.'

'So you stabbed her,' Béatrice said. She stepped away again.

'How did you know that?' He frowned, his clear blue eyes reflecting his surprise.

'She told me.'

'No, I killed her.'

'You stabbed her. I took her into a house and eased her passing.'

'That was kind. I will make sure you don't suffer.'

'You will kill me too?'

'I think you could be jealous. You may want the money back. Wait!' His frown deepened. 'You say you helped her: where did you get that money?'

'She gave it me.'

He laughed. 'She gave it all to you? And then you walked into me, and I can take it from you. Hah! That is perfect!'

'If you touch me, I'll kill you.'

'You can try, little maid. But I'm better equipped to defend myself than that fool with a beard, and I won't be distracted by your splendid figure.'

He stepped towards her, and she kept her eyes fixed on him. Curiously, she felt no fear. She had killed two men already in the last week. This man was no stronger or quicker than they were. He was no longer 'Alain', her protector: he was only another man seeking to use her, to steal from her and kill her.

No, she had no fear of such a man.

He took another step towards her and she moved back. Another, and she retreated again. 'Will you walk back to Barfleur?' he taunted.

'No.'

He darted forward, his hand under his cloak as he came, and pulled out his knife.

She turned and fled, towards Caen, towards the last people she had seen on the road.

He would know she was bolting in search of protection, just as she had run to him when he first met her. A man like him, a coward who would stab his own mother, would not comprehend a woman who was not terrified of him. He was after her like a greyhound seeing the hare run.

His high-pitched laugh sounded to her like the giggle of a demon, but she didn't care. He was only a man. She had nothing to fear from him. She had already killed two like him.

She ran on, her feet raising small clouds of dust as she went. The air seared her lungs. She pounded onwards, all the while hearing his panting breath draw nearer and nearer, until she could almost feel his hands about to grab at her clothing.

That was when she stopped, her legs bending like spanned bows, and she straightened and whipped round, the knife already in her hand.

He ran into her, and didn't feel her blade at first. Only when she grabbed his own knife-hand and twisted her little blade under his breast did he understand.

For a long moment the two stood, she breathing deeply, her eyes fixed on his face, while he stared back, panting. Then there was a sob in his breath, and he tottered towards her. She shoved with her knife, sawing the blade downwards, feeling it rasp against his flesh, and suddenly he collapsed.

She pulled the knife free, stepped away, and watched as he squirmed and started to wail as the pain in his belly grew.

CHAPTER SIXTEEN

22 July

The next morning, Archibald woke with a grunt.

The hammering and clattering had carried on ceaselessly through the night while the engineers worked on the bridge, curses flying regularly as tools or nails were dropped into the River Vire, but that wouldn't normally keep him awake. Archibald had learned early on, while training as a monk, that sleep should be snatched whenever possible. A monk's life was harsh enough without exhaustion to torment the soul.

He prepared himself as the rest of the King's host lumbered to their feet, swearing and bickering lethargically.

It was good to see how the vintaine with Berenger Fripper immediately set to making a fire and toasting their little cakes, he thought. Most men would break their fast later in the day, but these men saw to it that they had eaten before risking battle. That, to Archibald, was the sign of seasoned campaigners.

For him, a hunk of bread and the remains of the pottage from the night before were sufficient. Then, with a stretch and yawn that would have befitted a bear, he made his way to the river. He was thirsty, and he wanted to get there before the majority of the army. Too many pissed into the waters.

At the bank, he saw Welshmen and others filling their skins and pots. He went a short way upstream and slipped down the bank behind a little stand of trees, filling his pottle-pot. It held two quarts, and the mouth was small, so he must hold the barrel-shaped container under the water for a while to fill it. While he was there, he heard voices.

'You should be careful,' he heard a man say.

The voice was familiar, but he thought nothing of that. Right now he was concentrating on his water.

'Who are you to tell me to be careful?'

This second was a strange voice, but the accent was recognisable to any man in the King's army: it was a Welshman speaking. Idly, Archibald listened to their conversation.

'The boy said you attacked him. You know the one, the boy with the archers? He said you assaulted him and robbed him just before the ship set sail.'

'Him? We didn't hurt him. We only made fun of him. He wanted to join us in the army, and tried to bribe us to bring him. As if we would have a halfling like him with us in the midst in a battle!'

'Well, he says you assaulted him, and he's told other people that you did.'

Archibald frowned as he suddenly recognised the voice as Tyler's. Leaning closer, he listened more attentively, but it was too late. The voices moved on, the men walking away from him.

Archibald filled his pottle-pot and thrust the cork home with a slap of his palm.

That was interesting. He wondered who the boy was, and why Tyler had chosen to accuse him of spreading tales. Not that it was any of his concern. As something of an outcast himself, Archibald was less inclined to tell tales.

However, he disliked Mark Tyler. The man was up to something.

Grandarse roared and waved his hat to egg them on as the main body of infantry hurried past them over the bridge.

Sir John de Sully was one of the first men to cross it. He nodded to Grandarse, but gave a quick frown to see Jack Fletcher leading Berenger's vintaine. Later he would have to go and check on the vintener, to see how he fared from his wound, he reminded himself, before trotting towards the main gates. There he sat, resting his forearms on the crupper of his saddle, and studying the main walls with interest. 'Over here,' he called, waving to Grandarse and his men.

When they reached him, he pointed to the town.

'These walls are a mess. They have only recently been repaired – and that in a slapdash manner. You can see where they have expended their main efforts. There, there and there.' He pointed at the three cracks in the walls where rocks had been thrust into crevices in an effort to strengthen them. 'We should attack from here.'

'Yes, sir,' his esquire said.

A man-at-arms stared at the walls with dismay. 'You want to scale the wall *here*?'

'We have two choices: we can wait while the engineers construct trebuchets and other siege weaponry, all the while allowing King Philippe to prepare for us, or we can take it quickly. Do the men on the walls look like trained men-at-arms? No. If I am any judge, I would say that they are towns-folk. Specifically, townsfolk who are petrified of us, and with good reason. Richard, see to it that ladders are brought here.'

'Yes, sir,' his esquire said, and trotted back towards the bridge.

'We do not have the men or matériel to sit and become embroiled in a lengthy siege. Sometimes it is necessary to grasp the nettle,' Sir John said. Seeing a boy nearby, he whistled. 'You: come here!'

'Sir?' Ed had been unashamedly listening, eyeing the huge destrier with fascination and not a little fear. He had never been this close to such a massive beast before.

'Hold Aeton for me.'

Ed quailed, but held the reins as Sir John dismounted. The knight pulled on his bascinet, and soon his esquire was back, leading several men bearing ladders.

'Set them there,' Sir John instructed. 'Archers? Keep the men from the walls.'

Grandarse directed the fire of the centaine. One man at the battlements fell with a shriek, toppling back inside the town, and all the others at the walls immediately hid themselves.

'*UP!*' Sir John shouted, and as the first ladder clattered against the wall, he was already at it. Arrows flew over his head as he clambered up. The wall was tall, and he could feel the sweat soaking into his padded coif before he was halfway to the top.

His mail rattled, and inside his armour he was thoroughly uncomfortable. It added an edge to his excitement. He was at the battlements now. A man leaned through the embrasure to see what was happening, and the knight butted him with his helmet, then grabbed the man's collar and yanked at him. He fell, screaming, to the ground, as Sir John climbed in through the embrasure. In a moment he was on the walkway. A man was before him, a heavy sword gripped in his hands, but his mail shirt was ancient, and the rings stopped at his upper arm.

He tried to stab with his blade, but Sir John cut once. It took his hand off above the wrist, and while the man wailed, waving his stump in horror, Sir John booted him in the belly. He fell from the wall, and then the knight was at the next man.

This fellow at least was more experienced. He had sharp eyes in a square face, and he held his sword like an old friend. The blade wavered close to Sir John's belly, but his own sword was already in the *true gardant*, and as soon as the man thrust, Sir John parried and stabbed. He was in no hurry. All he need do was hold the wall while the rest of the army climbed after him.

Richard was soon at his side, and the two stood abreast, holding back the guards while more English fighters joined them. Soon there were twenty or more, and then Sir John gave the order to advance.

The French were unwilling to give way, but the English pushed forward, hacking and cutting. A crossbow was aimed at them, and Sir John saw one of his men clutch at a bolt in his skull before falling. A quarrel passed through another man's belly and threw him against the man behind him, who shrieked as the missile ended in his spine. Both slumped against the wall, but they were the last victims. The English held the whole of the upper wall, and while the defenders retreated to a tower at the corner, more ladders were brought and set down inside the town behind the wall. Soon forty or more were in the lane and running for the gates. Sir John gave one last push at the men before him, before going down a ladder himself.

'Open the gates!' he bellowed, standing in the main roadway. The men before him were reluctant to throw themselves into the fray. Barricades had been erected to hold back the English, but they were ineffective.

The gates were opened.

'My Lord,' he said as the Prince of Wales entered on his horse. 'Saint-Lô is ours.'

In the plain before the walls, Ed had delivered Aeton to the grooms, and since then had been running back and forth with sheaves of arrows, delivering them to the vintaine as the men kept up a relentless assault on the walls. Every time a man poked his head around a castellation, three or four arrows went whistling towards him.

When the vintaine began to run for the gate, Ed was with them. A swirl of smoke wafted before him, blinding him momentarily and concealing the street ahead, but it didn't matter. Not now. The town was theirs. No one could stop them.

His blood thrilled with the thought of killing a Frenchman. Any memory of the miserable plight of the ambushing militia man, and his inability to end his suffering, was banished as Ed pulled his dagger from its sheath and set off after the others.

'Not you, Donkey,' Geoff said, a spade-like hand planted on his breast. 'This is man's work, *boy*.'

'But I want—'

'I don't give a shit what you want, Donkey. I won't have you in here,' Geoff told him.

Ed was suddenly scared of him. The man who had been the most genial and protective of the whole vintaine was now threatening, his eyes black with anger, before he turned and was gone, hastening with the others into the town. Already Clip was further along the road, running with that strange, loping gait of his, and Jack was close behind – and then a fresh breeze filled the road with smoke and Ed was blinded once more.

Struck with indecision, Ed was buffeted by others running past, but then he set his jaw. He was a soldier, with as much right to be here as any.

The gateway held three skulls on spikes. A grim reminder that here the law held sway: malefactors would be punished. Their faces were blackened, strips of tanned leather clinging to the bone beneath, and the eyeless sockets were horrible. They seemed to be looking down at him, as though mocking him.

Lifting his chin in defiance, Ed strode beneath the gatehouse and into the streets of St-Lô.

Near the gate there was a tavern, and a pair of Englishmen issued from it, clutching small barrels. One was singing in a hoarse croak, while the other was giggling like a lunatic. It gave Ed the feeling that he was walking in a dream, hearing that mad laughter.

Along the lane, he saw two men kicking and beating a figure rolling on the ground. Ed could hear the man's cries. Time seemed to slow. Each step took an age, as though he was walking through heavy water, like the day he landed at the beach. He saw a woman, gripped by her elbows by one man while a second man ripped away her chemise and tunic, then grabbed her and began to thrust.

Bodies lay in clumps all about. Ed saw boys and a girl tangled together in a mess of death, tossed aside carelessly. Dogs and cats lay in their own blood – lots of dogs – near a little girl cowering behind a dead woman, watching the men passing by with eyes like pits of horror.

There was a metallic crack from the wall by his head, and he saw a crossbow bolt pinwheel away with the sound of a pigeon taking off, a chip of stone flying where it had hit.

That was when he suddenly seemed to lurch back to reality. The first barricades in the streets were being attacked by the vintaine, with Grandarse bellowing and roaring incomprehensibly; Geoff heaving at a great baulk of timber and hurling it aside; Clip darting up and around, loosing an arrow whenever he saw a face appear; other men swinging swords and axes with gusto. He saw a man's head lifted clean off his shoulders, to rise up into the air as though driven by the gush of blood that followed it in a fountain of death . . . Ed fell back stumbling into the wall, the acid hot in his throat at the nightmarish sights and sounds. He opened his mouth to sob, and an acrid vomit fell from his lips, the stench overpowering.

That was when he turned and fled. He ran and ran, away from the town, out to the bridge, and fell, and picked himself up, and fell again, sprawling, and only then did he begin to sob.

Because here, seeing the French people of that town as they died, he could not help himself. He didn't hate them – he mourned for them, too.

CHAPTER SEVENTEEN

Sitting on a piece of timber with a pad of cloth held to his shoulder, Berenger felt helpless. A carter, ambling over, said, 'Shame you're missing it all, friend. There'll be good loot in there.'

'Yes,' Berenger said. 'The town was a rich one.'

'Not for much longer,' the carter chuckled and walked on.

Berenger was still weak. He had tried to sleep, but his wound kept him awake. Every time he moved, the pain woke him. In the end he rose and walked about the camp, swearing to himself about the foolishness of standing by the bridge when he had known that crossbowmen were about.

By morning his temper was not improved. The sharp throbbing was unremitting now, and Berenger had to grit his teeth against it. He would have gone into the town with his men, but for the realisation that he couldn't fight. With this wound he would simply be a liability.

He waited grimly, watching as the men stormed the walls. It was clear that the professional English soldiers were cutting through the townspeople of St-Lô like knives through soft French cheese. Such people could not hope to defend themselves against trained men. A drunken archer from Roger's vintaine staggering back from town burdened with furs and a silver goblet gave him a long pull from a wineskin, giggling, and the rush of heavy wine on Berenger's empty stomach left him light-headed. Still, by the second gulp, some of the pain was alleviated.

He had moved to sit on a tree-trunk left by the joiners at the side of the road when he heard a familiar voice. 'Not dead yet, then?'

He looked up to see Geoff. 'Bored already with plunder?' he retaliated.

'Ah, you know how it is,' Geoff said easily, but his grey eyes were pained, and he wouldn't look directly at his vintener. Berenger knew that the worst atrocities were always unsettling. They dragged at a man's soul afterwards like lead.

Geoff sat on the ground beside Berenger. In one fist he held an earthenware pot, which he passed to Berenger, who sniffed and then drank.

'Sweet Jesus!' he said. 'What the hell is *that*?'

'Someone called it burned cider. It sure as hell puts hairs on your balls where none stood before,' Geoff said.

There was a wildness to him. A long, raking cut had sheared through his left sleeve and the flesh beneath it, and there was a short gash on his right shoulder as well as a new scratch under his left eye – but it wasn't the wounds that struck Berenger. The vintener had seen him after numerous other battles, but this was the first time he had seen such an expression of despair on his face.

'What is it, Geoff?'

'The King has decreed that, because the town held its gates against him, the men can lay it waste. The rich are to be ransomed, but all their property is forfeit. Much'll be burned.'

'He's making an example,' Berenger said, and took another swig.

He felt drunk already. At plenty of other battles he had joined in the plunder, stealing all he could before others did. It was all part of the business of war. But to see Geoff's face was to understand that this was a different kind of battle.

'It's worse even than that,' Geoff went on. 'At the gate were three skulls. The King heard they were knights executed for supporting him during the truce, when they should have been safe. The King's furious that his allies were murdered, so he's given the army a free hand. You know what that means: no mercy. All the women . . .'

'I see.'

Berenger put his hand on Geoff's shoulder. Geoff always missed his wife. He would whore with the others, but he never forgot his woman at home, and would not join in a rape. He only ever took women who were willing. Usually the English army was restrained, with most men anxious about punishments, but when they were set loose from the leash, English soldiers could be as brutish as the worst heathen.

'I saw two men with a little girl, Berenger,' Geoff whispered. 'I wanted to kill them.'

'Drink.'

Geoff took the pot, but didn't lift it to his lips. He stared moodily at the town as the first orange glows began to light the walls. Smoke was beginning to boil from the southern edge of St-Lô, tipping over the walls like a sea overwhelming a castle in the sand.

'I didn't come here to watch women and children being raped,' he said quietly. 'I believe in the King's authority, but how can he permit them to be violated in pursuit of his ambition? It's not right.'

Berenger pulled the pad from his shoulder and winced. 'It's his right if he wants to punish the townspeople. They showed him disrespect.'

He was about to continue when Grandarse and Clip appeared at the bridge. They stood, staring about them, and when they saw Berenger and Geoff, they began to walk towards them. Behind them, Berenger saw Will and a stranger: a little, bent man with a satchel over his shoulder.

'Didn't expect you back so quickly,' Geoff said. He remained staring at the town as a flurry of sparks rose from the farther side.

'Aye, well, we couldn't leave this old git suffering, could we, eh?' Grandarse said. 'How is it, Fripper?'

'It hurts,' Berenger said shortly.

'This man can help you. He's a leech. Not the best, from the look of his clothes, but at least he's alive – for now,' Grandarse said, shoving the stranger towards Berenger.

The old man peered at him, pulling the balled cloth from Berenger's shoulder and sniffing it with a frown. He opened his bag and began to rummage inside.

'Where's the Donkey?' Berenger asked, to take his mind from his shoulder as the man moved the material of his shirt aside. It hurt, but not so much as when he began to poke at the wound with a pair of tweezers. 'Hey!'

'Bits of your shirt are in the wound. You leave them, you die. You know gangrene? Must take all the shirt out.'

Berenger clenched his jaw as the man probed and pulled out tiny threads of linen. 'Well?'

'I haven't seen him, not for an age,' Grandarse said. 'Thought he was outside.'

'He was,' Geoff said. 'I wasn't going to have him in there while the town was taken. I told him to clear off.'

'I saw him in there at the first barricade,' Clip said. 'But when we took it, he was gone.'

Berenger gave an exasperated grunt. 'Come on, then. We'd better go and search for the daft lurdan.'

'Oh, no you don't,' Grandarse said. 'We went to the effort of finding this old bastard, and we're not letting you get up until he says you're fit. You'll stay here until he's done with you.'

'I can't sit here while—'

'Ye can and ye will, eh? Sit back and enjoy being pampered. We'll be back later.'

Berenger fretted, but in truth he felt so battered, the thought of rising again did not appeal. He watched his companions as they crossed the bridge again, and wished he could be with them. The thought of Donkey being injured or dead was oddly painful.

'Careful, that hurt!' he snarled as the leech delved too deeply.

The man muttered something which sounded like 'English children,' but when Berenger glared at him, the leech ignored him and continued with his delicate task.

When Ed came to himself he was down near the bank of the river. The sun was sinking now, and the area was lighted by a livid red glow from the town. He washed his face in water that sparkled, reflecting golden-yellow flames, and squatted with his hands over his eyes, shivering.

When he first came here, all he had longed for was to see Frenchmen being slain. Only a mound of their bodies could ever begin to compensate for his suffering. Or so he had thought. But the bodies in the road, the little girl hiding by her dead mother, the three murdered children . . . they weren't guilty. They were as innocent as he was.

His life had been so bound up with thoughts of revenge and hatred, he had never considered that he might reach a time like this, when his life's purpose was lost.

So why was he here, sitting at the side of a French river, while his friends and companions indulged in an orgy of murder and rape?

He drew his hands down and stared about him, still confused, lost amidst the madness of the sacking of St-Lô. Leaning down, he cupped water in his hands and rinsed his mouth once more. As he did so, he saw an arm float past.

Springing to his feet in horror, Ed retreated up the bank of the river again. It felt as though his mouth was stained indelibly with blood, and he fell and retched on all fours until his empty belly could convulse no more. Only then did he notice the man.

It was the Welshman, Erbin. He had a woman by her hair, and was half-dragging her back to the army camp. She was screaming and flailing with her fists, and the Welshman panted, 'Try that again, bitch, and you'll regret it!'

That was when he caught sight of Ed, and he hesitated. The woman's fist caught him at the temple, and he swore, then bunched his own fist and slammed it hard into her belly so that she collapsed, gasping for air, rolling with her hands over her stomach.

'You, boy! Come here!' he called, and he kicked the woman before crossing the ground towards him. 'You want to buy me another drink, eh? Is it still that you want to join the army, boy? You can join our group, if you want.'

He was grinning now, his dark eyes watchful and filled with a strange light. 'We can help you, boy. If you want to be with us, with the Prince's men.'

Ed remembered that soft voice from the tavern, the way that the men took his drinks, and then the crushing blows that fell upon him outside. He hadn't seen the man who assailed him, but Erbin's smile was enough to make him shake with terror.

'Or is it that you have been speaking about me and my friends behind our backs?' Erbin asked softly, approaching with alarming speed.

Ed shook his head, backing away as the Welshman came nearer, and then with a little bleat of terror, he turned and fled, back along the bank of the river, away from the bridge.

The Welshman took a few paces after him, but then spat. He returned to the woman curled up and moaning on the ground. 'Up, you bitch. He'll wait, but you have some men to entertain before you rest!'

CHAPTER EIGHTEEN

Geoff was tired. 'Damn his cods!' he muttered as he approached the town once more. 'Fool should have stayed back, like I said. What was he doing coming up here?'

But he thought he understood. Ed knew nothing of life. He was alone at the sack of a town, a terrifying experience for anyone. No wonder he wanted to remain with his vintaine.

Geoff stopped under the gateway to the town and stared about him. It was a scene of horror. At his feet was a baby with a crushed head. On his left a heap of bodies, some soldiers, some citizens, a few older women. Three English soldiers were removing everything of value from the dead. One man with bare feet was hopping on one leg while he tried to pull on a shoe from a corpse, swearing and laughing in equal measure.

Bodies lay everywhere, and more dangling where they had been hanged. Farther off, a small boy, perhaps four or five years old, stood and screamed, his hands twisting a scrap of cloth. Men walked past, ignoring him and his despair. Near him lay a woman.

Geoff paced slowly, his eyes fixed on her body. The sight captivated him. She had hair the same colour as his wife's; she had a similar build, and the wound in her throat looked like his wife Sarra's – the wound he had seen that terrible morning when he found her corpse waiting for him downstairs.

His ears were assailed by harsh laughter, the crackle and rush of flames taking hold, occasional clattering of weapons.

It was scenes like this which had driven his brother, Henry, to despise him. When he thought of Henry, Geoff wanted to remember the youth with the smiling face, but instead he saw the priest with haunted eyes and thin, pale features. He had looked at Geoff with sadness and regret, as though Geoff was responsible for every death, every body tormented beyond pain.

'All the Devils in Hell,' Henry had said one day, 'cannot butcher and torture so well as we poor souls.'

Not long after that, he had left, and Geoff had never seen him again. Once Geoff had heard from a friar that his brother sent his best wishes and prayed for him, but neither thought there was any hope for him.

Well, Geoff didn't want his prayers. He was strong enough. He would shout at the Devil and curse him when he died. He had no need of a priest's sympathy. Not even now, with his wife dead.

The thought made him stop, stock-still, in the road.

Two men ran from a house further up the street. They bore torches, and then stood watching the building with an eager glee, waiting. Soon a burst of flame rewarded their patience, and they began to dance, singing. Screams came from within.

It was suddenly too much. Geoff turned and hurried from the town. There was a stinging in his eyes, but not from the smoke.

He was almost at the bridge when something made him stop and look past the gates, along the line of the wall. There, he saw a familiar figure. 'Donkey?' he called.

The boy saw him, and suddenly he was pelting along the grass towards Geoff, a panicked boy who had seen too much, just like Henry all those years ago. He cannoned into Geoff like a rock from a trebuchet.

'What is it, boy?' the man said, not unkindly.

'Geoff, I, I didn't . . .' he faltered, 'I couldn't . . .'

'Was it the town? Now you know why I didn't want you to see all that.'

'No, it was out here. The Welshman.'

'What Welshman? Don't panic now,' Geoff said, and he gripped the boy's arms to calm him. 'It's all right, lad. You're safe now.'

But the sobbing wouldn't subside. Geoff could see how the shock overwhelmed him even as he carried Ed back over the bridge towards the wagons and Berenger.

Archibald the Gynour filled his water bottles and stood a while staring over the river at the fires, his mind empty. He had no sense of guilt or shame. This was not his city, and not his responsibility. He had taken no part in the sack.

He felt a fleeting regret. There would have been good stores of cash and plate in there, and along with all those lives, it was lost now forever. The enemy would suffer in any war, of course. Surely it was better that it was the French who suffered, rather than the English.

He was walking back to his wagon when he saw something lying in the debris at the side of the road. A body.

Old habits died hard with a man who had been a priest. He could contemplate with equanimity many deaths in the town over the water, but a body close to hand required his attention. Leaning down, Archibald pushed some of the rubbish from about the figure and felt a little pang when he saw the shock of hair. Turning the body over, he recognised the young groom who had helped him the other evening, and whom he had rewarded with a bowl of pottage.

The boy had a hoofprint on his breast. It looked as though he had been knocked down here in the rush to get to the bridge and attack the city. Possibly it was a destrier that struck him, and the rider didn't realise what had happened.

Archibald was not outraged at the death. Boys were as liable to die in battle as any man. Yet he was stung by the thought that the lad would not share his fireside again. What was his name? He couldn't remember.

He picked up the body and stared about him. He wanted to find him a suitable resting place – but where in this hell of fire and death was there somewhere for an innocent child?

Unaccountably, Archibald felt hot tears springing in his eyes as he stared down at the dead boy's face. He looked as if he was sleeping.

26 July

For Ed the days passed in a welter of noise and terror.

The men marched with a joyous demeanour, all but Berenger, who hissed and glared at the French leech at every twinge of pain.

The army was spread over a huge front three or four leagues in breadth, swallowing the countryside like a glutton. Houses, villages, towns – all were engulfed and left smouldering. Any people discovered there were left dead. Before them was green, fertile land with hamlets dotted about, a scene of pastoral calm; behind them lay Hell.

Not that the men displayed any concern about the destruction they had left in their wake. Grandarse sang his lewd songs, while Clip and Will joined in lustily with the choruses;

Geoff grinned and murmured the refrains, but he kept near Ed, who felt comforted by his presence. The others were too taken with the pleasures of the moment to be worried about their Donkey.

They were moving towards Cormolain, where the French Marshal and his men had retreated. King Edward and his son were keen to find him and break his force, since with the Marshal's men out of the way, they would have a clear route to Paris.

It was a continual grinding, misery for Ed. He staggered on, laden with loaves and some cheeses Grandarse and Clip had liberated. Farmsteads were put to the torch and fields of wheat burned, while cattle were brought to be slaughtered at night for all to eat. The French had killed many of them already, to deprive their enemy of food. Ed would never forget the sight of dead cattle in the fields, legs uppermost, bellies swollen with decay. Nor the stench of putrefaction. It would not leave him, but grew, so that he felt it was impregnated in his flesh, even unto his soul. The army was befouled. Each soldier carried the reek of death.

Last night they had reached this prominence and had slept a scant league or two from the great sprawl of Caen.

Ed lay awake, convinced that the following morning they would reach the city and repeat the scenes he had seen in St-Lô. It terrified him.

Just before dawn, the horns blared their command to rise and muster. The vintaine rose all about Ed, grunting, hawking, spitting, grumbling and cursing as only an English army could. Ed slowly climbed to his feet, and Clip, still half-asleep and looking for a tree to piss against, tripped over him. 'Watch where you're going,' he snarled, before staggering to an oak and untying his braies.

Ed waited with the others while the darkness cleared to a bright daylight. The men stood, leaning on bowstaves or polearms, metal caps on their heads, leather or quilted jacks tight against the chill air, and as Ed looked about them, he hoped to see a glimmer of pity, a show of sadness in any of their eyes.

He shivered; he saw none.

Caen.

They reached an open space late in the morning that afforded them an uninterrupted view. Berenger gave a low whistle at the sight.

'We won't take that in a hurry,' he said quietly.

It was a large city, lying in the curve of two rivers, with marshy land all about. The walls were formed from a gorgeous, pale cream-coloured rock that, in the early-morning sun, seemed to glow from within, like a city built for angels. To their left stood a great castle on a promontory, slightly above the city itself. The wall led from the castle around the city to the south and west, before meeting a strong abbey. A second abbey lay further beyond the castle. The yellow sun glinted from the rivers and streams that appeared to fill the space west of the city, beyond the abbeys. It was an enchanting sight.

Later, Ed would recall that first view and think that no city of angels deserved the rage of the English as this city would suffer it.

'What will happen?' he asked Berenger.

The vintener's wound was considerably improved, and Grandarse, impressed, had hired the leech to be their own bone-setter and medical expert during their march. The fellow, Jacob, was not overly keen, but when he saw a little of Grandarse's liberated wealth, his eyes grew round, and he exhibited more enthusiasm.

Berenger shrugged without thinking and winced. 'The King sent a messenger offering terms, but the city's thrown him in prison. That's not honourable: messengers are supposed to be secure. Especially him – the poor sod was an Augustinian. It's not right to treat a monk like that.'

Before the city walls, an army was forming. Ranks of men clad in drab tunics marched forward over the plain. Behind them came more, these with the symbols of their lords blazoned across their breasts, while their flags and banners fluttered gaily in the morning breeze.

'It looks a bloody strong city,' Geoff said doubtfully.

'Aye, but the King knows his business, eh,' Matt said. He was gazing at the fortifications with relish. 'Aye, and think of the women in there!'

'Are you so cunt-struck you can't see how high the walls are?' Clip demanded.

'Or that it's two cities,' Berenger said. He rolled his shoulder again experimentally, then regretted it. 'See? The nearer of the two is the old town, and behind it is the river, with a bridge to the new town beyond. That's where the merchants and rich folk will have their houses: that's where the money will be.'

'Why do you think that?' Ed asked.

'It's newer, boy. Only the rich can afford new houses.' He pulled a face. 'It's a natural island, isn't it? The rivers form a moat around that part of the city. Be a bastard to get to it, if not by the bridge.'

'So we have to take the old town first and cross the river.'

'That's about it,' Grandarse said. 'One good thing: we can avoid that damned castle on our way. They say it was built by William the Bastard, and he built the abbeys in shame for what he did to the English. One for monks, one for nuns, just to pray for his stinking soul, the black-hearted git.'

'Yeah,' Clip said sarcastically. 'We can avoid the castle. That'll make life *so* much easier. So all we have to do is attack sheer walls and break into the town, kill everyone and get to the new town – job done. Yeah. Ye'll all get slaughtered, you do understand that, don't ye?'

Grandarse and Geoff said simultaneously, 'Shut up, Clip.'

'Don't come whining to me when you're dead,' he said, unruffled. 'I've warned ye.'

CHAPTER NINETEEN

It was past noon before they had been bullied and shoved into battle formation, and now, with horns of archers on either flank, and the mass of infantry and knights in heavy battles in the middle, they began their slow march towards the town.

'Ed, bring the arrow cart,' Clip said. His bow was strung, and he walked along with a dozen shafts in his belt.

The others were already moving ahead as Ed grabbed the cart's handles. He knew that once the archers began to loose their weapons, he would be forced to run back and forth; he was already growing used to his role as Donkey for the vintaine.

'They're breaking!' Grandarse roared suddenly. 'Look at the cowardly bastards!'

Ed peered around him, and sure enough, some of the men at the rear of the French lines were running back to the gates. First one or two, then a group of ten or more, and then an entire battle on the right took up their weapons and fled.

'You've scared 'em already!' Grandarse bellowed, and a ripple of laughter spread along his centaine.

'Sod this!' Matt cried. 'We can get into the city right now, if we're fast. Look at them run!'

Berenger cast a quick look about at the men, swinging his arm to release the tension in his sore shoulder. 'Hold!' he ordered. 'There could be an ambush. Keep with the army.'

Geoff put his hand on Ed's shoulder. 'You stay back, boy,' he muttered, and then said louder, 'Frip, Matt's right. If we hurry, we can overtake the last bastards. A few of us to attack the gate, while our archers hold back the defence, and we could take the city. It's worth taking a chance, surely?'

Berenger chewed his lower lip, and looked over at Roger from the second vintaine, who was making a similar calculation. He came to a decision, and grinned.

'Geoff, Clip, Jon – you come with me to the gates with Roger's men. The rest of you, hold back and use your bows. Got it? Come on!'

Geoff ran with his arms pumping up and down. Bolts hissed nearby, one passing so close he heard it buzzing through the air like an angry wasp, but then he was at the gate.

He had a long knife and his sword in his hands, and as he reached the first of the French defenders, he stabbed the man through his jerkin and slashed at his throat. There was a cry, and he was past, staring only at the gates before him.

Nothing else mattered to him at that moment. His entire being was fixed upon those gates. Thoughts of his wife, his children, everything else . . . were gone. There was only him, and the men running with him, although whether they were English or French, he didn't care. All he cared about was the timbers and the men who stood over them. There were plenty of townspeople there, ready to slam the gates shut and shove the baulks of timber across in their slots to lock them. More men appeared on his right. One was panting and white-faced with fear, and Geoff realised this was no ally. The man made a half-hearted lunge with his sword, which Geoff knocked aside with ease, and then they were at the gate, and Geoff swung. He caught the man's throat, just a little nick, but the fellow squealed like a pig and dropped his sword. Geoff swung again, backhanded, and the man's throat was opened wide with a bubble of blood.

Geoff felt the exultation of battle flood his soul. A thrilling in the heart, a stark clarity in his sight and in his thoughts, a perfection of existence that knew no limits.

The gates began to close, and he thrust a shoulder at the nearest one. 'Here! Quick! Give me a hand!' he shouted at the top of his voice, and felt the timbers shake as three more men thudded into it. 'Archers! Loose!'

The gap between the two gates was shrinking, but with the sudden flight of arrows, someone must have panicked, for the gates moved a little. Then they stopped and, to the sound of bellowed commands from the other side, the gates inched shut by degrees.

But more and more Englishmen were arriving. Geoff felt a man slam into his back, and could hear the grunts of the French who tried to hold the gates. 'With me!' he roared, and stamped a foot in time with his thrusts. 'Now! One, two: *NOW*! One, two: *NOW*!'

Almost imperceptibly the great timber gates began to creak and jerk back in time with his shout and the stamping, shoving mass of men at his side and behind him. There was a gap of inches, but now it grew to a foot, then two, and suddenly there was space for a man to enter.

Berenger was at his side, heaving at the gates with all his might. '*Archers*! Aim through the gates!'

There was a flurry of feathers, a scream cut short, and the gates moved wider. Geoff could see into the city now, and he took a deep breath and gave a bellow with the effort as he set both fists, still clutching his weapons, on the gates and shoved for all he was worth. There was a distinct movement, and he heard Berenger shriek something as the vintener sprang through the gap.

'We're in!' Geoff screamed, and followed.

With the first panicky orders and the rush of men to the gates, Béatrice felt the fear return, but no longer was she smothered by it as if choking beneath a blanket of horror. She had been attacked by priest, felon and friend, and she had won. She knew that there was no one she could trust, so the assault of a foreign army added little to her sense of aloneness and separation. She was cursed, and she would remain so.

Alain she had discarded by the side of the road, kicking his body into bushes. He had still been alive, slobbering and drooling like a dying hound, begging and weeping weakly as she set her face to the city, thinking that here she would at last be safe, but even as she approached the gates she saw the feverish preparations. They feared the English. Decades of peace had left the citizens complacent and now they worked to make good the ravages of time.

Men scurried like slaves to repair broken walls, with hoists pulling up new stone. Carpenters worked on the old gates, while townspeople gathered wood to build palisades or dug new ditches outside the walls to strengthen their defences.

At the gates, the guards tried to refuse her entry.

'Please, I must come in,' she said to the porter at the gate, an harassed young man with a helmet that was too large for him.

'We don't want anyone else in here, no extra mouths to feed. You carry on, go east. You'll be safer there than here,' he said, his pale eyes staring out at the land all about.

She followed his gaze and saw the smoke again. So many fires! There was a curtain of smoke, and when it was drawn, they would see the English. It was enough to send a shiver of fear through her. 'I have no man,' she pleaded.

'It makes no difference. You must go – but be quick. You've heard what these English devils do to women? It's horrible,' the man said.

'Wait, please, sir,' she begged.

But only when she brought out the old woman's purse did he finally offer her space on the floor in his own home.

That was two days ago now. This morning the English had arrived, and the dread of what was to come settled over the city as tight as a winding sheet. Men and women huddled together for comfort, but she walked alone. This was divine vengeance, brought down upon her countrymen by a just God. He was punishing the people who conspired to see her father slain, who sought to rape and rob her. They deserved their fate.

The Count of Eu and the Lord of Tancarville had brought men to supplement the town's guard, and a force of Genoese crossbowmen were already lined up on the walls staring bleakly over the marshy lands before the town. Men-at-arms waited at street corners, looking up at the walls, wondering when the clash would come, and in their eyes she saw the fear of death.

She couldn't bear the wait, knowing that soon the English would arrive and the slaughter would begin. This delay, this anticipation, was oppressive. She longed for it to end. In the attack she knew she must die, but she welcomed the peace that would come after death.

There was a shout from above: three men in armour were bellowing down to the men at the road. A sense of certainty overwhelmed her: this was the end of the city. She turned and began to walk towards the bridge to the Île St-Jean, the island behind the walled town, past townsfolk filled with panic. The walls wouldn't hold the English. They were too fragile.

All knew it. They saw the mustered English: a vast number of men, a wave of blood and bone that would engulf Caen, drowning all within.

The Count's men-at-arms fell back, withdrawing from the walls and gates, and the townspeople were already hurrying along towards the Porte St-Pierre, the last gate before the bridge over the River Odon and the Île St-Jean.

At first it was an orderly retreat, then it became an urgent mob. Finally, as the men at the north gate began to call for help and the first English arrows lanced down on the poorly protected soldiers on the walls, it became a frantic stampede. A woman fell, a babe in her arms, and was trampled by men clad in heavy mail, who ignored her screams for help in their maddened race to get to the island and safety.

Béatrice watched the men pounding past and she felt the certainty assail her like a leaden maul: that way led to death.

A door was open. She entered a little house. There was a chamber over the fireplace, behind the chimney. She climbed into it, and concealed herself behind the flue. Shivering, she looked about her, drew her knees to her chin, and waited.

After a little while, tears began to fall. Only later did she realise she was mourning the imminent loss of her life.

Berenger saw a bearded face as he hurtled through the gap, and slashed at it. His sword carved a red gash along the man's eye and cheek, and he fell away, but Berenger was already turning to stab at the men heaving the gate closed. There were so many, he couldn't kill them all. He felt a shove, and realised Geoff was at his side. The two hacked and cut and, unable to defend themselves while holding the gate, the French fell away. The timbers slammed back against the wall of the gatehouse. Caught between wall and gate, a man gave a short cry as he was crushed, but Clip slipped a knife into his breast and he was silent.

Berenger and Geoff ran along the street behind the men from the gate. There was a horrible whistling in the air, and both ducked, but the men behind were too slow, and the quarrels found their marks. Berenger ran forward, leading fifteen. Roger was at the far side of the street, and more archers were pouring into the city through the same gate. A cry, and Berenger turned to see one of them clutching at a bolt stuck in his throat, the point protruding from his spine. He fell, feet kicking in his death-throes.

A sickening crunch, and a man near Berenger disappeared as a rock crushed him. More bolts flew, and then he saw a great mass of French troops holding a barricade. Even as Berenger rallied the men to move forward, another flight of bolts struck the front rank. They fell, and he had to step over the squirming, shrieking mass of their bodies to get to the enemy.

'For the King! For England!' he bellowed, and then he was trying to force his way forward.

But in the narrow streets, it was impossible to move. And as rocks and heavy bricks were hurled upon them from above, Berenger realised that this was a trap he could not escape.

Sir John de Sully was with the Earl of Warwick when the messenger rode up from the King.

'The King asks that you pull those archers from the gates, my Lord,' he gasped. 'He fears to lose too many. Can you urge them to retreat?'

Warwick was already bowing to the Prince. 'By your leave?'

'Yes, go – and hurry,' Edward of Woodstock said.

'Sir John, with me,' Warwick snapped, and the two hurried to their horses. They mounted and gathered their esquires and rode at a gallop down to the gate of the city, where they pushed their way inside.

It was mayhem. A thick crush of men, and Sir John wielded his sword as spears were thrust at him and Aeton, but in the press, it was impossible to aim accurately and the assaults failed.

He bellowed at the top of his voice for the men to pull back, but it was impossible to make those at the front of the heaving mass of slashing, hacking men hear him. He pressed forward with the men-at-arms, but in so doing, they were all soon engulfed by the battle. Barricades had been erected, and now the French were standing and making a furious defence at them. From his saddle, Sir John could see the southern gate which led to the bridge and gave entry to the suburbs.

Swords rose and fell, stabbing, parrying and cutting at an enemy that seemed to grow by the minute. A lance snagged at his coat of plates, and he cut at it, uninjured. At every moment, more Frenchmen were arriving – and when some fell, more took their places. Although he saw Genoese crossbowmen, they were wielding their weapons as hammers. He hoped that they were out of bolts.

It was just as the Earl of Warwick had the horns blow for retreat that Sir John saw six English archers hurrying along the edge of the buildings. They held torches, and flung them into the timbers and carts blocking the road. One bounced off, but the others began to ignite the barricades. A number of the French immediately set to throwing water on the flames, but as they ran to the river with buckets, they weakened the defence.

145

There was an unearthly scream, and as he peered over the heads of the men in the mêlée, Sir John saw a Frenchman leap from the top of one of the fired buildings. He fell, still shrieking, and landed on three English soldiers. The French gave a roar of defiance, but even as they did so, a small contingent of archers outflanked the barricades. Arrows fell in among them, and with the extra Englishmen rushing to join the fray, the balance tipped.

His orders were to withdraw the archers, but Sir John saw the opportunity and seized it. He leaped from Aeton and rushed the barricades, sword in hand. With a cry of *'For England, for Saint Boniface!'* he sprang over the collapsing defences and began to attack the men behind. The Earl of Warwick was at his side, and the two were joined by more archers, pushing the French back through the streets.

That was when Sir John saw before him the looming inner face of the wall and the gatehouse.

'To the bridge!' he roared, and heard the cry taken up on all sides.

'To the bridge!'

CHAPTER TWENTY

Sir John fought with a cold deliberation. There was little enough space in the narrow streets: a man must block each blow aimed at him, while shoving and forcing the defenders back.

Frenchmen tripped and fell, to be stabbed where they lay; men had their weapons fall from their hands as the blows of their assailants beat upon their heads, their arms, their shoulders. The men fought in a mixture of human excrement and urine, blood and offal, all mingling with the filth of the roadway to make a slippery, foul mud.

Sir John glanced about him and saw that the Earl was heavily pressed, but even as he sought to run to his aid, Sir Richard Talbot rushed to help. The Earl was soon relieved, and the French forced back by the fury of Talbot's attack. In an instant more men followed him, and the enemy soldiers threatening Sir John were encircled. They fought on until the last man was cut down. None asked for quarter.

They were at the bridge! Sir John hadn't expected to reach it so quickly, but as he ran after Talbot, he realised that they were running beneath the arch of the gatehouse. There was a little door, on which men were pounding with sword pommels and axes. French noblemen had rushed inside at the last moment, and the archers knew the value of a nobleman's ransom.

Sir John didn't care. Standing beyond the gates, he saw a man's face, one of those from the vintaine, and then he saw Berenger too, wielding his sword with economy and accuracy.

The French on the bridge were fighting with the determination borne of despair. None wanted to give up: they would fight to the very last man.

Then he saw Welshmen pouring into the roadway *behind* the French. They were rushing along the bridge, and the French didn't see their danger until it was too late and they were hemmed in. Some tried to surrender, but were cut to pieces where they stood. The others fought on with grim resolve. They knew that there would be no prisoners taken today.

Berenger had fought all the way here, with Geoff roaring and slashing beside him, while Clip seemed to be possessed by a frenzy, spinning and striking like a berserker. Will the Wisp was to his right, wielding his sword and dagger with lunatic disregard for his own safety.

The French were demoralised. They had expected to keep the English from their city. Their enemy's sudden advance had shocked the citizens. Driven back, they fell over themselves to get to the South Gate, and once there, their mistake was clear. They were attempting to hold the gates closed with timbers and the strength of their men, when the Welsh fell upon their rear.

Sodden from wading across the river, the Welsh fought with all their hearts, and the French defenders died not knowing which way to turn on the bridge's tight-packed street.

Amidst the French fleeing or dying on the road before him, Berenger moved forward. With Geoff on one side, and Clip, Will and Jon close behind, he made his way across the bridge and into the streets beyond.

Houses rose high overhead, some with jetties almost touching. There were shops and stalls here, and the English must fight whilst avoiding the dead and dying and the loose stones that lay about.

The road ahead was blocked by a rampart of carts, boxes, barrels and anything else that could be collected. This barrier had been thrown together in panic as the English approached, and here the fighting was brutal: a hand-to-hand combat that moved back and forth as men clung to each other, stabbing at any exposed body part, hacking with swords, knives and daggers. The injured must remain standing, for the crush was so tight that those who fell were soon trampled to death.

Berenger grappled with a heavy-set warrior wielding an axe, and when the man fell, Berenger felt himself tumble forward also, in a welter of other men. The French barrier had collapsed, and their defence with it. As soon as he was up again, Berenger bellowed his rallying cry.

In only a short time they were in the island town. The defenders melted away, and Berenger found himself panting in a road full of bodies. There was a moment's calm as he bent, resting his fists on his thighs, gazing about him.

His vintaine was all around him, while the fighting ahead mainly involved Welshmen throwing themselves into the fray, and fighting fearlessly. Occasionally a whistle and hiss would betray a passing crossbow quarrel, some of which found their mark in hapless victims further along the roadway.

A stone was thrown from a house, crushing a man's head, and a roar of defiance went up from the French. As he watched,

Berenger saw a group of seven Genoese rise, all with spanned crossbows. They fired a volley into the Welsh, and so close were they that almost all their missiles passed through their targets and injured more men behind.

''Ware the stone!' Berenger heard, and Will shoved him in the back. He stumbled, only just avoiding a large rock which crashed into the ground where he had been standing. Looking up, he saw two Frenchmen with a steel bar at the topmost level of the house, on the parapet of the wall, levering away the stones to send them tumbling onto the English below. A cold dread entered his bowels.

'Archers! Aloft!' he commanded.

Clip was quickest, and his first arrow took the nearer man under his chin. The fellow's head snapped up, and he danced on the dangerous wall for a moment, then dropped down. Before his body hit the ground, the second man was pierced by three more arrows, and he disappeared.

'Will: get more arrows. Send the Donkey,' Berenger said tersely, and Will was gone, haring back through the streets as Berenger ducked into a doorway.

There was a regular clatter of rocks and stones now, and when Berenger peered from his hiding place, he saw a Welsh spearman hit by a rock. It crushed his head like a ripe cherry, shearing away arm and shoulder. A second caught a man at his hip, and he fell, roaring with pain and disbelief. More crossbow bolts came flying down the street at belly-height, and Berenger saw two men thrown to the ground.

Will was not gone for long. He rushed to Berenger's side and ducked in, another quarrel missing him by mere inches.

'Donkey's fetching them,' he gasped.

'Good. We need to clear these bastard Genoese dogs,' Berenger snarled.

Will nodded, but he couldn't shoot from here without exposing himself. As another bolt hissed past, he took a deep breath and threw himself over to the other side of the road, slamming into a doorway. From there he steadied his bow, an arrow nocked ready. There was a zip as a bolt hurtled past Berenger's face and struck the doorframe.

For an instant, his heart stopped. Then he yelled, 'Will someone please get that bastard?'

There was a flurry of arrows, and he heard screams. Peering from his doorway he saw two Genoese squirming in agony on the ground, while another lay dead beside them. Shouting, Berenger leaped from his cover and pelted along the road. At a flash of movement, he ducked behind some barrels. He saw Clip and Will darting from the road as a flight of bolts hissed by. One man fell back against the men behind him, a bolt impaling him through his mail shirt. He fell to his rump, mouth moving uselessly as he stared at the bolt, before his eyes rolled up and he died.

'Heads down!' Berenger bawled at the top of his voice, jerking a thumb over his shoulder. 'Crossbows up there!'

Will was in a doorway and already had his bow ready. With his back to the wall, he bent his bow, peering for a target. At a movement, he loosed, and Berenger turned to see it fly, a flat trajectory, and strike a man in the skull at the barricade. He went down with the arrow embedded, the fletchings projecting like a decorated splinter.

Behind Will, behind a pillar, Clip was grinning evilly as he peered down the length of another arrow. A man moved, Clip loosed his arrow, and the man fell with a shrill shriek, the cloth-yard in the small of his back. Then the Genoese bowmen stood again. Berenger ducked back into the doorway

That was when he saw Ed running forward, his arms filled with sheaves of arrows.

'No, Donkey, stop!' he shouted, rising.

He saw Clip loose again, saw Will aiming – and then Will turned and saw the Donkey. He span, arms wide in warning, and Berenger was sure he heard Will's voice . . . and then three bolts struck Will, one after the other, in his buttock, his kidney, and one in his neck, and Will toppled to the ground, blood gushing from his mouth and nose.

Berenger stared, appalled. Will had been his friend for years. Berenger couldn't believe he was dead, killed by a Genoese shit of a mercenary. A mist of raw fury came down over him, and Berenger began to run, heedless of the bolts and stones flung at him. He clambered up the rampart and at the top he fought with a concentrated rage that brooked no impediment. A man before him cut at Berenger with frantic despair, but Berenger caught his blade on his sword's cross, dragged it down, punched him with his left fist, and shoved quickly with the blade. It sliced deep into the man's thigh, and he fell; another man was before him, and he held his sword like a man holding a snake, but Berenger's cut took off his hand and wrist; another man was behind him, and this one flew at him with a flurry of cuts like a whirling dancer – but a Welsh spearman behind Berenger stabbed at him, and the man fell with the blood pumping from his throat.

Berenger was over the rampart now, and killing, killing all the way. He kicked and punched, parried and cut, and when he reached a Genoese bowman, he took the man's head off in one sweep of his sword. All the way, he heard the wails and cries of terror as the English pursued the French through the streets. None had thought the English would reach this far, and there were no more barricades, no defences of any kind. Utterly lost, the defenders ran hither and thither, chased by laughing men brandishing spears, swords, long knives or even clubs. The slaughter continued long into the evening.

It was then, when Berenger found himself slumping against the wall of a church in the city again, that the black reaction came over him.

Looking about him, he saw bodies everywhere. Two men lay at his feet, both with gaping wounds. Nearby lay other men without arms, without heads, with their hamstrings cut, their corpses discarded like so much rubbish. The whole street reeked of death.

It was a scene of Hell.

'Dear Christ, what have we done?' he groaned.

He wanted to weep.

CHAPTER TWENTY-ONE

Sir John left the fighting tired but content. While he had not taken much in the way of loot, he was still alive and whole, which was all to the good. The only pain he acknowledged was a soreness in his shoulder and neck from wielding his sword. It had been hard work in that press, but they had won the day.

Dear God! he prayed, gazing back at the city. *You have granted us a marvellous success. To have conquered a city so strong as that in an afternoon!* It was truly a miraculous achievement.

He nodded to the guards outside the King's pavilion and entered to find King Edward stalking about it in a towering rage.

'Who do they think they are to thwart me?' he began, his pale blue eyes flashing with anger. 'They wanted to hold their gates against me – *me*! Only a few remain, shuttered up in the castle. Well, we can take our time over that. How many of our men are lost?'

Clerics scribbled urgently in ledgers. The Earl of Warwick stood looking over their shoulders with Sir Godfrey de Harcourt nearby. Three other knights stood huddled together as though in defence against the King's mood.

'I fear it is some hundreds,' Warwick said. 'Genoese archers did some harm, but the fighting was fierce – especially when we came to the bridge. The Welshmen were brave indeed to wade across the river and outflank the militia, but still, many archers were killed.'

'How many of my archers?'

'Three, perhaps four hundred, Your Majesty.'

'So many?'

The King's face went white. At first Sir John thought it was merely shock, but then he realised that this was pure, white-hot wrath. King Edward III had come to power with a sword in his fist, capturing his mother and her adulterous lover, Roger Mortimer. His choleric temper was forged in vengeance. Those who thwarted his ambition learned to their cost that a King's right should not be questioned.

'Three or four hundred of my archers are dead because of these bastards? We need those archers, my Lord! They are the strength of our army, in Christ's name!'

'We can make up the numbers, Your Majesty,' the Earl said calmly. He had been eating a hunk of bread, and now he tossed the crust to two hounds lying on a rug. The two bickered over it, and then one snapped at the other's throat and pinned him to the ground until he yelped. The winner took his prize, swallowing it in a quick gulp.

The King watched the two as Warwick continued.

'Send messages to your sheriffs and ask for more archers. They will understand the urgency. Besides, there were some who were late to the muster. Perhaps they will have arrived by now. It is not only these men today whom we have lost: there were others on the way. Now would be a good time to replenish your army with men as well as provisions.'

'Yes. You are right,' the King said, but his mind seemed elsewhere. He pointed to his hounds. 'See them? The fastest and boldest wins the treat. The greater overwhelms the lazier, more indolent brute – just as we shall defeat Philippe. We shall win the land and I shall take the crown. We have swallowed this town today. A swift attack, and our men proved their valour. In the same way we can take the whole of France, if the coward Philippe will ever dare to meet us.'

'We shall make such a din of war in all his land that he will be forced to meet us,' the Earl said comfortably.

Sir John was surprised to see the Earl so calm. He had expected Warwick to display more anger. After all, many of the archers thrown into that hectic fight had been his own vassals.

'We shall do that,' the King declared, and then he frowned. 'So many of my archers gone – that is a great shame. Not all were killed by the Genoese bastards?'

'No. When our fellows broke into the city, the citizens took to their roofs and hurled stones and other missiles down upon them. Those, along with the barricades and the militia fighting street-to-street, caused most of the injuries.'

'So the people of the city are guilty of all these murderous acts?' The King's voice grew cold again. 'You will give orders, my Lord. In punishment for their intolerable revolt against my honour, the people of this city shall pay a heavy price. The army may take what they want tonight: loot, women – *anything* – and be free of censure. And then I shall burn the city to the ground.

'Your Majesty, it shall be done.'

'Wait – a moment, please, my Lord?'

Sir John saw that Godfrey de Harcourt had interrupted before the Earl could put his orders into force. He was a shortish knight, with the dark hair and eyes of a Norman, a strong, square jaw, and heavy brows. Sir John knew him by sight: he was a wealthy landowner, but because he had declared his loyalty to Edward, he had been exiled from France. Sir John was wary about Normans, for he considered them prey to divided loyalties, and apt to change with the wind at a moment's notice, but this man seemed reliable enough. He had been enormously useful, Sir John had heard, in choosing the site of the English force's landing, and then deciding on which route the King should take. Now Sir Godfrey was pale.

'You wish to add something?'

'Your Highness, I beg that you curb your wrath. You brought me with you to advise you. Let me give you my opinion. I know these people. They are my people. You can destroy this city. It is yours, and if you wish to bring it down, you can do so. But I urge that you reconsider. It has already been sacked. There are no families which have not suffered the full brunt of your attack. They have seen their property taken, their animals slaughtered, their women raped, their treasure stolen. Many have lost their menfolk. They have suffered. But if you go further, sire, if you burn the place as well, you will have shown that you are utterly merciless. All the cities and towns between here and Paris will rise up and fight you. Why would they not? Where is the virtue in surrender, when the result is the same? At least if they fight, they will die with honour. So they will contest every town, every village, every hamlet, every street. You will never win another quick victory like that which you have won today. And that will cost you *more* time, and men! You say it is your urgent wish to assault Philippe? Then you have a need for haste. Delay here, and it will not aid your cause. If you have to fight every step on the way to Paris your army will be depleted, so that when you do meet Philippe, he will prove too strong. He may win the day, or you can choose to retreat from him, and that would not gain you respect.'

'Then what do you recommend?'

'This: your army has already made free with the city, so show them mercy, and others will submit to you. They will bring you food and wine. They will aid you. You own the city already. It is a poor thing, to destroy that which hundreds gave their lives to win.'

The King nodded slowly, but reluctantly, Sir John thought. He was not inclined to mercy. This was not a campaign to win over the loyalty of the Normans by showing clemency; it was a campaign of conquest.

The Earl of Warwick snorted and peered down at his torn surcoat. Blood adorned the bright red of his shield, and the yellow stripe that passed between the six crosses was ripped where swords had thrust at him.

'There is another aspect, Your Highness,' he said, clearing his throat. 'This is a good port. We may hope to win another, but for now, Caen could be used to resupply ourselves with men and provisions.'

'Which other do we hope to win?' Sir John asked, and for the first time in that meeting, he saw a smile break out over the King's face.

'Those bastard French at Calais protect pirates,' Edward said. 'I have long felt that, if we could, we should take Calais. Even if the French King refuses to fight me in France, he will change his mind when we lay siege to Calais. He cannot allow that city to fall without fighting.'

The town that night was a scene of riotous pleasure as the English and Welsh moved from one house to another, liberating them of wine and cider, furs, pewter and silver.

Ed wandered through it all in a daze, looking for the vintaine. He had lost them as they continued into the town, and now he gazed about with a growing sense of unreality. He was used to ribald singing and occasional fights from sailors in his home town of Portsmouth, but to see the army let off the leash in this way was like gaining a view of the inner circles of Hell. He saw men bending a shrieking woman over a table as they took her in turns. A man was on the floor, and Ed assumed it was the woman's husband. A thick pool of blood lay all about him from a terrible gash in his forehead.

A scream from further up the lane caught his attention, and he turned in time to see a woman running from a house, two men chasing after her with cups of wine spilling. She turned at a locked door, and as the men approached her, she drew a little eating-knife from her belt and, weeping, shouted something at them. Ed didn't understand her words, but it sounded like a plea. One of the men, laughing, went to her, but cursed when he felt the prick of her blade. He drew a long dagger and began to slash at her, long, raking cuts that sliced into her and opened her belly, her breast, and then her throat. She fell, wailing, and Ed watched helplessly as the man kicked her slowly moving body, hurling vile abuse, until his friend called him away.

Ed could not drag his eyes from her. She was only about twenty, if that, and her long dark hair was unbraided, falling from beneath her coif to lie in disarray over her shoulders. As he watched her, he saw her eyes rise to his. There was no expression in her face, only a dumb acceptance, as though he was like all the others, the men who had raped her and killed her. He was no better, because he was a man. She swallowed and he thought he saw a tear run down her cheek, but then she sighed, and her entire body sagged, as though her soul had been sucked from her in that moment.

He couldn't bear to see any more. He turned and fled through the streets, now fitfully lighted by occasional bonfires or by burning houses, away from her accusing eyes. That was how it had felt as she looked at him, as though he was just one more man like those others. He was no better.

That must be how all the English were viewed, he thought. These people could only see the English through the glass of their own experience. Men and women slaughtered like beasts, their city pulled apart around them, the richest merchants captured and held for ransom while their daughters were despoiled.

A group of men burst from a building ahead, and he slunk into the darkness, feeling afraid. Somewhere in the city were Berenger, Geoff and Clip, and he should find them. With them he would be safe, but not here. Out here in the streets was no place for a boy like him. Not tonight. Not ever.

The flickering lights showed him another long alley, and he hurriedly slipped into it, his bare feet slapping through the puddles and ordure, until he came to a broader thoroughfare. He cautiously poked his head around the corner, and gazed up and down. He heard footsteps approaching, and singing. Returning to his little alley, he waited anxiously, until a group of men appeared. There were two archers in the front, English, and he felt the relief flare in his breast. They didn't seem too drunk or dangerous.

There was a movement, and he saw a woman at the street opposite, her hair all awry, eyes wild.

Ed was transfixed. She was a pretty woman, much older than him, but in her fear for her safety he felt she was a kindred soul. In a moment the men would see her, and they would rape and kill her, just as they had the French maid – and just as the French had killed his mother.

He would not allow it.

Without further thought, he stepped into the road, jerking his head at her to show she should conceal herself again.

By the second jerk of his head, she had disappeared, and now he found himself facing the group – and too late he realised that the archers were separate. They were already past him, and now he was confronted by the men behind: the Welsh spearmen.

'Another French pup!' one cried, and he was soon ringed by them, many speaking out in their uncouth tongue. A few laughed and chattered in English, and he called to them, pointing out that he was English and with the army himself.

It didn't help. One of them, Owain, an ill-favoured man with black eyes and brows that formed a single dark line, bared his teeth in a laugh, and pulled out a long dagger. He pointed at Ed, saying something he couldn't understand, and then a man came and gripped Ed's arm and pulled him forward.

'Wait! No! Leave me alone,' he said desperately. 'I'm English! Remember? You saw me at the tavern at Portsmouth? I bought you ale!'

One uncoiled a rope and threw it over a beam projecting from a house. He took one end and made a noose, all the while grinning at Ed.

Erbin appeared from a nearby house and stared at Ed with a smile spreading over his face. He was chewing at a lump of cheese, and in his hand was a short knife. 'Yes, we remember Portsmouth. But you have been dropping us in the midden, haven't you, boy? You said we attacked you and robbed you, you lying little *shit*!'

As he spoke he came closer, his eyes reflecting the glittering flames from a burning house.

'You did!' Ed burst out. 'It was the vintaine who found me after your robbery!'

'Go swyve your mother!' Erbin sneered. 'You are a pain in the arse, boy. Owain, kill him!'

Ed was dragged, shouting in terror, his eyes fixed on that fearful loop, while Erbin strode off into the night. Ed tried to draw his head away as the laughing hangman attempted to slip it around his neck. In the end, a cuff left him so dazed that his knees would have buckled, were it not for the man holding his elbows. They set the noose in place.

He felt the hemp tighten, and he screamed at them, but then his hands were released, and he tried to scrabble at the cord. He couldn't grip it. The rope was too tight. He could not touch the ground, and he began kicking and bucking. The rope was fast against his throat, just under his jaw, the knot beneath his left ear, forcing his head to the side, and every kick he gave made it tighter. In his panic, he had no conscious thought of the rope, nor of his little dagger in its sheath; rational thoughts were flown. All he could think of was the breath that hurt like a thousand dagger cuts as he tried to breathe. His throat was closing, and his lungs wouldn't work. His eyes, wildly staring at his murderers, were full of anguish as he tried to move his belly to bring in just a little air, enough for one breath. One breath could last a lifetime, and he craved a breeze to pass into his nostrils. But his nostrils were burning hot, and there was nothing to cool them.

Beneath him, Owain was laughing, he saw. *Laughing*.

CHAPTER TWENTY-TWO

Béatrice saw the boy grabbed, and it was enough to make her flee. She ran swiftly, ignoring the pebbles and shards of broken pottery that flayed her feet.

The boy had saved her. He had given her the chance of life.

All this long day she had been trying to find somewhere safe in the madness of the city. Her hiding place had been secure, until a man had thrown a burning torch into the house and she was forced into the open again. The hopes she had nurtured on the long walk here, of escaping English brutality, had turned to ashes. She was no better off here than she would have been in the fields and woods. In fact, she was less safe. In the countryside she could run away, as she had from Alain before slaying him.

Here she was enclosed by walls and rivers. It was an unnatural place, a city of death. Even that poor boy would soon be dead. She wished there was something she could do to save him.

Pelting along, she turned a corner and found herself confronted by fifteen men. Their bows and clothing declared them to be English, and she stopped, staring and gaping. And then an idea formed in her mind. She might still be able to save the boy.

'*Vite! Vite!*' she pleaded, and turned to race back to the boy.

Ed glimpsed movement, but he was beyond caring. He swung gently, spinning slowly as the hempen cord creaked.

Two men were striding forward, then running. More came behind them. One Welshman was thrust aside, hurled into a second, and both were slammed to the ground; Owain turned suddenly, and his body was run through with a steel blade that appeared through his back, waving and moving as the swordsman wriggled and jerked it. It was Berenger, Ed saw, Berenger with a snarl of fury fixed to his face, who booted the man away. And then Ed found he was falling, blessedly, to the ground, and the rope loosened, and he could gasp with his almost-crushed throat burning like a chimney over a hot fire.

'I . . .' He was caught between coughing and vomiting.

'Quiet, boy,' Geoff said kindly. 'You're safe now. We won't let them do anything else to you.'

Ed looked about him as Geoff rubbed gently at his bruised neck. Clip stood with his sword at the breast of the nearest Welshman, as if sorely tempted to slip it into him. Jack had hold of another, his dagger at the man's shoulder, ready to thrust down into his heart. Berenger stood beside Owain's body, his sword bloody. 'Are you all right, Donkey? Did these shites do anything else to you?'

Ed tried to stand, but he couldn't. His legs wouldn't support his weight. 'I . . . I thought I . . .'

'It's all right, lad,' Geoff said, his curious, hissing voice sounding malevolent and dangerous as he glanced about him at the Welshmen. 'They'll never try this again, I swear.'

'How did you find me?'

'She saved you, boy. Without her, you'd be dead,' Berenger said, pointing. The Welsh, he saw, were listening, but he disregarded them. If he had taken a little more care, he would have saved Béatrice a great deal of grief in the coming days.

Gil was saying harshly, 'And if you were dead, Donkey, we'd have destroyed all of these Welsh cunts too.'

Ed stared at Béatrice and tried to smile. When he swallowed, however, it felt as though he still had the rope about his neck.

A moment later, he was being picked up and carried away, while the vintaine gathered together behind him, and he clung to Geoff like a child as he was borne away, back to their lodgings.

Archibald was at his wagon when the vintaine returned, Berenger and the other men looking weary, Geoff carrying the boy.

'What happened to *him*?' Archibald asked.

Berenger turned to him a face full of pain. He looked at the gynour searchingly, then glanced down at the pot on his little fire.

'Master Fripper, be seated,' Archibald said with gruff understanding. 'I should be glad to share some little of my pottage with you.'

'No. I'm fine,' Berenger said.

Archibald sighed. It was often the way of other men that they would avoid the Serpentine: gynours who spent their lives working with the strange black powder.

'Master, you are alive,' Archibald said. 'Remember that, my friend.'

'Aye.'

Berenger walked away, and Archibald watched him go. Gradually he became aware of a young woman watching him.

'Yes?'

She too stared at him, then at his pottage.

He shrugged. 'If you want some, you can have some, maid.'

She approached him warily.

Béatrice had followed the vintaine as they made their way back to the camp. There was nothing in the town to tempt her to remain.

This gynour appeared amiable enough. A great bear of a man, and with the marks and stains of powder burns on his arms. His clothes were pocked and burned, as was his old coif, but he smiled and she felt he was no threat. She sat opposite him at his fire, and although she sipped some of his soup, she didn't get within arm's reach.

'Don't be scared of me, maid. I'm not going to hurt you,' Archibald said.

'What makes you think I fear you?' she asked.

'Most do, when they see my clothes,' Archibald said. 'It makes men and women think I'm a sorcerer.'

She nodded. There were many who had felt the same about her father. Perhaps that was why someone had sought to condemn him: fear of his skill with powder? She cleaned her bowl. The pottage was weak fare, but her belly was so empty after the last week that it was welcome and sufficient. When she was done, she rose and walked backwards, keeping her eyes on him.

'Fare well, maid,' he called, but then he was out of her sight and she was in the midst of the English army camp.

The army was bewildering in its enormity. All about her, men were working. Bakers kneaded dough and bellowed at boys commanded to light ovens, while butchers slaughtered and skinned and jointed, and wagons and carts brought ale and wine from the plundered stores of the city. It could have been a market, were it not for the occasional screams and sobs of the wounded as leeches did their best and the butcher-surgeons removed limbs from their traumatised owners.

She felt a thousand eyes upon her, but no one made any attempt to seduce her. The men were all too busy.

'Hello. Who're you?'

Béatrice turned to find herself being studied by a short, slim woman with fair hair and a narrow, elfin face. She spoke with a heavy accent.

'I am called Béatrice.'

'Are you a marching wife?'

'Certainly not!'

'No need to take that attitude, maid. It's not a bad life for us.'

Béatrice shook her head.

'Do you have a man? I can find you one, if you want,' the woman went on. 'It's just while the army's here. And it's better than being really married. I tried that.'

'You give yourself to any man?' Béatrice said. For her, it was little better than whoring.

'What do you take me for?' the woman asked indignantly. 'No, I've my man, and you can have yours. We give them comfort, that's all. What's wrong with that?'

Béatrice eyed her doubtfully. 'No. I cannot do that.' The thought of having a man pawing at her, slobbering over her, filled her with revulsion. Visions of the peasant who had tried to rob her and Alain sprang into her mind.

'It comes natural enough,' the woman said with a little smirk.

'Leave her,' Archibald said. He walked between the two, and the blonde stalked off, tossing her head. Turning to Béatrice, Archibald told her. 'If you want to stay with me, I can give you food, and I won't want anything in return.'

She stepped away.

'Maid,' he continued, 'this is an army. You aren't safe here with men getting drunk and foolish. I have reason to stay sober.'

'Because of your powder.'

'Yes,' he agreed, surprised. 'You know of such things?'

She gave him a thin smile. 'My father was a powder-maker.'

28 July

Two days later, Ed was up early.

The horror of his hanging had marked him. He kept his eyes lowered, terrified lest a man might take offence. He had learned quickly that grown men could behave like demons. Although the vintaine had saved him, they were still warriors. The blood staining their clothes was proof of their ferocity when roused, and that knowledge stayed with him as he fetched water, wandered the plain searching for arrows, or helped stir the pot for their pottage. All the while, his throat was sore, inside and out. He could scarcely speak without pain.

When he returned to their camp with water, he found the vintaine huddled together at the back of their cart. Even Grandarse was there, watching approvingly.

Berenger held a blanket, which he spread over the ground. He took an inordinate amount of time to smooth it so that there were no ripples and folds, and set stones at each corner to hold it in place.

'What is it?' Ed croaked to Geoff.

'Hush, Donkey! Watch and learn.'

Ed stacked his sheaves with the others beside the cart. It was still empty, and while he watched, he saw Berenger open a large pack and spread all the items within about the blanket.

'That's Will's stuff,' Ed managed, frowning.

'Aye. Now shut up.'

Not a word was spoken as Berenger took up Will's dagger in its sheath, his short sword, his bow with its distinctive pattern of grain, and set them down on the blanket.

Grandarse was the first to move. He lumbered over and stood peering down at the items. Finally, he reached down and picked up a little eating-knife. He weighed it in his hand, his mouth drawn down at the corners as he fiddled, pulling at the blade, testing its fit in the handle, before taking his own little knife from his belt and placing it on the blanket. 'Mine is getting old,' he muttered.

Berenger nodded towards Geoff, who glanced at Ed and walked forward. There was a little cross on a leather thong, which he took up. 'He used to wear this all day,' he said, and removed his own, placing it on the cloth before pulling the thong over his head.

Ed watched as each man went to the blanket, one after the other. Matt took a wooden cup and dropped his own cracked one in its place; Jack chose a dagger and nodded grimly to himself, placing his own in the spot whence it came; the long knife went to Eliot, who exchanged it silently with his own; a cloak went to Jon Furrier, who grunted that his was thread-bare, although Ed could see nothing different in the two; a brooch was picked up by Oliver; Luke took Will's shoes; the bent knife-blade which Will had used to carve bowls and cups was taken by Walt. Before long, Ed had witnessed almost everything that Will had possessed being taken by the others.

Geoff prodded Ed in the back. 'Go on, Donkey. You take something.'

'I don't want to!' Ed said hoarsely. He felt a slight supersti-tious alarm, as though the ghost of Will the Wisp might come back to haunt him for stealing his belongings. 'I'll take what I need from the French.'

Berenger explained, 'Donkey, we aren't stealing anything. All this stuff will go. Better to take something worthwhile.'

'I don't need anything.'

'Your purse?'

Ed shook his head, but as Berenger stared at him, he reluctantly fumbled with the cords binding his old purse to his belt. He dropped it on the blanket and snatched up Will's old purse. There were only three pennies in it, but that didn't matter. Ed tied the thongs to his belt, eyeing Berenger defiantly, then turned and strode away.

'You think they were behaving as thieves, don't you?'

Ed turned at the sound of Archibald's voice. The gynour was sitting at the bank of the little stream that passed by the village. Béatrice smiled at Ed shyly as he took his seat near them and began to hurl stones into the water.

'It was horrible,' he said. 'They just stole whatever they wanted.'

'You really believe that?' Archibald said.

Béatrice gave a chuckle. It was a breathy little sound, and she gazed at the water for a moment before reaching into her tunic. On a cord there hung a simple wooden cross from a leather thong. It was much like the one Will had worn, and which Geoff had taken. 'See this?'

'Yes.'

'It was my father's. Now it is all that I have that remains of him.'

'What happened to him?'

'He was arrested by the King's men. They thought he was a traitor. He had said he wasn't sure that it would be worse to be ruled by an efficient English King than a foolhardy French one, or something like that, and he was reported for his words. They came for him and took him away. I gave him my cross so he could pray to Jesus, and took this. But it is all I have of him or my family now. All else was taken from me, and destroyed.'

'What of it?' Ed still didn't understand.

Archibald looked at him. 'William the Wisp was their friend, can you not see that? They were all fond of him.'

Ed threw another stone. It was true that there was no theft, for all the items they removed from the blanket were exchanged with their own. The blanket was as full after they had taken the goods as it had been beforehand.

'The maid is right. When he died, it left a hole in their hearts. So they swapped a thing of theirs for a thing of his, so that they would not forget him.'

She nodded. 'Don't judge them harshly. They remember their companion: they keep a part of him with them forever.'

'Perhaps,' Ed grudgingly allowed.

She saw a tear fall down his cheek. His pain and sorrow were so intense, she looked away, not wishing to intrude on his misery. In her mind's eye she saw the axeman hacking off her father's limbs, and fingered his cross for comfort.

But Ed was not thinking of Wisp. He was remembering his mother on that fateful day when his entire family was wiped out.

CHAPTER TWENTY-THREE

It was some hours later. By his fire, Archibald watched as Berenger stood, staring down at Wisp's sorry pile of goods.

'Master Fripper,' he called. 'Would you like a sup of wine?'

He saw the vintener give him a sharp glance, but then he nodded and crossed the grass to meet the gynour. 'That would be welcome, master.'

'It's a good wine. Sweet as a good bishop's.'

'It is good,' Berenger agreed, taking Archibald's mazer and sipping. 'If you want, we have some bread and meats.'

'Ah, the food that has been liberated from the city,' Archibald said, leaning back against his wagon-wheel with satisfaction. 'A man could grow fat in this land.'

Berenger nodded. 'It is a good land. I pity the poor souls living here.'

'Aye, well, peasants and burgesses alike should accept our King.'

'Perhaps they will.' Berenger was quiet a moment, rubbing his sore shoulder, and then said, 'My apologies for refusing your offer earlier.'

'You had suffered loss.'

'It was a hard battle.'

'Aren't they all?'

'I was here before. I thought then how beautiful the lands were. I never thought I'd return and burn them.'

Archibald cast an eye at him. 'What were you doing here?'

'Travelling with a man to Italy. A rich man.'

'I have a feeling there is more you could tell me.'

'Maybe another day,' Berenger said. 'Some tales can get a man into trouble.'

'Ah, well, that is very true. Such as a story that a boy is spreading malicious rumours.'

'What do you mean?'

'I heard that your boy was hurt?'

'The Welsh tried to hang him.'

'Perhaps they thought he was deliberately slandering them,' Archibald said and explained what he had overheard.

'I will speak with him. If he *has* been talking in that way of the Welsh . . .' Berenger looked at him. 'What of you?'

'Me?'

'What is your story?'

Archibald smiled. 'You and I are not so dissimilar.'

'Eh? What do you mean?'

'Only that you and I are both running from something. Isn't that true of almost all the men here?'

'I don't know what you mean,' Berenger said, bridling. He passed the mazer back and was about to rise, but Archibald restrained him and refilled the mazer.

'Friend, I meant no insult. But almost everyone here is escaping something or someone. A woman, a job, a money-lender . . . the reasons for their presence here are many. Those with a happy woman at home are rare. They would be at home else, at her side.'

Berenger reluctantly took the mazer from him, with a doubtful sucking at his teeth.

'I am not your enemy, Master Fripper. I am a gynour, and I know my reputation, but I'm *not* evil.'

Berenger gave a short grin. 'I never thought you were. I'm not superstitious.'

'You have a wife?'

'No. I've known only the King's army since I was a boy, not yet eleven years old. My father was servant to Sir Hugh le Despenser. When the Marcher lords fought with Sir Hugh, Father was killed and my mother raped and murdered. Good King Edward, our King's father, sought to protect me. King Edward II was a great man, kind and honourable. I grew up in his household, moving about the country with him, as though I was his legal ward.'

'Because you were orphaned.'

'Because my father died defending Sir Hugh's lands. Sir Hugh was the King's best friend and closest adviser.'

'So the King protected you?'

'And later, I protected him.'

'How so?'

'During the rebellion I fought for him. I was there when he was caught and brought back to England. And later, I was with him when he was imprisoned.'

'And when he died?' Archibald asked.

Berenger shot him a look. 'I don't know if he's dead yet. That is why I know this area. I walked it with him sixteen, seventeen years ago, all the way to Avignon to see the Pope. God save his memory: King Edward II was as good a man as any I have ever known.' Berenger held up his mazer in a silent toast. 'The King gave me some money, and I lived here in France for a time, but I missed England, so returned. Since then, about eleven years ago, I have been a soldier for the new King.'

'You came straight to the army after that, then?'

'No. First I was arrested and held as a traitor'

'What? *Why?*' Archibald choked on his wine.

'Some said I was involved in murdering his father, but our King heard that I always loved his father, and he pardoned me and had me released.'

'But no wife.'

'The army is my family: the vintaine contains my brothers. I am proud to be one of them.'

'That is a fascinating tale. Do you think the old King is yet alive?'

'I am sure he is dead. And that is good. He was old, and his son, God save him, would not need the complication of a father appearing and demanding his throne back!'

'True enough.'

'And now,' Berenger said, finishing the wine, 'I must return to the men. I thank you for your hospitality.'

'And I thank you for your candour.'

'Aye, well, some secrets are too ancient to be kept.'

'And watch out for the boy.'

Berenger was about to respond, when he saw Sir John de Sully.

'Berenger Fripper, I have been told to take you in chains.'

'*What?*' Berenger sprang to his feet.

'Our good Lord the Prince of Wales has heard that you feloniously slew one of his men, a respected fighter with his spearmen. His men all assert that you killed him.'

'I did.'

'Ah!' Sir John looked at him. 'Very good, Berenger. I know you. As you reminded me, we once walked together on a long journey. So, if you killed this man, you will have had a reason, I hope?'

'They'd caught our young boy and were hanging him. We had to kill the Prince's man to get to Ed and release him.'

'So you say they were tormenting your young mascot, and you took offence? I can understand that. However, His Highness is inordinately fond of his title, you know, and of the men of his Principality.'

'The Welsh were going to kill him. The proof is there on his neck, where the rope bruised and burned him.'

'Was he worth your life?' Sir John asked.

'Without him, we'd have run out of arrows in the battle. Would the Prince prefer to have lost Caen and more archers because of a lack of weapons?' Berenger asked. 'I protected our boy against those who tried to murder him. One stood in my way and I had to kill him. It's as simple as that.'

'I will speak to the Prince and we shall see what comes of it. Meanwhile, my friend, I recommend that you keep yourself out of the way as much as possible in the days to come.'

Geoff had noticed Ed's mood.

The boy had been quiet and withdrawn for days. His throat was healing, and the livid blue-black mark was turning to green and gold at the edges, but he looked like a beaten hound, slouching around with his head down: the picture of despondency.

'What is it, boy?' he asked. 'What's troubling you?'

Ed jumped at his voice. 'I was thinking of all the French in the town,' he said. His voice faltered. 'So many dead.'

'You were the boy who once told us that the only good Frenchman was a dead one,' Geoff reminded him.

'That was because . . .'

'What?'

'My parents were killed by French pirates when I was a boy,' Ed burst out. He didn't want Geoff's sympathy, but he couldn't keep his story hidden any longer. 'My father was out fishing when they arrived in several big ships, and they landed and killed everyone. My father, mother, brother – all slaughtered. And for nothing!'

He could picture the scene in his mind's eye now: the ships beaching, one with a gonne in the prow that boomed and belched flames and death at the unarmed men on the beach. Horror-struck, he saw his father's friends hacked down by pirates as they stood mending nets. Others were cut down by the evil flying balls from the gonne or from the deadly bolts from crossbows.

'So that's why you hate the French,' Geoff said.

'I have always hated them. I wanted to come here to kill as many as I could, but now I see them, it's hard to hate them. They look like us!'

Berenger had been sitting in the dark of a tree's shadow. 'It's a good lesson to learn, boy,' he put in. 'All people are the same, deep down.'

'But if you know that, how can you go on killing them?'

Geoff rose suddenly. 'God will know which are His own when He receives their spirits. Look around you. The good people of that city will be in a better place this night.'

The Prince's lodging was in a merchant's sumptuous house in the old city, and it was already full of his commanders. Sir John had been summoned, which surely meant that there was news about the French army.

This was a new, modern building, with chimneys and glazed windows, and Sir John eyed the place covetously. Even now, after the army had been through every chamber before the Prince could commandeer it, there were still beautiful paintings on the whitewashed walls. Scenes of biblical events, pictures of angels sitting over base sins, and one glorious tapestry which depicted the Battle of Charlemagne against the massed hordes of the Saracens.

Sir John would have taken that first. It would suit his manor at Ashreigny.

'You like that?' the Earl of Warwick asked. He was sitting at a table, sipping wine from a mazer. The Prince and his bodyguards had not yet arrived.

'It is magnificent, my Lord.'

'Perhaps in years to come they'll have to replace it with our King's battle against Philippe.'

'You believe it will come to that?'

'That we shall finally crush them when the French meet us in battle? Yes, with God's help.'

'Yes,' Sir John said.

'You sound doubtful?'

'We have tried to bring him to battle many times before.'

'This time we shall make such a noise that even Philippe must hear it and try to stop us. And if our chevauchée fails, we shall go to Calais and lay siege to it. Philippe cannot dare to leave Calais to endure a lengthy siege. He will come and rescue the city. He must.'

Sir John nodded. He was too old to be concerned about riding into battle. He had done so many times. Sometimes the outcome had been magnificent, but he could still recall other, less happy days – the disaster of Bannockburn, for instance. He had no wish for a repeat of that. But in recent years Edward III had brought the English to one victory after another. Even on the sea the English succeeded, no matter what the odds.

The French had the largest army in Christendom: thousands of knights and well-armed men who could be called upon. There was no doubt that they must beat the English if they met on equal terms. However, the English had superb archers. The French had encountered English archers before, but never on such a massive scale as King Edward planned.

'We shall whip them,' the Earl said smugly.

There came the sound of marching and the rattle of armour and mail, and the door opened to show the Prince. He looked around the commanders with a firm eye.

'My friends, I am glad to see you all here. Where is Northampton? Oh, there you are, my Lord. We have news. Apparently our friend Philippe is gathering men to defy us. Excellent! He has no idea what he is going to find, does he? Page, fetch wine for my guests. Quick about it.'

'Where is he, Your Highness?' the Earl of Warwick asked.

'He has met with his men at Rouen. The Oriflamme is to be raised against us, apparently, so when we defeat him, we shall be proving ourselves invincible compared with his ancestors. It will be a glorious battle, my friends!' he said, breaking into a broad grin.

The wine arrived, and the Prince had all their goblets filled, then proposed a toast: 'To the ruin of Philippe and the two crowns united!'

Sir John raised his goblet and prayed silently to St Boniface for his aid in the coming battles. They would be hard, he had no doubt. Yet he found himself warming to this young Prince.

Perhaps Edward of Woodstock was not so callow as Sir John had feared.

CHAPTER TWENTY-FOUR

Clip had traded some fur for a small sack of oats, which he had brought back from the coast like a war trophy. It was stored carefully in the vintaine's box in the cart, and that night the men squatted contentedly at their fires and watched as their little oaten cakes cooked.

Berenger was still in pain. The scabs covering the wound in his shoulder had pulled away during the fighting for Caen. He lifted his shirt to look at it, but before he could do so, the old leech arrived at his side and studied the wound carefully.

'I'm all right,' Berenger said gruffly.

'Which is more than we will be,' Geoff said. He had removed his cake from the fireside and now stood eating it, watching how the leech probed and tested.

'What is that supposed to mean?'

'It's all wrong to have that girl come with us. She will bring bad luck – you know that. Wisp told us all that we were taking a course that would end in disaster, and he was proven right.'

180

'She saved the Donkey, Geoff. It could— *will you stop doing that, you clumsy old goat!*'

The leech gave Berenger a contemptuous sneer and continued with his ministrations.

'If Grandarse hears what Wisp said – you know, about the chevauchée being doomed when he saw that cat – he'd have her out on her ear in a blink, you know that.'

'What's it got to do with Grandarse?'

'We have the boy with us. I like the Donkey, but he isn't exactly blessed with fortune, is he? He's hardly a safe mascot.'

'If we discard the fool, he'll be dead in a day.'

'He is bringing us bad luck, and so is the girl.'

'What?'

'You can't trust women, you know that.'

'I never thought to hear you say that. You are always so happy with your wife.'

'Yes, well . . . I *was*.'

Berenger gave him a close look. 'Is there something wrong, Geoff?'

Geoff looked up again. 'Frip, all women are the same, and this French one's more dangerous than most. She loiters with us, but she isn't one of us. She's French.'

'So?'

'I could get rid of her: no one need know – no one.'

'No! Leave her. I will see what I can do. And don't mention her or Wisp's words to Grandarse.'

'If you're sure,' Geoff said.

He left Fripper there, staring sadly at the fire while the leech, all but forgotten now, muttered to himself, mopping and cleaning the wound.

Geoff nodded grimly. The French bitch had to go. If

181

Frip wouldn't do it, he would have to take on the job himself.

At the Prince's lodging, Sir John listened as the commanders moved on to a discussion of the King's plan of campaign.

'We shall be leaving here early in the morning. Be ready before dawn,' the Prince said.

'We march in our normal battle order?' Sir John asked.

'Yes. We will lay waste to the broadest area. Our men will devastate every farm, village, town in our path. The people must be shown that Philippe cannot protect them, therefore to be safe, they must enter our King's Peace.'

'I heard that Bayeux tried that yesterday,' the Earl of Northampton said. He scratched his ear. 'Did you hear of that, my Lord?'

The Prince chuckled with delight. 'Absolutely! The city was so petrified of our army that they sent fifteen of their bourgeois to meet the King. They hadn't seen a single Englishman threaten them, but the news of our rampages across the countryside were clearly too shocking for them to wait for us to come and take their city – even though we have already passed it!'

'Did the King accept their allegiance?' Sir John said.

The Earl of Northampton laughed. 'No, he was much too sharp for that. He refused it. Politely, but firmly. He told them that he was not going to leave men dotted about the country to garrison little towns and cities like theirs; he was marching to fight their King, so he could not promise to protect them – yet. However, he would be glad to take their oaths of allegiance and protect them fully once Philippe has been defeated.'

All present laughed at that. Soon afterwards the men were dismissed, and each returned to his own billet. While the Prince was still in a happy, cheerful mood, Sir John sought him out.

'Your Majesty, there is one matter I should wish to discuss: Berenger Fripper.'

'You have caught him already? Good.'

'I know where he is, my Lord. However, I would not have him punished.'

'Where will the army's discipline be without the guilty being punished?'

'This was a matter of army discipline. The Welshmen had captured Fripper's servant. They were hanging him.'

'Why? What had he done?'

'Nothing. He was merely a source of entertainment.'

'I see.' The Prince looked at the Earl of Warwick.

The Earl glanced at Sir John, frowning. 'Is this the vintener who was injured at the gates of St Lô?' he asked.

'Yes, my Lord. He was there even though he had been injured before.'

'Then I know him. He is a good fighter, and bold, too. I would make more use of him, Your Highness. Put him in the front line where he can show his mettle.'

'Very well. But I shall not be so lenient in future,' the Prince declared. And then he broke into a broad smile again. 'Tomorrow we start to search for Philippe, my friends! It's marvellous, isn't it?'

3 August

It was the end of a weary day's marching when Sir John de Sully next saw the centaine.

He rode forward to meet them. Nodding to Grandarse, he said, 'How are your men?'

All about them, soldiers could be heard bickering and grumbling. The old man looked up at him from beneath his bushy eyebrows.

'They'll serve,' he replied.

'What of the boy with Fripper's men?'

'He's well enough: he fetches and carries when ordered.'

Sir John dismounted. He could see Clip returning from a foraging expedition with a cockerel and a hen. He grinned to himself: Fripper's vintaine was experienced in all the arts of war.

Patting his rounsey's shoulder, he noticed the woman leading the old nag at the cart.

'Who is she?' he demanded.

'Just a French slut. In Caen, our boy suffered from the Welsh. They nearly killed him.'

'So I heard.'

'This wench saw him and drew us to him. Without her, the boy would be dead.'

'So she is wife to the vintaine.' Sir John smiled. He knew how 'wives' could be adopted. Half the female followers in the army had chosen to be wives for the course of the campaign.

'Rather, she is the sister,' Grandarse said reprovingly. 'Aye, the lads decided that she had saved our mascot and it'd be bad fortune to harm her after that. So they adopted her and took her as their ward. I doubt any of 'em would think to touch her. Besides, she can cook and sew better than Eliot or Matt, and she makes a good pottage.'

Sir John eyed the girl. She was a sullen-looking mare, he thought, with her down-drawn mouth and dark eyes, but if she kept the vintaine happy, he was content. 'Very well – but make sure she doesn't cause any arguments. We both know how women can sow dissent.' As he spoke, he caught a glimpse of Geoff's expression. The fellow was watching the woman with a mistrustful expression.

'I wouldn't have any of that, Sir John,' Grandarse said. 'I'd take her as my own marching wife before I let the men turn to fighting over her.'

His words distracted Sir John. 'You? By Christ's pain, man, you'd crush the poor maid,' the elderly knight chuckled. 'Your belly is vast as a tun of wine, man. That would be a cruel way to kill her!'

Grandarse was grinning widely and about to respond when there came a cry from the sentries.

Sir John rose to his feet and watched as Berenger darted over to the sentries. They pointed, and Berenger peered into the distance with fierce concentration.

'What is it, Fripper?' Grandarse called.

He wanted to say, 'How the fuck can I tell?' but it was best not to remind Sir John that his eyes could see little further than half a bow-shot. He muttered to the guards before responding: 'Two men. They could be priests from their clothing. Riding at speed.'

'Frip, send four of your archers to meet them,' Grandarse called. There was no need for more men than that. If the two riders were alone, they could be little danger to the English.

Sir John made his way to join Berenger and the sentries. 'They look well-enough fed to be priests,' he said thoughtfully as the men approached.

Berenger nodded without speaking. He was still studying the roads, the trees and grasses for any sign of enemies.

The two were cardinals, from their dress. Berenger noticed Archibald glaring at the two with deep distrust. It made him wonder again about Archibald's background. Still, there was no time to speculate now.

'Good Sir Knight,' the first said as he reached the line of sentries and archers, but looking directly at Sir John.

He was at least fifty years old, with a weather-bronzed face and cunning little blue eyes that flitted hither and thither as if counting how many soldiers were in the army. 'I am Cardinal Pietro of Piacenza, and this is my companion, Cardinal Roger. We are here to see your King. I expect safe passage to his presence.'

'Berenger, bring two men,' Sir John said.

With Jack and Will, Berenger was soon marching, while Sir John ambled along beside the cardinals on his rounsey. Berenger watched the countryside as he strode along. All knew that Popes tended to support the French and had done ever since the Popes moved to Avignon from Rome. He listened as Sir John spoke with them, ears straining unashamedly for a clue about their visit.

'You have proposals for the King?' Sir John asked.

'What we have is for his ears only. The Pope is alarmed at the rancour that your army is causing here in France. It is not to be borne that royal cousins should fight in such a manner,' Pietro said. He had a tone of resentful disdain, as though it was far beneath his dignity to discuss such affairs with a mere knight.

'Perhaps the Pope would be better advised to support the wronged party,' Sir John said, making Berenger grin.

'It is not the French King who has invaded his cousin's lands,' the Cardinal spat. 'The wrong is upon one side.'

'When we took Caen, there were many interesting records,' Sir John said. He spurred his mount until he was alongside the Cardinal. 'You know what was in there? Plans for Philippe, who calls himself King, to invade England. All written up and sealed and signed. If we had not come here to prevent him, our lands would be laid waste just as we do now. This is a war of self-defence.'

'A war of self-defence in which the people are being slaughtered,' the Cardinal declared icily.

'God is with us. The Crown belongs to Edward,' Sir John said comfortably.

Berenger smiled grimly to himself. It was true. King Edward was the son of Isabella of France who had married Edward II. When her brothers died without issue, the crown should have passed to her son, but the French nobility barred him by creating a new law so that the crown could not pass through the female line. Edward III was disinherited. All England knew that. Their King had been robbed.

Not that it mattered to Berenger. All he knew was, he was happy to be serving his King.

It was not an easy journey. The English army marched on a broad front, and now it was some fourteen miles across. The King was a good league from where the vintaine had stopped, and Berenger was relieved when they came to a group of Welsh spearmen. He recognised their leader.

Sir John rode to him. 'Erbin, I place these Cardinals in your care. You are charged to take them to the King as swiftly as you may, and to treat them with all courtesy while they bide with you. They are messengers from the Pope.'

'We will look after them as we would our own kin,' Erbin said, staring at Berenger.

As Berenger turned to go back with Sir John and the archers, all the while he thought he could feel Erbin's eyes aiming at his back, like spanned crossbows.

CHAPTER TWENTY-FIVE

Tyler saw the Donkey as he walked to fetch water. The boy had grown since Mark first saw him. Then, he'd been a confused, anxious little fellow, easy to strike in the dark and rob.

Tyler had thought, when he first saw Ed here in the army, that he would be denounced, proved to be a thief and punished. That would be bad here, under the rigours of martial law. The army knew few punishments: there was only execution and flogging. That was why he had been forced to invent the stories.

He had told the Welsh contingent about Ed, suggesting that the boy had been spreading malicious rumours about them, and when that didn't immediately succeed, he began embellishing his tales. It was a shame that the Welsh hadn't managed to hang him properly in the city, but there was still time.

For himself, Tyler was content. He had managed to collect a considerable amount of plunder in the last towns and cities, and his pack was growing heavy; and while he was still nervous that the lad might remember his face from that fight in the alleyway, still he reckoned that the Welsh would do his bidding.

And meantime, no one suspected him of having anything to do with it.

Yes, life was good.

Le Neubourg, 6 August

Many of the knights and men-at-arms joined the King that morning for Mass, and Sir John was impressed by the sight of the noblemen. It was the first time he had seen all of them gathered together in one place, and as he stood in the middle of the church's nave, he was almost awed.

However in one corner he caught a flash of red, and when he peered, he saw the two Cardinals. Both bent their heads and prayed and participated in the service as a good priest should, but Sir John saw the poisonous glances that both directed towards the King. This gave him cause for concern. He would not like to see the King alone with them, for even Cardinals had been known to commit murder.

After the service, he became aware of the Earl of Warwick standing at the doorway and beckoning him. Sir John crossed the floor, pushing past other noblemen who huddled, chatting, laughing and gambling. 'My Lord?'

'Come with me. The King wishes for your company.'

The King had taken a large hall not far from the church, and when Sir John entered after the Earl, King Edward was shrugging off his cloak.

Now in his thirty-fifth year, the King was tall and powerful. Training in the saddle and with weapons had lent him a muscular frame. Long fair hair and his thick moustache and beard framed handsome features. His air of grave concentration gave him an aura of authority.

Sir John cast a look about the room as the King seated

himself and took a goblet of wine from his page. The King's pages were ranged at the walls, ready to satisfy his every whim, and to the left stood several men-at-arms as bodyguards.

'Sir John, come here, I pray,' the King said quietly. His voice was calm, but there was an underlying tension.

'Sire?'

'Some days ago, two Cardinals arrived here. They are emissaries from the Pope, come here to try to negotiate a truce between me and Philippe. I hear that they saw you?'

'Yes, my Lord, I escorted them.'

'Did you bring them to me?'

'No, my Lord. When we reached the Welsh, we left the Cardinals in their care.'

'I see.'

Sir John was confused. He glanced to the Earl, but the latter was keeping his face as carefully blank as a child's accused of filching a biscuit. Sir John dared not ask the meaning of the King's words.

'Bring them in!' the King called after a moment. He waved Sir John and the Earl away, and they walked back to the wall.

After a few moments the two Cardinals were led into the hall through the main entrance from the screens.

Pietro paused in the doorway, either to take stock of the men in the chamber, or to emphasise his importance before walking in; Sir John wasn't sure which. Then the two Cardinals strode forward until they were just before the King.

'Your Majesty, we have been waiting three days to see you,' Pietro said. His face was rigid with control, but it was clear that his mood was not as calm as his outward appearance might seem to a casual witness. He was filled with a rage that was almost overwhelming him.

'I have been busy, my Lord,' the King said as he studied the men before him. 'You have messages for me?'

'We rode here in great haste to communicate the Pope's alarm at your continued harassment of your cousin the King Philippe.'

'My *harassment*?' King Edward repeated.

'How many of his subjects have you slain already? You persecute the people of this country, and when—'

'I would remind you, Cardinal, that for many years the French King has attempted to prise from me my possessions in France. First he invaded Guyenne, and demanded the whole of Aquitaine. He has threatened invasions and—'

'This is nonsensical! Invade England? Philippe has no such intention.' The men's eyes shot to Sir John as he spoke.

Edward snapped his fingers and an esquire stepped forward, passing him a sealed roll. The King unrolled it. 'Plans for the invasion of England, with the enthusiastic support of Norman shipmasters, including how to despoil England and bring back her treasure. These plans are dated eight years ago. And you tell me he has no such intention?'

'It must be in retaliation for your numerous assaults against him and his Kingdom. You realise that he is already, even now, bringing together all his vassals to destroy you?'

'We await him.'

'You think this ragtag army will be adequate to stop his advance? You have no idea of your danger! The greatest army in Christendom gathers outside Rouen. King Philippe has proclaimed the *arrière-ban*. You know what that means? Every fighting man of military age hastens to meet him. You have what – ten, perhaps fifteen thousand men? The King of France can demand five times that paltry number! You have some hundreds of knights, but he has thousands. When battle commences, you will be overwhelmed. He will destroy your forces utterly. Who then will protect your people? Who will save your towns and cities, when the French army takes its revenge for all that your men have done here in Normandy?'

'And your suggestion?'

'The Holy Father wishes you to cease this violent *chevauchée*. There can be no purpose served by continuing this terrible war.'

'I have a crown to claim.'

'You have no claim. Your father proved he was vassal to the King of France, and you also.'

'My claim to the throne is stronger than that of the Valois!' Edward roared. He stood, towering over the Cardinal, who took a pace back in the face of his anger. 'You say that I should retreat, that I should *bow* to the King of France? A true king would have fought me when I landed before. He has never sought to meet me in battle or protect his people. *He* is no king!'

'You should have returned to negotiate with the Pope.'

'The Pope demands that I accept the same territory as my father held. This illegitimate King has stolen my lands! I will not accept merely the return of stolen goods. I demand *more*! I will take this kingdom at the point of my sword. It is mine, and I am here, in the sight of God, to reclaim it.'

'The Pope demands that you let us negotiate with the French King on your behalf. We require that you agree, that you remain here, and cease your appalling depredations.'

'Cease my depredations? This Philippe has sponsored the Scottish to harry the whole of the north of my kingdom, and has already taken my territories in Guyenne, and you tell *me* to cease? By God, I shall not!'

'We shall ensure that you have all your lands returned to you. Ponthieu, the Dukedom of Aquitaine, all the lands you seek.'

'To be held free of the French crown? My own to command?' Edward challenged.

Pietro's eyes narrowed warily. 'To be returned to you as your father held them, naturally.'

'As fiefs of the French King, therefore. You think I came here with the largest army England has fielded to become vassal to a king whose right to the throne I dispute? Do I *look* like a fool?'

The other Cardinal broke in. 'The Pope would seek to have you and France ally yourselves in a crusade – do you not see that your squabble here prevents Christendom from regaining Holy Jerusalem? We could take back the City from the heathen. Your grandsire was a strong, powerful knight, and he aided the Christians of Outremer with his crusade . . .'

'You seek a crusade? I say this, Cardinal: I will be happy to consider a crusade – once the matter of my inheritance and my crown is resolved.'

'I *demand*, in the name of the Pope, that you cease this strife!' Pietro snapped. 'You will see your forces hacked to pieces if you dare continue. God Himself abhors this appalling strife. You must desist.'

'You "*demand*"?' King Edward stared at him, his head lowered, for a long moment. Then he held out his hand. 'Where are your papers?'

'What?'

'You will have letters of authority to demand action of me. Where are they?'

Pietro exchanged a glance with his companion, and then met the King's gaze with resolution. 'We have no need of papers. You recognise our rank and position. You will obey us as Princes of the Church.'

'You have no papers. I do not recognise your authority.'

'Your Majesty, I—'

'The interview is concluded, Cardinal. You may leave us. Do not be tempted to argue further. I will brook no more discussion. You have no place here.'

'Then before I depart I must ask for the loan of a horse.'

'A horse?'

'Your men stole our beasts when we arrived here,' Pietro stated, holding his temper in check with difficulty. 'The uncouth devils with spears.'

'I will have a mount provided for each of you. Now, begone! I have much to deal with.'

The Cardinals nodded, glanced at each other, and then turned and made their way from the room.

King Edward beckoned an esquire and muttered to him. The man hurried off after the two prelates. When they were alone again, the King sat once more and stared at the floor. Then, slamming his fist on the arm of his chair, he said in a furious hiss, 'How *dare* they! How *dare* those piss-pots come here and command me when they have not even a letter of authority between them? Be damned to them!'

'What now, my liege?' the Earl asked.

'Now? In God's name, my Lord, we find the French King and bring him to battle! Tomorrow we advance to Rouen.'

7 August

Berenger's shoulder was much improved. The soreness was faded, and when he caught sight of the old leech, there was a grudging respect in his eyes. Never before had he known a man so competent at curing wounds.

This morning they had risen as usual before dawn, the camp grumbling awake in the cool greyness, while the sergeants and vinteners walked about bellowing their orders, counting their men, kicking the recalcitrant awake, and generally making themselves annoying.

Grandarse had always preferred a more leisurely approach. He rested while Berenger and the other vinteners bullied and cajoled their men to their posts, and then came along to stare at them sourly.

'A fine riot of pisshead tart-ticklers you look,' he grunted. He hoisted his hosen up beneath his belted tunic and puffed out his cheeks. 'Bugger-all sleep last night, me. I could do with a decent bed again, and a fine wench to warm it.'

Clip called out, 'You could always try Ed's young strumpet. She'd keep you fresh enough. A little draggle-tail like that would ruin a night's sleep!'

'Ah, go piss in the wind,' Grandarse said. He glanced around at the girl.

Berenger thought she was losing a little of her fear of them now. At first she must have assumed that she would be raped when the men brought her to their tented shelters, but no one had laid a finger on her, not when they understood she had saved Ed's life. Even the usually hard-bitten Jon Furrier had gruffly passed her a cloak one night when the air was chill and she lay huddled and shivering.

And yet the girl made Berenger uncomfortable. There was some knowledge in her – a look of measuring confidence, such as an assassin might give – that made him anxious. It must also have been Geoff's words. It took little more than a comment like his, mentioning 'witch' to cause distrust and fear.

For now, she had helped them, and saved Ed, and that was enough for the men in the vintaine, so it would have to be enough for Berenger too.

On the order, he helped the others stow their goods. A fine

collection of plunder they were acquiring, and there was some good food in the cart alongside the arrows and bow-staves. The nag that pulled the cart was a tormented, bony old beast, and by common tacit agreement, the vintaine had allowed the woman to take its head. Now, some days later, she and the horse were almost inseparable.

'Fripper, take five and scout ahead. The rest of you, take a bow each and five arrows. If you see anything, the usual rules. Bellow out for help.'

Berenger pointed to Clip, Geoff, Matt, Eliot and Jon. They took their bows and made their way forward as the mists began to clear. There was a little wood ahead, and a mixed shaw which was thick at this time of year. Soon the villagers from all about would come here and cut it back, selecting the different types of wood that they needed: some for making hurdles, some for baskets, some for staffs and handles for tools. Little would go to waste. It reminded the vintener with a sharp pang of his own home, so many hundreds of miles away. 'Too many leagues behind me,' he muttered, and promised himself he would go home again. One day.

They pushed through the trees and then, up ahead, there was the little town of Elbeuf. 'Tell Grandarse we can see the town,' Berenger said, leaning his good shoulder against a tree.

It was a peaceful scene. Smoke wound up from chimneys and fires, and there, in the midst of the plain, was the thick, curling silver of a great river.

'That it?' Grandarse demanded. He had lumbered up even as Berenger took in the view.

'There can't be another river that large,' the vintener said. 'It's got to be the Seine.'

'Good!' Grandarse said, pleased. 'There'll be cause for cele-bration soon.'

'What's all that?' Clip had joined them, and was peering ahead through the haze.

Here the River Seine came due west, towards the English, but at Elbeuf it curled north and then east again in a tight loop. Continuing east and then northwards, it flowed up to the old city of Rouen. Usually this city would be much like London, full of noise and bustle, and there would be a fog of smoke over the town as the traveller approached. But today, from many miles away, there was a thicker smudge in the sky east of the town.

Berenger felt the stirrings of nervous excitement. 'That's where the French army waits for us.'

CHAPTER TWENTY-SIX

The vintaine continued almost to the River Seine. On this side there was a small suburb.

Orders were given to torch the place. Soon flames were shooting up into the sky, and Berenger watched as men cavorted and cheered at the face-scorching fires. The whole of the countryside was blanketed in smoke. Orange-red sparks danced on the dry fields of wheat under a choking fog, and Berenger coughed as the fumes passed over him. He looked up briefly as Ed sat beside him.

'What is it?' Berenger asked, toying with his dagger. He was whittling a stick into the likeness of a bird's head. He had given it a cruel beak, and now he was trying to smooth the brow to give it the look of an eagle.

'All this flame. It seems wasteful.'

'It's war, boy. War *is* wasteful.'

'But why destroy the crops? Shouldn't we let the people harvest it first? Otherwise, what will become of them? And if we burn it, *we* can't use it. Where is the sense in that?'

'Donkey, there's no sense. It's *dampnum*,' Berenger said. 'We destroy everything so the people daren't return, not until they have agreed to live under the rule of King Edward. If they refuse, they lose everything. It's a hard lesson, but an important one.'

'And if our enemy does the same?'

'They must choose which army scares them the more,' Berenger said brusquely. Why did the boy pester him with his doubts and questions? He carved again, and this time his knife went home too deeply, and a jagged splinter of wood sheared from the bird's skull. Berenger sucked at his teeth in annoyance, then thrust his dagger back into its sheath and rose, saying, 'And sometimes the poor bastard peasants make the wrong choice.'

'What will they do here?'

Berenger looked at the flames, weariness heavy on him. 'Mostly, they will die.'

Ed wandered disconsolately to the gynour's cart. Béatrice was there with the old horse, stroking its head and murmuring words that only the beast could understand.

In Béatrice's eyes the boy had seen a deep sorrow, and here, in the midst of the destruction, he felt sure he knew why.

'I'm sorry,' he muttered. He saw she had golden glints in her brown eyes – a strange, bright gleam. At first he thought there were tears forming, but her voice was steady.

'For what?' she asked.

He was startled. 'For the damage, the burning,' he said with a wave of his arm that encompassed the fiery fields.

'This is nothing. *C'est rien*. I would burn more,' she said with a coldness that sent a shiver of ice into his bowels. He recoiled.

'These are your people,' he said.

'I have no people,' she said. 'They killed my father and they tried to kill me. I hate them.' She turned away, and her face was fixed on the fires all about them. 'Now it is my turn for revenge.'

'Fripper, get up off your arse!' Grandarse called.

To Berenger he was a humorous sight: red in the face, and smeared with smudges where a store of pitch had caught light. Sooty clumps had gathered on all the men nearby and made each sweaty face as dark as a Moor's. His jerkin was ripped where a falling timber had caught it.

'What now?'

'There's a force riding to the bridge at Rouen to see what the Frenchies are doing.' He spat. 'Ach, my mouth tastes like a blacksmith's taken a piss in it! All this smoke and shite in the air! Sir John de Sully is going: you'll be with his private guard. I want to know what's happening up there. There'll be some hobelars riding with him, I dare say, so you won't be alone. Take my pony.'

Berenger nodded and wandered to the cart. The bowstaves were kept in waxed sleeves to protect them from the weather, and he slid three out before he found one without a knot or imperfection. He bound it with cord so it slipped over his shoulder, then took a sheaf of arrows and went to find Grandarse's pony. It was a recalcitrant beast at the best of times, and Berenger had to ram his thumb hard into its belly before he could tighten the cinch-strap. 'Cross me, you miserable git, and I'll make you into a bloody stew,' he muttered as he jerked the girth sharply.

'You are joining us, Master Fripper?' the knight enquired when Berenger trotted over to the party.

'Sir John,' Berenger said. He glanced about the rest of the men.

There were forty armed archers on horseback and ten men-at-arms. Sir John was not the only knight. Berenger recognised Sir Thomas Holland: when they took Caen, it was Sir Thomas who had accepted the surrender of the French Marshal, Sir Robert Bertrand, at the gatehouse. He was smiling now, chatting merrily with the others, as Sir John lifted his arm and called the men to ride off.

On all sides were the proofs of the English rampage. Bodies lay in the roads near their homes. At one door he saw a pale, skinny little girl with a skull-like face watching as the party rode past. The house behind her was gone: it was merely three walls with no roof, and at her feet lay two adults, so cut about and bloodied that Berenger could not tell whether they were men or women.

The sight depressed him immeasurably. He remembered his talk with the Donkey, discussing the choices of the local people, whether they would survive when two armies trampled and burned their lands. Seeing this waste made him feel more sympathy for the French peasants than for the army in which he served. He could happily fight on the battlefield; killing another man who was trying to kill him was easy. When he stood in a wall with other Englishmen, with his pike or spear pointing at the enemy charging him, he felt exultation in his heart. It was what he was good at. He knew it. He had survived battles with the Scottish and the French, and although he had known fear, he had swallowed it and fought on.

That was the measure of a man, someone once said to him: not that he was fearful of battle, but that he conquered his fear and continued to grapple and stab. There was a sensation that came from nowhere else, when he fought. A kind of thrill in the blood, an excitement that was a part of his body, not a mere 'feeling'. When a warrior wielded his sword in the line with his comrades, when he felt the first slashes of the weapons that were aimed at his death, when he felt the bite as his own sword leaped into a man's throat or breast and caught a bone, there was an exhilaration that was almost religious.

But to see *this* – the ravaging of a vill with the peasants lying ruined in the dirt like rats caught by dogs; to see good, solid homes burned and fallen down, the grain stores broken into and their precious stocks trampled into the mud, the few possessions smashed and despoiled – to see that, was to know shame. There was no pride in this, no glory or jubilation. It was simply the strong, conquering the weak. And while many would look on these poor people as mere chattels to be killed or let live, Berenger could see in them the faces of people he had known when he was a boy. He felt befouled by this pointless aggression and slaughter.

'There it is,' Sir John said.

He had taken them north to the westward bend in the river, before following it downstream towards Rouen, and now they could see the town before them.

It was similar in size, Berenger thought, to Caen, but this would be a harder town to break. The Seine curled about it, and without access to a bridge it was clear that the English would struggle to cross so wide a river.

'With me, my friends,' Sir John called, and broke into a gentle canter. 'Can you see all the men at the city walls? They are alert, in any case. Halloo! What is this?'

They were closer now, and they could clearly see the workers scurrying all over the one bridge. Berenger saw men with axes and hammers, and even as he watched, a great baulk of timber slowly leaned over and began to topple from the vertical.

There was a hill or rise in the land a mile, perhaps two, from the river, and the knights went to the top with the hobelars following after. When they reached the top, Sir Thomas Holland whistled. 'Look!'

Beyond the town Berenger saw a vast, sprawling mess of tents and makeshift covers, standing higgledy-piggledy in the pastures north and east of Rouen itself.

'There is the French army, then,' said Sir John. He leaned back against the cantle and stared. 'I confess, I do not think I have seen so many men gathered together in one place before. We shall need to select our ground carefully.'

'Come, Sir John,' Sir Thomas said. He reached over and tapped his mail gauntlet against the older knight's bascinet. 'The more French there are, the greater the glory. Do you not know that if the French do not outnumber us five to one, it is an unfair fight? We have fifteen thousand men, so to make it right, the French needs must have at least seventy-five thousand. Ah, me! I do not think they have enough. It will be a battle as lambs to the slaughter!'

Sir John smiled thinly, but said nothing. Berenger was glad to be fighting under Sir John rather than the younger, more hotheaded knight.

They rode off down the hill to go and study the works more closely.

It was clear that the English army would not be able to cross the bridge. It was already largely dismantled, and by the time the English arrived in force, would be broken down entirely. Even as they watched, another span of timbers fell away and floated off, a raft in the river.

'Is there a ford?' Sir Thomas asked. He was behaving like a rache who has seen the quarry, Berenger thought privately.

'Go and look, Fripper,' Sir John said, and Berenger trotted closer.

In many towns and cities, there was a toll to pay on a bridge, and men would often ride to a ford where, for the cost of sodden feet and hosen, they could cross the river for free. You could always see where a ford lay because of the tracks leading to it, the bare soil where the grass had been worn away. Here there was nothing.

He was still at the bank when he heard the sound of horses, and when he turned, he saw Sir Thomas had joined him.

'Well, Master Fripper, that is a brave sight, is it not?'

'There's no ford I can see.'

'Surely there must be something.'

'If there was, I reckon we'd have trouble trying to use it,' Berenger said. 'It would only take a few men to defend the crossing, even if we outnumbered them. At a place like this, they could let us cross and pick us off as we approached the far bank. We'd be sitting targets.'

'Oh, come now! Do you really think we couldn't force our way past them if that was our intention?'

'Sir, I think we'd lose half our army, and the other half would be slain as they tried to enter the town.'

The knight glanced at him, a confident smile on his face. Then he gave a whoop, spurred his horse and galloped off to the bridge itself. Three men were hurrying to it from a little cottage, and Sir Thomas aimed straight for them.

'Sweet Jesu, what will he do now?' Berenger muttered, and kicked his own beast to follow. Two other men-at-arms and a knight also pelted off after Sir Thomas.

Sir Thomas drew his sword and as he reached the men, he hacked viciously three times, whirling his horse and trampling their bodies. When Berenger arrived, Sir Thomas and another knight were fighting with four more Frenchmen. A pair of Frenchmen with spears arrived, and began jabbing and prodding at the horses, trying to unsettle them, but Sir Thomas managed to withdraw, then ride around so as to attack them from behind. He nearly succeeded, but the men realised their danger and ran for the river, plunging in and swimming for the other side. One of them made it, gasping as he crawled up the far bank. The second, however, disappeared. The weight of his mail, or the strong current of the river was too much for him.

When the little battle was over, Sir Thomas stood up in his stirrups, and bellowed at the French on the other bank.

'St George for King Edward! If any of you dare to meet us, we are ready!'

CHAPTER TWENTY-SEVEN

Sir Thomas had been cheered by the action, and he continued to joke and be merry with the other men as they jogged along. Sir John de Sully looked less sanguine, however, and Berenger saw him keeping a constant lookout for ambushes.

He was distracted by Richard Bakere, the knight's esquire, saying, 'Master Berenger, my lord would speak with you.'

Berenger nodded and urged his pony to trot up to the knight. 'Sir John – you wanted me?'

'You and I are not so young as some in this army,' Sir John said. 'I remember the ride to Avignon; our old King trusted you as a solid fighting man. You are little changed, I think. I like to know that men I am selecting are sound.'

'What do you mean?'

'This war has one purpose, my friend: to crush the French army. We have enough archers to make every French infantry-man look like a hedgehog, and with luck our bodkin arrows will prick any French knight who tries to charge us, but some may escape even our clothyards. Of course, we have other weapons to throw them into confusion, God willing, but there are so many of these damned Frenchmen! You saw the size of their army at Rouen. If all should fail, we will have to act with caution.'

'You mean that we should consider retreat?' Berenger said. The idea did not appeal. The army that turned and fled was invariably the army that was destroyed. No man could fight while taking to his heels.

'Do I look like a faithless coward?' Sir John snapped. 'No. I mean that we must look to the defence of our King and Prince. We have many young knights and esquires among us who are less experienced in battle than you or I. We know not to race ahead of our companions because we see a tempting target. Others do not, and are often surrounded and overwhelmed.'

'We rarely lose unless we are taken by surprise,' Berenger noted.

Sir John's flash of anger was already flown. 'True enough, my friend. However, the bridge at Rouen is gone. The French will be fools if they do not seek to destroy other bridges with the aim of preventing our crossing – *except* at the place of King Philippe's choice. When we have the opportunity, a few hotheads may rush over, then find themselves in a trap. It would only take a small force to throw our army into disarray. Think: a force of a thousand archers and men, crossing at a suitable point, and then enclosed and wiped out. All France would see that the English were not invincible, and our men would lose heart. They would feel that their King's star was waning, and mutterings would begin. Many would accuse the King of foolishness in seeking the crown, and some might even desert his cause.'

'So what do you suggest?'

'No more than this: keep an eye on your men. You will serve me directly, and I will bring you to support the Prince. He is our hope and future. We have to protect him at all costs.'

'At all costs,' Berenger repeated softly.

'You understand, don't you? Keep your men on a tight rein. If there is a need for military prowess, we shall form a resolute band. But we cannot afford to risk archers committing themselves like at Caen, or see men like Sir Thomas rushing in willy nilly.'

'No, sir.'

'I have fought in many battles, Fripper. At Halidon Hill we crippled the Scottish and left the main part of their army dead on the grass, because we English held our line. We didn't break our ranks, but held together as the Scottish attacked. It was just as they had done to us at Bannockburn, when *they* held the ground and we charged them, and were destroyed.'

'You were there?'

'It was my first battle, and my worst. But it showed me the importance of discipline.' He threw a stern glance at Berenger. 'At Caen we could have lost everything. The archers rushed ahead and yes, we took the city. But if the French had set traps in the walled town, things could have turned out very differently. If the Welsh had not succeeded in their flanking attack, if the archers were held at the gatehouse, if there had been more barricades that held up our men, if the citizens began to drop more rocks and missiles on our fellows . . . it would have gone ill for us.'

'I was there.'

'I know. And I am saying this because you are not usually foolhardy. Next time, wait until your King has drawn together all his forces before you take such a risk. Otherwise you could be responsible for the destruction of the English, and of your

King's ambitions. So, if you see a fool like Sir Thomas rush off to fight, next time, leave him to get on with it.'

'He could have died without our support.'

'Then so be it. It is worth losing one rash fool compared with losing the battle. We need steadiness in the army.'

'Aye, Sir John.' Berenger looked at him with respect mingled with relief. His nagging concerns about the leadership of the army had been quelled.

'Now return and find your men. I will speak with you again very soon.'

'I have bread and wine here, boy. We lack meat, more's the shame, but there is some thick pottage left over from last night, if you want some. We can soon heat it up.'

Archibald bent to the fire again, and Ed saw that he had made small loaves of bread which were sitting on top of a steel disk over the embers. The glorious scent of newly baked bread mingled with the odour of brimstone.

'What is that smell?' Ed asked.

'Don't worry about it. I use this same pan to test my mixtures sometimes. A little of the smell gets into the metal, I suppose,' Archibald said.

Ed nodded, joining him at the fire. 'Is Béatrice here?'

'She's gone off somewhere, boy. Don't worry about her.'

'I do, though. If you'd seen the way that the Welsh treated her . . .'

'I did, remember? But they will think twice about doing anything to her while she's with me.'

'I've heard rumours, rumours that . . .' Ed stammered. He felt foolish even mentioning it.

'That I'm in league with the Devil, I suppose.'

'Yes.'

'I can make magic, of course. You may see that one day.'

'Oh.'

'And I am considered so foul by the Lord God, that I must be ostracised and excommunicated.'

'I hadn't heard that, but—'

'And my soul is doomed. Oh, and so are those of any who join with me. Like you.'

'I . . .' Ed looked into the fire. In his heart he felt sure that he could see demons deep in the flames, leering at him.

Archibald suddenly gave an explosion of laughter.

'Boy, it's ballocks! I am a man like any other. I am a Christian, and I go to the altar like you every day. There is nothing to fear from me. They say I make magic. What they mean is, they don't understand how I do things *without* magic.'

He pulled out a platter of wood, and slid the bread onto it. 'Go on, boy, eat. You see, what I do is make use of modern arts. I learned from a clever religious man many years ago how to make the black powder. It is a marvellous powder, full of energy and excitement. It makes flashes and flames, it lights the sky, if you want it to. In years to come, it will be seen as the means of giving princes power. Because no matter how highborn, no matter how wealthy, a man with a bag of powder at his side will be your equal.'

'How can you say that? *Powder?*'

'Watch and learn, boy!'

The gynour rose and walked over to the wagon. He took up a leather satchel, inside which was a waxed bag like a small wineskin. Bringing this back to the fireside, he pulled out the cork and poured a small amount into his hand. Thick black flakes of powder appeared, and Ed peered at them closely.

'It looks like the dust from the roadside after the rains have panned the mud and wagons have crushed it,' he said.

'Aye. And I make it in much the same way, very carefully mingling the three elements – clean charcoal, brimstone and saltpetre. I have made it from other ingredients, but those three, mixed in the correct proportion, give you the real powder. After that, I wet the mixture into a thick pottage, and then leave to dry on wooden racks in the sun. Never by a fire! Later, I crumble it – gently, very gently – in a large mortar, and finally, I am left with this glorious, God-given residue: *black powder*. Look!'

The gynour threw the powder into the fire. There was a sizzling flash, and a roiling cloud of blue-black smoke rose from the fire like a small thundercloud.

Ed did not see it. He had leaped away, yelping: *'Christ Jesus, save me!'*

Archibald laughed at his shock, setting his little flask on the ground beside him.

'Don't panic! It is quite safe,' Béatrice said, walking up to them and sitting near the fire. 'It is only the powder he uses in his guns.'

'I know. It was a gun like that which killed my father,' Ed said brokenly.

Soon they had reached the outer limits of the camp. At first, the sentries on duty were suspicious of the little cavalcade, but before long Berenger was back with Grandarse and the men, squatting at the fireside and dunking pieces of rough, unleavened bread in a watery pottage.

'How was it?' Geoff asked.

'Not bad. They have a lot of men up there,' Berenger said, looking at Grandarse.

The latter pulled a face. 'Aye, the buggers are likely thinking they can roll us up like a tapestry and throw us into the sea.'

'If they can gather together well enough, that would be likely. You wouldn't believe how many there were.'

Jack grunted. 'What of it? We're worth any number of French churls.'

'They won't get through us,' Matt agreed.

'We'll all get slaughtered,' Clip said gloomily. Then: 'What? Why're ye all looking at me like that?'

'Shut up, Clip,' Berenger said.

Grandarse heaved his bulk up, scratching his cods. 'Aye, well, there may be many of them, but there are enough ugly bastards here with us, too. Ach, I need a piss.'

Berenger dipped bread into his pottage. 'I hope you're right.'

At a tree, Grandarse lifted his chemise and pulled down his braies to water the grass. Over his shoulder he called, 'Listen to you, man. You've lost your senses! You think we can't beat a bunch of Frenchies? Most will be local levies without training or weapons to protect themselves, let alone hurt us. There'll be some mercenaries, maybe some Genoese – look how useful they were at Caen! And knights. Well, if we take our own position and hold it, we'll keep them away, too.'

Berenger was about to make a comment when there was a sudden scream. He sprang up, his bowl of pottage falling into the fire and spattering and hissing. Ramming the last of his bread into his mouth, he set hand to sword and ran towards the scream, while Grandarse roared and swore, slapping at his damp thigh and trying to pull his braies up as he lumbered after his vintener.

Béatrice had not lost her instinctive distrust of men. Archibald she could tolerate, in the way that a child could put up with the annoying attentions of a generous uncle. The gynour, she felt sure, was unlikely to rape her. His genial manner appeared genuine. Ed, too, was no danger. But that was not the case with other men in the English camp. She could feel their lascivious gazes on her.

'Come, maid, food,' Archibald said. He held a large bowl aloft.

She took it slowly, and began to eat. Once, a year or more ago, she had found a stray dog, and although it was ravenous and wanted the tidbits she held out, it was afraid to approach too close. She felt like that wild brute herself now. Distrustful, hungry, ready to bite.

After their meal, Archibald toyed with the leather flask.

'What is this powder?' Ed asked.

'It is called the Serpentine,' Archibald said. 'You let the fire get to my wagon here, and have one of the barrels there get scorched, and you'll level this forest!'

Ed's lip was curled. 'I know that smell,' he muttered.

'Few don't. You are used to the powder?' Archibald enquired of Béatrice.

She nodded. 'I told you. My father was a merchant of powders. He made it, and I learned how to make it from him.'

'Maid, I think you are my perfect woman,' Archibald smiled.

Shortly afterwards he settled, his hat over his eyes, his back against a tree. Béatrice took herself a short distance from him, almost under the wagon. Ed went to join her, and she covered them in a cloak, snuggling up tightly.

It was late when she heard the footsteps. In the gloom she could see nothing. Then there were figures, flitting softly from tree to tree. She thought them wraiths, but then one went to the side of Archibald, and she heard a thud as that person struck him on the pate. Instantly his breathing changed to a shallow snore.

'Ed, *vite*! Flee!' she hissed. 'The Welsh, they are here!'

He goggled momentarily, and then she saw an awful comprehension in his eyes. As though she could read his mind, she guessed he was thinking of the women in Caen, the wives and daughters littering the roadside. She saw him clench his jaw and frown.

There was no time to argue with him. He was prepared to fight and die in the attempt to protect her.

As he rose, Béatrice snatched up a stone and brought it down against his skull. It was for his own sake. She pushed him under the cart, and while there, she came across Archibald's little powder flask. She quickly dropped it beneath her tunic, and was straightening when Erbin and two men grabbed her legs and pulled her out. She tried to snatch at her knife, but they had gripped her firmly, a hand clapped over her mouth.

'Not a sound, witch, or you'll suffer more pain than you knew could exist in this world or the next!' Erbin breathed in her ear.

Gritting her teeth, she thought how, with her knife, she would have stabbed and slashed at them until no flesh remained, until she had smothered the grass all about in their blood and gore. But when she glanced back and saw Ed's body, she felt relief that, once again, she had saved him. She hadn't stopped her father's death, but she had saved Ed from dying: she had submitted to her own capture in order to protect him.

And then, suddenly, she felt a lurch in her belly. For the first time since killing the priest, she felt defenceless and was overcome by a blind, unreasoning terror as Erbin and the men pulled her away from the safety of the wagon and deep into the darker recesses of the forest.

CHAPTER TWENTY-EIGHT

Berenger and the others soon reached the little copse in which Archibald parked his wagon. Ed was leaning against the wagon's wheel, a hand to his brow. It was his scream they had heard. 'They took her, they took her!' he moaned.

'Who took her?'

'The Welshmen! They came and took Béatrice!'

'Shit!' Heedless of Grandarse's shouts for him to slow down, and despite Sir John's recent talk about the need to act prudently, Berenger pelted through the undergrowth to where the Welshmen had made their camp.

The Welsh had taken a large yard area near a farm. They had a series of fires on the go, with rabbits and a lamb spitted and roasting. The men were drinking and laughing, some holding valuable mazers with chased silver rims, some chewing on pieces of meat.

Berenger did not pause to think. He strode into their midst, anger sending ripples down his spine. Clenching his fists, he demanded, 'Where is your captain? Where is he?'

'Why?' asked Erbin. 'Oh, it's you: the murderer. What do *you* want?'

'Your men have taken a woman of ours.'

'A whore?'

'She is our woman,' Berenger said. 'Your men were seen taking her.'

'Who saw them?'

'The boy.'

'Oh, him.' Erbin shrugged contemptuously. 'He would say anything to insult the Welsh. Look at the stories he's made up about us already. Perhaps it was a screech-owl that scared the brat. There are many about here.'

Berenger was tempted to grab his sword and hold it to the man's throat. He was maddeningly smug. 'Don't try my patience, Erbin. Where is she?'

'I couldn't say. If you have lost your goose, you should go and search for her.' The man squatted insolently by the fire. 'Perhaps she is back in your bed already?'

Two men strolled towards Berenger. One was grinning inanely, and toying with the hilt of a short sword; the other wore a scowl of hatred.

Berenger suddenly felt foolish. How stupid of him, to have rushed here without anyone to back him up. He was at the mercy of the Welsh. If they were to kill him, they would be perfectly within their rights, defending themselves against a crazed attacker.

Erbin stood now and smiled. 'What, Englishman, do you mean to remain here and drink our wine?' he jeered. 'Have some and be merry! But you care little for your wench if you leave her to her fate while you enjoy yourself here.'

Berenger took a pace back, but as he did so he became aware of more steps behind him and he froze with the certainty that a

Welshman was blocking his escape. Then he recognised Geoff's voice, saying, 'What now, Frip?'

'I don't know,' Berenger admitted.

'I'm bloody soaked, me,' Grandarse grumbled. 'When that scream came, I was nearly beshitten. Taking a piss, and hearing that sort of row, it's a wonder I didn't cut off me tarse I was in such a hurry to tie me braies!'

'Since you have not taken her,' Berenger called to Erbin, 'you won't mind us staying for some drink and food, as comrades who share at ease.'

'Nay,' Erbin said, looking at Berenger coolly. 'You accused us, and that was an insult. On second thoughts, I think you should go now before I call the guards to report you. Go on – fuck off. The wench is probably back there already, wondering where you have got to.

Berenger glanced at Geoff. 'What do you think?'

'I think he's talking ballocks, Frip.'

Berenger had risked his life many times for money and the chance of winning a butt of wine. If he were to attack Erbin, he felt sure there was a good chance he would die, but what of that? To die trying to save the girl who had herself saved their Donkey was a good trade. He saw Geoff give a wolfish grin, and felt his own face crack into a smile. He was just about to shout and launch himself at Erbin when Grandarse put his hand to his breast.

'No, lads. If you do that, we'll all hang. Leave these Welsh fellows alone.'

'Why?' Berenger said. He was ready for action.

'Fripper, you had Sir John save you once before when you killed one of these pieces of shit. Don't expect him to do so again.'

'I don't know,' Berenger had his eyes fixed on Erbin. That was the man, if it came to blows, whom he would kill first.

There was something cold and feline in Erbin's eyes. Something unnatural.

'What now?' Geoff murmured from the side of his mouth.

'Ballocksed if I know,' Berenger said with a shamefaced chuckle. There was nothing they could do but retreat. It was one thing if these Welshmen leaped upon them and brought matters to a head, but if they did nothing and stood back while the Englishmen remained here, it was a stalemate. No one would support them if they caused an affray in the middle of the Welsh camp.

All because of that woman, too. All this trouble over a French tart who wasn't even a 'wife' to any of them.

Geoff said, 'If she was here, we'd have heard her by now, Berenger.'

'He's got a point, Fripper. If they've killed her, it's too late to do anything about it now,' Grandarse added.

'All right, I know,' Berenger said. But he was reluctant to leave, and possibly abandon her to her fate. *She had saved Ed*, he told himself.

There came to his ears a noise, a pop and hiss like a loud hiccup. All heard it. Erbin's eyes slid away towards a door set in the wall on their right, and a sudden, shrill scream came from within.

Berenger stepped forward, slammed the cross of his sword into Erbin's face hard enough to feel the nose break, and then span to his side. His sword was at the throat of the nearer Welshman, and the second was stepping away from Geoff's point, arms held up defensively.

'Wait here, Grandarse,' Berenger snapped, and was about to make his way to the chamber, but there was no need.

She appeared in the doorway, her face blank. Her mouth was moving, as though she was whispering something, but Berenger could hear not a single word.

The Welsh drew away from her, averting their faces, one covering his eyes as she came out and walked forward, her feet scarcely rustling the grasses, until she drew level with Berenger. She looked like a woman who had peered into Hell itself, and who had lost her mind. She then continued on her way, passing behind Grandarse and Geoff, leaving the clearing and continuing on towards the vintaine's camp beyond the copse.

Berenger felt a shiver run down his spine. There was the distinct odour of brimstone about her. The men in the camp huddled anxiously near the fire as if men afrighted by a ghost or a vampire, casting agitated glances all about them. And all the while, shrieks of agony came from the little room.

Berenger, still clutching his sword, saw a man stumble from the room, his hands to his face.

'I'm blind! The bitch blinded me!' he cried.

Ed was sitting back, feeling sick to his core, while Archibald ministered to him, when she returned.

'Béatrice? Are you all right?' Archibald asked. Each syllable threatened to shatter his own bruised skull.

She said nothing, merely squatted on her haunches at the fireside, staring at the flames. Then she pulled out the flask and placed it on the ground near Archibald, away from the fire.

'They took me into their room and left me tied up. They said I was to satisfy all of them. But my hands were in front of me. I poured powder into a drinking horn, and put stones and sand on top. I wanted to kill them. When the vintener came, a man was sent to hold me still and quiet. I sat down and shivered, and asked him to stir the flames and make the fire warmer. When he did, I threw the horn into the fire. It exploded, right beneath his face.'

'You did well, maid,' Archibald said, but he thought something had broken. Something deep inside her that had been fine and strong was rent apart and would never be mended.

He stood, fetched a thick blanket and, barely touching the woman, draped it over her shoulders. He poured water into a pot and set it on the fire to boil. Tipping some strong wine into a large cup, he topped it up with the steaming water, stirred in a dollop of honey and passed it to her. She took it without looking up, but at least she sipped it.

Something about its warmth or taste communicated with her. She looked about her as if startled, wondering where she was, but then stared at the ground, and Archibald was saddened to see her misery. It made his own eyes well up.

'Maid, you're safe now,' he said gruffly.

'No. I will never be safe,' she said, and began to weep.

'You know what she is?' Erbin said. He stood at Berenger's shoulder now. 'She has already killed one of mine, at Caen, when she called you to aid your bratchet. Now she has blinded another of my men. She will bring bad luck to us all. You understand me? She is evil, man. A witch. You saw her cursing us. We have to destroy her.'

The man in the room was being tended to at the fire. His face was a mass of blood where the flesh had been burned, and his eyes were mere bloody caverns. He sobbed and moaned as the men tried to comfort him.

'She had something, and it exploded in my face! It all blew up! I can't see anything!'

Erbin spat. 'Someone shut him up.'

'This is your fault. *You* took her,' Berenger said, although he felt his flesh creep at the inhuman sounds coming from her victim. 'Leave her alone. If you do anything more, if you look at her, let alone touch her, I will command her to curse you with all the fervour at her command.'

'It is not just us,' Erbin called as Berenger rejoined Grandarse and Geoff and set off for their camp. 'It's the whole army. You think a bitch like her will comfort you in your beds? While you're swyving her, you'll be seeing to the end of all of us! We'll all die here!'

Berenger continued on his way as the Welshman shouted after them, his words growing more overwrought as the English left the Welsh camp behind.

'You hear me? You will see to the ruin of the whole army if you keep her! She's evil! She's a witch!'

Grandarse stopped and looked back at Erbin through the trees. 'You hear that? Daft bugger has had his pate beaten once too often, hasn't he? He's brain-dead. Witch, my arse! What, does he think a witch would come here just to annoy *him*?' His tone was light, but there was a frown on his face. His superstitious soul rebelled at the thought of harbouring a witch. 'Eh? Berenger?'

'Yeah, what do *you* think, Frip?' Geoff asked.

Berenger looked at them both. 'She feared – rightly – that she was to be raped, by the whole lot of them, so she defended herself as best she might. That's all. They captured her and imprisoned her in that little chamber. We all heard her being taken.'

'Aye, but if she is a witch . . .' Grandarse growled.

'If she is, she'll likely strengthen us. We haven't done anything but try to help her, so the wench would have no cause to want to harm us,' Berenger said with finality.

They entered the edge of their camp and Grandarse and Geoff strode to the fire, squatting near the heat.

Berenger found his own attention moving to Archibald and the wagon. There was a small fire, and Berenger could see Ed sitting there beside Béatrice. The sight of her reminded him of Erbin's hissed words: 'She is evil, man. A witch.'

'Ballocks to the lot of it,' he sighed tiredly, and stepped around the men in the camp, over to his own belongings, and there he lay down.

At a sudden snapping of twigs, he looked up again and felt a shiver of unease when he saw that Béatrice was staring straight at him, as though she could read his every thought.

CHAPTER TWENTY-NINE

8 August

Berenger slept uneasily that night. When the vintaine was called to stand-to the next morning, he could not help but look to where he had last seen Béatrice and the Donkey, but they were not there. Of course they weren't. They had their own duties to attend to. Archibald, however, was there and he waved amiably.

As Grandarse wandered up and down the line counting the men, Berenger saw a movement over his shoulder. It was the Donkey, with Béatrice. She moved so elegantly, it was like watching a woman skating on a frozen lake, but he felt a flicker of alarm at the sight of her. He could see again the face of Erbin, flames lighting his features with an unwholesome orange glow as he made his stark accusation: 'She is evil, man: a witch.'

There was something unsettling about her; something other-worldly, he thought. But it was time to put such ideas away and concentrate on the job in hand.

*   *   *

Overnight, fires had raged through many farmsteads, almost up to the walls of Rouen itself. The land was scorched. Only the skeletons of trees stood in copses and woods, stark and bare, all the undergrowth gone. Such wanton damage must be evil in the eyes of God, but to Berenger it was the way of war, and he could no more change how warriors fought than turn back the tide.

Sir John called him to join a scouting party. The bridge at Rouen, they found, was completely demolished. At the farther side of the river a group of men stood guard, and the French herald trotted to the riverbank, from where he could shout across to them to convey his King's message.

'This is a pretty nonsense,' Sir John muttered.

'Sir?' Berenger said.

'The King asks if the French will join in battle, but look about you: is there any point? The French have surrendered the western bank of the Seine, and now wait over there to contest any attempt to cross.'

'Are you sure?' Berenger said doubtfully, thinking of the army King Philippe had at his disposal.

'He wants to ensure that we are utterly crushed when he fights us,' Sir John said. 'He will wait until he has all his might here, and he can close his fist around all of us.'

'Then what can we do?'

'Torment him to the extent that he finally agrees to fight us here, or find another bridge before he has his camp struck. We could make our way to the next bridge and take it, then cross the river and find a suitable field to fight him.'

'And if we don't?'

Sir John looked at him. 'Pray that we do,' he said curtly.

'When we were here before . . .' Berenger began.

'Eh?'

Berenger looked at the knight. Sir John was shrewd, and his memory was undimmed. 'Sir, when we were here with William of Wales sixteen years ago or more, we saw many lands over here.'

Sir John said nothing, but looked about him carefully. 'You should forget William le Walleys,' he said quietly.

They both knew why. Their charge, 'William', was in fact the man they had sworn to serve all his life: King Edward II. But he had been declared dead in Berkeley Castle, and his son had taken the throne thinking, in his grief, that he was come into his inheritance. No King would wish to be reminded that he took his crown while his father was yet breathing. That was an offence against God.

'I know, Sir John,' Berenger said. 'But I recall good flat plains and fields to the north, when we crossed the water to come here.'

Sir John nodded. 'I too recall those plains. There were some that would serve us well today, but,' he sighed, 'they are all too far away. We need a good field here to bring the French to battle. We have to *force* them to fight.'

They stood with the herald waiting for the answer until the sun was grinding its way to its meridian. When it came, Sir John gritted his teeth.

'So, it is as I thought. He waits for the rest of his men. Only when he outnumbers us by tens of thousands will he risk trial by battle. We shall be hard-pressed when he finally agrees to wage war against us.'

Berenger returned to the camp that night to find the men in a wary mood, on the alert for any new threat from the Welsh.

For her part, Béatrice worked on, fetching fodder and drink for the horse, helping Archibald move his gear and make some supper. Keeping busy was key, she thought.

'Careful with that,' Archibald said at one point.

She looked down. A man had given them a pair of coneys, and she had skinned them with a knife Archibald had lent her. Now she saw that she had been about to set the blade to rest on top of a barrel. Archibald nodded as she took the knife and set it aside.

'Don't want to risk any sparks with that barrel,' he said. 'You know better than that.'

She nodded, and shortly afterwards, he lumbered off.

It was a little later that Berenger appeared. He stood anxiously for a few moments, and then cleared his throat. 'Maid?'

Her thoughts had been far away. Now she looked up with the alarm of a hart hearing a hunter. 'Yes?'

'I have not spoken to you since . . .' he wanted to say, 'since we came to the Welsh camp', but couldn't. He felt the need to prove that Geoff was entirely wrong about her, but looking down into her anxious eyes, he found himself wondering how anyone could think evil of her. She looked so innocent.

'You need fear nothing from me,' he said.

'I know. You came to save me.'

'Ed cried out and alerted us. I was worried about you. Did they say why they had taken you?'

'At first I thought it was because they wanted to offend you. But then I heard the man they called Erbin tell another to "find the boy and kill him", but they could not find him as I had hidden him under Archibald's cart, so they took me instead.'

Berenger considered that. The Donkey had been struck down. 'If the Welsh had wanted to kill him, he was easy prey. Who knocked him down?'

She looked at him very straight. 'I did. I knew they would kill him.' There was a fresh tear glistening in the corner of her eye.

'You knocked him down to protect him. That was kind of you,' Berenger said more gently, but he was still unsure whether he could trust her. Her coolness, her distance, all spoke of her strangeness. He wasn't used to women like this.

He jerked his head in the direction of the Welsh. 'Did you hear what Erbin said to me? He said you were a witch.'

'What of you, vintener? What do you think?' she said, her voice lowered.

She looked so young, but so full of knowledge and despair, that any idea of her being a witch was simply preposterous. Yet if she were a witch, surely she would be able to appear in any guise she wished – including that of a young woman. Every year Berenger watched the Passion plays, and he knew that some witches had the skill of dissimulation. Perhaps *that* was her magic: an ability to change her appearance at will, to confuse and frustrate men?

'I don't know what to think,' he said truthfully. 'But I do know you'd be safer away from us. If Erbin and his men want you, they will know where to find you if you stay with us.'

'You are telling me to leave the army?' she asked, and for the first time he saw a hint of vulnerability. There was a tiny flaring of her nostrils, a tremor at her eyelid, that betrayed her inner fears.

'No. But we must see if there's a place in the army where you'll be safer,' he said.

'I feel safe here,' she said.

'With the Serpentine?' Berenger said, glancing down at Archibald who was snoring, his back against a cart's wheel. 'Sweet Jesus, even Erbin would be safer than him!'

9 August

The English struck camp in the pre-dawn light of the Wednesday, and Berenger and his men were told to scout the lands to south and east.

There was a sense of urgency in the camp as he took up his bow and set off. Men were scurrying about, gathering their belongings and packing. Berenger saw Erbin at the copse as he threw his pack into the back of the cart. Béatrice was there already, stroking the long nose of their old nag and murmuring softly, so that the brute nuzzled at her throat. She met Berenger's gaze with a calm nod, but when she saw Erbin, her eyes hardened.

They were off before full dawn. The land about the Seine was dark and misty, but as they started their journey, the sun broke through and filled all the river's plain with a pale golden glow, as if the ground itself was lighted by an inner fire.

Berenger and the men made good progress. They hurried forward, for once without complaints. Grandarse had made it plain that the first man to grumble aloud would be flogged, and there was something in his manner that convinced the men to pay heed.

It was perhaps six leagues to Pont-de-l'Arche, and Berenger and the others covered much of the distance at a trot, closely followed by the main bulk of the army.

The land here was flat, and Berenger, sweating in the heat and parched as the dust rose on all sides, kept a wary eye over the river. Sir John de Sully's words came back to him, and the thought that they might be prevented from crossing was always present in his mind.

The town came into view, and his heart quailed. A strong fortress had sprung up on this side of the river to protect the bridge that brought so much trade and wealth to the citizens. It had a good wall, and towers rose to a great height. It would not be easy to storm this quickly, but storm it they must, if they were to take the bridge.

Sir John de Sully met Berenger as they approached.

'A strong fortress, Master,' the knight called.

'Aye, Sir John.' Berenger squinted at the walls against the bright sunshine. 'It'd take a good week to conquer, even if the French King had not massed an army nearby.'

'And they can use the bridge to reinforce the place,' Sir John noted. 'Yes. This will not be easy.'

Berenger was surprised to see that for once the knight appeared concerned. 'We shall cross, though, even if not here.'

'When, though – and where?'

Ed the Donkey trailed behind the men. He was happier walking alongside the cart with Béatrice, and even when the men began to halt, staring at their latest target, the walled town of Pont-de-L'Arche, he continued to trudge along beside her. In his mind, he was back at home in England, sitting in a tavern with a mug of ale in his hand, singing and hiccoughing along with the tunes as men sang of the sea and of fishing. Those had been happy days, despite the loneliness of being an orphan.

It was with surprise that he heard the sudden blaring of the horns, the call to arms. The archers stopped to string their bows, and gathered at the side of the cart to grab spare strings, bracers, tabs and arrows, and he hastened to assist them, startled out of his lethargy.

A shout from the men-at-arms, and soldiers rushed back to the wagons, collecting ladders of all sizes. There was little chatter and no laughter now. No one was happy at the thought of trying to clamber up a ladder thrown against a high wall while defenders aimed missiles from above, or poured burning oil upon them all. Men's faces were drawn and their hands twitched, Ed noticed. Little nervous tuggings at belts or buckles, a hand sometimes rising to a cheek or an eye, sometimes pulling at a bottom lip or an earlobe as if to aid concentration.

There came the dull pounding of drums, and as trumpets blew, the first men began to run for the walls.

Archers were already positioned in their order of a staggered harrow, with wedges of men rather than straight lines, in order that each man in the fore should have the maximum field of fire. On command they could direct their aim from left to right without impeding each other's shooting. Already now the archers were bending their bows, drawing and loosing a deadly storm upon the walls. As they drew and released, the arrows rose thick in the sky.

It was beautiful – and horrifying, Ed thought.

'Daft beggars!'

He turned to see Archibald sitting on the bench of his wagon a few feet away, his thumbs tucked into his apron, thoughtfully studying the walls.

'Sorry, Master?'

'We can't capture that place. It's too massive for us to scale the walls quickly, and if we don't, there's no possibility of taking it before the French army arrives.' Archibald set his head to one side. 'If only I had time, maybe a barrel or two to spare, and a few engineers to dig beneath that wall there, I could set it and tamp it, and make such a blast as would be spoken of for a hundred years!' He grinned happily at the thought.

Ed shivered. He remembered the snaking, hissing line of burning powder. 'You think you could?'

'Given the powder, I could raze the whole town to the ground,' Archibald said, and then winked. 'But I would need a lot of powder, you understand!'

Ed nodded without comprehending. 'I hate it,' he said.

'What, my powder?'

'I saw it kill my father,' Ed said quietly.

Before Archibald could reply, they both heard the bellowing from Grandarse to 'Get your skinny little backside moving, you son of a Winchester strumpet!' and Ed sprang to the cart and the sheaves of arrows.

The men were sending prodigious numbers of arrows at the town. Ed hurried, planting arrows before Clip and scarcely keeping up with his rate of fire, while other men were glad just to have a sheaf dropped into the wicker baskets standing before them.

Ed hastened back and forth, but even as he did so, he saw that there was movement on the north bank of the river. 'Look!' he told the vintener.

Berenger followed his pointing finger, and gave a groan at the sight of the French army. 'They're already here.'

CHAPTER THIRTY

The attack failed. Strong walls, with adequate men to defend them, meant they needed siege engines and much more time. Attacking without these things was pointless.

'It was never going to happen,' Archibald said.

Berenger looked up. The vintaine had slogged its way along a rough road that made all the carts creak and crash. They had stopped now at a small wood, and the army's transports were being formed into a defensive ring in case of attack. Archibald's wagon was lumbering backwards, shoved by any helpers they could find, making more noise than all the others put together. Even as he spoke, it gave a dreadful thundering report as it fell into a rut.

Archibald froze for a moment, concerned, then relaxed. 'Yes, Vintener, it's a heavy beast, this wagon,' he grinned. 'It has my toys in it.'

Berenger could sense the men around him shrinking back. No one liked the 'toys' a man like Archibald played with.

'You are a gynour, aren't you?' Geoff asked.

'And expert with Serpentine, aye.'

Berenger felt his skin crawl. He had never come to terms with cannons. An arrow that whistled through the air to cleanly puncture a man was one thing: a tube that vomited flame and stone and tore men limb from limb was something else altogether.

'Well, I reckon we could have taken the place,' he declared. 'It only required a little luck, just as we had at Caen.'

'Not with the men they had inside Pont-de-l'Arche. No, it'll soon grow a great deal more troublesome to take a fair-sized town or city. They will all be stocked with food now, expecting a siege, and they'll have brought in all the men from miles around to form their militia.'

'So we should all go home, you mean?' Berenger gave a twisted grin. 'Tell that to the King – if you dare.'

'Perhaps I should,' Archibald said with a chuckle. Then his eyes became shrewd little flints of blue. 'Your boy Ed – he seems a bit lost.'

'What of it?'

Archibald's confidence seemed to fade. He looked down at his hands for a moment. 'Let me take him. I will protect him. I could do with a boy to help.'

'Sorry, my friend, but we need him. He gathers up our supplies and brings them in battle.'

'It will be a while before my toys are needed in battle. But a lad who can cook, see to the oxen and horses, a boy who can help me load and unload, that would be useful. In battle you can have him back.'

'Why do you want him so badly?'

'Because, as I said, he looks lost.' Archibald added quietly, 'He reminds me of how I was once, Master Archer.'

'Aye, and me,' Berenger said, equally quietly.

The wagons and carts were formed into a rough circle now, and the horses were herded into the middle to rest the night. Berenger looked up at the gynour and suggested, 'Come back to our fire and we'll speak further.'

'Do you think he wants to learn about guns?' Archibald asked.

Berenger grinned. 'He wants to learn how to kill the French.'

Archibald nodded. 'He dislikes my powder. He said he saw his father killed by it. Perhaps that is both why he hates the French and powder too.'

'Perhaps.'

Archibald turned shrewd eyes on Berenger again. 'Meanwhile, you are keen to be freed from the young woman. What have you got against her, exactly?'

Berenger shrugged. 'The girl is trouble. She's making the men fractious. The boy is a soothing influence on her and she on him. It seems better to me to let them both go together than to try to keep just one.'

'I have no need for a whore.'

'All the better,' Berenger muttered, thinking of the Welshman in the darkened room.

Archibald considered for a moment before nodding. He spat on his hand. 'A contract, then, Vintener.'

Berenger gazed up at him, and spat on his own hand. They shook on the arrangement.

'Although how I'm to tell the boy . . .' Berenger wondered.

It was easier than he had feared.

'Come here, boy,' Archibald said later that evening, and Ed obediently went to him.

Berenger gestured to the gynour. 'This man has offered to look after you on the journey, Donkey. What do you think?'

'You don't want me in the vintaine any more?'

'It's not that. He has a need of an extra man, and he says he will defend you from the Welsh.'

'One man will protect me better than the vintaine?'

Berenger nodded. 'We are sent to scout, we are sent on patrol, we are sent to take our part as sentries. At all those times you are left to your own devices without protection. With a man like this one here, I think you will be safer. You will be with him all the time.'

'I don't want to.'

'It's the powder, isn't it, boy?' Archibald asked quietly.

Ed looked away, but finally mumbled, 'Yes.'

Archibald was gentle. 'You said your father was killed by the powder. What happened?'

'He was fishing. French pirates came and attacked us. They sailed straight into our harbour at Portsmouth, up the river, and they had cannons that blasted boats apart. I saw my father. The gonne hit him . . .'

Archibald glanced at Berenger. 'So that explains why you would see all Frenchmen killed.'

'And why you wanted to kill them yourself,' Berenger said. 'Well, boy, this way you'll be safer, so that perhaps in years to come you will yourself have become a brave warrior.'

'How will I be safer with powder all about me?'

Archibald gave a beatific smile and gulped a mouthful of wine. 'You'll be fine. And remember, my son, when a Welshman is confronted by a man who holds in his head the word of the Lord, that Welsh sinner is confused and baffled.'

'I don't understand.'

'Once, my child, there was a servant of God. He worked hard, but found that his opinion of his comrades was sinking. Those, he discovered, who should have spent their lives praying for the souls of their flocks, were more keen on seeking ever better viands and wines. And his faith in their ministry was put to the test. However, he found a friend in a man who understood the dark arts of forming powders, and he learned the same skills. After a while, he bethought himself to leave his abbey and make his way in the world. If your Welsh friends try to assail us, they will be thwarted and shamed by our stalwart defence.'

'You used to be a monk?'

'Did I say so?' Archibald enquired.

'I'm not sure,' Berenger said. 'Did you?'

'The Good Lord will make all clear, I dare say,' Archibald said.

'I want the truth, Gynour.'

'Don't we all, my friend? But reflect, how many of us are here from a desire to help the King, and how many come here because of troubles they wish to escape?'

With a grin, he stood. 'Come, boy. And bring the French slut with you. It seems I won a pair for the price of one!'

11 August

They were all exhausted.

The army which had set out so full of hope was dog tired. Marching eleven miles a day was no hardship, but every day they were forced to try to attack a town.

After their failure at Pont-de-l'Arche, they had marched on to the rich town of Louviers and set it alight. The town was already empty when they arrived, and it was obvious that other towns would also be evacuated. After that, they went to Vernon and destroyed the fortress, although the town itself repelled their attacks; then it was Mantes, and now Meulan – but at each town the guards were ready and prepared to fight. Here, the bridge had been thrown down at the southern side, but the English could not reach it because of a strong bastion full of men who kept up a withering hail of crossbow bolts when the English attempted to assault their walls. They suffered several casualties, and a sudden, unexpected sortie caught several unawares and saw more men killed. In the end the English withdrew, furious and bitter to be denied the crossing once more.

'It is the French plan, to keep us to this side and prevent our crossing the Seine,' Sir John said to Berenger when he stopped to talk to them after their failed assault. 'Their King seeks to tie us to this shore, and keep his major towns and cities free from us.'

'What will we do?'

'Carry on. If we continue upstream, we shall eventually find a place to cross,' Sir John said comfortingly, but there was a line of anxiety on his brow that had not been there before.

Next day, Berenger woke with a sense of grim certainty. They would never manage to break free from this land, he felt. It was as though there was a curse on the army.

The thought was instantly squashed, but he could not help but cast a look once more at the group with the gynour. Béatrice was sitting with Ed, laughing in her quiet way at something Archibald had said, his beard wagging as he chuckled, while Ed sat by and smiled. Most of the Donkey's tension had faded from him, and now he was a great deal calmer. In a battle, he moved with speed to rearm the men in the vintaine, and Berenger had to confess that Grandarse was right. The boy had turned into a useful member of their team.

'What today, then, Frip?' Clip called from the line.

'Wait and you'll find out,' Berenger said.

It was a part of the reason for their tiredness: not only were they all marching eleven miles each day, but with the whole army spread over a broad front, men were forced to walk further and further in order to raze the widest area. Even now, in the early morning, the stench of smoke was in their faces.

'Well, I hope we're not going to be told to run off south and burn more peasants out of their homes. A man gets bored with that.'

'And there's bugger-all profit in it,' Jack added.

Berenger stared at the land ahead. While he tried to control his feelings in front of the men, he couldn't lie to himself. For some time now he had decided that this march was less a principled advance to a great battle than a raid against the innocent inhabitants of the country. It was the kind of assault, in fact, that could be performed by an outlaw. God Himself must look down in despair to see such devastation for so little reason.

'What about turning back? We've collected plenty of plunder. Even the King must be happy with what he won from Caen,' Clip said. 'We can't stay here forever.'

Sir John and his esquire appeared as he spoke, and Berenger snarled, 'Shut up, and listen!' as the knight paused in front of them.

'Master Fripper, we are to march again today,' Sir John said, and he looked over the vintaine. 'I would be glad to have you and your men at my side.'

Grandarse drew himself up to his full height. 'If it pleases you, Sir John, I'm sure that I can afford to lose one vintaine from my complement,' he said. 'But when it comes to a fight, I'll need 'em back. What do you plan? A scout?'

'No. We have a new battle formation today,' Sir John said. 'We march together, and your men will not be far from you, but if there is a need of defence up at the river's edge, I would have some men with me.'

'Oh, at the river?' Grandarse said, and Berenger could have chuckled at his crestfallen expression. He had thought Berenger and his men were to run further away to scout the land again. As it was, if they were to remain near the river, they would be hanging back from most of the army.

'Yes. Look!'

The archers peered over their shoulders at a strange sight.

Red banners had been raised by King Edward's heralds and esquires. The flags must be waved gently to show them clearly, for the wind was non-existent, but they were in full view of the French who stood at the northern bank of the river.

Berenger felt a spark of warmth deep in his belly. 'So, we march, sir?'

'As soon as the order comes. And then we wait and hope, eh?'

'Yes, sir.'

At the wagon, Ed and Béatrice had no idea what the banners signified.

'What do they mean? Are we to surrender?' Ed asked anxiously.

'Surrender?' Archibald laughed heartily. 'No, boy! They mean we're ready and waiting. They say we expect to fight: here, *today*! If the French don't come to find us, we'll call them cowards, and not worth the country they claim as their own!'

CHAPTER THIRTY-ONE

Sir John stood in the broad space before the King's great pavilion along with all the nobles and barons of the army. He had been called to a Council of War.

The King marched from the entrance to his pavilion with his armour gleaming, his son Edward of Woodstock behind him. A dais had been erected from some boards placed over barrels, and the two stood on this.

For a man who had been thwarted in his every attempt to cross the river and come to blows with the French, the King showed little sign of frustration. Instead, he looked about his men with a smile. Some he acknowledged with a tilt of his head and a wink, and when he caught sight of Sir John, his smile broadened.

'Sir John, are you still with us? A man of your age should be enjoying a life of comfort with your grandchildren at your feet, not coming out on escapades such as this!'

'I would be happy, my Lord, to rest my weary bones, were my King content. But since he chooses to seek justice, I must burnish my armour and sharpen my swords. My wife will speak with you later, I doubt me not, about the importance of allowing your knights to rest!'

'When you are ready, old friend, let me know and I shall personally purchase you your corrody!'

Sir John grinned. He would not be ready to take a pension for many years.

'My Lords, Barons, good knights, we find ourselves at an impasse. We are here, south of the Seine, while our good cousin, the King of France, tarries at the other side. He remains quaking in his tent!

'We have given him every opportunity to meet us on the field of battle. We are ready today, should he desire it! But he has more pressing engagements. Perhaps he must haggle over some more Genoese galleys to replace the ships we burned at Sluys, or he wishes to buy some more crossbowmen to supplement his meagre army?

'For his army *is* meagre. It looks vast, a prodigious number of men and beasts. You can see them, if you wish! They are all there on the other side of the river. Yet it must be composed of men too feeble to fight us! We have raised the red banners of war to offer him battle. Look! They are all about us even now!

'More, we have marched only two leagues today, and for good reason. We are now in-between two bridges, those of Mantes and Poissy, of course. The good King prefers us not to cross to his side, and bars the bridges to us. Those he cannot, he tears down in his frenzy of destruction. He prefers to ravage his land to save it from us! With the red banners aloft, we have given him time to cross the river after us. Yet he has chosen not to do so.'

The King paused and looked about the faces before him once more. Then his head lowered on his shoulders and his eyes narrowed.

'He blocks us, he believes, by taking down his bridges and denying us the crossing. I say, God is with us, and with His help, we shall cross this river.'

His face cleared. 'There are still feats of arms to cheer us. Only a few days ago, Sir Robert Ferrers crossed the river in a rowing-boat and so vigorously did he assault the castle at La Roche Guyon that he persuaded the castellan there that the whole of the English army was upon him. The castle was surrendered to him! If that is what a small force of Englishmen in a rowing-boat can achieve, think what prodigious feats of arms we can achieve as an army!'

That raised a belly-laugh. The fact was, every man there was confident in his training and experience.

'The King of France has received bad news,' the King continued in a low growl. 'He has learned that another English army threatens his arse, advancing from Flanders. That is another reason why he is nervous to meet us here, because he doesn't know what is happening behind him. And while he leaves us to our own devices, I intend to increase the shame heaped upon his head. We shall leave such a swathe of devastation behind us that even the coward who rules this land realises he can no longer with honour evade battle. The territory we are entering is the King's favourite. He will learn that it is better to confront an enemy than leave him to rampage. And then, if he still persists in avoiding us, we shall assault Paris itself!'

He raised his arms and now he roared: 'We fight to prove who is the lawful King of this land! With you, my friends and comrades, I can prove to the world that my cause is just!'

While the assembled men cheered, drawing swords and waving them with jubilation, Sir John cocked an eye at the Earl of Warwick. The Earl glanced back at him with a dry smile on his face.

'Well?' Sir John asked as they fell into step walking from the meeting.

The Earl said, 'He has waited too many years to fight this war.'

'And now he can feel the prize within his grasp.'

'He has felt it before,' the Earl said, 'but the French refused to fight.'

'I was there. I recall it clearly.'

'His policy this time is to try to meet the army coming down from Flanders.'

'So we *must* cross the river.'

'Yes. And the French most certainly do not want that, so they keep us on the southern side and demolish all the bridges ahead of us.'

'A holding action. But how long will he wish to keep us at bay?'

The Earl shrugged, his face growing serious. 'Until he can call up all his fighting men. He has warriors besieging Aiguillon under Duke John of Normandy. If they were brought back to Paris, even the French King must think himself strong enough to attack us.'

'You think that's what he will do?'

'If I were the French King, I would hold the river with small forces and bring the rest of my army over to this side, and block our route to Paris. Meanwhile, his army under Duke John would hasten towards us and increase his forces.'

'So the French will wait for us?'

'Yes,' the Earl said. Then he grinned. 'You think he would launch an attack on us? He's never tried to fight an offensive war. That is the English way, but the French always defend, or hit quickly and run away, like their attacks at Plymouth, Southampton and Portsmouth in recent years. No, he will draw his troops up on a strong battlefield and wait for us. Depend upon it.'

'I shall,' Sir John said. 'And hope that we find a bridge open so that we may retake the initiative as soon as possible.'

12 August

Marching and burning. Days of pointless destruction, of savage encounters with Frenchmen bravely trying to hold back an army that was insatiable in its hunger. Like a glutton, it trampled over the land and engulfed all, leaving behind a burning waste where nothing moved but cinders and ashes sluggishly stirred by the wind.

And then, one day at noon, on a hillside, Berenger found Clip standing, leaning on his unstrung bow and staring ahead. 'What is it?'

'Frip! There it is! We're bloody here! It's bloody Paris!'

Berenger forgot his sore feet and blisters as he stared through the misty air. There, beyond the bends in the river, he could see towers and walls, the glitter of glass and gilded statues. It stood like a city of the imagination, as though floating in the air, insubstantial as a wisp of smoke, and yet as Berenger stared, he could feel its awesome power and strength. Paris was the centre of chivalry for Christendom, the centre of beauty and authority, a pearl sitting in the lush countryside, the whitened mass of the Louvre standing over the western edge of the walls, a vast abbey before them, the towers of Notre-Dame rising to the skies behind.

'Grandarse? Look here,' he called.

There were suburbs on the English side, protected by a high wall, but the true wealth lay north, defended by the French army. It was safe while the English could not cross the Seine, but the Parisians were not to know that. This was a catastrophe. They had no experience of an English host appearing to threaten their city and their existence. Within those walls the populace would be terrified.

The rest of their vintaine, and Roger's, came and gathered with them, all staring in astonishment at the city.

Grandarse scratched his cods. 'That's it? Bugger, but we could take that in an afternoon, us. Ye'll have to walk a bit faster to get to it before night though. Must be twenty mile if it's a league.'

'Come, we can get to it tomorrow. There's no hurry,' Clip said.

Jack was still staring hungrily. 'They say that there's gold in the streets there. When we're inside, any man among us could take enough to live like a lord for the rest of his life. Think of that.'

Wat was standing with a wistful expression on his face. 'I'll make my wife proud of me again with the money I'll bring back to her.'

'Is that right?' Clip said sarcastically. 'Look over there, at the north of the river. Isn't that an army? So before you count your profits, man, just bear in mind that you'll probably die in the attack. Aye, ye'll all be slaughtered.'

'To take a place like that, even if you die trying, that would be good enough,' Jon Furrier said wistfully. 'What a victory that would be, eh?'

'What about you, Ed?' Clip said. 'Can you see the advantage of our war now?'

'I – I don't know. My family's dead. All the gold in the world won't replace them.'

Geoff shook his head. 'No – and this time I won't have you risking your life in the streets, remember, Donkey.'

'Very true!' Archibald called from his wagon. 'I need you fit and healthy to carry my loads, boy.'

'I know,' Ed said, and was silent.

Berenger noticed that the boy was staring at Béatrice.

She herself was gazing at the city – with a look of such hatred that it made the vintener's spine tingle.

When they settled for the night, Geoff sat beside Berenger with a large skin of wine, which he passed to him. 'You look like you could do with a drink,' he said.

Berenger allowed a good mouthful to pour into his mouth. 'Good wine,' he acknowledged.

'Only the best for the abbot, eh?' Geoff said, smacking his lips. 'Good enough for me, anyway.'

'Yeah.'

They were silent for a moment, and then Berenger sighed and grunted, 'Come on, then. What's on your mind?'

'I'm worried,' Geoff confessed. 'We need to cross that damned river, but ever since we reached it, things have gone from bad to worse. I don't like it.'

Berenger gave a snort of derision. 'Bad to worse? Our vintaine's still strong. We only lost Will and James, and the way things are, we'll come to the gates of Paris with all our men, God willing.'

'You think so? That city's like London, Frip. You think you could storm London with an army like this? If Londoners wanted you, you could enter, but if they barred all the gates, what then? We can't sit outside for a long siege, can we? We don't have miners to bring the towers down, nor the siege train to batter the walls. The French army is larger already, and grows daily. Philippe intends to crush us.'

'What of it? We intend to crush him too. One side will win: our fate is in the hands of God.'

'So long as we don't carry the seed of our failure in amongst us.'

'What does that mean?' Berenger demanded.

'The woman,' he said flatly. 'I heard Erbin just as you did. He said that she was a witch, and the more I watch her, the more I think he's right. I wish we'd left her with the Welsh.'

'You're talking shite. That's villeiny-saying, that is. Drink some more.'

'Did you see her expression when she saw Paris? If she was staring at the murderer of her own child, she could not look more filled with loathing.'

'So what? Maybe she caught sight of your face!'

'You know the Welsh. They are said to have more feeling for evil than we English.'

'They're said to be superstitious gits, more like.'

'You can scoff, but you get Matt and Eliot on a dark night and tell them there's a vampire nearby and see how they cower!'

Berenger didn't laugh. In his heart he knew that there were such things as witches and evil spirits. No man could doubt that, not when the priests were so full of stories of the harm such unnatural creatures could do. He found it difficult to believe that Béatrice was a witch, but the look on her face when she saw Paris in the distance, the lack of sympathy for those who were her countrymen, while the English slaughtered so many, that was legitimate cause for reflection.

'All those bridges, and we cannot win a single one,' he muttered. 'There must be one soon.'

'What if there isn't? Maybe it's all because of her.'

'You think she has cursed us? Why?'

'How should I know?'

'Geoff, she's happy with us. You saved her from the Welsh at the camp, and we saved her in the city. Look at her: she hardly looks like a woman who is driven by hatred of *us*, does she?

She's driven by hatred of the French. In any case, it's resolved now. Archibald is looking after her.'

'Perhaps that's it. God is disgusted by her because she has nothing to do with her own people,' Geoff said. 'She's brought us nothing but bad luck. Before her, we went through French towns like a dagger through water. Since she came, we've failed in all we've attempted.'

'So far as I'm concerned,' Berenger said with finality, 'she's been a breath of fresh air. I like her.'

'I know,' Geoff said, his quiet response more worrying than his earlier bluster. 'Many do, Frip. That's how witches snare their victims.'

CHAPTER THIRTY-TWO

13 August

Berenger slept badly that night. It seemed as though every time he snoozed, he saw Béatrice. Once he dreamed she was standing at his head with a dagger in her hands, ready to plunge it into his throat, and he rolled over and woke up in a panic. A guard cast a suspicious look at him from the far side of the camp.

They rose before dawn as usual, and Berenger found himself peering about in a search for her. Geoff's words had unsettled him. In the end he spotted her at the far side of Archibald's wagon. At least she was some distance away, he thought, recalling the dream with a shudder.

Today their orders were to march straight on. The town of Poissy lay some three miles distant; there had been a bridge there, although whether it still existed was a question that few dared ask.

An air of grim resolution hung over them. Those who had set out filled with the thrill of battle and glory had gradually been ground down by their long march. All knew that the King had intended crossing the Seine many miles before this, and the continued slog south and east had eroded the optimism of even the youngest. There were irritable words between men who only a few days before had been firm friends. The journey was bringing all low.

The only beam of hope was the possibility of the capture of Paris, Berenger reckoned. The men were speaking openly about the wealth inside the city; having enriched themselves at St-Lô and Caen, they spoke of the fabled treasures of Paris with a greed that rivalled that of any Pope.

Berenger did not share their excitement. He had an old soldier's respect for his enemy. No matter how good the land, how skilled the troops with their weapons, it was still the case that a momentary failing on the part of the war-leaders could throw all into disarray and disaster. Today, as he looked over to the opposite bank, he was aware only of the strength of the French position. A small force was all that would be needed to defend the far banks against English troops trying to wade across, even if a ford were to be found. A few hundred men could hold off the English for a long, long time.

He shook himself. A pox on that! This army would cross somehow, and they would fight their way back home. And if the French army tried to cut them to pieces, so be it.

As the order to move came, he shrugged his pack over his back and joined the rest of the men. All the while his eyes were not on the road, but on the small force of men-at-arms on the opposite shore. Their mail gleamed merrily in the sunshine and their tunics were bright, clean and colourful, as they ambled gently along the northern bank of the river, matching the pace of the English. Soon, they stopped and began to break their fast, and Berenger watched them jealously. He could do with some decent food inside him, too.

They entered a small wood, and Berenger heard a large animal blundering through the undergrowth some yards away. There was a narrow trail cut through, and he watched it warily. Long ago, he had seen an esquire stab a boar with his spear, but the damned brute ran on and on, driving the spear through his body and then continuing up the shaft until he reached the esquire and gored him horribly. The man had killed his boar, but he died in the attempt.

Berenger carried on through the forest, until they at last reached the further edge, and stood looking down on the town of Poissy.

It was a town of ghosts.

Poissy was deserted.

Berenger waved a hand at Geoff, who nodded and ran ahead with Clip and Eliot. They stopped at a low wall, peering over into what appeared to be the main street, arrows nocked and ready. Berenger followed them, with Luke and Gil behind him. Grandarse and Matt and Oliver were over on the left, while the rest spread out in a line behind them.

There was a clatter, and instantly sixteen bows bent, the arrows pointing at Ed, who paled and shook his head, bleating as he grabbed the sheaves of arrows he had dropped when he tripped.

Berenger grunted his relief, and gazed ahead. A broad street led towards the river, and he and the others clambered over the wall and made their way along it, edgily staring along their arrows at empty windows and doorways.

He had never known such utter desolation. There was nothing: not the sound of a baby crying, not the creak of a wagon's wheel, not the chatter of women washing – nothing but an occasional exclamation as a crow or rook rose, complaining at their interruption of the peace. Clip, startled stupid by a sudden explosion of sound at his feet, let fly and spitted a pigeon. It fell, the arrow clattering loudly on the stony roadway.

'You stupid bugger,' Grandarse called out. 'Next time, fall on your own fucking arrow and save us the bloody trouble!'

Clip pulled a face and tugged his arrow free. It was gory, and he wiped it on his sleeve before pensively picking up the bird and stuffing it inside his shirt.

They gradually made their way through the town until, at last, they approached the river.

Berenger saw the piles where the bridge had once stood and felt his heart sink. A man from Roger's vintaine cried, 'Another failure, by Christ's pain! Look at it!'

It was the first time Berenger had seen Geoff lost for words, but now he wiped a hand over his brow and sighed deeply. 'Perhaps there's another bridge near, Frip?'

Berenger pointed at the far bank. A group of French soldiery stood there, jeering; two dropped their hosen and braies to display their arses. 'You think they'd bother to wait if they thought we could force our way over somewhere else?'

Clip, offended by their antics, loosed an experimental arrow, and struck a man in the groin. He fell, shrieking like a stuck pig, and Clip received several buffets of congratulation about the head in return. Grinning, he muttered modestly that it was nothing.

Meanwhile, Jack had been studying the shattered bridge. Many of the timbers from the bridge still bobbed in the water, caught against the piles. 'Frip, look!' he cried. 'The piles are pretty intact. We could have planks set on them, then a light man could run across on those timbers.'

Berenger looked. 'Do you know what? He's right. Clip, you're the lightest – do you want to try it?'

'Swyve your mother and your sister, Frip. You show me how, and I'll be pleased to, but if you think you'll get me to test that with my own life, you can call on the Devil first!'

Berenger grinned. 'Ed, go and find Archibald and bring him here – quickly.'

'What is it, Fripper?' Grandarse demanded.

'The piles are all there, all of them. We could rebuild the bridge – if the King had a mind,' Berenger said. And for the first time in days he felt the return of excitement.

The vintaine camped there at Poissy while other vintaines and centaines were sprawled as far as St-Germain, only three leagues from Paris. Berenger stood with Archibald at the water's edge.

'What do you think?'

'My expertise lies more in the destruction of bridges,' Archibald said, but he frowned thoughtfully at the timbers. 'The piles are all solid enough, aren't they?'

'They look it,' Berenger agreed.

'What do you want me to do?' Archibald asked.

'You must know the best carpenters and joiners. Who should we ask to look at this? The King's own man?'

'He's a good fellow,' Archibald smiled, 'but he's more used to being given the best timbers and a perfect site to construct his efforts. This needs a good bodger.'

'A what?'

'Someone who'll take what he's given and make some-thing worthwhile. I know just the man. Miserable devil, but he's talented. He makes the *talaria*, the trestles the gonnes rest on.'

It took only a short time to track down the man, a squat, ugly Cornishman with a perpetual scowl, who glared at the piles as though they had personally offended him.

'There's sod-all to work on here,' he said with exasperation. 'What idiot thought up this idea, eh? Was it you, Archibald? How are we expected to fix this? Look at it! It's just a mess of bits and pieces of trash. It'll be like building a bridge from bloody hedge-trimmings and twigs! A complete waste of time.'

'So you can't do it,' Archibald said, his voice carrying just a hint of contempt.

'Did I say that? Did I bloody say that? Did I? *Did I?*' the engineer demanded truculently. 'You hear me say that, did you? *No!* So shut your gob and let me think!'

He stood, hands on his hips for a long time, staring at the river. At last, he pursed his lips firmly and turned away from the water.

'Right! Pinch and Hon, go and chop down the biggest bleeding tree you can find. You lot, come here. I need all the joiners I can lay my hands on. We can work on the planks that are already there for now, and then peg a tree to firm it up, before we can lay the new bed in place. Got me?'

Berenger and Archibald sat down to watch. Clip had recently come across a hastily abandoned house that still had loaves left in the bread oven, and he had liberated them for the vintaine. Jack in turn had located a cellar full of wine, and the vintaine was in cheery mood as they gathered to observe the engineers' labours. Several times the carpenters cast sour looks at them as they laughed whenever a man failed to fix his plank to the bridge securely. When one man fell into the water, their delight was so uproarious that Matt began to choke on a crust of bread and had to be pounded on the back. Luckily the joiner in question was soon hauled from the water.

A shout went up as the tree appeared, and the Cornishman ran off to supervise its working. A pit had been found in a joiner's yard, and the tree was manhandled to it, while a team of workmen set to sawing the trunk into planks. It took them from noon until Vespers, but by then Berenger was surprised to see cut and shaped planks being carried to the river. There were enough to span the remaining distance from the bridge to the far bank.

'Come on, then, you idle gits. Think you can sit about all sodding day while we do all the hard work?' the engineer demanded.

'We don't have orders to cross,' Clip said.

'Ballocks to that, you little drop of piss! You think the King will be happy to learn that we builded him a bridge and some lazy bunch of shits couldn't be bothered to get off their flabby arses to defend the bridgehead? Now fuck off over there – *and keep your eyes open!*'

Berenger could see the logic of his words, but he grumbled as much as the others as he made his way reluctantly to the bridge.

'Be careful, Master Fripper!' Archibald called.

Berenger nodded. 'Aye. Bows ready, lads,' he said, stringing his own. He grabbed an arrow and nocked it, taking a deep breath.

The first part was firm enough, where the original bridge had survived, and each plank was firmly set in place. After this, for about fifty feet or so, the engineers had constructed a pair of rails, one riding each set of piles. Berenger carefully ascended the leftmost runner, and gently tested the set of the timber. It was firmly fixed.

Jack came after him, and as Berenger reached the middle of the first span between piles, stepping with the caution of a man

MICHAEL JECKS

desperate to keep his balance, Jack jumped up and down, making Berenger turn and glare. 'You do that again and I'll personally cut out your liver!' he snarled as the tremors moved in waves through the soles of his feet. Jack merely grinned.

Far below he could see the murky waters of the Seine. The more he looked at it, the further away the water seemed, until he could almost persuade himself that the bridge was rising, and that to fall would be to die, instantly.

He turned his eyes from the view beneath and stared ahead, walking faster. There was a rushing in his ears, and he wasn't sure whether it was the sound of the river below or the blood in his veins. Certainly he felt lightheaded and slightly dizzy as he hurried over the last few feet. With his feet on solid ground once more, he took a long, shivering breath, and wiped a hand over a forehead that had grown unaccountably clammy.

Jack joined him, laughing. 'That was fun! I want to go again!'

'Shut up!' Berenger snapped. The vintaine was soon with them, and more men were arriving by the minute. On the bridge, men hammered pegs into planks, fitting a stronger path. Grandarse shouted and pointed, and Berenger nodded. The land rose from here. They must keep a lookout.

'Geoff, Jack – go and take a look from up there,' he said.

He watched the two hurry up the sandy bank and turned his attention to the rest of the men. 'All of you must go and . . .' he began, but he got no further, because then he heard Geoff blowing the alarm on his horn '. . . *support Geoff*,' he bellowed, and ran at the bank himself, roaring over his shoulder: 'Donkey, bring arrows!'

CHAPTER THIRTY-THREE

At the top of the bank, Geoff was already drawing, aiming and loosing his arrows.

'Sweet Mother Mary,' Berenger said with shock. There, on the plain before them, was a party of Frenchmen.

'There's at least a thousand men on horse, and double that on foot, Vintener. What shall we do?' Geoff panted. He drew again, aimed, loosed, and the arrow plunged into one of the leading horsemen.

'By the Son of God, I don't know,' Berenger spat. He had nocked his own first arrow, and it flew straight and true into the breast of a horse. The beast collapsed, ploughing into the soil, throwing the man-at-arms from its back and forcing horses behind to swerve. Two crashed together, and another knight was knocked out of his saddle.

'Donkey, where are you?' Berenger roared, and loosed again. When he dared cast a glance behind him, he saw no sign of Ed, but there was better news.

Sir John and the Earl of Northampton were already crossing

the bridge with two dozen knights. They were soon over the river, and Berenger could feel the solid drumbeat of their hooves as they took the bank at a canter, paused at the top, and then, with spears ready, plunged on towards the French.

Sir John blew out his cheeks at the sight of the French. A thousand men on horseback – a force capable of smashing the tiny English defence and trampling the archers into the ground. Already there were cries of defiance to rally the French, and the dust was rising from their hooves as they began to charge.

Foolish, his brain told him as he lowered the visor on his bascinet. His new conical helmet clung closely to his skull at both cheeks. It was laced with thongs to his mail coif, and with the visor in place, he felt impregnable. He had his eyes fixed on the enemy approaching, and already he could see that there were a few hotheads racing out in front.

It was a big mistake, he knew. He had been present in enough battles to know the importance of riding at the side of one's neighbour, so that the ponderous weight of the horses and men should slam into their opponents simultaneously. Begin the gallop too early, and many horses would compete with each other, a few throwing caution to the winds and racing onwards to ride into the enemy's ranks one at a time, losing the impetus that was the strength of the cavalry attack. No, better to wait and, at the perfect moment, launch a united assault.

They were already trotting forward, each man eyeing his neighbour and keeping his mount in check, while the French hammered towards them. Closer, closer . . . and the Earl gave a bellow. The knights began to canter, and then, with the French only a matter of yards away, the gallop started.

Sir John wanted to sing. His blood was hot, and a tingle of exultation tickled the base of his spine as he leaned down, his spear pointing at the man charging at him. There was a clash as that man collided with his neighbour, and suddenly there was another man before him. The French onslaught was hampered: with so few enemies to fight, they were riding on a line that was constricting, as the knights to left and right unsuccessfully tried to find a target.

Closer, closer, closer . . . the thunder of the hooves was beating a tattoo in Sir John's helmet, and then the clash – and his spear was shivered to pieces as the man before him disappeared in a welter of blood.

He dropped the butt of the lance and drew his sword, whirling Aeton round and aiming for three Frenchmen who had encircled the Earl.

'*Saint Boniface!*' he bawled, and rode in amongst them. A man turned to face him, and Sir John thrust. He felt his sword crunch through the man's mouth, through teeth and bone, and then the point snagged. He jerked it free and the man fell with a gurgling scream that was cut off as a horse trampled his head.

A second man appeared to his left, and Sir John rode at him, Aeton taking the man's horse with his breast, tumbling man and steed to the ground. Sir John wheeled and rode at the gallop to a pair of French men-at-arms who were approaching warily. One charged, and his sword hacked, catching Sir John's left arm. He instantly lost all sensation in his fingers, but before he could try to bring the man to battle, he was on the second, and he saw an opening beneath the man's armpit where there was no mail. Their swords clashed, and the blow sent a tremor up his arm into his shoulder, but already his point was down and he shoved forward, feeling his tip cleave through flesh, tearing and slicing. The man's head fell back, and his eyes opened wide as his horse trotted away, carrying its master's corpse.

Sir John turned to meet his first opponent, and saw that he too was riding away. However, there were four Frenchmen clustering about a desperate esquire, who whirled his sword and slammed it into the head or body of any man who came too close. Sir John swung his sword at the back of the neck of the nearest one, who slumped in agony; Sir John swung again, backhanded, and caught another man beneath the chin. His chainmail protected him, but he choked, and Sir John's blow threw him from his horse.

Another man was fighting with the esquire, and Sir John spurred towards him. He caught him unawares, his sword smashing into his forearm. The blow broke his arm beneath the mail, and he dropped his own sword. Between them, Sir John and the esquire beat at him until he fell, his face bloody and ruined.

And then it was over. Sir John turned to stare at the French force, but all he could see was bodies in the grass. Those who had been on horseback were either dead or riding away at speed. More English horsemen were chasing after the infantry, and many already lay twitching.

'Sir John,' the Earl said, lifting his own visor. 'I call that an excellent defence of our bridgehead. I thank you for your aid.'

'My Lord, I am glad I was here to assist,' Sir John said. He eyed the bodies on the ground. 'We need as many of our men as possible to hold this bank. I shall stay and ensure that we do so.'

The Earl expressed his gratitude and rode off back the way they had come, while Sir John stared about him.

'Berenger? I would be grateful if you would ask your men to see to all these bodies. Count them and despoil them, but most of all, make sure they are all dead.'

14 August

The bridge was completed. All through the night engineers had struggled and lifted, sawed, hammered and cursed, and the result was a bridge that could take the weight of the entire army, as well as the wagons and carts.

For his part, Berenger was bone tired. He hadn't slept well, expecting a counter-attack at any moment. The news that he and the rest of Grandarse's men were to hold the north bank he greeted with something near relief. Others would go to burn the towns and manors all about, but Berenger and his vintaine could rest and keep watch from the bridgehead.

As the first men began to ride out, Sir John de Sully was at their head. Behind him straggled a party of fifty, archers and men-at-arms. He paused as he passed Berenger.

'Master Fripper, your men fought well last evening. I congratulate you.'

'We saw you kill several,' Berenger replied.

'There were enough for all of us, eh? And there will be plenty more. That's why I'm riding north, to see how far from us the French are, and what they are doing.'

'What of the south?'

'The King has ordered everything to be burned south of Paris, especially the manor of Montjoye. That was King Philippe's favourite, apparently.' He turned and pointed to a billowing cloud of smoke. 'That was it, I think, there.'

Berenger felt a shiver of anticipation. 'The French have plenty of reason to want to fight us.'

'Aye. They have that. Which is why I'd ask you to keep your eyes on the horizon for me and my esquire Bakere here. If you see us riding back in haste, nock your arrows!'

'We shall, my Lord. Godspeed!'

The knight nodded and held his hand aloft. With his hand a blade, he pointed forward and the party trotted off to the north. Somewhere out there lay the mass of the French army, and it was crucial to know whether they would attack from the north, or would circle round Paris to come at the English from the south.

Setting sentries, Berenger sent Clip to forage for food, while Geoff made the fire.

'We've no sticks,' Geoff said. 'I'll fetch some more.'

'Good,' Berenger said flatly. His brain felt leaden, and he sat down with his back to the cart's wheel, letting his head rest against the spokes with relief.

He could not help but think that their enterprise was teetering on a knife's edge. On the one side lay disaster, on the other, perhaps more disaster. Geoff was still convinced it was down to that Frenchwoman, Béatrice. Placing her with Archibald had not cured Geoff's suspicions. He did not trust her, and the Welshman's words were constantly pricking at him, he said. Perhaps Berenger should trust Geoff's judgement and warn others. Tell Grandarse – or perhaps say something to Sir John? There were enough priests, from that ferocious fighter, the Bishop of Durham, down to vicars from London and the Scottish Marches. Any number of them would listen with sympathy to a man's honest concerns about the woman.

'Be careful Geoff. Don't stray too far – and make sure to keep away from that woman,' he mumbled and yawned profoundly. His eyes were already shut, and as his mouth closed, his breathing became shallow and noisy.

'Sleep well, Vintener,' Geoff murmured as he turned and began to make his way up the slope of the bank. There was a copse over on the left, a scant half-mile away, which should provide him with firewood.

*   *   *

In the midst of the little wood, Geoff saw a small building.

Others would have been about here already, he knew – scouts, pillagers and idlers trying to avoid hard work at the bridge, but nevertheless there was no point taking risks. He set his hand to his sword and drew it slowly from the scabbard, holding it low, ready to cut upwards at the first sign of danger. Stepping cautiously, avoiding the twigs and bits of broken timber that lay all about, he made his way to the door.

It was no farm building or storehouse, he discovered: it was a little chapel. The cross over the gable was crooked, as though the priest had set it up himself with scant knowledge of carpentry, but it was a tidy little building. As he approached, there was a cry, and glancing up, he saw a black bird, a raven or crow, sitting on the cross and staring down at him with its beady eye. It was unsettling.

At the door, Geoff pushed gently. There was a slight scraping as the timbers scratched their way over the threshold, but the hinges had been well smeared with grease, and made no sound. Geoff entered warily, his sword higher, his left hand flat near his belly, ready to knock away an assailant's weapon.

A scrabbling sound made him turn. There, near the altar, there was a little, low doorway, and he stared, listening intently. A quiet step, then another, and he scowled. There was someone in there, he was sure. He walked on tip-toes along the nave's flags, and when he reached the door, he peered inside.

'Maid, what are you doing here?' he said when he saw Béatrice. She was kneeling before a crucifix with her hands clasped, the picture of piety. From his vantage point, he could see the nape of her neck, and was struck by the beauty of her soft, pale skin. He added gruffly, 'You should be careful in places like this. I thought you might be a French spy.'

Startled, she rose, staring at him, her eyes wild with fear. Her head was bared, her hair awry, and to him she looked like a creature of the forest, a spirit of nature. It made him feel nervous, as though she was more dangerous than he could see.

Yet at the same time he felt his tarse swelling. Her rapid breathing made her breasts swell against the thin material of her tunic, and he couldn't help but stare. It had been so long. He had not lain with a woman since the day he found his wife's body. The day his life had ended. Suddenly the longing became uncontrollable.

She stood and backed away from him.

'Don't run! I won't hurt you,' he said, his voice thick with lust. He wanted to hold her and feel her body next to his.

His tone alarmed her still more, he saw. She shook her head, before trying to bolt from the room. He put his hand to her, but she drew away, backing to the wall.

'No! Please don't!' she cried.

'I won't hurt you,' he repeated, and he meant it – yet he felt a dreadful emptiness in him. The memory of his own wife back in England, the horror of the deaths ... This young Frenchwoman could give him some much-needed solace. He wanted it. He *deserved* it.

Unconvinced, she suddenly darted forward in an attempt to escape. He tried to grab her by the arm, not to harm her, but just to hold her still so he could explain that he wanted only to talk. But his hand missed. Instead he grasped a fold of cloth, which ripped with a deafening sound that desecrated the chapel. The two stood, her panting like an injured cat, him stock-still, his eyes fixed on the softness of her bared breast. With a moan, he leaned forward, his mouth open.

Her hand raked down his cheek, narrowly missing his eye, and he roared with surprise and shock. Purely by reflex, he punched her in the face, so that her head snapped back, and she fell to the ground, unconscious. He knelt and put a trembling hand towards her breast. He could have taken her like the slut he knew she was, but before his hand touched her, his eyes rose. There, before him like a marker on the road to Hell, he saw the crucifix on the wall, and he stopped, staring, his hand inches from her.

He clenched his fist and remained there, staring at Christ's sad face. Then, leaving Béatrice still slumped on the floor, he walked to the altar and knelt. Gradually his body became racked with dry, heaving sobs.

CHAPTER THIRTY-FOUR

Berenger was startled awake by the sound of weeping as Béatrice ran into the camp area, staring about her wildly, clutching her tunic to her breast.

'Sweet Mother of God,' he cried, and clumsily climbed to his feet, fumbling for his sword. 'What's happened? Who is it? Where?'

He ran to the slope and stared out over the lip of the bank. Luke was standing sentry, and he shook his head baffled. 'She was out there, near those woods, Fripper. I saw her come out, and she began running. You saw what she looked like. Sobbing, she was, the whole way. And her tit hanging out.'

'Is there any sign of the French over there?' Berenger demanded, scowling at the woods as if daring them to conceal his enemies.

'No. Geoff went in there a while back, but I haven't seen him come out yet.'

'Geoff? Very well. Call out if you see anything suspicious.'

266

Berenger turned and went back to where the woman knelt, shuddering, clinging to Donkey. 'What's the matter with her?'

Ed looked up, distraught. 'Look at her! Can't you see? She's been raped, or someone tried to rape her. Are the Welsh out there?'

'Non, non. Ce n'est pas . . . C'est rien. Rien.'

She was still weeping, her face hidden in Ed's chest, one hand clutching the material to cover her modesty.

'"Nothing"? Looks like a lot more than "nothing" to me,' Berenger said.

She looked up, and then stiffened.

Berenger span around to see Geoff, an armful of sticks and branches in his arms, enter the camp. He set them all down carefully at the fire's side, squatted and began to break them ready for burning.

Berenger couldn't believe that Geoff would have done anything to her. A man terrified of a witch wouldn't try to rape her.

Béatrice deliberately spat in Geoff's direction before averting her face.

'Christ's pain, Geoff,' Berenger said.

Outside Paris, Sir John had left Aeton with his esquire and made his way to St-Germain, where the French King had recently built a vast new palace for himself. The land all about was his favourite hunting estate. King Edward had ensconced himself inside, while Edward of Woodstock had taken the old palace alongside.

Sir John found the palace filled with men, and more were outside, laughing and toasting each other.

'My Lord Warwick? What is happening?' Sir John asked. The evident jubilation of the men-at-arms outside was almost alarming. It reminded him of the febrile atmosphere of an army before a foolhardy charge, when all the men drank themselves stupid so as not to face up to the disaster to come.

'Sir John, the French King has agreed to do battle!'

Sir John stared, his mind whirling at the news. 'Where? Does he say when?'

'Our King will soon tell us.'

They were forced to wait while the senior bannerets and lords arrived. The space was much like a glad May morning, with the cheery atmosphere and flags fluttering overhead, but at last there was a sudden hush. A troop of men with pikes marched from the palace and cleared a passage from the main doors. The King strode out, waving to his cheering officers as he went, until he reached a wagon and climbed atop, his arms aloft.

'My Lords, good knights, friends! I hope and trust you are all as happy with the passage of our army as I am, but soon you shall have reason for still more joy at our successes! For today we have received a letter from our good cousin, the man who calls himself King of France. Would you like to hear what he says? Shall I read it to you?'

There was a chorus of cheers at that, and arms were raised as the knights bellowed support for their King and enthusiasm to hear what Philippe had written.

'Hold! Hold! Very well, listen, and I shall read it to you,' King Edward said. He raised a scroll. 'He says: "Dear cousin, King of England and Wales, and . . ." well, you don't want the preliminaries, do you? Let us get to the meat of the dish. He says: "You who want to conquer this land . . ." Is he not most rude? He calls me his "most dishonourable and disloyal vassal". I am glad he realises I do not intend to be loyal to *him*! He says he will meet us for battle. He wishes us to go to him, north of Poissy or some field south of Paris, on Thursday, Saturday,

Sunday or Tuesday following the Feast of the Annunciation. What say you? Should we agree to fight him on these days?'

There was a roar of support at this. Fists and drawn weapons were waved in the air, and a man set up a chant of 'Battle, battle, battle!' that was taken up by several other knights, stamping their feet or slapping their breasts in time to the cries.

Sir John did not feel the same enthusiasm. 'He wants us to meet him at a time and place of his choosing? Philippe will prepare the land and expects us to march to him to our deaths? Perhaps the French King has learned strategy.'

'You would avoid his trap?' the Earl asked.

'I would.'

'Silence, my friends! Please, hold!' the King bellowed, and a herald nodded to a pair of esquires, who blew three loud blasts on their horns.

When the tumult had subsided somewhat, the King lowered his head and cast about, looking at the men before him.

'My friends, I say *no*! No, we shall not accede to this man's demands. What? He wants us to "cease in the depredations against my people, cease to burn the lands", et cetera. Should we stop our profitable investigations of his favourite manors? I say again, *no*! He says, we may meet him here, or there, when it suits him. I say, we have offered him battle all the long miles from La Hogue to here, and he has refused us. I was content to accept battle wherever he decided, but he did not come. I wanted to cross the Seine to fight him, but he tore down the bridges or garrisoned the towns so that we might not reach him. And now, now we are all-powerful, he asks us to agree to *his* terms?'

King Edward paused and stared about him with a slow deliberation, meeting the eyes of his knights and barons as though testing their will-power.

'Gentlemen, I will burn and destroy everything he most values here. All his manors, even this splendid palace here, the Palais du Roy, and the other over there where my son rests. He asks: Where shall he find us? And I say: Look for the smoke. Look for the fires. That is where I shall be. Listen for the sound of mourning and weeping. *That is where I shall be!* And when *we* desire it, we shall stop at a place of *our* choosing, where we may offer battle. But should I take his commands to fight at such a place and such a time, when he desires it? Then indeed should I be accused of being a false vassal, for only a vassal would agree to terms from his lord in such manner. I shall not. I shall not. *I SHALL NOT*! I am King of England and of France. I shall continue rewarding those who demonstrate their fealty, punishing those who are faithless! And I will take this land with your aid, my friends, my noble companions. This *chevauchée* shall be remembered through the centuries, I swear!'

The Earl nodded as the men erupted once more in bellows of support. He commented drily, 'Well, it would appear he agrees with you, Sir John.'

'I am glad to hear it. I think that his conclusion is correct.'

'Which is?'

'The French wish us to stop burning and looting. They offer nothing, only a battle at some time in the future, if we are good enough to accept it, when they have overwhelming force.'

The Earl eyed him. He himself was thirty years old, so thirty years younger than Sir John. There was no disputing the fact that Sir John had more experience of war, of success and shameful disaster and failure, than he did. 'They will say that we run, that when they offer us a battle, we avoid them.'

'Yes, they will,' Sir John agreed. 'For a while, a little while. But we shall seek and find ourselves a more accommodating site for a battle than a flat field on which the French may encircle us and destroy us at their leisure. Has he responded already to the French King?'

'Yes. The Bishop of Meaux came to deliver it, and he has been sent back with an offer of a truce for the morrow. The Feast of the Annunciation will be celebrated in peace – and the day after, we shall be ready for war.'

Sir John nodded. He recalled speaking with Berenger earlier. In his mind's eye he pictured a field north of the Somme: a sloping hill with strong woods behind. A perfect place for siting a defence against even massive foes.

'We are ready now, but we need the right field,' he said, 'not somewhere selected by the French. A place with a hill where we can set our archers, where we can assault the enemy with impunity, a place where they must attack on one line of approach. A field where we must win.'

That night, Geoff sat apart from the rest of the vintaine as they ate their meal. He cast wary glances towards Berenger and the others, chewing his portion of hard bread until at last the vintener rose and walked away from the fire, crouching at his side, still carrying his bowl. He didn't meet Geoff's eyes, but dipped a crust into his pottage and sucked it.

'Well?'

'It's not true.'

'Did you rape her?'

'You know me better than that.'

'How well does any man know another?' Berenger muttered.

'Look at me, Frip! I am the same man you joked with yesterday.'

'Aye, very well. What happened up there, Geoff?'

Geoff wouldn't speak for a time. Then: 'Frip, when did the Devil last try to tempt you?'

'Me?' Berenger frowned. 'What do you mean?'

'Have you never been tempted?'

'I've seen Him in many men after a battle, but no, I don't think He's ever tempted me. Neither in battle nor with a woman.'

'The Devil tries to tempt me all the time.'

'But he has easier targets,' Berenger objected. 'There are men who only need a push to go and murder a nun or monk. Why would he take you on, when there is such easy prey?'

'I know the Devil is here – and out there today, I saw His skill. She is the Devil's own, Frip.'

Berenger began to smile, but he caught a glimpse of Geoff's expression. 'What happened up there?'

'In the woods there's a chapel. I saw her in there, and I wanted to talk to her. That was all, I swear. But she didn't trust me, and I suppose that got my blood up. I wanted to make her stop and listen to me.'

'You raped her?'

'No. I could have, Frip, if I'd wanted to. But I didn't. I just tried to hold her back, and she gave me this scratch. I was furious, but I let her alone.'

'It's between you and her, Geoff. But if I could, I'd have you stay right away from her from now on.'

'I know, Frip, and I will. I don't want to go anywhere near her. She has been touched by the Devil. That's why I was tempted, because *he* tempted me. Just like . . .'

'What?'

Geoff shook his head. He couldn't tell Berenger about his wife and the boys. It was still too raw. Their screams still filled his nightmares. 'Nothing. I'll leave her alone.'

'You'd better. The others may find it hard to swallow, that the Devil suddenly came and forced you. They believe her.'

'All I know is, I won't sleep easy while she's still here. The thought of her blade at my throat is with me all the while.'

Sitting at his own fire, Archibald watched Geoff from beneath beetling brows. Béatrice sat near him, her own eyes fixed upon the fire, arms huddled about her upper body. Her eyes had streamed with tears earlier, and left pale tracks in the dirt that masked her features. She had been so near to forgetting the Welsh attack, that to see her in this state again was upsetting.

'Ed, take this to her,' Archibald said, passing him a goatskin full of wine.

The boy took her the wine, and she looked at Archibald and ducked her head in gratitude, tipping it up and drinking deep.

'That's right, maid,' he said. 'Drink it away. And be assured, I won't let him near you again.'

'He will never touch me again!' she hissed.

'You need not worry. Just stay here with me and the vintaine. I am sorry this happened while you were under my protection. You should have told me you were going up there.'

'I saw the chapel, it seemed right to go,' she whispered.

'Aye, possibly. But we have priests aplenty here in the army. Any of them could have shriven you or said a Mass.'

'I wanted some peace to pray for my family.'

'What happened to them?' Archibald asked, thinking it might help her, to talk about it.

Hesitantly at first, Béatrice began to tell her story. Gradually, her voice strengthened and her pride shone through.

'I was the daughter of Simon Pouillet, of Argenteuil. We were a happy family. He made powder for gonnes – like you, m'sieur.'

'Just call me Archibald,' he said gently.

273

'I had a spoiled life. We lived well, and often had friends of importance come to stay. Well, last year my father had a party for those who had helped him over the past twelve months. He invited his brother, and lots of members of the guilds came to dine with us.

'My mother was always proud of her cooking and her brewing, and she laid on a wonderful feast. The men grew merry, and my father was praised for his hospitality. But during the meal, someone mentioned the King of England and his demands. My father made a silly remark. He said: "Perhaps France would benefit from a King who ruled well and wisely, even if he were English, rather than being ruled badly by Philippe." It was a joke – a jest. No one took it seriously.'

She wept, her face in her hands. That was the last time her family had been together, happy, free, prosperous and comfortable. She could remember the long table, her mother at the side of her father, all their guests in their finery, the servants moving quietly and efficiently between them, serving the large messes of stews, the pies with gravy oozing, the honeyed larks, the mixed dishes and beautiful sweetmeats. How everyone had laughed and sung and danced and enjoyed themselves. And then . . .

'The first I knew something was wrong was the knock at our door two days later. There was the sound of mailed fists against the timbers, and then the door burst open and men poured in. They took my father, and when my brother tried to stop them, they beat him over the head with a cudgel. My mother was screaming – *I* was screaming. The maids were terrified, and the bottler and our manservants did not know what to do. How could they?'

'What happened, maid?' Archibald asked.

'They took him. He was held in a gaol overnight, and we heard later that – that they took him to Montfaucon. There they hanged him on a hook in the butchers' slaughterhouse, and hacked him apart while he . . .'

'Enough, maid,' Archibald said. 'You poor thing!'

She sniffed, not daring to look at him. His voice was breaking, and she knew that in his face she would see sympathy. But she didn't want it. Béatrice was strong. She wanted no man's compassion. All she wanted was the means to protect herself.

'So that's why you have no feeling for your people, then?' he said.

She nodded, head hanging. There was nothing left in her now, she felt drained. And then she did look up. Archibald was weeping, and the sight made something tear in her soul. Her eyes filled with tears, and she began to sob. The attack by Geoff had been more unsettling than the attempted rape by the priest or even her capture by the Welsh, because she had come to feel secure with the Englishmen. It made her misery all the worse, knowing that one of them had broken that bond of trust.

'Maid, you are perfectly safe here,' Archibald said. 'No one will try to attack you, and if they do, I will protect you. Do you believe me?'

'Yes,' she said, to please him.

'Good. You stay near to me from now on, and you'll be fine. I have ways of protecting you that these fellows couldn't dream of.'

She nodded, but in her heart she knew he was wrong. There was nowhere in France where she could be safe again. She would have to create her own safety – and only she knew how to do that.

CHAPTER THIRTY-FIVE

15 August

Berenger slept badly again that night. Ever and anon he would startle awake and stare about him, and each time he would see the figure of Geoff, sitting on a tree-trunk nearby, staring at the shapes of Béatrice and the Donkey, lying together for warmth under the gynour's cart.

That morning, the army rose early as usual, but as it was the Feast Day of the Virgin Mary and a day of truce, the men had fewer duties and could make the most of their leisure. Even as the vintaine stood-to with their weapons ready, there were raucous cries from other units where the men were already letting off steam.

The cheerful atmosphere spread to everyone except Geoff, who sat apart and did not join in. For the others there was a lightening of hearts at the thought that there was no risk to their lives today. Clip acted like an apprentice after consuming a gallon of ale, and playing tricks on the others. He spent much of the morning trying to pin a strip of parchment with a picture of a donkey badly etched in charcoal on Jack's back without success; then he attempted to persuade the other men that it would be amusing to pick up Berenger and dunk him in the river. He was fortunate to fail in that ambition too.

In the middle of the morning, a wagon rumbled into their encampment and a beaming archer on the bed waved a horn cup at the men, crying, 'Ale from the King!'

There was a rush to the wagon, the men carrying cups, mazers, horns, even two men with heavy goblets, filling them and drinking quickly before returning and refilling them. The man leading the wagon tried to draw away, but his stony expression eased once Clip and Oliver had pressed a cup on him and insisted on refilling it at intervals while he took up station by their fire and regaled the men with tales of the miserliness of other units who had held back with their ale allocations, refusing to whet his thirst.

Berenger saw Geoff standing and drinking near the cart. He was not actively shunned by the other men, but kept himself aloof. Probably all, at one time or another, had participated in the rape of women in the towns through which they had passed to get here, but Geoff's attempt to abuse Béatrice had offended their sense of hospitality. They had welcomed her as a guest in their midst, and she should have been safe.

'You all right?' he said as he passed near Geoff.

'Aye, I'm well enough. I just wish *she* was far away from us, that's all.'

Not long after this Berenger saw the lumbering bulk of Archibald approaching.

'Vintener, I hope I see you well?' the gynour said pleasantly.

'I'm well enough.'

'Let me make your life easier. The maid – she is terrified of your men after the attack on her. I'll keep her under my wing, as we agreed; this time, she will not leave my sight.'

'If she is content, that sounds a good idea.'

'But advise your men to keep away from my camp, eh? The powder I use is unstable stuff. If a man were to sneak over and try to molest the girl . . . well, the powder could react badly.'

'I understand. None of my men will try to harm her, I can swear, Gynour.'

'I am glad to hear it.' Archibald moved away, but not before darting a look at Geoff, an expression of loathing darkening his usually amiable features.

16 August

It was a little past dawn the next morning when Sir John de Sully trotted up with his esquire.

'I hope I see you well, Master Fripper?' he called, reining in his horse and casting a glance along the men of the vintaine. 'Your fellows all look hale and hearty. I trust they are rested and ready for whatever the day might bring?'

There was a ripple of laughter along the line at that. Even Berenger allowed himself a smile. 'Aye, we'll do, Sir John. Is there news?'

'Yes, and all good. The French have moved. Last afternoon they marched through Paris to the south of the city. They are waiting for us now at the vineyards of Bourg-la-Reine.'

There was a muttering amongst the men at that. Some were excited; others who had hoped for a short, sharp raid and a quick return home afterwards, looked less happy.

'How many?' Berenger asked.

'Frenchmen? Oh, thousands, Fripper. Many more than us.'

'I see.' Berenger glanced at his men. Geoff stood alone; he remained sullen – ashamed of his actions but convinced more than ever. Although several of the other men wore expressions of concern, there was no overt alarm. The vintaine had fought before. All the men knew the risks and rewards of battle.

Clip heaved a sigh. 'Aye, well, ye'll all get murdered. That's a fact.'

'Hit him, someone,' Eliot called, and Matt, who stood at Clip's side, clumped him over the head.

'Hoy! What was that for?' Clip demanded.

'Purely personal enjoyment,' Matt replied.

'Shut up, lads,' Berenger said flatly. 'So, Sir John, are we to march to the city?'

'The French have chosen a marvellous site, with rising land leading to their position. It is protected on both flanks, I hear, with trees and thick undergrowth to prevent a charge, and they have Genoese mercenaries to bring down all our men from a great distance.'

Berenger pulled a face. The thought of charging into the Genoese arrow-storm did not appeal. He had fought in battles like that. Invariably it was better to be on the defensive than the attacking side.

Sir John gave a loud chuckle at his expression. 'You think our King was joking when he said he would not meet the French at a time and place of their choosing? No, Fripper. We do not fight today. Instead, we are to cross the river and march north.'

'I thought we were here to fight the French, Sir John,' Geoff called out, frowning.

'Aye, but at a time of *our* choosing – not theirs,' Sir John replied. He nodded to Berenger and spurred away.

*   *   *

It took little time to strike camp. After the last weeks they were well-practised at packing their belongings and stowing cook-pots and bedrolls, blankets and bags into the back of the cart, along with the bows and arrows.

'Wonder how the Donkey is,' Clip said as he threw his little haversack in with the others.

'Why? You never cared about him while he was here,' Geoff said.

'He had his uses. Good at fetching and carrying, he was, so long as there weren't any Welsh around.'

'Did you see the Welshman's face?' Geoff said quietly. 'After she flung the powder into the fire. I've never seen anything like it.'

Matt nodded. He was on her side. He liked women. Always had. 'She was in the right. That bastard was going to rape her – our maid, the girl who saved our Donkey. Then all the other men would take their turn. The Welsh bastard deserved all he got!'

'She stole that powder from Archibald,' Geoff persisted. 'Those damned gynours are more in league with the Devil than His own demons! I hate the smell of brimstone. That poor Welshman. He had no eyes left, did he?'

'He should have left Béatrice alone,' Matt said unsympathetically. 'They were all planning to have their fun with her. It's one thing to take a wench from a town after an assault, but they knew she was with us. I wouldn't see her molested by a bunch of hairy-arsed sheep-swivers. It makes them worse than the French!'

'I'm just glad the wench isn't here any more,' Geoff grumbled on. 'She's a witch. She threatens all our—'

'Oh, change the song, Master Millerson,' Matt sighed. 'I've heard that refrain too often. She's no more a witch than I am!'

'She is bringing bad fortune.'

'Ballocks! She helped the leech to nurse our vintener. Look at him! You can hardly see he was injured.'

'Yes – and isn't that proof enough?' Geoff snarled.

'No,' Matt said. He leaned against the cart's wheel and studied Geoff. 'The fact is, the girl is innocent. We're not suffering disaster. Our army is safe still, and when we meet the French, God willing, we shall carry the field.'

'Why do you protect her?' Clip intervened. 'She's only another little wench with a plump arse.'

'Why? Because she came to us freely. She didn't come to bargain her safety. When she saw us first, it was to save the Donkey, and after that, she stayed because she trusted us,' Matt said, looking meaningfully at Geoff.

Geoff coloured. 'Are you saying I—'

'I'm saying nothing, Geoff. But you did betray her trust, didn't you?'

'She would have been worth a tumble though,' Clip said with a sidelong glance at Geoff.

'Shut up!' he rasped.

'Go on! We all saw her tit!' Clip taunted him. 'How was she? Did you only get a quick fondle, or was she keen enough as well?'

Geoff's bitterness and frustration boiled over. In a moment he had spun about, grabbed Clip's cotte and shoved hard, thrusting the other man up against the wagon, Geoff's elbow at his throat. Eyes wild, Clip saw Geoff's fist clench, ready to pound his face, and felt for his knife to defend himself.

'Enough! *Enough*!' Berenger bellowed, shoving Geoff away. 'There are thousands of Frenchmen waiting to kill us – do you want to do their work for them? Geoff, back! *Back*! Clip, take your hand off your knife right now. I won't have fighting in my vintaine!'

'He went mental,' Clip said, rubbing at his throat. 'Just because he got his hand up that French tart's skirt, he tried to kill me!'

'Get moving!' Berenger said, pushing him forwards. 'We're supposed to be marching.'

He turned to face Geoff, who wouldn't meet his look, but mumbled, 'I'm sorry, Frip. It won't happen again.'

'Fucking right it won't, Geoff. Because if it does, I'll have you flogged!'

They were within sight of the great cathedral town of Beauvais when they stopped for the night. Berenger set the guards and took a turn around the perimeter before he went to the fires and hunkered down at the side of Geoff and Matt.

'All well?' Matt asked.

'I hope so,' Berenger said, glancing at Geoff. 'You all right now?'

Geoff sighed. 'It won't happen again, Frip, like I said. I'm sorry, but he kept on needling me.'

'About the maid?'

'Yes. And I won't have it.'

'You'll bloody have to, Geoff. If you don't, the King will see you dangle! This is an army, man! You need to contain your anger.'

'So you said.'

'I'll say it again and again if I think there's any risk of another outburst like that,' Berenger said.

Matt snorted and hawked. 'Any news?'

'The smoke behind us was the bridge going up in flames,' Berenger told him. 'The French won't be able to follow us that way. They'll have to march through Paris to come out this side of the Seine, and then they'll head straight for us, I suppose. They won't want us to harm any more towns or cities.'

'Do you think they'll actually come to blows with us this time?' Matt said. He felt for his sword's hilt with an anticipatory grin. 'This hanging about is hard on a man. I want to get the fight over with so we can concentrate on plunder!'

'I think we've tugged the French King's beard so hard, it's made his eyes water,' Berenger said.

'Beard? I think it was his short and curlies, Frip.' Matt laughed.

'Well, he's bound to take action now. If he doesn't, none of his people will respect him ever again.'

They were sitting on a little hillock, next to a small stand of beech trees. From here they could see in the far distance a darkening grey cloud where the smoke from the town rose. As the light began to fade, Matt got up, rubbing his arse.

'I'm off to find a small skin of wine and take my ease. After all, if you're right, I may not have many more chances, eh?'

As he wandered off back down towards their camp, Berenger looked over at Geoff, sitting moodily nearby.

'What is it, Geoff? You can tell me. This chevauchée has brought you low.'

'It's just that Frenchwoman,' Geoff said. He took a deep breath, closing his eyes. Remembering.

There were so many regrets when a man reached his age. So many opportunities lost, so many hollow challenges that could have been better ignored, so many dreams that had been discarded as reality came and thrust them away.

'You just want to go home, old friend. When you get there and see your woman again, you'll be content,' Berenger said soothingly.

'Aye.'

Geoff thought of her now: Sarra, his wife.

'She was a grubby young thing when I met her, you know,' he said. 'A peasant-daughter from the next vill – lean, potent, with a pair of breasts that swung at every step, and an arse like puppies in a sack. And so pretty: an oval face with catlike hazel eyes, and a wicked, beckoning look to her. I fell in love with her the first moment I saw her.'

'You married her a long time ago.'

'It was the Feast of Saint John the Baptist, fourteen, fifteen years ago. Her father wouldn't let me near, so we met in a little leaf-strewn clearing in the trees, and there we straightway made love. There was no discussion, no lengthy negotiation. We both knew that we were meant to be married.

'After that, things moved swiftly. We made our vows there in the leaves, in front of friends, before visiting the doddery old fool of a priest, who blessed us at the church door. Afterwards, he declared that it was the first wedding he had legitimised for a couple in love.'

He remembered it all. 'You know, when I was told to go and fight the Scots, I was dead keen. And when I returned – Christ's pains! – Sarra was so glad to have me return, it was a day before she allowed me from our bed!'

'You are lucky, Geoff. I've never found a woman like that.'

'I never had reason to doubt her affection.' Never, in all those years, he told himself wonderingly.

Berenger was called away by Matt, and when he was alone, Geoff remained, staring into the distance.

She had always been there to look after him: the one fixed point of his life. Until the beginning of summer, when he met Edith.

Young, fresh, wriggling and gorgeous as a summer's morning, she worked in the tavern, and all the men adored her. Her ivory skin, her rich auburn hair, the perfect roses of her lips.

She was sweet and taut and soft and bitter, and he longed for her when he was away from her in a way that tormented his soul. Sarra, in comparison, looked like a worn-out drudge.

At his neglect, Sarra grew sharp, with a poisonous tongue that could slay a saint. It made his visits to the tavern to see Edith all the more delightful. Until that day when he wandered home drunk, after spending the day with her, and Sarra tore into him. She shouldn't have done that. It wasn't her *place* to demand, to insult him and say that he was whoring with all the sluts in the alehouses. She shouldn't have spoken to him like that. No man could keep his anger under control, when provoked like that.

The next morning, he found her down behind the table, her throat cut. And the memory returned – of their shouting, their fighting, her spitting at him, raking at his face with fingers like claws, kicking and punching at him, her face twisted into a mask of hatred while their little boys watched.

That was why he never joined in the rapes in the towns; that was why he couldn't take Béatrice by force when he had the chance. Not because he didn't want to, but because every time he took a woman, he saw his Sarra's eyes, her dead eyes, looking back at him accusingly.

CHAPTER THIRTY-SIX

17 August

'Up! The lot of you: *up!*'

Berenger was awake at the first shout. Before the second, he was on his feet, sword in hand.

All around him, men were yawning, rubbing their eyes and grumbling in the gloom. This was not their usual routine. Most mornings, it would be Berenger moving about them kicking the occasional figure, beating on a pot or shouting. Today, however, Grandarse and Sir John's esquire were hurrying about the camp, waking everyone.

'What's the matter?' Berenger demanded.

'We're to break camp,' Richard Bakere said tersely.

'You heard him,' Grandarse snapped. '*Now!* We're leaving the wagon train and anything unnecessary. Bring all the oxen and horses, but the heavy ballocks are to be left behind.'

Berenger felt the words hit him in the belly. 'Leave the wagon train? The enemy are that close?'

'The mother-swyving sons of whores have already closed on us. We're told to find ourselves horses or ponies, anything with four legs we can steal to get away from here. I'd cut their throats if we could stop and fight, you lads would shoot 'em so full of arrows they'd look like my lady's pin-cushion, but the fact is, they are a large army, and we are depleted. Damn their black souls, but I didn't think they'd catch us so speedily!'

Grandarse was already off again, swearing and shouting at Roger's vintaine, and Berenger walked to a tree and pulled down his hosen, pissing long while trying to come to terms with the news.

'Will they catch us, do you think?' Matt asked quietly, taking his post at the tree a moment or two later.

'If they're on the same plain, they may, I suppose. It's ludicrous to think that they'd risk it though,' Berenger said.

'Is that the view of my friend the vintener, or the politics of a commander?' Matt grinned. 'I am a man, Frip. I can take the truth.'

'Very well. If they can, they will fall on us like wolves on a flock. But we still have our King and his advisers. You know what they say: if five Englishmen were attacked by fifteen French it would be an unfair fight, like five wolves attacked by fifteen sheep.'

'Aye, but these sheep have steel fangs and mail for fleece!'

Berenger shrugged. 'I cannot think of the last time the French managed to assault us and win. Can you?'

Clip overheard them, and called out gleefully, 'Aye, if they get much closer, they'll murder the lot of us. We'll all be slain!'

Matt spat on the grass at his feet. 'I'll bloody murder you myself if they don't manage it first,' he said.

*   *   *

They were soon ready, packed and off.

Berenger watched the horizon closely as he rode his small black and white pony. They had found him in a field as they marched past, and then two decent rounseys at a stable, but Berenger took one look at the rounseys and decided to stick with the pony. It was less distance to fall. Together with the other beasts they had already found, these were enough for half the vintaine to ride. Those without horses padded along on the grass, for the most part complaining loudly that their legs ached.

Before they had covered a league, Matt had stopped and pulled off his shoe, saying he had a thorn in his foot, and Berenger saw that the shoe had almost no sole. The upper was flapping uselessly. Matt was not the only man to go near-barefoot though, and before long many others would be too.

The path they took was clearly used by villagers moving their cattle, and soon they found themselves in a small town.

It was a quiet little place. Smoke still rose from a hearth in one cottage, but the whole place was deserted. Only one ancient dog barked for a while, until one of the vintaine hit him with an axe handle.

'Is there any drink?' Clip demanded, hurrying into the nearest house.

There was little enough of anything. They moved cautiously, taking cover when a flight of duck flew overhead, jumping when a cock crowed, constantly fearing attack. Berenger whispered and hissed his commands, convinced that the French had encircled them by their quick marching and were already here.

Soon Berenger heard a loud noise from behind. A column of their own men was advancing, along with the lumbering wagons of Archibald, the Donkey and Béatrice marching at its side. On a whim, he walked to greet them.

'Is he treating you well?' he asked of the boy.

'He's very kind,' Ed replied. But his face was thinner, and his eyes looked larger than ever.

'Have you eaten?' Berenger asked, shooting a suspicious look at the rotund Archibald.

'Eaten, Master Fripper?' the gynour replied. 'Damn me if he has. Why should he eat?'

'I didn't supply you with a slave to be starved!' Berenger snarled, and would have leaped onto the wagon to grab the man, but the Donkey put out a hand to prevent him.

'No, Master, he hasn't eaten either. No one has brought us any food.'

'Is that true?'

'It's often the way,' the gynour shrugged. Then he looked very directly at Berenger, and jerked his head towards Béatrice. 'It's normal, Vintener. The others don't like men like me. They think that since I smell of the Devil, the Devil can look to my meals! Eh? So, if you have a crust or two of bread, I'd be glad of it. Failing that, a half-ox would meet my own needs, washed down with a tun of good French wine!'

Berenger looked at Béatrice and back to Archibald again. It was clear that this was an invention to protect her feelings. Archibald and his little cavalcade had no food because too many of the soldiers feared her. Rumours that she could be a witch were widespread. Berenger grinned. 'I don't have much, but you can share in our fortunes. Would you ride with us in the front?'

'I don't know about that,' Archibald said. 'I've heard it's dangerous to be at the point of the spear. But if you mean to tell me that there is more food to be had there, I'll gladly chance my safety.'

Before Berenger could respond, a sly voice intruded. 'Be careful of him, Master Gynour. That vintener is dangerous to know. People die around him.'

He turned to see that a party of Welshmen had caught up with them. Ed shrank away, and Béatrice moved until her back was at the wagon's side. She fumbled at her belt, feeling for her knife.

'Stop that, child, or you'll cause more disturbance than you would wish,' Archibald said firmly. He eyed the Welsh with contained belligerence.

The Welshman sneered at him and moved on past, their long ragged cloaks trailing.

Archibald watched them disappear, saying, 'If I were to get myself in a tight spot, I shouldn't like to have to rely on *them*. We had more trouble from them last night.'

'What happened?'

'That turd Erbin offered to purchase young Béatrice for the sum of one loaf and a bowl of pottage. When I told them where to go, they took away their food and we were left hungry.'

'They didn't try to attack you again?'

Archibald gave a cold smile. 'I think they have learned that it's not a good idea to try to surprise folks with experience of black powder.'

After that, Berenger kept close to Archibald's wagon. If there were to be an ambush, it could become a stronghold for the men when arrows began to fly.

There was no sign of the French army as yet. Lulled by the sounds of squeaking harnesses, the rattle of pans and chains, the steady tramping of many feet, he began to lose the sense of urgency, and instead listened to the men talking.

'We're not to halt, they say. But if we don't, how can we forage?' Matt was saying.

Geoff contributed, 'It's bad enough that the food has run out. We are starving when the villages all about here have food in plenty.'

'Aye, how can a man fight on an empty stomach?' Eliot said sadly.

'Does it matter? You're all going to die soon, anyway,' Clip said. Then: 'Ouch!'

Matt spoke with an innocent voice. 'What, did you hurt yourself?'

'You hit my pate!'

'You viciously butted my elbow with your head, Clip, I think you'll find.'

'Aye, well, we'll see who's left laughing when the French are done with you,' Clip muttered in his nasal whine.

'Will you shut up saying that!'

Berenger could tell that these were not the usual gripes and grumbles: the men were beginning to feel anxious.

Beckoning Matt, he pulled him to one side. 'The men. What's their temper?'

'You can hear what they're saying, Frip. They aren't happy. Nor am I, for that matter. For one thing, they're hungry.'

'They've been on short rations before.'

'It ain't just that. They're worried about the French, too. Come on, Frip, you know what they're like: they had an easy march of it from the landing to Paris, and they reckoned the whole thing would be a piece of cake. Now they see there'll be a serious fight.'

'The King told us as much when we embarked. They knew he meant to catch the French.'

'Yes. But now it looks like it's us who'll be caught. We could be engaged in the open on the plains before we can even form our battles. If the French get us, before we're good and ready, we'll be buggered. You want that? I know I don't.'

'Distract the men. Occupy them with thoughts of women and wine at the next town.'

'Which is that?'

'I don't know,' Berenger admitted.

'I'll do what I can.'

'And get them to speed up. The King has ordered that we should all hurry.'

'Has he?' Jack looked at him sharply. 'The French must be very close, then.'

'Why else would we have left the wagons behind?'

'Yeah, but if the King's worried we're—'

'No one's worried. It's just the way things are. We have to reach the river as soon as possible before we get cut off. Once we cross the Somme, we'll be home and dry – it's country the King knows well.'

'Aye, well, I'll try to buck them up,' Matt said, rising.

'Do that. We don't want the daft sods getting themselves panicked.'

'Panicked?' Matt repeated with a sidelong grin. 'We're in a foreign land, without food or supplies, and the biggest army in the whole of Christendom is heading for us, hoping to beat us bloody and break our pates, but, there's *nothing to worry about*.' His smile disappeared, like water soaking into sand. 'I'll do my best, Frip, but I can't perform sodding miracles.'

CHAPTER THIRTY-SEVEN

That afternoon, it all went to pot.

For once, Berenger and the others were not in the lead as the army rumbled, squeaked and thumped its way north and west. Other scouts were sent to spy out ahead, and more men on horseback clattered by, throwing clods of soil in all directions as they passed, carrying messages to the King or from him to his son. Every so often, a white-faced archer or esquire would hurtle back from the front with news. Whether it was of sightings of the French army or not, Berenger could not tell.

But the fighting – he knew when that started.

There were three vintaines of Grandarse's century up ahead of them when it kicked off. At first there was a series of shouts and orders, then the blast of dozens of horns.

'Frip!' Geoff cried.

'Archers, string your bows!' Berenger roared. 'Clip! Fetch arrows: *now*! Donkey, help him!'

Ed the Donkey stared mulishly, but a kick from Archibald almost sent him sprawling. 'You think this is a holiday? You want to argue whether you work for him or not? Get moving and make sure there's an army to fight with!'

Berenger gave him a quick grin, then hared off to see what had happened. There came the pounding of hooves, and a whey-faced youth rode back from the front, reining in late when Berenger held up his hands.

'Hold! What is the alarm?'

'Ambush! Those French cunts are slaughtering us!' There were perhaps four dozen of them, he told Berenger and Geoff, nestled together in the ruins of a little cottage, with some crossbowmen lying further up in a deep ditch at the side of the road. As the first of the English had ridden down the lane towards the village, a sudden shock of arrows had slammed into the front rank. Six men were downed and two horses, and then, as the English began to edge forward, more bolts flew, and three more men were impaled.

'We'll have to get around them,' the rider declared, his voice shaking. 'I'm to fetch help.'

Berenger let him go. The lad was petrified, and would be no help in a fight. Better to let him take his terror with him, lest he infect the rest of the men.

'Come on!' he said, and his vintaine pressed forward in his wake.

There was not much cover here: on their left, a large shaw of mixed trees and bushes, on their right, a pasture spreading out towards a stream. Cattle and some sheep were grazing, warily eyeing the intruders. Occasional bushes and trees stood between them and the houses ahead.

The ambush was set in a hamlet; there was a chapel and five cottages, with the grey line of the roadway passing on between all.

'Where are they?' Geoff muttered as the two crouched low. Matt joined them on Berenger's right, kneeling and peering ahead with narrowed eyes.

'Can *you* see anything?' Berenger asked, his own eyes fixed.

'There's something at that window,' Geoff breathed, pointing to the second house on their left. 'And I think I saw someone in the ditch at the side of the road. But it could have been a flower moving in the wind.'

'Wind, my arse,' Berenger said. There was not a breath of air. Even the dust from the roadway hung in the air behind them to show their path.

'Are they trained, or local militia?' Matt said.

'They have a good position,' Geoff considered.

'That may be because they live here and don't want to give up without a fight,' Berenger said.

'I say, lay down a strong assault with our arrows, and run in on 'em,' Jack said. 'We can do it if we're fast.'

'If they're trained, the first men will be killed,' Berenger said.

'So make sure your friends are in the second rank,' Geoff said grimly. 'I don't fear the bastards.'

Berenger nodded, and then called to the rest of his men.

Behind them was the Welsh contingent, and then two more English vintaines. Roger and his men were there, and he and Berenger agreed a plan. Two vintaines of archers drew up in two formations, like arrow-heads pointing at the village.

'Nock!'

A ripple of movement as the archers brought up their arrows.

'Draw!'

The men bent their backs, their bows creaking under the strain as the clothyard arrows were aimed up into the sky.

'Loose!'

A whirring and whistling, and the arrows rose into the air, and as they went, the archers were already nocking again. This second flight took to the air before the first had plummeted to the ground. A third flight, and even as they soared, Berenger and Geoff and the rest of the vintaine, along with the Welsh, were racing over the road as fast as their legs would bear them.

There was a scream as an English arrow found its mark, and then a figure rose from the side of the road, hesitated, and turned and fled. Three arrows were sent after him, but none found its mark. Another man appeared – only a youth, this; an arrow struck him in the groin and he fell down, squirming horribly, a thin shriek of agony cutting through the whistle and thud of arrows striking the ground.

'To me!' Berenger bellowed, pounding across the road.

All sound faded. He could feel the blood thundering in his veins, the metallic taste of blood in his throat, and he was aware of an all-encompassing desperation to get to the other side before he could be struck down.

Yet there was more than mere desperation. There was a sense of the justness of this. He was a warrior, and this – here, now – was his duty, his life, his love. He wanted to cross the road safely because this was his vocation: to run, to charge . . . and to kill.

The arrows ceased, and suddenly he could hear noises again: the rasp of breath – it was his own – the slap of boots and bare feet, the rattle and chink of mail, shrieks of terror, the solid thwack of bolts striking flesh, screams of pain.

A man sprang from the ground before him, and Berenger swung his sword, wounding his assailant in the throat. He fell, and Berenger leaped over the ditch, making for the houses where they had seen the men at the windows. An English arrow sped past his shoulder and he saw it continue in through an open window, saw the figure inside stumble; then a bolt loosed down at the ground near Berenger's feet, but he scarcely registered it as he ran at full tilt.

Behind him, the Welshmen were hacking at bodies on the ground, although their leader was looking about him for fresh targets. When he saw Berenger, he pointed, but did not direct his men to join the English. Instead, they held back.

Berenger saw and gritted his teeth. He was being left to be caught and slaughtered. From the room inside the house, he heard a man's voice. He sounded terrified, and Berenger slammed his pommel against the window's shutter twice, hard, shouting: *'Surrender!'*

His only answer was a pair of bolts sent flying towards the English. In a sudden rage, he threw himself bodily through the window.

It was a gloomy chamber, but he made out three figures. Two were trying to span their crossbows, while the third handed out bolts from a satchel. The first bowman Berenger caught as he fell in through the window, the point of his sword entering under the fellow's ribcage and opening his gut. He shrieked like a snared rabbit, and fell back, hands moving frantically as he tried to push back the glistening intestines; Berenger tumbled to the floor and rolled, grunting as he clambered back to his feet. The third man was wielding his bolt like a dagger, and he thrust at Berenger's face, but Berenger's sword slashed, and the man's hand fell away, flapping on the ground like an injured bird. A fine spray of blood briefly blinded Berenger. Then the second bowman flung his crossbow at him and raced for the door. Berenger tried to get to him, but the hand-less loader obstructed him. He had to stab the man in the breast to get past, and as he did so, he saw his quarry escape through the open doorway, running for dear life. With brilliant timing, an arrow fell lazily from the clear sky and slammed right into his spine, causing him to drop like a pigeon hit by a slingshot.

Geoff appeared in the doorway, his bow still in his hand, and peered in cautiously.

Berenger had turned to look at the wounded. The hand-less one was only a boy, and the crossbowman not much older. He was struggling with the coils of his belly, all his attention on his opened gut, a boy of perhaps fourteen years, with a thin, long face and blue eyes that streamed tears.

It took just one heavy blow to open his skull and release him from his suffering. Berenger felt exhausted. He walked a short way from the chamber and slumped against the wall, staring out to the north.

When he had launched himself into that room, he had assumed that there were adult men in there, trying to kill him and the others. It was a fair fight. But then to discover that they were so young shamed him. They should not have been fighting him and his men.

'They were boys, Geoff. Not fully grown! And now they're dead. What in Christ's name were they doing, trying to hold up our army? Were they mad?'

As he spoke, Ed ran up through the doorway, his arms full of arrows.

Berenger stared at him. 'So – does your heart good, does it, to see these poor dead French boys, the same age as yourself?'

Ed gazed back at him, and Berenger was surprised to see tears begin to run through the grime of his cheeks. With a sob, the Donkey threw the arrows to the ground and fled from the chamber.

'The little sod's spent so much time telling me how the only good Frenchman is a dead one, and I've had enough of it,' Berenger ranted, forgetting that Ed's view had changed over the past weeks. 'Look at these poor devils. Not one is old enough to wear a beard, in Christ's name! Does the country have no men to fight us? Must France depend upon children?' He was enraged.

'I don't give a clipped penny for them,' Geoff said thinly. 'They killed Matt. He's dead, too.'

Berenger went with Geoff and the others to Matt's body, Ed trailing in their wake.

Matt's face registered only surprise. There was no horror or shock in his eyes, as if he had died instantly as the bolt struck him.

'He was a good fellow,' Geoff said quietly.

'He was a randy old git,' Jack muttered, but he wiped at his eye as though rubbing away some grit.

'He was our randy old git though,' Geoff amended.

'A sound judgement,' Eliot said. Then: 'In the meantime, my friends, there are more men up there.'

'Shit!' Geoff said. 'These bastard French seem to have discovered their courage at last.'

'What did I tell ye? Ye'll all be slaughtered afore long,' Clip waited.

'Shut up, you bastard,' Geoff and Jack said in unison.

'Makes you think about Wisp,' Eliot said slowly. 'I mean, he said it as soon as he saw that body, didn't he? How we'd all get killed. How none of us would go home.'

'That's not what he said,' Berenger snapped. 'He was just alarmed, that was all.'

'It was that cat hanging. He said it was a witch's pet, that's what he said,' Geoff said.

'Aye, and we all heard him say that we were doomed, and the French would find us and destroy us,' Jon Furrier said glumly.

'It's all that woman,' Geoff said. 'We should tell Grandarse about her.'

'Tell him what?' Berenger said. 'That she retaliated when a Welshman tried to rape her? That she was saved when they tried to attack her again? That she was nearly raped by one of our own?'

'Even if she isn't a witch, she's bringing bad luck on the whole army,' Geoff said. 'She should be—'

'*No!*' The Donkey pushed his way to the front. 'That's wrong! Béatrice is gentle and kind. She wouldn't do anything to cause us hardship.'

'Maybe she would, and maybe she wouldn't. But having a witch in our company puts the whole army at risk,' Geoff looked around at the other men standing nearby and said earnestly: 'God will not allow an army to prevail when it keeps such people in the ranks.'

'Leave her alone!' Ed declared wildly.

'Silence, boy,' Geoff said with irritation. 'This is a matter for men.'

'No, it isn't. It's for God, just as He will see the validity of the King's claim to the throne and support him,' Berenger said.

'If she stays in the army, the French will crush us,' Geoff stated. 'We all know how large is the host raised against us. If God wills it, we could fight with His strength and win. Were His support to weaken, His resolve would also falter. Keeping a woman like her with us – that would stop Him wanting to aid us. He would withdraw, and then the French must win. With so many men at their command, we cannot succeed.'

'Well, they haven't done too well so far,' Berenger commented, pulling at his hosen. 'Now cut the ballocks and let's get back to work. Geoff, you take the left, Jack, you're on the right. Eliot, you stay with me. The rest of you, spread out along the line and we'll go and get these bastards. Don't forget to leave a good gap between each of you.'

There was grumbling, especially from Clip, but then the men gradually formed their line and began to stride forward, past the houses and beyond.

Berenger could not help but stare back at the house where he had killed the boys. It would be many long nights before he forgot them. This chevauchée was turning into a nightmare. Only a few weeks ago, the men had been cheerful, enthusiastic. Now he could see in their faces only a weary determination to slog on somehow.

They all felt the same rising despair. It was hard to believe that they would return home triumphant – or return at all.

CHAPTER THIRTY-EIGHT

Berenger asked Geoff and Jack to pick up Matt's body and put it in the cart.

'No! I'll take him!'

Berenger was surprised to see Clip barging the other two out of his way. Tears ran down Clip's face as he stood a moment over Matt, and then he bent and gathered up the body. He carried his comrade to the cart and gently laid him in it, standing a while with his hand resting on Matt's breast.

'I want a priest for him,' he said.

'We'll find him a priest later,' Berenger said.

'I want him seen to – properly, mind.'

Geoff put a hand on his back. 'We will, Clip. We'll make sure he has a good burial.'

Clip nodded, and walked away to sit on a fallen log, his head bowed.

Berenger exchanged a look with Geoff. Neither had thought that Clip was so attached to Matt.

While the injured had their wounds seen to, Sir John de Sully's esquire came riding up.

'Sir John needs your help, Vintener,' he said. 'There's fighting at the next town.'

'We're already in the middle of a fight, Richard,' Berenger said sharply.

'The King's orders are that no one should delay. The whole army is moving slowly because of the vanguard, and now some of the Prince's men are attacking a town even though they've been ordered to leave it. Sir John asks that you join him, so that you can help persuade these fools to leave their plunder, and come away. If the army is halted, the French will overtake us – and that will mean the death of us all!'

Berenger glanced at the others. Geoff shrugged, while Jack stood and shouldered his weapons, saying philosophically, 'Aye, well, we won't get anywhere by sitting on our arses.'

Clip spat into the dirt at his feet with a display of petulance. 'Why *us* again, eh? Why do they keep on sending *us* whenever there's another battle? Haven't we already done enough? Matt's hardly cold, and they want us to go risk our lives again?'

The esquire was about to comment, but Berenger gave him a warning shake of the head.

Clip rose to his feet, muttering all the while, 'Aye, well, we'll all get ourselves slaughtered. You do know that? We'll all be murdered by the bastard French.'

'Not you, Clip,' Berenger said, as he pulled his sword loose and examined the blade. 'You're the one they count on to single-handedly ruin the army's morale.'

'Aye, it's a knack I have.'

They mounted their ponies, and soon were rattling along behind the esquire towards the next town, Vessencourt.

It was obvious that they were too late. Smoke was gathered and balled by the gusting winds, looking like thick clumps of fleece, dirty and grey, before being whisked away. All about, they could smell the charring and scorched grounds, while amidst that were other odours: the tang of sweet, burned meat, the foulness of feathers and fur, a disgusting concoction that assailed the nostrils like a noisome poison.

Across the plain, they could see the devastation as they approached. Sir John stood in the midst of the ruin staring about him with a gleaming fury in his eyes. Berenger had never seen him so angry.

'You see this? All this? They came here at the middle of the day to rob and pillage, as though we have all the time in the world to enjoy taking women! It was hardly a town worth the name, but the fools came here to plunder, and for that they were prepared to risk their lives and our entire enterprise. Damn their souls! God rot them!'

'Where are they now?' Berenger said.

'God in His heaven must know, but I'll be damned if I do!' Sir John shouted, infuriated. He calmed himself with an effort. 'We will have to follow their trail. Richard, do you return to my Lord Warwick and ask that we have more men to curtail this meandering, and then hurry back with them. We shall have to try to find these fools and pull them back to the army. However, Richard, make it clear that the army must continue. Let my Lord the Prince know that another few men must be set to scout ahead, until we are returned.'

'I shall, Sir John.'

'Then ride, man, ride! What are you hanging about for? Be fleet! Master Fripper, I depend upon you and your men. Come!'

The trail was not hard to follow. The men who had burned Vessencourt had left a broad path of devastation in their wake.

A road of mud and dirt over ten yards wide stretched away into the distance before them. They set their ponies' heads to the north and cantered on.

Occasional farmsteads and hamlets were sprinkled over the flat landscape. Most were ablaze, the thatch sending up thick, greenish yellow fumes that caught in a man's throat and made him choke. Worse was the ever present odour of burned pork. It had nothing to do with pigs: this was the smell of roasting human flesh.

'How many men are missing?' Berenger asked Sir John.

'Maybe four centuries. Enough to make all this damned mess. But the fools will be slaughtered if they try to take a town. Especially since they'll be roaring drunk by now.'

There was no need to explain his words. Every few yards as they rode, they passed little jugs or barrels that had been discarded. Clearly the men had stolen all the drink from the houses they had plundered.

It was a league or more further on when they came across the first stragglers.

'Hoi!' Sir John bellowed, and clapped spurs to his rounsey. There ahead were four or five men staggering along under a weight of goods. Berenger kicked his pony into a trot to catch up with him.

'What are you men doing up here?' Sir John bawled as he reined in before the men.

To Berenger they had the appearance of peasants who had been called to muster for the first time. One man he recognised: a tall fellow with a sullen expression who carried a strung bow, while the others were happily drunk and oblivious.

'My Lord?' one asked, hiccuping. A friend of his was giggling beside him, and he slapped away his proffered cask of wine. 'We are following our comrades.'

The man whose cask had been rejected gave a long, loud belch. 'There's good pickings up here. We'll all be rich men.'

'You will be rich and dead,' Sir John declared flatly. 'You are guilty of abandoning the King's host without permission, and engaging yourselves on a wild hunt for plunder on your own account. For that the penalty is death.'

While the other men appeared to sober swiftly, the taller, sullen man spoke. 'Why should we take *your* word for that, Sir Knight? You come here and tell us we're in the wrong but it's what we're here for, isn't it? To ravage the land just as the King has so far. We're doing his job for him. He should be grateful.'

'Your King has ordered you to make all haste to beat the French to the Somme, and you and your companions are putting us all in jeopardy by delaying him. You are giving the French a chance to catch us.'

'Then we can go on to the next bridge,' the man said truculently.

'Like we did on the way to Paris, you mean?' Sir John said his tone mildly.

Berenger remembered the fellow now: Mark Tyler was his name. God, the day he and Roger had sat and discussed their new recruits seemed an age ago. He eyed the man warily.

'Well, Archer, return to the army and be swift about it, and I will forget your insubordination,' Sir John said.

'Go swyve a goat,' Tyler said. He squared up to Sir John's horse. 'I don't know who you are, but why shouldn't we go after the rest of our vintaine?'

'You refuse a knight's order?' Sir John demanded.

Tyler grinned. 'Come with us to Beauvais! There are rich takings there, so we've heard. Good wine, money, furs, gold, everything. Come with us, and we'll all be wealthier than the dreams of a prince!'

Berenger was getting impatient. 'Tyler, do you realise this knight is one of the Prince's own advisers? You idiot! You place your life in peril. Even if you carry on, the town is well-defended and the French army is approaching. Our army may succeed in crossing the Somme if we are swift, but the way things are, I doubt it. Come! There is nothing for us here. Not today.'

Tyler nodded reluctantly. 'Very well.'

'Where are the rest of the men?' Berenger asked.

'Follow the tracks,' Tyler shrugged, at which Sir John nodded and rode away. As Berenger was about to ride off after him, Tyler stepped forward. 'Master, before you go, can you spare one or two men to help us with our baggage? The cart is broken, and we have a great deal to carry. It's mostly provisions, master, not treasure. If you send me two men, I will let them bring half away with them.'

Berenger considered. The men were all hungry, as he was himself. He looked over his shoulder and called, 'Walt and Gil: come here.'

He gave them instructions to help Tyler and his drunken companions, and then to head back to the vintaine, as fast as possible, before dark. The first few yards on his own, Berenger felt deeply uncomfortable, as though a man had painted a target upon his back, and he half-expected a clothyard arrow to bury itself in his spine at any moment.

He was also anxious about what he might find when they caught up with the rest of the renegades. It might not be so easy to cow them.

'Hoi!'

Berenger turned to see Gil waving. 'What?'

'Leave the Donkey with us. We'll have need of someone to help carry the stuff.'

Berenger glanced at Ed. The lad was downcast. His eyes were red-rimmed and glittered as if he had a fever. 'Ed? Do you want to go with them?'

'I'll go where you tell me, sir. I'm only a porter, after all. I have no opinions or feelings. I'm just here to fetch and carry.'

'Then *go*! Obey Gil and Walt. They are responsible for you,' Berenger snapped.

Before he turned back to the trail, he watched the boy shamble off towards the other group of men with a strange presentiment of loss. It was almost as though he was saying farewell to an old comrade rather than a foolish youth who had been continual source of petty annoyance.

'Damn him!' he muttered, and turned to the trail once more.

Only later would he come to regret that decision, when he realised the full horror and danger involved.

CHAPTER THIRTY-NINE

Ed found the going hard. Although he had no shoes, his feet were toughened, and the stones and pebbles caused him little trouble, but the speed that Tyler reckoned was necessary was difficult to cope with. The party hurried on, heading north and west, to avoid Beauvais altogether and so come upon the Somme farther to the west.

Tyler had made up his mind to be friendly, and he chatted and told jokes as they made their way along the rough tracks, soon reducing Gil and Walt to helpless laughter, but Ed remained unamused. There was an underlying cruelty about this man that Ed disliked and distrusted.

True, the same could be said for most of the men in the army. They were trained killers, when all was said and done. Yet the majority – apart from the Welsh men of Erbin's vintaine – had shown him sympathy and kindness, Ed thought.

'You all right, lad?' Gil said now, breaking into his thoughts.

'My feet are sore, my shoulders chafe from these bags and my belly aches from hunger – but I won't die of any of them,' Ed said.

'You have a good sense of humour, boy. It's lucky, we all need it here.'

Yes, it was true that the kindness of men like Gil and Walt and Jack, and poor Will and Matt, was often gruff, yet it was kindly given, and that was the most important thing for Ed. He was beginning to feel, for the first time ever, as though he was a wanted, useful member of the vintaine. Gil hadn't needed to ask for him, but had done so anyway.

Only Berenger didn't appreciate him.

'My thanks for asking for me to come with you,' Ed said.

Gil looked down at him with a twisted smile. 'You didn't want to go with Berenger, did you?'

'He's the bastard son of a Winchester goose,' Ed mimicked.

'Son of a whore, eh? Your language is developing nicely,' Gil chuckled. 'Why do you think that?'

'Because I can say and do nothing that will please him. Anything I do say, he derides or pulls to pieces to make me look foolish. Today, after that fight, he insulted me. I don't deserve that: it's not fair. I don't even report to him any more. I am with the gynour, with Archibald, not with the vintaine, but does he show me any kindness or mercy? No!'

'You know he was once like you?'

'Who, Berenger?'

'Aye. His parents were killed, and he would have died too, if the King hadn't taken pity and seen to him. He saw his mother killed, and his father, so I heard. He doesn't like to have youngsters with him in battle now, and if he must have them, he dislikes those who speak too much of killing. He believes it's better for boys to be spared the sight of death, and also the risk of their own death.'

'What of it? I'm no *boy*!'

'Today he killed three boys. You should try to understand him. It was hard for him. I wouldn't care, I've killed too many – but Fripper is different. He feels each one.'

'You think so?'

'I know so. None of us want to wage war on the young, Ed. If you meet a man with a sword and kill him in a fair fight, that is good. It warms the heart. To learn that you have killed a youngster does not.'

'I came here to slay as many French people as possible. They killed my family, and I wanted revenge – but now we are committing the same atrocities they did against us.'

'Good!' Gil said with approval. He slapped Ed's back so hard, the boy almost fell. 'You're learning. Perhaps you will become a soldier yourself. If you do, make sure you avoid the same mistakes so many others make.' His face grew bleak and he stared into the distance.

'What, killing the young?'

'Aye – and of being found out,' he murmured.

Geoff rode along with a feeling of disquiet. It was good to have something to occupy his mind other than Béatrice. The others were treating him once more as they had before. But still, this area felt dangerous.

The roadway was broad, and every so often they would find that the plain had a little rise, with cleared land for pasture or planting, but for much of the way, the trail they followed took them through woods and stands of trees, perfect for ambushes. It was a relief when at last they came out into the open and saw before them the broad sweep of a fresh road.

'Christ Jesus!' Jack swore under his breath, and Geoff followed the direction of his gaze, seeing a strong, walled town before them. There was already a fight going on. Clear on the air they could hear the din of battle: shouting, screaming, the clash of weapons and the thundering of a siege-weapon against the gates.

'They have moved on faster than I expected,' Sir John said wearily. 'Look at that! It'll be well nigh impossible to extricate them once they feel that they have a modicum of success. Those fools think that they can blunder their way inside without trouble.'

'Then we'd best hurry and call them away,' Berenger said.

Geoff saw his eyes go to him, and he nodded at once. 'Yes. I'm ready.'

'Ride on, then – and Jack, you go too. We'll be along shortly.'

'I will ride with them,' Sir John said.

'I would advise against it,' Berenger said. 'Better that they see it's only men like themselves, more poor warriors, than a rich knight.'

'Fair enough,' Sir John said. 'So, what now? Ride on towards the town?'

'I think so.'

That was the last Geoff heard as he and Jack trotted off. 'Look out for Frenchmen,' he muttered, and Jack nodded.

The land was prodigiously flat here, Geoff noted. Large ripples were the closest things to hills, but were nothing compared with the hills of his native lands.

He missed his home. The thick woods and forests, the swift-flowing streams and brooks, the hills with their pastures for the hill-farmers and shepherds, the strips in the communal fields. He could almost smell the thick loamy soil near his home, the house in the woods not far from the Avon, in which he had fathered his children with his wife.

But he would never see them again. The thought made his throat close up, and he had to wipe at his eyes with a terrible sadness.

They were close to the town now, and Jack rose in his stirrups, shouting and waving his arm. It was enough to distract Geoff from his grim mood, and he began to copy his companion.

The men at the walls turned to glare at the newcomers. They had worked hard, in the short time they had been here. Palisades and a number of scaling ladders had been constructed of timber liberated from the nearby woods. A siege engine had been thrown together, brought from King Edward's siege train, from the look of it. And on all sides men bellowed and fired arrows at the Frenchmen who dared show themselves at the walls. A team worked with a huge ram resting on a wagon, slamming it at the gates with abandon, while stones hurtled towards them from above. Even as Geoff and Jack reached the men, there was a gout of flame as a vat of oil was tipped over them, but luckily only two were superficially burned. The others dropped their holds and ran away a short distance until the worst of the flames were burned through, and then they went back to their charred wagon and ram.

'Who's in charge here?' Geoff demanded of the first man.

He was a heavy-set fellow with a round bearded face and an almost entirely bald head. 'Who wants to know?' he replied.

Geoff jerked a thumb over his shoulder. 'Sir John de Sully, knight banneret, on behalf of Edward of Woodstock.'

'Really? And why would my Lord Edward be so interested in us here then, eh?'

'What is your name?'

'I am Ham of Bristelmestune, master, and I'm the vintener of this group of felons and cut-throats,' he grinned.

'Well, Master Ham, you should know that the King's express orders are that the whole army should be moving because the French army is too close to us already. And if we don't keep moving, they will overtake us.'

'Who cares?' The man snapped his fingers dismissively. 'If they come, we'll fight 'em. You know we can beat the French on any battlefield – we've shown that already. Let 'em come and see what happens when they meet a real army.'

'Yeah, and if they were to appear here – right now – the whole French army surrounding you here, and beating you like a hammer beating a nail against the town's walls, do you really think you'd survive? Are your brains in your tarse that you think you can fight the whole of the French army on ground that suits them, not us?'

As he spoke, Geoff was aware of the man's eyes going behind him, and he thought that the rest of the vintaine with Sir John had come to join them. It was suitable timing, he thought, just as he mentioned the idea of the sudden appearance of the French.

Ham turned and bellowed orders. Then he pulled off his metal cap. 'You could have warned us,' he hissed to Geoff.

Geoff shrugged. 'I relayed the King's orders, that's all. Get a move on.'

'We'll come with all speed. Tell my Lord Edward of Woodstock that we'll extricate ourselves as quickly as we can.'

Geoff nodded, turned his pony – then sat gaping.

The whole of the English army had appeared behind him, and now straggled in a ragged column over the plain.

Ed felt his legs beginning to falter. They had already covered so many miles in the last few days since leaving Paris, and now, with the load he was carrying, and the weariness of the long distance, he felt as though he must fall with every stumble.

It was a relief when Tyler gave a shout and the little party stopped. There ahead were more men – a second party of English soldiers who had been scouring the land for provisions.

'How much further?' Ed asked as he allowed his load to tumble to the ground.

'Until we find the army? I don't know,' Gil admitted, but before he could say more, Tyler called out.

'There is a monastery two miles north of us. It has a rich tithe barn, with stores from the area, and there are cattle and pigs for the taking. What do you say?'

'We were told to return to the army,' Ed said.

'Yes,' Gil said. 'But if we find more food and drink, that won't matter.'

'Is that all that is in his mind?' Ed asked.

'It's a monastery,' Gil said. 'Any man's mind will turn to gold and silver: but there could be food too.' ·

'I don't like this,' Ed confessed. 'God will not reward us if we attack His churches.'

'He won't object to us taking a little food and drink from these priests and monks,' Gil said reassuringly. 'He will know we need to eat to be able to do His work, and it's only natural that we should seek food from any source.'

Ed was not convinced. So now another monastery was to be sacked and looted.

To his mind, the English were now the criminals. And he was one of them.

Berenger was glad to see Geoff and Jack return. They rode along with the rest of the army, for once not scouting for the enemy at the front, but in the midst of the main groups of fighting men.

'There are benefits to being in the lead, you see,' Sir John chuckled. The dust from thousands of boots and hooves was rising all around them in a cloud, clawing their way up Berenger's nostrils and irritating his eyes with tiny particles of grit.

'Damn this dust!' Sir John muttered under his breath. How are your men?'

Berenger shot him a look. 'They are well enough. The marching is getting to them, and it's hard to see long-standing comrades die. We've lost several now.'

'I know of Will and . . . that man James. Who else?'

'Matt died today. And of the newer recruits we collected in the last muster, three or four are dead. Two others are badly injured. One will come back, the other won't.'

'So, of twenty, you've lost five or six?'

'We never were twenty. When we left Portsmouth we were four under our number. Now, we're half-strength.'

'The boy?'

'Yes. But he's gone, too.' Berenger met Sir John's stare. 'He had some trouble with the Welshmen, as I told you. In Caen, after the sack, they found him and tried to hang him. Apparently they mistreated him before he met us, before we sailed, and they held a grudge, or wanted to silence him.'

'Oh, yes. That was why you attacked them, I recall.'

'I was in a black rage that they should try to murder one of my men. I would do it again.'

'You would be a poor leader of men, were you not to take their health and well-being in hand. And avenge them in death.'

'I do my best for them,' Berenger said.

Sir John nodded. 'It is no more than I would expect.' His eyes suddenly widened. 'What is that?'

Ahead, and a little to the north, was another thick column of smoke. The wind caught at it and tugged it this way and that, but the pall was so thick and oily that it still remained hanging over the whole area.

Sir John studied it for some while, and then he beckoned his esquire. 'Richard, go and ask the Prince if we may ride to investigate that. It is far from our line of march. None of our men should be there. Suggest that we and two vintaines should go and reconnoitre.'

'Sir.'

The esquire wheeled his horse and cantered back to where Edward of Woodstock rode with the Earl of Warwick. Soon he was back.

'Sir John, the Prince thanks you for your observation. He says he would be grateful if we could go and investigate.'

'Good! Berenger, you come with me, and bring your men. We'll take Roger and his vintaine too,' Sir John said. He glanced at his esquire. 'We can ride and investigate, and if there is nothing, at least we shall have escaped this damned dust for a while,' he added.

They took their horses across the path of a swearing, furious wagon-master, and thence up a gentle rise to the top of a broad hillock. In the distance they could plainly see a series of large buildings enclosed by low walls.

'It's a monastery,' Richard said. 'If those are our men, they will pay a heavy price for this. The King wants no insults to God this late in the campaign.'

'God?' Sir John snorted. 'More to the point, the King wants as few English archers wasted in individual mercenary engagements as possible. He needs every single man. And he does *not* wish to be held up here, with the French breathing down our necks. If those are Englishmen, they will live to regret their actions for the rest of their lives. Although that may not prove to be a very long time.'

CHAPTER FORTY

Later, sitting muzzily in the dark with a goblet of wine, Berenger would remember every moment of that afternoon.

Even as he cantered under the monastery's gatehouse, Berenger had a premonition of disaster. Just inside, three bodies were sprawled in the dirt. Avoiding them, the vintaine rode in past the outbuildings and towards the main convent.

All about the grass, they saw, were more bodies – lay-brothers who had tried to defend their church and cloister, but had failed. Some had been pierced by arrows, while others had been beaten to death or stabbed. Fighting and killing those who were all but incapable of defending themselves was the action of outlaws, Berenger thought in disgust, not a disciplined army.

At a doorway, a porter lay draped over the steps. Berenger dismounted, and with Sir John and Geoff, he marched inside.

From the abbot's chamber upstairs there came the sound of ribald celebration. Sir John drew his sword and, with a quick look at the men behind him, took the stairs in a rush.

At the top there was an already open door, and inside they found a party of thirty men.

All were drunk. A pair were dancing on the abbot's table; beneath it lay the body of a man. A piper played a tune, beating time with his tambour, while others capered and sang, all brandishing goblets and cups which they refilled from the cask set on the sideboard. The cushions and hallings that had been hanging on the walls to keep the room warm, were thrown to the floor, and a man was pissing on them as Sir John entered. He turned, mouth agape, at the intrusion, but before he could make a comment, Sir John's gauntleted fist smashed his lips against his teeth, and he crashed into the cupboard. Pewter and plate rattled and fell to the ground in a discordant cacophony, as though a box of hand-bells had been thrown on to a granite slab.

The piping, drumming and singing tapered off, and all the men in the room turned to stare at Sir John. He lifted his sword and pointed it at the men on the table. 'Get down!'

'What's this? Come to get your own share, my Lord Knight?' a sarcastic voice called. It was Tyler.

'All in this room are guilty of looting and disobeying the King's command,' Sir John announced. 'You will leave this chamber at once.'

'This is our victory, Sir Knight,' Tyler said in his sneering tone. 'You want us out, you'll have to pay us to go!'

There were some muttered assents to this, and heads were set nodding.

Sir John called to Berenger's men, and Jack and Geoff entered. Without needing to ask, they grabbed the nearest man and flung him bodily down the staircase. After that example, the men ignored Tyler's exhortations and followed down the stairs themselves. None was in a fit state to argue their cause.

Amongst the men Sir John saw three he recognised, and he glanced at Berenger, whose face was filled with misery. Shaking his head, the vintener walked outside, waiting until Gil appeared.

'What were *you* doing here, Gil?'

Gil's faded blue eyes were almost grey, and although he was sober, he looked washed-out and anxious. 'We helped them, just as you said.'

'You knew your orders, didn't you? You knew no one was to attack a town or manor, but to keep moving, to prevent the French from catching up with us. What did you think would happen?'

The men were marched from the abbey's grounds. Geoff and Jack were despatched by Berenger to see if anyone had survived the assault, but even Geoff looked shocked at the sights in the cloister.

'Two men in there, they'd been tied to a wall and crucified. They were tortured first. Frip,' he said in a quiet voice. 'I've never seen things like that before. They didn't even choose the sort of men who would know where any treasure would be stored, but just grabbed anyone: servants or lay-brothers, from the look of them.'

Berenger had the captives herded back towards the army. When they arrived, the marching troops were commanded to halt, and a passageway was opened for the renegades. Riding slowly down it, Berenger saw the Prince approaching beside his father from the far end of the corridor. The King, a tall, handsome man in his middle years, was known for a sense of humour. But today there was no smile on his face. Today, he was bitterly angry.

He held up his hand to halt his escort.

'Is it true, what my son has told me?'

Sir John allowed his rounsey to side-step to expose the men with Tyler behind him. Berenger watched as the King allowed his gaze to fall upon each of the bound men in turn. 'Where were they?'

Sir John took a breath and cleared his throat reluctantly. 'At the monastery over there, Your Magesty. All inside were slain. Some tried to defend their convent, but they were cut down. I think no monks or lay-brothers survived.'

'And for what?' the King demanded in a low, furious voice.

'We sought to wage war with fear, just as you told us,' Tyler said boldly. 'You brought us all here to fight a war of *dampnum*. You told us to attack towns and cities, farms and villages. We continued what you told us to do.'

'I gave orders that the whole army was to ignore tempting targets today, and should ride with determination to the Somme. That was the sole purpose of our day, to make it to the river before the French get there. It will be our purpose tomorrow too. We must prevent ourselves from being trapped here. But you decided to slow us, to entertain your own base greed for profit. By your treachery, you may have cost us more than treasure!'

'Sire, we did what you wanted us to do all the way here! How were we to know that this one day you would choose to alter your plans?'

'Silence! I will not debate with you about this act of callous treachery! You have betrayed my trust: Sir John, have them form a line.'

Sir John nodded and motioned to his esquire. 'Do as your King bids.'

The men were forced from their horses, and pushed and shoved into a line. Men armed with bills kept them in their places.

King Edward motioned, and the men at his side rode forward a few paces. On the King's left was the Earl of Warwick, and he now pointed with his baton to more foot-soldiers. They marched up, bills at the ready.

'These men have broken my command,' the King declared, his voice singing out in the silence. 'They knowingly rode out on adventure for their own benefit. Their greed has endangered our army, for their arrogance caused us delay, and our enemy is hard on our heels. For this there has to be a punishment that fits the severity of their offences. The first man will step to the left, the second to the right, the third to the left, and so on through the men in the line. Those on the right shall be reduced to the rank of the foot-archers and their money shall be stopped at that level. They will have to prove their loyalty afresh.'

He paused while the men were prodded and beaten into their new lines, and then the foot-soldiers marched down between the two lines and separated them.

The King stared at the second line.

'These other men shall be executed now.'

Ed listened to the King's words with breathless disbelief.

When the men had all been marched back to the army, he had thought that there would be a court, an opportunity to explain – and yet here he was, with the sentence of death on him!

He looked about him frantically as he realised the full awfulness of his situation. When they were forced into a line, he had shuffled between Gil and Walt. There, with their two solid forms before and behind, he had felt safe. It was like standing between the walls of an fortress. He was out of sight – and that meant he was out of mind.

And then he heard the King's judgement, and suddenly his confidence was stripped away as he realised his danger. Men came marching down the line, pulling a man to the left, then to the right, and as they came closer and closer, Ed saw that Gil, in front of him, and Walt behind, would both be pulled out to one side, leaving him on the other.

He wanted to ask to be allowed to stay with his friends, but the man tugged him away, and he found himself on one side of a polearm held across a guard's chest, while beyond he could see Gil and Walt. The polearm was one of many forming an impenetrable fence, and the look in the guard's face told Ed that any pleading would be useless.

And then he heard the King's pronouncement.

Time slowed to a heartbeat's drum-pace. He found his gaze moving helplessly from side to side, trying to seek an escape, already knowing that there was none. A horn blast sounded clear on the air, and he knew that shortly he would be marched away.

A shiver convulsed his frame. Tears wanted to spring, but the full shock of his situation seemed to prevent them. He was soon to be executed, and he couldn't even plead his innocence. God stood by, waiting for his supplication, but he could not move his lips.

While they had been gathering the men from the abbey, the King had sent a team of engineers to construct a large gallows-tree.

Three tree-trunks had been cut and conveyed to the army's flank. Now they were embedded vertically in the French earth in a triangular formation. From the top of each trunk, a strong plank ran to the next one. Thus, by linking the three tree-trunks, a triangle of planks stood some fifteen feet from the ground.

Now men threw coils of rope up and over the planks, seven to each plank, and a pair of hardy men looped and knotted these until each rope had a noose of sorts dangling.

No need for formality here. The King had issued his commands, and for men held under martial law, there was no higher authority. The first of the men in Ed's line was pulled forward. A thong was quickly lashed about his hands behind his back, a noose placed over his throat, and then to the command of a vintener, three men hauled hard on the other end of the rope, and the man was slowly lifted into the air, his face reddening, eyes bulging, legs kicking and thrashing in the manner so familiar to those who had witnessed men dancing the Tyburn Jig before.

Berenger watched the second man. He had already soiled himself, and when he was hoisted aloft, his kicking spread ordure over the observers. Some laughed to see their comrades bespattered, and there were ribald comments as the third went up. This one had managed to release his hands, and now he clung to the rope at his throat, desperately clawing at the cord. Berenger had seen men fight the rope before. Inevitably their attempts failed, but not before they had raked the flesh at the rope into a bloody mess where fingernails had scraped away the skin of their necks.

It was a foul way to die, he told himself. When he looked along the line and saw Ed, a sense of melancholy settled on his spirit. Gil was in the first line of men, standing and watching the frail little form of their Donkey as the King's men pushed and shoved Ed and the others towards the gallows.

Ed found himself pushed forwards to his doom. To his side, the guilty men from the abbey who had been spared were watching. Some looked away; one had his hands over his eyes – but many just stared without compassion. Tyler himself was there, Ed saw, with a look of indifference on his face. There was no sympathy for the men who had followed him so willingly to the abbey and who now dangled, moving gently as the jerking of their legs lessened and gradually stilled.

Near him was Gil, who stared back at Ed despairingly.

Eleven were up now, and the twelfth was being hoisted up. The man in front of Ed would be next. All of a sudden, the man whirled around, punched the nearest guard and fled, weaving and ducking to evade his pursuers. His run was ended suddenly as a bill swung and caught his leg. With a shrill squeal, much like an injured rabbit's, the man was felled. He tried to rise, but he had broken a leg, and now his screams of agony rose over all the other sounds. The guards moved in to grab him . . .

. . . And Ed felt a hand at his shoulder.

'Boy! Donkey! Swyve your mother, boy! *Move!*'

He heard the urgently hissed command and allowed himself to be pulled back, and to his confusion, was tugged away from the line and concealed behind the guards, while Gil took his place in the line.

'But . . . what . . .?' he managed.

Gil gave him a twisted smile. 'You remember what I said to you, Donkey? You be a good soldier, if you make it that far. Don't do as the rest of us have. *Understand?*'

The limping man was pulled bodily up to the ropes, his left leg dragging in the dirt, his face full of terror, staring up at the ropes and hanging bodies. A noose was placed over his head, and soon his shrieking was cut off with a hideous gurgling as he tried to breathe. When his legs jerked, his shattered left leg moved irrationally, like a puppet's, bending forward and sideways as well as back.

Ed witnessed it all, and now, as he saw men take Gil's arms and pull him, unresisting, to the next noose he heard a burst of laughter. When he turned and stared, traumatised, he saw the King's household sitting mounted on their great beasts, drinking wine from richly chased mazers. Only the King himself appeared to be watching his soldiers as they hanged, his eyes dark and bleak below his thick brows.

When he turned his attention back to Gil, Ed saw that his companion was already in the air, his face growing purple as he span gently on the wind. When he revolved, his eyes sought out Ed's, communicating an especial urgency.

Ed went forward to him, and as the body turned, he jumped up and grabbed Gil's legs, using his own weight to try to snap his neck, or at least hasten his end. His eyes screwed tight shut, Ed clung there, as his tears fell.

It was the only means he had of repaying the debt.

CHAPTER FORTY-ONE

18 August

Ed slept fitfully and only woke fully when most of the camp had already risen. He had passed the night beneath the wagon of the gynour, and felt worn out. His eyes were sore from weeping, and he had a feeling of guilt that would not pass. Every time he closed his eyes during the night, he saw Gil's body as it slowly revolved, dangling above him.

He sat up, rubbing his eyes. When he woke in the night, Béatrice had been beside him, but she was gone now. He rolled up the thick sheepskin that had softened the ground, and slid himself into the cold, dark, pre-dawn light.

'Oh, so you're awake then?' Archibald demanded. The gynour was sitting near a fire at a safe distance from the wagon, his eyes twinkling in the light. For an instant, when a flame rose, his eyes glowed red, and Ed felt a superstitious dread at the sight. He almost recoiled.

'God's blood!' he gasped.

MICHAEL JECKS

'Calm down, boy. I'm not the Devil! And you should not
take the Lord's name in vain.'

'I don't think He's going to care what happens to me now',
Ed said miserably. The memories of the previous day came
flooding back. The destruction and killing – and Gil dying to
save Ed's life. 'He must hate me.'

'You think the Lord would desert you when you need His
help most? He will care, if you behave. But, not if you behave
as you did yesterday though.'

Ed scowled as the old man eyed him seriously. 'I wasn't
there to loot and kill,' he explained. 'It was just difficult to get
away when all those men started. I didn't *want* to be there.'

'That, boy, is the excuse of the felon through the years. "It
wasn't me, I didn't want to do it, they *made* me." If that is the
best you can say, perhaps you should keep your excuses to
yourself.'

It was true – and Ed was unpleasantly aware of his guilt. The
double guilt of having joined in at the destruction of the abbey
and then, having been convicted, allowing another man to take
his place at the gallows.

Gil: why had he done that? Pulled Ed from the queue of
death, and put himself forward instead? It made no sense. As
far as Ed was aware, Gil had never shown him too much in the
way of kindness. It was incomprehensible.

'What do we do today?' he asked, keen to change the
subject.

'What do we do?' Archibald stared at him with a smile.
'Why, boy, we ride, or walk, to where the King tells us. Our life
is very simple, after all. We march when we are told, and at
some time in the near future, we shall stop. And then we shall
fight.'

*   *   *

328

They were up and moving before the dawn, to Berenger's relief. The men of the vintaine were sullen, and he could sense a simmering resentment.

'What's the matter with the whoresons today, Fripper?' Grandarse asked as he jogged along uncomfortably on his pony. 'From the expressions on their faces anyone would think they'd been told all the wine was drunk.'

'It's something to do with the death of Gil yesterday.'

'Tell them he was a fool and shouldn't have gone plundering on his own account, then,' Grandarse said unsympathetically and rode on.

But it wasn't only that, Berenger knew. As he rode, he caught little glances from the men, meaningful looks at the wagons behind them, and muttering.

Geoff and Jack were a short distance in front, and he saw them talking. However, the pair were very quiet in their speech, and when Geoff noticed Berenger watching them, he hissed something, and spurred his little beast away.

Berenger kicked his pony to a shambling trot, and soon caught up with Jack. 'Come on, tell me what's going on, he said.'

'It's nothing, Frip. Just talk.'

'Good. If it's nothing, you won't mind telling me.'

Jack had known Berenger for many years now, and was not afraid to say, 'You think I'm a child to be forced to speak?'

'I think you're man enough to understand that your vintener needs to know if there's something boiling in the minds of the men.'

Jack lifted an eyebrow at that. 'This isn't to do with you, Frip.'

'It's to do with my vintaine. That means it *is* to do with me,' Berenger snapped.

'Aye, well,' Jack said easily.

The two rode along for a while in silence, and then Jack gave a sigh of submission. 'Look, as usual, it's the woman. Geoff is still convinced that since she appeared, we've had a run of bad luck. And we can all see that for ourselves, can't we? When we first arrived here, we enjoyed success no matter where we went, but soon after we took her in, things went downhill. The long march to Paris, the wait down there, hoping to meet the French King in battle, and then the return all the way up here. Ever since she appeared, we've been harried by the French. And look at us now! Riding *away* from them at the double. I don't get it.'

'Our King knows his work,' Berenger said sternly. 'He is picking the best time and place. What, would you prefer he sat back and waited for the French to dictate to us? Or that we charged them when they had a good defensive position? Don't be moon-struck!'

'It's not moon-struck to notice that since that woman turned up, we've been afflicted – and now Matt and Gil are dead too. Explain that away, if you can, Frip. The men don't like it, and they don't like her.'

'But what can they do about it?'

'If someone were to denounce her as a witch, perhaps our problems would fade away,' Jack said.

Berenger gave a gasp of disgust. 'So you'd see the girl taken and burned at the stake just to satisfy the—'

'*No*. Not to satisfy the baser wishes of the mob,' Jack interrupted. 'If it meant that the vintaine and the army grew more easy, I'd kill her myself, Frip, and so should you.'

He was deadly serious. His dark eyes held Berenger's for a moment, and then he looked away, studying the land ahead of them.

'I don't like the thought of killing a woman any more than the next man, course I don't, but I've had to do it in the past – when told to, when the silly bitches have tried to attack us. It was self-defence – kill or be killed. *And this is no different.* She's a threat to us, to the army. Frip, you need to get a grip. You seem to be unworried by her. Well, I tell you now: she worries the rest of us.'

Berenger heard him out then said, 'I'd think it was more to do with Geoff than her. Béatrice seems a bit strange, certainly, but I'd wager that she is no threat to the army, nor to the vintaine. If I thought she was dangerous, like you say, I'd kill her myself.'

It was true. He could not risk the coherence of his vintaine to protect some French wench just because she had a pretty smile.

He allowed his pony to fall behind, aware now of a gnawing doubt.

What if the men were right?

'Fripper, there are reports that some damned Frenchmen are trying to delay us,' Sir John said. 'Take your lads up there, to the woods, and have a good look around, eh? The others aren't so experienced in looking for trouble as your fellows.'

It had sounded so innocuous when Sir John put it like that: 'Some damned Frenchmen' – a handful of men somewhere up ahead. Berenger remembered those words later, as he stood amid the shambles of their fight.

He had been pleased that the vintaine would be occupied and prevented from brooding. It was also good to have them away from the Prince and his men. Berenger was nervous around the King's son. He always felt that an ill-considered comment could result in a hanging, and while he was comfortable with holding his own counsel in the presence of barons and lords, he knew that some of his men were less than guarded in their speech. Clip, for instance, never cared who heard his moaning and whining, and Jack positively revelled in insulting nobles. He had a knack for finding those who were too dim to realise he was making fools of them, but one day, no doubt, he would trip up – and then Berenger and the vintaine would be down another man.

Today in particular, Geoff was in a rebellious mood and Berenger knew that he would have to persuade Geoff to hold his tongue or risk disorder.

At least being at the front of the army would keep the men out of sight and sound of the nobles.

He led the way through the press. It wasn't easy. The army here was restricted by woods on one side, and the archers on their horses were singing and laughing, oblivious to Berenger's vintaine. The noise of raucous men-at-arms shouting over the rattles and rumbles of the heavy wagons, the cookpots and chests banging and crashing, the light clinking of mail and chains of harnesses, the squeaks and groans of leatherwork – all added to the colossal din of an army on the move.

In the end, Berenger chose the simple expedient of blowing a good blast on his horn, and gesturing wildly when surprised faces were turned to him.

It took a while, but at last he was alongside Geoff.

'I want you to take the left when we get to the front,' he said.

'All right, Frip.' His tone was flat; undemonstrative.

Berenger sighed. 'Look, Geoff, I know what you think of her, and I can understand it. I felt like that myself, eh?'

'You were right. Everyone who has anything to do with her dies, Frip. Before long, I'll die too, and then you'll *have* to do something about her – before she kills you too. Even our leech won't mend you then.'

'When I was unwell, she nursed me,' Berenger pointed out. 'I'll not see her killed because of superstition.'

'There was a time when you'd have taken my word and not called it superstition,' Geoff said.

'There was a time when you'd have been more careful about how you labelled people,' Berenger said grimly.

'Perhaps.'

'So you won't shut up about her?'

'No. The rest of the vintaine agrees with me. When we stop tonight, we'll denounce her to Grandarse. We won't see the rest of the army's march endangered by her. She is either in league with the Devil or she's His unwitting helper. Either way, she's lethal.'

'You can't really believe that!'

Geoff turned very deliberately and studied his face. 'What is it, Frip? Are you after her for yourself? I wouldn't touch her, not with your tarse, if that's what you're worried about. You can have her, if you really want her.'

'I *don't* want her.'

'I know what it's like to want a woman, after all.'

'You have a woman at home. You have no need of a wench like Béatrice,' Berenger said, baffled.

'I did.'

'You did? What does that mean?' Berenger suddenly realised. 'What – do you mean she's dead? You never said anything.'

Geoff took a deep breath. 'Frip . . .' he began, but then there was a shout from in front, and their eyes moved to the source.

From the woods to their left, a mass of French foot-soldiers had suddenly burst out. A flurry of bolts and arrows whirred and hissed through the air, and the men in the van were tumbled to the ground. The air was immediately full of the screams of those shocked by the sudden violent assault, and the harsh battle-cries of their attackers.

'Shit on a stick!' Geoff cried.

'Wait! Geoff, with me!' Berenger said.

As the men bunched together, a path opened to their left, and Berenger shouted at the rest of the vintaine until all had acknowledged him, and then led the way through the gap. It took only a short time to canter clumsily through the low undergrowth. They were beyond the French assault here, and Berenger lifted his hand. Throwing himself from the saddle, he immediately bent his bow. He had only a few arrows, and he must make his mark.

While the others dismounted and strung their weapons, he pulled out an arrow, nocking it and eyeing the French ambush. Men still poured from the woods, but there were not so many as he had thought. This was not the army he had feared, but a small party determined to slow the English advance. Or was it a retreat? he wondered. He glanced from side to side, then found a target – a burly man armed with a heavy axe. He drew his bow and aimed. Already the men were ranged on either side of him, most with their bows bent.

'Ready?' he called, and there was a grunt from his vintaine as all concentrated on their targets.

'*Loose!*' he roared, and their arrows sped forward.

CHAPTER FORTY-TWO

They were so close that the arrows flew for only a moment. Then, like a man clapping his hands, they struck the leather jerkins of the Frenchmen. Some were hurled back by the impact; others reeled, their hands going to their flanks, while more stared dumbly. The axeman darted forward a moment before Berenger released his missile, and his arrow took another man in the head. The arrow passed almost entirely through his skull, and the fellow dropped like a rabbit hit by a slingshot's bullet. And then the axeman saw Berenger and the others.

Berenger drew a second arrow, but as he nocked it, he realised that the axeman had drawn the attention of French crossbowmen to his vintaine. Bolts were being aimed even as he drew, and he had to pause, shouting, ''Ware archers in the woods! Crossbowmen in the trees!' before seeing a Genoese man with a heavy crossbow lifting it to his cheek. Berenger quickly adjusted for the range and loosed, and had the satisfaction of seeing him collapse.

There was the din of battle all about them: shouts and screams, horses whinnying in fear. More than one had been hit by the bolts that missed the vintaine. Men were ducking as the steel-tipped nightmares whisked past, hissing like geese in angry flight.

And then he saw the man with the axe again. He was running straight at him, the axe gripped high, screaming shrilly like an enraged boar, all thought of personal danger cast aside in his maddened desire to kill the Englishman.

Berenger aimed another arrow at the man, but as it flew, the fellow took a springing leap to the side to avoid a large rock in his path. The arrow passed through his flank, but he sped on, hardly noticing its passage. His black eyes were fixed on Berenger with a terrible purpose, his teeth bared like a man insane with rage.

Then he was on Berenger, his axe swooping down. Berenger only just had time to lift his bow to defend himself. With an explosion like a thunderclap, the bow snapped in two, and the broken spring threw Berenger's arms wide. In an instant, the axe was back and hurtling towards his bared breast, and Berenger's only defence this time was to throw himself backwards, away from that wicked blade. He stumbled on a tussock of grass and landed on his back, winded, trying to roll away as the axe was raised again.

And then a lance speared the axe-man perfectly in the centre of his breast, and he was driven back as Sir John's massive charger continued on. His body was deposited on the ground, jerking in its death-throes and a thick gout of blood came from his mouth as a second horse trampled him on its way to the ambush.

The battle for now was over for Berenger, who let his head sink back to the grasses and closed his eyes, so exhausted for the moment that he might as well have been dead. Before him, he could hear the sudden screams and cries as a mass of cavalry joined together to charge into the French flank, and then there were only cheers as the English celebrated their victory, strolling amongst the fallen Frenchmen and ensuring they were all dead before looting them.

Berenger could have kept his eyes shut and slept for a week, he thought. And then there was a whining voice near to his ear. 'Aye, well, the old bastard's survived, then.'

'Me, you mean?'

'Who else, Frip?' Jack rumbled, but there was an odd note in his voice.

Berenger opened his eyes to find Jack and Clip at his side, while Eliot and Jon went systematically from one Frenchman to another, gathering up their purses and bringing them back to the vintaine. Walt and Luke stood a little way away, bows ready with arrows nocked, in case more men should appear from within the woods.

It was then that he caught sight of Geoff. He was sitting with his back to a tree, a bolt in his upper left breast. He gave a twisted grin as Berenger caught his eye, before leaning his head back against the tree, his face contorted with pain.

Geoff regained consciousness with a scream. There was a red-hot sensation in his left shoulder and breast; as soon as he moved, pain shot through his entire left side, making the breath shudder in his throat. It felt as though someone had thrust a heated brand thrust into his flesh and was twisting it.

'Keep still, you dog's turd,' he heard a man hiss, and he looked around to see Jack at his side, gripping his arms and holding him in place. Berenger was at his feet, sitting on his ankles, and above him was a figure with a cloth.

'Keep her away from me!' he panted, but then saw her reach down to his face. He jerked his head away, and wept as the movement made his injury complain again. 'Keep her away, damn your soul, Jack Fletcher, or I'll kill you!'

'Shut up, fool,' Berenger called. 'She has already nursed you all the way here, when we thought you would die. You would indeed be dead, were it not for her.'

'I don't want her help,' Geoff declared, but they paid no heed to his complaints. 'She's a witch. She has to be brought before the priests! She should be burned!'

Jack gripped his arms more tightly, until his fingers were as painful as vices slowly squeezing. 'Shut up, Geoff. Didn't you hear him? It's Béatrice who's kept you alive.'

Looking about, Geoff saw that it was full night, and the flames from a nearby fire licked Berenger's face with an orange-red tint and made him look demonic. The same lurid light cast a glow over Béatrice's features, but as he stared at her, he saw the lines of pain and worry at her brow. She looked less evil than Berenger, he thought to himself, and then he wondered how he must look himself. In the light of the fire, he knew he must look just like Berenger, and his life justified it: he *was* evil.

She washed his wound, then smeared some liquid over it, before placing a thick lump of cloth over it. Geoff had to grit his teeth as she pressed.

'It's not as bad as it could have been,' Berenger said while Béatrice mopped the sweat from Geoff's brow. 'The leech managed to pull the bolt from your shoulder, but it snapped, and splinters were left behind. It was Béatrice who worked them out this morning.'

'Where are we?' Geoff tried to look round, but the movement made him clench his jaws and groan in agony.

'Not far from where you got this,' Berenger said tiredly. 'The bastards managed to harry us just enough. We were held up for a while, making sure that the woods were safe.'

Berenger saw that Béatrice was finished with her ministrations. She was standing nearby, wiping the hair from her face with the back of her hand, then glancing about her. There were four other men with serious injuries, and at the moan and sob from one of them, she hurried away.

'There were no more attacks, no,' Berenger said. He relinquished his hold on Geoff's legs, and rolled over to relax on the grass nearby. 'But that doesn't matter. It means we've been held up again. Tomorrow, we will have to make better progress.'

Geoff nodded, but his eyes were on Béatrice. 'You let her look after me? She could have—'

'Of all those injured, only the men she looked after are still alive,' Berenger rasped. 'Jack is telling everyone. The vintaine won't support any move against her. If you wish to die, I will keep her away, but make sure you die quietly. There are four other injured men over there, and she is saving their lives while you rebuff her aid!'

19 August

The next day, Geoff felt as though he was suffering the torments of the damned.

He had been loaded into the archers' cart early in the morning, and there he was forced to wobble from side to side as the army made its lumbering way towards the Somme.

His shoulder was immensely painful, and every so often when there was a halt, Béatrice would appear, wiping at his forehead. The old leech from St-Lô came with her a couple of times, and muttered to himself about 'English children' as he washed the wound and smeared cooling egg-white over it. 'If you will fight with filthy peasants, what more can you expect?' he demanded at one point, before shrugging to himself. 'And you are no cleaner yourself, that is the problem,' he added.

'Why are you here?' Geoff demanded of Béatrice when the army had halted to rest the mounts and take some much-needed sustenance. She had come to tend to him. 'You know I am no friend of yours.'

'You are ill. And you remind me of a man,' she said.

'Who?'

'My father.'

'Where is he?'

She looked away. 'He is dead. They cut him into tiny pieces, and then cast them into a pit at Montfaucon. For a comment made in jest.'

'You saw this?'

'I was not permitted,' she said, leaning down and wiping the beads of sweat from his brow. 'My father sent me away. He hoped that Normandy would be safe for us.'

'And then we landed.'

'The people of Barfleur did not trust me. Neighbours heard that my father was the victim of the King's injustice, so they came and accused me. The daughter of a traitor must herself be a traitor, they said. That was why my uncle sent me away, to a little village where he knew an old widow-woman, Hélène. She took me in, and for a while everything went well. But Hélène grew ill. She died, unshriven, poor lady, because when the priest arrived, he wanted me to whore for him before he would hear her confession. He said he would tell all the villagers that I was a witch if I did not let him . . .' She stopped and wiped her eyes. Sniffing, she returned to her work, wringing out the cloth in cool water and reapplying it to Geoff's brow. 'He refused to take my answer. He tried to force me – and then I stabbed him.'

Geoff watched her closely. 'We found that cottage. We found him.'

'He deserved to die. Some knights took Hélène's body to the church for me, and then I left. The next day you and your army arrived and I felt sure that you would try to do to me what the priest had wished to do, so I fled. And I continued to run until I reached St-Lô, and there you found me.'

'What of the cat?'

'My cat?'

'Someone hanged a black cat and fired the place.'

'I burned it down because I didn't want anyone to benefit from it,' Béatrice said. 'I am sorry about the cat though. He didn't deserve to die.'

'We thought he was your link to the Devil,' Geoff said.

'My link to the Devil?' she repeated, and amusement gleamed in her eyes for a moment or two. In that time, he saw not a fearsome witch, but a pretty young girl about to laugh for pure joy. But then her expression hardened again.

'I am sorry about the chapel,' he said.

'I don't care. My life is already over.'

He gave a dry chuckle. 'As is mine. I have no family now. All is lost.'

'You had a wife?'

'Yes. She is dead,' he said, remembering how her body had caved in when his knife entered her throat. The way she stared up at him as her eyes faded. All because of the ale; all because he was infatuated with a tart from a tavern. He had killed his wife while he was enraged, and the next morning he did not even remember until he found her body. And then the bodies of his sons. He had killed his entire family in his drunken rage and frustration. Perhaps he had reasoned with the logic of a drunk-ard that, if his family were all gone, he could take Edith for his own and could start a fresh life with her. He shuddered as a vision of Sarra and the boys returned to his mind, their faces blanched, lips blue, eyes dead and flat – and instantly felt Béatrice's cool hand on his brow.

'I'm all right,' he gasped. 'Just remembering things.' Tears stood in his eyes.

'Why did you attack me?' she asked.

'I . . . I was desperate. Lonely. And then I saw you, and the sight inflamed me. I was mad, I think.'

There were calls and horns blown and the vintaine rose, ready for the afternoon's march.

'I must go,' she said.

'I thank you. My life is yours now.'

'Perhaps I will have need of it before long,' she said, and was gone.

CHAPTER FORTY-THREE

21 August

Berenger had spent an unsatisfactory day with his men, riding to and fro across the line of march of the army – and now, at last, they were approaching the river.

The carts made a hellish din as they rattled and crashed over the ruts and stones of the tracks. Every so often there would be a short scream as the injured inside them were thrown around, making broken bones move and wounds reopen. Two more men had died from their injuries, and three from a sickness that had spread to many in the army.

It was always the way. Berenger had never yet seen as many men killed in battle as had died from disease. This time, perhaps because the men were moving continually, the illnesses were fewer. It was an interesting thought.

Uppermost in his mind, however, was the whereabouts of the French.

Every day for the last three they had been attacked by groups of militia, but these were uncoordinated assaults. It was the main force that Berenger feared, yet the French had not been sighted.

It was alarming. The English were suffering. Those marching on foot had boots that were worn through, and several men had given up on them, casting them aside or stuffing them in their packs in the hope of finding some leather to mend them with before too long.

In Berenger's mind, there was an ever-ready presence just over the horizon: the French King with his enormous army. And when the first troops of that mighty host appeared, the English had best be ready and waiting or, as Clip foretold, they would all be slaughtered.

He had no idea how many men the French could muster, but everyone knew that with King Philippe's funds, he could hire the most proficient mercenaries from Genoa, Saxony and beyond. There truly was no defence, unless the English could find a perfect piece of land for a battle: an area where they could install themselves to their own satisfaction.

Sir John had mentioned this himself. He had ridden up behind Berenger late yesterday morning, and the vintener had seen how the strain of the last few days was affecting the old knight.

'How are the men, Fripper?'

'Well enough, Sir John.'

'Good. Let's hope this nonsense will soon be over and done with. We need to cross this damned river. Once we are over the other side, then will I be content.'

Sir John cast an eye at Berenger. 'You reminded me of the land north of here. Once we're across the Somme, I recall the ideal place where we could settle and wait for the French to meet us. Do you remember a vill called Crécy? A broad plain, sweeping down from a curved hill. If the French were to ride into that horseshoe, and we were on the hill, few of them would make it to our lines.'

Berenger nodded thoughtfully. He recalled the place. 'Is the enemy far away?'

'No. Not far enough! We don't want to meet the French too soon. That could spell disaster.' Sir John's old eyes were fretful. 'If we are forced to a battle here, God Himself knows how it will go, and who will win the day. But once over there, then we shall be safe.'

Safe. It was a word that returned to Berenger now, as he led his vintaine at a brisk trot a mile in advance of the main body of the army.

The vintaine's scouting had been reduced after their mauling three days ago. Other men had been called to the front to take their place temporarily, to allow them a little peace and recovery time. Today they were back at the front again.

'It's wrong, that's all I'm saying. We'll all be slaughtered.'

Berenger didn't bother to look up. 'What is, Clip?'

'It's not right, that's all.'

'We've done our bit, haven't we? Why can't we ride at the back, or with the King and his bodyguard? We've lost too many men already – do they want to see us wiped out?'

'Stop your blathering,' Jack said.

'It ain't blather, you bastard! You want to die here, you go ahead. It's fine by me. But I don't see why I should be stuck up here with—'

Jack bit his thumb at him, grinning.

'And that's your answer, is it?' Clip demanded shrilly. 'You reckon you can just insult me, and I won't—'

'Clip,' Berenger said wearily, 'Shut the fuck up! If you want to go and complain to the King back there, he'll be delighted to

345

hear your comments, I'm sure. But for now, I'm tired of your whining.'

'It's not fair, that's all I'm saying,' Clip muttered. 'Why are we always riding ahead, scouting for the army?'

Jack laughed. 'What are you complaining about? Look over your shoulder, man. There are fifteen thousand Englishmen at your back, and when you meet a Frenchman, all he's going to see is the number of men here to protect you: a king's host, with knights and English archers. He'll take one look at that lot, crap himself, drop his sword and flee.'

'At least it's not much further,' Berenger said appeasingly.

'How do we know that?' Clip moaned. 'It could be another hundred miles, for all we know.'

'No. We've been travelling too long already. The river isn't too far now.'

'How do you know that?' Clip said, his tone tempered by hope.

'I have been here before. Many years ago.'

'Oh. So how long will it be?'

'*Enough*, Clip! We'll be at the river in less than a day, I think. Now shut your trap – you're giving me earache.'

He did recall this land. The plains were familiar. It was a long time ago that he had last been here, but with the journey the memories flooded back. He recognised a village, now smouldering where English troops had set fire to the houses.

'When?'

'Eh?' Berenger was jerked back to the present.

'When were you here last?' Clip said.

'Sixteen years ago. Last time I saw it, people were working in the fields; the horses were set to pasture. There were children laughing, darting in among the trees at the edge, playing catch-as-catch-can.'

Yes. And King Edward II had thrown a coin to them, and the children had scurried for it gleefully. It was a happy scene.

'See? I can inspire joy in the hearts of the innocent,' the King had said sadly. 'Even if I have lost wife, son, throne and realm.'

Sixteen years ago, Berenger had been – what? Twenty? That was when he had fled England, travelling first to Avignon, thence to Italy.

'So long as we make it there,' Clip said gloomily.

Berenger frowned. 'What now?'

'I doubt many of us will ever reach home. Not with the witch still among us.'

'Without her nursing, Geoff would be dead by now.'

'He's dying anyway,' Clip said. 'He won't make it to England. You've seen how his face is. He's got a fever.'

'It'll break. He'll recover,' Berenger said.

'You think so?'

It hadn't crossed his mind that Geoff could die. Geoff was always there, an essential cog in the machine that was the vintaine. Without him, Berenger thought, the team would fall apart.

'He'll be fine,' he repeated, but he glanced over his shoulder towards the cart in which Geoff bounced. He could see that Béatrice was sitting in the cart still, her long hair concealed beneath a coif. It was tempting to go back and check on him, just to make sure that Geoff was truly all right.

He needed the miller's son alive.

'The river!'

The army straggled over a wide area as they ambled onwards, like men walking or riding in their sleep. On hearing the cry, Berenger saw Jack lurch, startled, and Clip almost tumbled from his mount.

347

Ahead, a scout was pointing and waving urgently.

'See that, Jack?' Berenger said. 'What is it?'

Jack peered through the dust that the rider had stirred; beyond was a sparkling and glinting. 'I don't know.'

The gleams were so faint, they could have been the sun sparkling on water, Berenger thought. Perhaps that was it: they had reached the river at last! With a quick thrill of fear, something struck him: the sun was behind them. Surely if it were a river, there would be less glittering? Besides, these glimmers looked to be too high. Any water would be low against the land.

That was when he realised what he could see, and recognised their danger. In that instant, he felt his bowels must empty.

'*VINTAINE, TO ME*!' he bellowed. 'It's the French, and they're coming straight at us!'

There was a sudden hush, and his men paused and looked at him, then back at the greyness ahead. 'Where?' someone asked.

Later, Berenger could have sworn that they sat stationary on their mounts for an age. Once, long ago, he had sat at the side of his village's pond and observed a strange, repulsive brown creature that climbed from the slime and ooze, to pause, gripping the reeds. Then, fascinated, he watched as the skin split, and gradually a brilliant, colourful body appeared. The wings were crumpled and useless, he saw, and he thought that they must somehow have been crushed, but then they gradually expanded, their appearance flattened and became shaped, and he realised that this was a magnificent dragonfly.

It had taken an age before the creature was able to fly away, and today he measured the time between the appearance of the rider and the sight of the men approaching them in a similar manner. In truth, he knew they came quickly. He saw men-at-arms in armour, lance-points shining in the afternoon sun . . .

and then suddenly they were ploughing through the vintaine, and the air was full of the shouts of the wounded, and screams and bellows as men tried to escape from the enemy. Berenger saw Jack avoid one lance, and then slam his bow at the face of another rider. He ducked too, but his aim was thrown off and he missed his own mark.

Berenger felt a lance-tip cut along his ribs but by a miracle, beyond the fine razor's slash, there was no damage. He looked up, just in time to see a second horse pounding towards him. He tried to jerk his mount out of the way, but the pony appeared spellbound by the terrifying sight of the other beast and the lance, and froze. Berenger yanked at the reins with such gusto that he fell half from the saddle. He felt a great shudder run through the horse, then heard a loud crack. The lance, aiming for him, had dropped when he fell, and speared his mount instead, the lance snapping as the rider galloped on.

He kicked his feet free from the stirrups as the little pony collapsed to its knees, blood gushing from its nostrils, and dodged swiftly aside as the beast collapsed, rolling, hooves flailing in the air.

Berenger could not afford to spend time to put the brute out of its misery. His sword in his fist, he stared about him. It seemed that the French were already gone. They had ridden through the midst of the scouts, killing many, and then continued on for a short distance, but when they caught sight of the main body of the army, they turned about and returned northwards.

Unknowing, Berenger knelt and gave thanks, his forehead resting on his sword's cross.

'You'd better hurry,' Jack said. 'They'll be back soon.'

'Back?' Berenger said, still dazed.

CHAPTER FORTY-FOUR

There was little time for the army to respond, but as Berenger bellowed to the men nearby to dismount and string their bows, he was aware of movements behind him as more men rode to his side and flanks. In a surprisingly short time, there were two hundred or more archers, bows strung and ready, their arrows near to hand.

'Frip, take these!' he heard, and turned to see the Donkey carrying an armload of arrows.

'Dump them here, lad,' Berenger said gratefully.

'You think I have time to clean your mess for you?' the Donkey responded with a grin. 'Take them and be damned. I have to take these to other men.'

Ed dropped the arrows, and Berenger quickly stabbed them into the ground a short way away so he could snatch them up in a hurry. It wasn't as efficient as having them in a wicker quiver before him as he preferred, but it was a great deal better than nothing. He counted quickly. Three-and-twenty arrows. Not enough, but they would suffice, with luck.

The enemy were coming on still. There were perhaps a thousand of them, and from the way they approached, they were reluctant to come to blows. Not trained men-at-arms, then, like the group which had first appeared and killed his pony. These were likely local levies, or perhaps just men from about the plain who were distraught at the devastation inflicted on their lands. Albeit unused to war, their anger and despair were enough to make them a force to reckon with.

'*ARCHERS*!' Berenger recognised Grandarse's stentorian bellow. 'Hold your ground!'

It was good advice. Some had considered moving forward to try to pick off the occasional Frenchman as they came into range, but by so doing they would weaken the force's impact.

Berenger's blood was thundering in his head like a horse's hooves in full gallop. His training told him that he was safe, for there were more archers appearing at his sides, and he knew that with so many bowmen, only a massive army could reach them . . . but still there was this dread anticipation of battle. He looked over to where his pony had been rolling, and saw that he was quite dead, his legs curved over his body. One eye appeared to stare at him reproachfully. The broken spear still projected from his breast, and the ground about him was black with his blood.

'Sorry,' he said, and felt unaccountably sad. Tears threatened his eyes and he dashed them away irritably. It was nothing: a pony. He was only sad because it had been a comfortable little thing, and he would miss the brute's broad back for the rest of the march.

'*Archers! Nock!*' Grandarse bawled.

Berenger took the nearest arrow and flicked the dirt from the tip. These were bodkins: sharp, pointed arrows, designed to penetrate mail and leather and stab the body beneath. A prick from one of these would be enough to pin a man to his horse, or to the ground.

'Archers! Draw!'

The enemy were approaching quickly now. A few bolder spirits had egged on the rest to throw themselves on the invaders, and now men raced towards them, seven or eight on ponies, but the rest on foot, hurtling towards the English with savage determination.

'Archers! LOOSE!'

Berenger felt the jerk as the string snapped forward, and saw the arrow bend and twist as it leaped up, the fletchings catching the air and coming alive. He saw it rise as he reached for his second and nocked the horn to the string, and saw it plummet as he drew again, feeling his eyelashes catch the string as he blinked . . . and then that arrow was flying, and he was reaching for the next.

An archer like Berenger could loose six arrows a minute easily. Three hundred men meant eighteen hundred arrows. And all those arrows would strike in the midst of the men coming towards them. Even as he watched, he saw the first arrows find their marks, and a rank of men disappeared. One moment they were running at full tilt, the next they were fallen. Unconsciously, the Frenchmen clumped together as their companions died, bunching up for comfort in the face of this hideous airborne onslaught, but by doing so, they made themselves into easy targets. The next flight of arrows slammed into them – and more men tumbled and fell. They gathered together again, and the next flight reduced their numbers yet further.

Few Frenchmen succeeded in reaching the English. Those who did, exhausted by their long race, were easily overwhelmed and dispatched, and as Berenger stared out over the plain, he suddenly had the feeling that things would improve. They would win. They would return to England.

But then the shrill cries and sobs reminded him of his duty, and he and the other men drew their long knives and went to end the suffering of the men on the field.

Sir John was glad to be asked to go and test the defences.

After the French militia had tried to bring the English to battle, the English army had been delayed once more, collecting arrows from the field, despatching the enemy wounded, and reforming their men into a line of march. If their intention had been to hold up the English, the French militia could hardly have succeeded more effectively, Sir John thought, but he kept the thought to himself.

The army would continue to Airaines, the Earl of Warwick told him, but Sir John must ride north, to the Somme, and test the defences. It was vital that the English army found a means of crossing the river. They must not be constrained as they had been at the Seine, but must punch their way over and continue up to the county of Ponthieu.

'Those lands were the King's own until this damned war,' Warwick said. 'Once we are there, our situation will improve.'

'Because of the people? You think we can win more men to the King's flag?' Sir John asked.

'Perhaps some, although I wouldn't trust any of the locals that much. You can never tell how a peasant's mind will work. No, I was thinking more that we know that territory. There are places where we can use the land to our advantage.'

'I see.'

The Earl nodded. 'The King used to own Ponthieu, and he has ridden over it, as have his advisers. We all know it. There are plenty of places where we can take on a French army many times the size of ours and utterly destroy it. It's been the idea all along, to harry the French and Philippe until he felt compelled to do something to remove us and our threat. We wanted him to chase us up here and into Ponthieu. Our only concern is that he may have already managed to leap beyond us. If he has, and he's blocked our path into the north,' the Earl said, his face grim, 'then we shall find the next days rather more exciting than we had hoped.'

Now, taking with him a party of six men-at-arms, Richard, and three vintaines of archers, Sir John was riding to the Somme.

'Where do we ride first?' his esquire asked.

'Due north. There was a bridge there, I think. Then we look for other crossings, whether bridges or fords, and gain an impression of the defences, such as they are.'

'And if the defences are strong?'

Sir John didn't answer.

They rode on and found the bridge – or where it had stood. It had been destroyed in recent days, and would not be easy to rebuild. The pilings had been removed, so another attempt to throw a tree over the waters would fail.

Riding westwards, following the line of the river, Sir John began to appreciate the immensity of the task before them. The Somme, it appeared, was impassable. It would have taken all the engineers in the army weeks to construct a bridge strong enough to let them all over, and as for fords, they were a forlorn hope. Nowhere were the waters shallow enough to allow the horses over, let alone the wagons and special weaponry.

The knight thought of his old manors at Iddesleigh and Rookford and wished he was there now. His wife would be working in the dairy at this time of day, making the most of the cool room to leave the cheeses to settle. He could see her in his mind's eye, lifting the heavy buckets and filling the pans, or stirring the curds, bending backwards to ease the strain after churning the butter.

He should be there with her. This journey was a fool's errand. A man of Sir John's age ought to be at his manor, enjoying the twilight of his life, not putting his life in peril.

When this chevauchée was ended, he vowed, he would return and never leave his shores again. But for now, he had to concentrate on surviving. It was very likely that he would *not* make it back to England. And that belief began to grow stronger as they rode on.

Most bridges they came across had been systematically destroyed, bar a few – but those all had many men guarding them. At two bridges there were fortified towns, and their strong encircling walls stood between the army and the bridges. It would require enormous resources to lay siege to them before anyone could cross the bridges behind. And if there was one asset which the English army lacked, it was time. The longer they were held here, without escape, the more likely it was that the French would be able to impose a stranglehold on all provisions, water and other necessities. The army would be bottled up, with the river on one side, the sea on the other, and no hope of escape.

This was futile. They were all doomed.

It was dark when they returned to the army at Airaines and reported to the Earl of Warwick.

'Well?' he demanded.

They were standing in the hall of a great house commandeered by the Royal Family, and the Prince was present, his advisers all about him; however, the thicker cluster of men stood about the other man: the King.

The King smiled, nodding encouragingly to the knight. 'Sir John, I know you have been busily scouting the river for us. Tell us your conclusions.'

The Prince and his household looked on hopefully, while the King maintained his steady gaze.

'Your Royal Highness, my Lords, we rode to the bridge at Long, north of here, and thence took the road westwards to Abbeville and beyond. Every undefendable bridge is thrown down and destroyed. The smaller ones are guarded by large forces that would make any passage enormously difficult. Abbeville and Amiens are well guarded, with French soldiers installed. Both have walls as strong as any fortress, and enough men and provisions to hold them for longer than we could spend investing them.'

'It is as I feared, then. The French reached the river before us,' the King said heavily.

'I fear so, my Lord. We carried on in the hope of finding another place to cross. I had thought that there could be a ford farther up towards the estuary, but my hopes were dashed.'

'Do you mean to say that we cannot cross the river?'

'The land becomes ever more marshy, with patches of sedge and reed and treacherous sands. It is possible that there is somewhere nearer the sea where we may cross, but I saw no sign of anywhere suitable. If we could pass through Longpré, or perhaps Fontaine-sur-Somme, we might be able to reach the river, but any such passage would be hard-fought. There is no doubt that the French are determined to keep us here.'

'And that is no surprise. We are trapped. The river before us, the sea behind us, and the army of the French approaching. Philippe will know that we have run short of food. Without supplies, our men will grow weak. Without an escape, this will

357

be our grave. But take heart!' the King said. 'God is with us. We *shall* cross this river.'

'I do not see where,' Sir John said quietly.

'Neither do I, Sir John. But there is a crossing – there must be. All we need to do is *find* it.'

CHAPTER FORTY-FIVE

22 August

Before dawn Berenger saw Grandarse appear, lumbering through the cool mists like a misshapen goblin from a nightmare. His face was twisted into a scowl, and Berenger could see his mouth moving as he muttered dark imprecations.

'All right, where are the lads?' he said as he came closer.

'Standing ready,' Berenger answered. 'What is it?'

Grandarse gave him a look from beneath beetling brows. 'They'll be glad to know we have a nice new job.'

'Oh yes?'

'We have to cross the river, right? But because we took our ballocking time to get here, the mother-swyving French reached it first,' Grandarse explained. 'They have men at every crossing from here to bloody Dover!'

Berenger listened as Grandarse told him of Sir John's ride. 'It'll be a fight, then,' he said.

'We'll have to try to get through the buggers, over the bridge, and out to the plains beyond. If we don't, we know what'll happen.'

There was no need for him to elaborate. All soldiers knew what the outcome would be for an army squeezed against natural obstacles by an implacable and more numerous enemy.

'Is there nowhere we could fight them around here?' Berenger asked hopefully.

'No. The King is desperate to cross the river. This is the last place he wants to fight his battle,' Grandarse said.

Berenger felt his hope dashed like a wave against rocks, and he turned away bitterly. 'I see.'

Clip had overheard them, and this was his cue. 'Sweet Jesus!' he burst out. 'He told us the whole point of coming here was to fucking *fight*! He believed in his cause so strongly, he brought the biggest army he's ever mustered, with the sole intention of forcing the French to come and attack us, didn't he? What was the fucking point of it if, as soon as they are near, we turn and run? We were demanding our battle all the way to Paris, and since then we've done everything we could to avoid it. They offered to fight us outside Paris, and he brought us all the way up to here. Now we have the French at our tail, we should turn, like a boar held at bay, and show our tusks!'

'Run at them to be spitted on the hunter's lance, you reckon, Clip?' Grandarse snarled. 'Get your brain working, man! You have it stuck in your arse from what you're saying. You think we should fight them here? Look about you! See the reeds, the flat marshes? There's no stable ground for a fight. Aye, the King wants his battle, but not here, not just outside Paris, nor anywhere else when he's not perfectly certain of the land. He has places in mind only a day or two's march from here.'

'Huh!' Clip said grumpily. 'I'm thinking this was just another quick dash to France to win booty, and he never meant to force the French to battle. I've seen little enough fighting spirit.'

'You keep your mouth shut!' Grandarse hissed, and Clip sullenly moved away.

When he was gone, Grandarse turned to Berenger. 'Get a grip on your lads, Frip. If they hear Clip moaning on like this, they'll lose heart – and men without hope don't win wars. Remember that! If you want to get back to England safe and well, the only way you'll do it is by keeping up the spirits of your boys. Don't let them whine and bellyache.'

'I'll do my best,' Berenger said. About him figures were moving in the wreaths of mist. 'What now?'

'We are the most proficient team, Frip, didn't you know?' Grandarse said with a sour leer. 'Who else would Sir John and the Earl of Warwick ask for when they need scouts? We're to be the first to go and force the crossing. It'll be glory all the way for us, man!'

'Ballocks,' Berenger muttered.

'Why us? Doesn't the King have any other poor buggers he doesn't like?' Jon Furrier said.

They were crouched on the ground nearby as Berenger, on one knee, told them the news.

'We'll all get killed this day,' Clip said with a twisted grin, and for the first time, Berenger wondered if he was speaking from conviction.

'We *won't* all get killed. You can, Clip, you thieving scrote,' Berenger said, 'but I'm going to get back. And when I reach home, I'll have a bag full of French gold to buy myself a little cottage, and I'll sit back while my woman cooks for me and brews the best ale in Warwick. I'm sure of one bloody thing, lads, and that is that I am not going to lie in French soil. I shall be going back – and so will the rest of you, *if* you're careful.'

'How do we do that?' Jon demanded. 'At the front, we'll be cut down like saplings.'

'We'll do what we do best, my friend. We'll fight side-by-side, and we'll protect each other. I'll get the Donkey back to help us. With him to bring us more arrows, we can keep up a steady fire against any enemy. Perhaps we can draw them to attack us, and use our bows to hold them off?'

'We can try,' Clip said, 'but they'd only do that if they were fools, and so far, Frip, they haven't shown much stupidity, have they? They've not risked their men in all-out attacks like we want. Not once. This French King knows his way around a fight.'

'Aye, the King may, but his men down here may not. Who knows but that the man at the bridge here isn't some long-headed fool with no understanding of combat? Remember how we took St-Lô? Who would have thought we could have stormed the place so quickly? Half a day and it was ours, wasn't it? If they'd held the gates against us, we'd not have done that so quickly or so well, but because the townspeople were scared and pulled back to the island, we took it. We can do the same here.'

'Aye, Frip. So long as the defenders have an idiot in charge like those at St-Lô,' Jon observed drily.

'Let's hope they do then. Right, lads, the main thing is, keep together, look after each other, don't panic, and we'll all make it home.'

'Yeah, right,' sighed Clip.

It was deeply unsettling when he didn't repeat his usual whining warning. That was the moment when Berenger knew that Clip really believed they would all die. Looking at the rest of his surviving vintaine, Berenger could see that they all had the same thought.

*   *   *

The village was called Hangest-sur-Somme, Berenger heard later. A scruffy little collection of cottages and small houses at the side of the river amidst the marshes and reeds. Behind it, the grey, broad mass of the river made its sluggish progress towards the sea. If Berenger could, he would willingly have stolen a boat to escape to the sea. No matter what Grandarse said, he reckoned the chevauchée was in its last hours. The might of the French army was out there somewhere, whether to the north or due east, he didn't know, but he was certain now, no matter what he said to the vintaine, that their raid was ending.

They approached Hangest with the Earl of Warwick on his horse, a collection of men-at-arms all about him, while the archers plodded along behind, Grandarse in the lead. Berenger and Roger's men were to be in the front rank: 'Aye, same as usual,' as Clip grumbled.

'You scared of 'em?' Tyler sneered.

Berenger glanced at Roger. If he'd had his way, Tyler would have been punished for his looting when Gil was hanged, but for now all the archers were needed. Still, when he had an opportunity, Berenger vowed to himself that he would see Tyler pay the debt.

As they drew nearer to the village, the bridge came into full view, and they rode towards it with a stirring of hope.

'Have they forgotten this one, Frip?' Clip asked.

'No,' Berenger said, but even he felt optimistic. So far, whenever there had been a danger of their being caught in the open by the French, they had somehow managed to salvage a miracle. Perhaps the French had indeed forgotten this one bridge. If so, they could quickly storm across and form a defensive position on the other bank, just as they had before crossing the Seine, and then the rest of the army could join them. It was a delicious thought. He could almost taste the sweet glory of victory in his mouth.

'Come on, Clip,' Jack called. 'Aren't you going to remind us that we'll all die?'

'Aye, well,' Clip said. He looked uncomfortable.

'Clip?' Jack went on. 'If you don't curse us, you old shit, we'll blame you when things go wrong.'

But Clip said nothing. Berenger felt his elation dissipate like morning mist as the other men exchanged glances and began to chew at their lips or fiddle with their kit. They were all growing convinced that Clip's attitude was prophetic. If he didn't dare complain about their death, it was for good reason.

'Come on, boys!' Berenger said. Jack and a couple of men rallied, but others remained looking nervous, their eyes hooded.

Three men in armour trotted forward. They passed around the edge of a couple of cottages, and the rest of the men watched them in anticipation, all praying that the way to the bridge was clear and safe.

But as they were passing the last cottage, they suddenly stopped. One horse reared, and the second man drew his sword and began to charge, while the third wheeled round and rode back at full gallop.

He didn't make it. As he pelted past the houses, there was a flurry of movement. He was crouched low over his mount's neck, but that was not enough to save him. The men all saw the explosion of blood from his mouth. A crossbow bolt had hit him low in the back, and must have ridden through his mail and up into his breast. He clung on desperately, then slowly rolled from his horse. Of the other two, nothing could be seen, but their disappearance was enough warning.

'*Archers!* Forward!' Sir John shouted, and Berenger looked to either side at his men. They were all glowering, including Clip.

'Keep close, lads,' Berenger said. 'Remember, shoot fast and shoot well. Donkey, you need to hurry, understand me? Just keep bringing fresh arrows, no matter what. Right, boys, here we go!'

He clapped spurs to his new pony, a sturdy little brute with an evil temper, and the whole mass of archers rode down to join the Earl and his household. Sir John was there, but he broke away from the Earl to join his archers, his esquire at his side.

'Don't worry about them, Fripper,' he said. 'These look to me like Genoese or some other mercenaries. If you scare them with your arrows, we can win through them!'

There was a suppressed excitement about him as he spoke, and Berenger felt his own spirits lift. The knight's enthusiasm was infectious. The men stood stringing bows, while boys came to take the reins and lead the horses away.

Ahead of them, the men of the village had decided that the need for concealment was past. Dozens of crossbowmen darted out and sheltered behind the great pavise shields gripped in place by their companions. Behind them, ranks of spearmen stood clumped in reluctant, uneven lines, and behind them, the men-at-arms sat on their horses, the great beasts pawing at the ground, eager for the battle to begin.

Each English archer had a quiver, which they set on the ground before them. All strung their bows and stood ready, while Donkey and Béatrice brought the cart nearer and began to dispense arrows. Sir John and Richard Bakere remained on horseback and cajoled and bullied succeeding groups of archers into their positions, leaving a good space between them, through which the men-at-arms could ride.

'Archers, are you ready?' Sir John roared. 'Nock arrows!'

There was a ripple of movement. Berenger felt the smooth click as his arrow was attached to the string.

'Archers, draw!'

The familiar tension tugging at his back muscles, shoulder muscles, belly muscles. The taut almost-pain at the base of his neck as the string came back and tickled his eyelashes. He felt the strain of the bow in his left hand, felt the urgent keenness of the arrow to be released. The point of the arrow, sleek, black, gleaming silver where it had been sharpened, was aimed up at a cloud, over the cottage some hundred and fifty yards away.

'Loose!'

CHAPTER FORTY-SIX

The release ran through Berenger's body, from both arms to his back, along his spine. The bow gave a lurch, and the arrow sped on its way, and as he watched its path, he saw the hundreds of identical arrows leaping up into the sky on all sides, their passage marked by a low sound like a strong wind in a forest. He grabbed another arrow and fitted it to the string, drew and loosed, and again, and again. The noise of fletchings taking to the air was all about him, the thrumming as each string slipped from its tab filled his ears until all he could sense was the noise of their launch and flight.

'*Archers!* To me!'

Suddenly there was the rattle and thunder of horses cantering, and Berenger turned to see that the Earl and his household were pounding towards the village.

Grandarse was roaring now: 'Come on, boys! You going to leave the knights and esquires to take all the glory! Berenger, Roger, follow me! Let's get our own!'

He began to lurch off down the hill after the men-at-arms, and Berenger picked up his quiver and slung it over his shoulder as he set off after the old warrior, waving to his men. 'Come on, Clip. Jack, get a move on!'

The crossbowmen were withdrawing already, and the Earl and his men were almost at the lance-men. But then the line of foot-soldiers parted, and the French horsemen sprang through.

Berenger ran now. His bow and quiver were held to him under his left hand, while his right reached for his long dagger's hilt. It should be knife-work from here, he thought, but even as he did so, the trap was sprung.

Where before there had been thirty or more men-at-arms on horseback on the French side, now he saw a fresh body of knights and esquires appear from between the houses. It was a second, stronger party designed, Berenger suddenly realised, to cut off the Earl and his men.

Even as he had the thought, a bolt whirred past his ear like a blackbird rocketing away from danger. That sound brought him to his senses. He stopped and studied the battlefield. There were more crossbowmen in the roadway now, to block any attempt at rescue. The rest of the French were determinedly heading for the Earl's men.

He heard a cough, and when he glanced to his side, he saw Roger gazing at a bolt's fletchings embedded in his chest. He looked at Berenger and choked, and a great gush of blood came from his mouth, and then he retched and collapsed, writhing.

Berenger stared in shock. Roger had always seemed impervious to the darts and blades of the enemy. Another bolt flew past.

'Swyve a goat, these bastards are getting serious!' Clip said.

It was enough to bring Berenger to his senses.

'Archers! *Archers!* To me! To me! Nock!'

He set his quiver on the ground and put arrow to string.

'Aim for the horsemen of the French. Take them in the back if you may! We have to support the Earl and his men!'

He stared to either side. *'Archers: draw!'*

A man three further along from him gave a strangled cry and fell back, a bolt jutting from his brow.

'Archers: loose!'

A flurry of arrows rose into the air and plunged down towards the French, and before they could strike, a second wave was heading after them. Berenger drew his bow a third time, and another mass of wood and steel was launched on its way.

The arrows did their work. French men-at-arms suddenly found that their steel protection was punctured, or badly dented, by the hideous, hard points of arrows from behind. Berenger saw a man hit in the head who rode, his arm held high with a sword gripped in his fist, away from the fight, and continue until lost from sight. Another was struck in the neck, near the spine, and seemed to fly into a frenzy, his gauntleted hands reaching around with desperation to try to pluck the barb from him. Two English knights hacked at him until he fell. A third was hit by two arrows in the lower back, and fell forwards over his horse's neck until a man with an axe beheaded him with two blows.

'With me!' Berenger shouted. With three arrows in his hand and a fourth on his string, he ran towards the Genoese. A man stood to aim his crossbow, but three arrows launched at him made him flinch, and his bolt flew high overhead. At his side, a second man took aim, but an arrow struck him in the eye and he was thrown to the ground. Then the Genoese took flight.

Berenger stopped, trying to control his breathing, and took aim at a large man with a flowing red beard. His helmet was open-faced, and he fought like a berserker of old, his sword leaping and dancing in his hand as he tried to belabour Sir John and the Earl. Berenger's arrow sprang forth and struck him in the throat, and he fell back with the point of the arrow protuding inches from the back of his helmet.

Jack was beside him again now, muttering, 'They don't pay us enough, Frip, fuck 'em!'

'Stop your moaning, you old git,' Berenger managed through gritted teeth as he held the string back, the point of his cloth-yard arrow aiming at a French man-at-arms who was riding towards the archers. He took a low aim, and saw it strike the man's horse in the breast. It managed only three more steps before its heart burst, and the steed crumpled to the ground, forelegs folding to the knees, and the brute's chin striking the roadway. There was a crack like a tree-limb breaking as the neck snapped, and the rider was hurled from the saddle to land in the dirt. He rose, shaking his head, but Clip was already at him, and his dagger went into the man's eye. He fell, legs kicking, blood spraying and smothering Clip, who swore and quickly dashed it away.

Berenger could see the French were wilting away. The Genoese crossbowmen had taken to their heels and were disappearing beyond the village, but even as they went, Berenger's glee was dispelled. More men on horseback were cantering towards them: men-at-arms, with their metal gleaming blue-black and silver, pennants fluttering from their spears. And with their arrival, the Genoese took heart again. He saw them turn, crouching to span their weapons, and then loading and aiming while protected behind walls.

'Frip, we can't take this place,' Jack panted at his side.

'We can't leave the knights!' Berenger responded.

'Then we'll all die,' Clip shouted. For once there was no whining edge to his voice, only determination. 'Frip, we *have* to get out of this!'

Berenger stood torn, but before he could decide, Grandarse appeared at his side. He had a long, raking cut on his arm, and he stood breathing stertorously as he studied the men struggling in the road before him. The dust rose, enveloping the scene, and only the clanging, crashing and bellowings of rage and agony could be heard.

'Sod this,' he muttered. Then: 'Frip, get your men back. This we cannot win.'

They withdrew to a hamlet halfway back to the main army, where the men rested and sat to patch their wounds. Of the archers, a quarter had been injured, although only fifteen had died. A little while after the last of the archers had slumped to the ground, Berenger heard cantering horses and turned to see the remaining English men-at-arms riding towards them, a body of French knights in hot pursuit.

'*Archers!*' he shouted, and gathered together three vintaines. They waited until their men-at-arms were safe, and then released four flights of arrows. Seven men fell not to rise again, and three more were punctured, the arrows punching through their armour – and when the French saw the archers standing at the ridge, they gave up on the chase, turning and riding away.

'I owe you and your men a debt of gratitude,' the Earl said, eyeing the retreating French. His face and armour were bespattered with blood, but he appeared uninjured. 'They bested us, damn their souls! They bested us well.'

'So we cannot take the bridge here?' Grandarse said.

'They have too many men, and reserves. It would drain our army to force a path. No, we shall find a better crossing-point. Pont-Rémy is supposed to have a good bridge. We shall try that. Gather your men.'

'Aye, sir. Berenger? You've complained about your manpower. Take Roger's vintaine and mix it with yours.'

The town of Pont-Rémy was less than two leagues away, and the archers wearily remounted and followed the Somme's banks.

Berenger found himself riding beside Grandarse.

'Well?' his centener asked. 'How are the men?'

'They'll cope.'

'Will you, Frip?'

'I'll be fine. You've known me long enough.'

'Aye. And you've known me, you daft bugger. Doesn't mean you won't see me start to complain soon. This whole campaign's gone to cock.'

'We'll get through it.'

'Will we? I wish I had your faith.'

Berenger stared at him. It was the first time he had heard Grandarse make a negative comment, and it was crushing. He had tried to keep his spirits up, but if Grandarse himself considered their position hopeless, there was nothing more to say.

Approaching the town, they saw the forces ranged against them.

'Sweet Jesus!' Grandarse grunted. 'Did I not tell you, Frip? How in God's name can we pit ourselves against an enormous host like that, eh?'

There were two main forces, one flag neither recognised, while the second was familiar to both of them.

'John of Hainault! I'd like to get my hands round his throat, the back-sliding, dishonest, treacherous git,' Grandarse said with feeling.

Berenger couldn't disagree. John of Hainault had been the King's ally until recently, but there was no honour in the man's soul. He would go wherever he thought he would gain the most. And right now, that was with the French.

In the course of their march, more men-at-arms had joined the English, and now there were over a hundred knights and esquires riding with the archers. It was good to see so many with them, but viewing the men ranged against them, Berenger felt his belly contract. It was his own, personal premonition of disaster.

CHAPTER FORTY-SEVEN

Sir John de Sully listened as the Earl discussed with his captains how best to force the French from their path. In the end, the Earl's view prevailed. The archers were placed in two triangular formations on either side of the road, and they were ordered to begin loosing their missiles as soon as the men-at-arms were ready.

Sitting in the saddle with his back resting against the cantle, Sir John eyed the enemy shrewdly. 'Easy, Aeton,' he said, patting the beast's neck. 'Not long now.'

There were so many of them! Too many. Men-at-arms of all ranks waited on horseback, while before them stood foot-soldiers armed with pikes, lances and bills. They would be able to defend themselves without trouble. There was a slightly weaker point in the line over to the right, he noticed, where the English might be able to charge through . . . but even as he thought this, more packed the space.

Usually, he would aim to charge, force a way through, and cause havoc behind their lines. A few knights ranging widely behind an army could quickly destroy what confidence that force originally held. But today, to break through that rigid-looking line would be almost impossible.

He let his eyes move over the men at either side, wondering how their courage would hold.

It was a simple fact that Englishmen were better trained and tested in war. That did not mean that the French were not equally bold and courageous, only that the English could sometimes perform prodigious feats of arms against overwhelming odds. All had heard of the brilliant efforts of men like Sir Walter Manny and Sir Thomas Dagworth. No one could be in any doubt as to the worth of Englishmen in war, but that did not mean that they were invincible. The French possessed more knights, more men-at-arms, more foot-soldiers and more weapons than the English. And the English were tired. They had been marching for weeks already, and with few provisions over recent miles, while the French could rely on every town or city for resupply.

It was not a comforting thought.

There was a horn blast, taken up by many others. Sir John gripped his lance, staring up at the strong shaft, assessing its strength. If the wood was strong, with a straight grain, the weapon would do.

A second blast, and the first men began to move off down the hill. The shallow gradient would give them no great advantage, but every element that could support them must be used.

The Earl had picked his position with skill – a sweeping plain leading to the French cavalry, with no woods or hedges in which to conceal crossbowmen or an ambush. With luck, they would have a clear ride to the French. There they could fight, and in an open battle, Sir John was content to think that an Englishman against three French were reasonable odds. The English had a hotter fire in the belly than their enemies.

'Forward!' the cries came, and his mount was already trotting. He held Aeton back. As ever, it was vital that all should ride as a single force, striking their targets in one massive, shattering pack.

The enemy were moving too, men and horses jogging gently up to meet the English. A dusty mist rose from their hooves. The ground here was, for once, dry and unaffected by the marshland that soaked so much of this land. Sir John was glad of that. He detested marshland and bog. It was disturbing to riders and horses alike. A charger crossing a mire could stumble or fall very easily.

This was no time to worry about how the beasts would cope with the ground, he chided himself. His attention must be fixed entirely on the charge and making sure that his team worked well with the rest of the knights and esquires. He cast one quick, final glance round to make sure that Richard was on his station, a little behind and to Sir John's left, protecting his flank, while Simon was there a few yards behind, riding the second destrier in case Aeton was killed or injured in the initial press.

But that was all he had time for – and then they were riding for the French.

Sir John could feel the great muscles coiling in Aeton's back and thighs, and the sense of power that exuded from the charger's body was thrilling. The air was in his face, and there was a ripple and crack from the flags and pennants as the men rode, and a metallic rasp as a coat of plates moved against a mail shirt. All the sounds of an army moving into battle mingled in his mind and were soon drowned out by the steady thundering of hooves beating at the ground in a threnody for the dead.

Aeton knew his position and his task. He lowered his head, shaking his mane, and increased his pace as the English began to charge. Sir John must merely maintain his seat and grip his lance. And then there was a ripple of light as the knights and esquires lowered their lance-points, and his too came down to point at a man hundreds of feet from him.

Sir John felt the old exultation, as though his entire being was thrilling with the glory of the moment.

But then a jolt hit him from his left. A man and horse had thundered into him. His lance was pushed from his target, and Aeton was slammed aside.

The charge was wrecked!

Berenger saw the disaster from his vantage point as he loosed his arrows.

A rank of Genoese archers riposted, and there was a rattle and crash as many English men-at-arms were felled. Horses reared and plunged, their riders clinging to them as the barbs of the quarrels stung. The Genoese were aiming for the brutes rather than the knights. Bring down their destriers, and the knights were helpless.

Sir John and his esquire were both at the fore as the English knights charged, and Berenger caught a glimpse of their lances dropping, ready to spit their enemies, but even as they did so, a man-at-arms behind them was hit in the breast. The quarrel stood out like an obscene splinter, and he tried to pull at it. It must have been enormously painful.

As he struggled with the foul missile, the rider's horse drifted across the rest of the knights, crashed into Sir John's steed, distracting Richard and knocking both men into the soldiers beside them. At the crucial moment, just as the charge was developing, the mass of horses and men that should have slammed into the enemy as a coherent, solid unit, was broken into a series of small groups that eddied about the French line like ripples of water cast against rock. Their gallop was ineffective, and they were forced to cast aside their lances and resort to war-hammers, axes and swords, hacking and beating at the men in the line, trying desperately to break through.

Then Berenger saw an opportunity. He discarded his bow and pulled out his sword. *'To me! Archers! To me!'* he roared. And with that, he began running to the men struggling in the roadway.

Sir John wheeled and thundered on again.

He glimpsed a man ahead – a Frenchman in a garish red and green tunic, who was racing to meet him . . . and then the man was only yards away and Sir John felt an enormous punch at his right shoulder, and he was rocked back against the cantle. His spear was cracked along its length, and snapped, and he saw a brief burst of livid red as his spear embedded itself in the man's breast.

As the second wave of French riders appeared in front of him, he tugged at his sword, hacking down at a hand that appeared too near to his saddle, and then at a face; more men were before him, and he clapped spurs to Aeton. The great brute reared, hooves flailing, and Sir John saw a man's head crushed, while another took the full force of Aeton's weight on his chest. The charger dropped again, and Sir John felt Aeton's legs propel them forward into the press.

It was a grand mêlée, the sort of battle a knight would dream of. Men cut at each other, with barely space to wield their weapons. Some hewed without seeing more than a momentary glimpse of an enemy, and hoped their blows would not go astray. Others were heedless, striking friends and foe alike, driven by an insane rage against any who could dare stand against them. Some were petrified with horror and fear, beshit-ten, squealing within their visored helmets, while others sang with the pure joy of it. This was what men were born for: to fight and die.

Sir John had seen enough battles. He neither sang nor screamed. His sole purpose was to win through this battle and see the next. He rode from one place to another, using Aeton's mass to blunder men aside, driving his enemies before him with his sword, or his war-hammer, if they came up on his left side.

Two ringing buffets hit his helmet, and he felt the metal slam against the thick, padded war-coif he wore beneath. The first blow nearly forced him from his saddle, the second was enough to knock his helmet crooked, but he ducked away and pushed it up again. When he turned, he saw that a Frenchman had been thrown from his horse by Richard. His esquire held up a fist in salute, before the two hurried towards a fresh enemy.

There was a knight beside him now, a man whom Sir John vaguely remembered – his arms were more easily brought to mind than his face – who suddenly erupted with blood. A crossbow bolt had slammed between the bars of his visor, and he fell to the ground, his armour clattering. His horse continued on, eyes wild and rolling, careless of his danger. The knight in front of Sir John – Sir Lawrence of Evesham, he recalled – reeled in his saddle, arms outstretched like a man crucified. An esquire rode past him on a charger, screaming as the blood pumped from a great wound in his neck, showering all in his path.

The obscene fantasy continued. A man stood on the ground before him, shaking his arm with futile horror. The forearm and hand were missing, and with every flail, blood was spattered onto the men about him. Sir John shoved his sword at a face, but even as he felt his blade clash uselessly on the side of the fellow's helmet, missing the flesh completely, he felt the resounding crash as a war-hammer cracked against the back of his own helmet. He almost fell from Aeton, but had just enough will to keep his place in the saddle; and then Aeton kicked, and when he glanced, Sir John saw that the great destrier's hooves had caught a man's thigh and the flank of his horse, crushing them. The French man-at-arms was slumped from shock and agony, and Sir John could see the greyish-white bone protruding from his hosen.

With his head pounding, Sir John roared his defiance, and spurred Aeton into the press once more.

CHAPTER FORTY-EIGHT

The Earl and his bodyguard had found a weak point and were exploiting it. Berenger made straight for them, the breath burning his throat. His lungs were on fire, and his legs were wooden and clumsy from marching and lack of food. Before he was halfway there, his foot skidded on a patch of loose pebbles, and he nearly fell, jarring his ankle. After that, he had to move more slowly as a stabbing pain rose into his calf.

It was the delay that saved his life. When he looked again at the front line, disaster had struck.

The archers had streamed off ahead of him, and he was hobbling after them, when he saw them race back towards him. Some had their bows with them still, and these few halted and began to fire. Others threw theirs aside and simply fled.

The French had unleashed a wave of their own cavalry. Most thundered at the English men-at-arms, but a large number were making straight for the despised archers, and as he stared, dumbstruck, he saw men flung up into the air, screaming, their arms and legs moving like strange, inhuman creatures.

He saw one lad, the tip of a lance sprouting from his cotte; he beat at it with his hands like a maid slapping away a wasp. The knight who had impaled him flicked his wrist to free his weapon, and the boy was thrown into the crowd like a piece of carrion.

Berenger saw no more. Here in the open, the men were unprotected, and he bitterly regretted his urge to support the Earl and Sir John. Turning, he tried to make his way back to his bow, but he was stumbling now, and knew he would fail. His ankle was too painful, and the French destriers were gaining too quickly.

'Here!'

It was Jack. Before Berenger could argue, the sturdy archer grabbed his sword arm and pulled it about his own neck. His other arm went around Berenger's waist, and he half-supported, half-carried the vintener back up the hill. As they were stumbling on, the sound of drumming hooves came to them.

A ditch gaped at the side of the roadway. Jack dived into it, pulling Berenger with him. The two scurried farther along the ditch, and the men-at-arms at their heels missed them, cantering on, laughing and jeering as they went, killing only the easier targets in the road before them.

The two men were up and hurrying again as soon as the French had passed. Berenger saw the place where they had left the cart and hobbled over to it, grabbing a fresh bow stave and looping a new string to it. With a strung bow, he felt more confident.

Jack had his own bow in his hands, and he snatched up a sheaf of arrows as Berenger gazed about them.

'Frip!' Jack shouted, pointing.

The French had turned and spotted them, and were already cantering back towards them. Berenger counted some two and twenty, and although three were knights, the others were men-at-arms in lighter armour. 'Leave the knights. Kill the others,' he grated, then nocked and drew. He loosed, and saw with satisfaction the arrow strike a man squarely in the breast. The man slumped, but the rest still came on. Other archers had joined the two of them now, and there were five, then six arrows striking at a time. A pair of horses on the right fell, while a third went berserk, whirling, trying to escape a barbed arrow embedded in its breast, and then the remaining men were almost upon them.

At the last moment, Berenger managed to hit the man nearest him. The arrow flew straight and true, piercing the armour at his right shoulder, and with a screech of pain, the man dropped his lance. He aimed his mount at Berenger, but even as he did so, the ground moved beneath Berenger's feet. He thought there was a landslide or some fresh catastrophe, for it felt as though the earth itself was rejecting the men squabbling on its soil. And then a great roar came from behind him, and he felt the wash as destriers galloped past.

It was the remainder of the English. They had fought their way free from the encircling French forces, and while they were much depleted, they were full of a killing rage. Returning to the archers, they saw the small number of French knights and sprang at them like wolves on a herd of deer.

Berenger saw Sir John ride straight at a man-at-arms, his sword out. He passed by the French lance-tip with negligent disdain and shoved his sword-point in under the man's chin. There was a moment when it looked as though the sword must be jerked from his grasp, but then he wrenched it free as he passed his opponent, and a gout of blood erupted from the man's throat. The latter's lance fell from his hands as he lifted them to his wound as though to stem the flow. He rode on, past Berenger, only to fall a few yards further on.

The rest of the French fought on doggedly, and the English were too exhausted to keep them at bay. Before long, the adversaries were parted and the French rode off with many a cat-call and jeer.

'You know what? I don't think we'll cross here after all,' Jack said.

23 August

The two vintaines were not mingled yet. Roger's men obeyed their orders, but the two groups of men still sat huddled quietly about their own fires.

No one was of a mood to joke or bicker for once, which was the proof, had Berenger needed it, that their morale was low. It was rare enough to see an archer quiet at evening time, but now, as they all began to stir in the early dawn light, he was aware of a profound dismay amongst them.

It was not fear: rather, it was the realisation that their chances of escaping the French net were growing ever more remote. While none of them admitted to being scared, that was not to say that they didn't appreciate the gravity of their position. With the main French army approaching, they must escape over the Somme or die. And all attempts had failed. Apart from the two in which Berenger and his men had participated, there had been two more, one at Longpré and another at Fontaine; there too, the English army had run into larger forces and been pushed back. At each confrontation the English had suffered considerable losses, and after the last attempt, the order had gone out to cease trying. The army could not afford to lose any more men.

'We've no chance,' Clip said. He was hunched down in front of the fire as usual, holding his hands to the flames and staring morosely into the embers. 'I thought when we came to the

King's own territories, the people would welcome us. They all said the folks here were fond of him, didn't they? And what do we get? Grateful thanks from the people, offers of food, and their prettiest daughters? Not bloody likely. No instead we get a lance up our arse.'

Berenger snorted, tightening a strip of linen about his sore ankle. It was already feeling a lot better, but he would be limping for days. 'Apart from you, Clip – as usual,' he said bitterly.

It was true enough. Clip was the only man amongst them who was uninjured after their attacks the day before. Even Jack had taken a stab in his thigh from an unhorsed Frenchman.

'Some of us know where to put our feet,' Clip retorted scornfully. 'You'd do well to remember that, Frip.'

'He's right,' Luke said. 'What were they thinking of, bringing us all the way up here?'

'Quiet!' Berenger said. He glared as a large, bulky figure approached.

'What were they thinking of?' Archibald repeated, amused. He walked to their circle, his eyes on their fire, and stood there, his smile twisting his magnificent moustache. 'They were thinking how to win, that's what they were thinking. They wanted the French King to be so humiliated by our march over his lands and territories, by the sight of the fires and devastation, by the daily news of how you lot laid waste to all his manors, that he would be forced to set off after us. It worked, didn't it? And now, our King is looking for the best place to settle this once and for all.'

'To see his army cut to pieces, I suppose,' Jack sneered. 'Look at the fucking state of us! It's all right for the King and his friends to be captured and ransomed. They will be safe enough. But what about us? There's no money in ransom for ordinary churls like us. We'll all be beheaded or hanged, or used for target practice by the Genoese. It's one thing to gamble when you aren't risking your own life.'

'Be still, Jack,' Berenger said.

'No, let him speak,' Archibald said, unruffled. He was still smiling. 'Master, you should know that your King and his advisers take your health and fitness very seriously. He knows that without your being able to draw a bow, he will never win France. And he desires France more than anything else in his life.'

'Well he won't have it, not unless he finds us food and a fresh crossing over the river.'

'It's only a river,' Archibald said with confidence. 'There will be a way.'

'Even if do we find a crossing,' Clip put in grimly, 'do you really think the French will let us over? We'll be cut to pieces on both sides of the water, and no one will survive.'

'Does he ever stop his whining?' Archibald enquired mildly to Berenger.

'Not to my knowledge.'

'He must be a trial to you.'

'Hey!' Clip objected. 'You may think this is a matter for jesting, Master Gynour, but we stand to die here. So unless you can make use of your friend the Devil and sort out a miracle to rescue us, I think you should start to plan for meeting your friend face to face.'

'You think I am a friend of the Devil?'

'Everyone says so. It's obvious.'

Archibald eyed him very coldly and seriously for a moment. The other members of the vintaine looked away.

'Clip, just be quiet,' Berenger said. He was unsettled. There was something odd about this large gynour with his calm self-possession even now, in the face of the odds ranged against them. 'He didn't mean it,' he added to Archibald.

'Oh yes, he did,' Archibald said. He stared at all the men in turn. 'And so he should, because it's not a story I have ever bothered to contest. But if I was a friend to the Devil and prayed to Him, I would be scorched by touching a cross, wouldn't I?' He pulled from beneath his chemise a battered little cross of wood. At its side, dangling from the same thong, was a pilgrim badge: a pewter shell for St James of Compostela. He kissed them. 'You see, fool? I am as much a Christian as you. But there are some arts which men can learn without too much effort, and I have learned much about my powders. So, if you want to believe that I am a crazed worshipper of the Devil, you carry on.'

'He is a fool, Gynour,' Berenger said. With his good foot he poked at Clip, who fell over with a muttered curse. 'Sit by our fire, and take some food with us. We have some flour.'

'Flour?' The gynour's smile returned. 'I would be glad of a little. Do you have salt?'

Berenger was about to shake his head when he saw Archibald pull a small leather purse from under his chemise. 'Do you keep all your belongings in there?'

'My cross, my badge, my salt and my tinder.'

Berenger nodded to Oliver, who took flour from their communal bag, one handful per man, and placed it in the wooden bowl. He added water sparingly, and mixed it together with a little of the salt. Soon he had a thick dough, which he moulded into one ball per man, and squashed flat. Each man took one and set his upon a stone at the fireside. They all waited and watched in companionable silence, turning their little cakes every so often, until each was cooked to the satisfaction of the owner and gradually withdrawn from the heat to cool.

The gynour took his and held it between his hands while still piping hot. Looking up at Berenger, he nodded. 'I'm most

387

CHAPTER FORTY-NINE

It was still early when the warning horns blew, and the army was ordered to march once more.

'What is it now?' Berenger demanded of Grandarse, who appeared just as the first mists were beginning to disperse.

'You want to complain? Speak to the French! The bastards almost caught the King at breaking his fast. He and his officers had to leave their meals, so don't expect them to be in a good and friendly frame of mind when you see them.'

But for all his dire words, when Berenger saw the Prince and Sir John with the Earl of Warwick, the three were laughing and making jests at each other's expense. It could have been a show to keep the spirits of their men from flagging, but he somehow doubted it.

He had a fresh little pony, whose rider had died at the river yesterday, and he jogged along with less discomfort than he had experienced the day before. Perhaps it was the sight of the cheerful party of war-leaders, perhaps it was Archibald's conviction: whatever the reason, he felt happier than he had for days.

To add to his good mood, Geoff had recovered enough to give up his place in the cart to another injured archer who was in greater need. While he refused to mount a pony, saying, 'God gave me these legs for a reason,' and walked along at the side of the others, Geoff seemed more at peace with himself than he had been for some weeks. His attitude towards Béatrice was now that of a man who accepted her place and importance in their team. He even, once, offered her a share of his food.

It was late in the morning when they reached Oisemont, the local market town. Unfortunately, the people there were not willing to give it up to the English.

'Oh, God's teeth!' Geoff said when he saw the gates.

Before them, drawn up in irregular formation, stood the townspeople. A scratch force of all the young men of the area, clutching hedging and ditching tools fitted to long ash-poles, stood between the English and their city.

'They'll not survive above an hour,' Jack said. 'Silly shite-for-wits.'

Berenger felt sympathy for the townspeople as the English men-at-arms gathered, chuckling and teasing each other about the sport they were about to enjoy. Esquires and valets tightened buckles and fixings, making sure all was ready for their encounter, but the knights could not treat this seriously. It was one thing to charge a line of French cavalry, and quite another to gallop at a force of fearful citizens from a market town who had neither the training nor the weapons to pose a challenge.

At last, with many a humorous parting shot at the men all around, the Earl and his household, augmented by as many other knights as were gathered nearby, set off at a brisk trot. The rest of the army, without halting, continued on their way. There was no need for archers today. This was sport for the knights and nobles alone.

Berenger saw Sir John as he passed. The old knight was the only one who was not affected by the light-hearted mood. He acknowledged Berenger, but rode on without smiling, tugging his visor down over his face.

Sir John grimaced at the sight of the line of scrawny youths anxiously gripping homemade weapons, casting many a longing glance back towards the city gates and safety. He could see them all so clearly, and it made him wonder how his own folk would cope, were they to be thrown out before the gates at Exeter, or perhaps to hold a line before Crediton or Hatherleigh, while a force of French horse hurtled towards them. They would fare no better than these poor young fools.

The charge began when they were a few tens of yards from the townsmen. There were no archers to speak of in Oisemont, no Genoese bowmen to break the charge and pick off riders from any distance. The few archers they did have were armed with lightweight hunting bows more suited to foxes or deer than men in armour. Sir John was hit by two arrows, but the thick barbed arrowheads made no impression on his steel.

And then they were in. His lance's first thrust caught two men, a young lad in front, who was speared through the breast, and the man behind, who was pierced in his groin. Both writhed and screamed as he tried to flick their bodies over his head, but their weight together was too much for the lance. After a moment's bending, it suddenly snapped with a sound like a craky of war going off, and the two Oisemontians fell.

The scenes were appalling: it was wholesale slaughter. Sir John's sword flashing wetly with oily blood running along the blade, dripping from his gauntlet.

He felt sick. Where was the honour in this assault on a group of men who were obviously used to nothing more ferocious than a brawl with their fists in a tavern? They had no experience of meeting steel and cavalry. The English were disciplined and trained. To attack men such as these was little better than murder.

Sir John was ashamed as he lifted his sword and brought it down onto the head of a boy near him. The sword passed cleanly through his skull, shearing off the back of it, entire. On to the next, a fellow who could not yet have been twenty years old, who stood weeping with panic. He fell with Sir John's sword in his face. Another boy, another slash, another mother's lad dead. He was not a warrior today; he was a butcher.

Over the rattle of his armour, the noise of the battle, he became aware of another sound: a high ululation. At first he thought it could be the drawbridge, but there was none; then, perhaps a port-cullis, but that was not moving either. It was only later that he realised it was hundreds of women wailing to see their husbands, brothers and sons being slaughtered before their eyes.

It was a 'victory', but it felt as much of a defeat as their doomed attempts to cross the Somme.

By the middle of the afternoon, the army was on the move again, leaving a blackened graveyard where once Oisemont had stood. There had been few opportunities for plunder, but never mind that. Berenger and the others were glad to be leaving the place behind.

The French were within a few miles, and the river was still two leagues to their north, but there were no bridges. Berenger had little doubt that their end would not be long in coming.

He was happy that the men had enough flour for a cake a day each for the next three days, but after that they would be down to the same hard commons as the rest of the army.

The ground was already turning to marsh. Those with no shoes were collecting leeches, and the men were fed up with the clouds of mosquitoes and flies that settled on them. As they marched, all Berenger could hear was the regular slapping as men tried to kill as many of the insects as possible, but as soon as one was killed, three more would settle, their bites driving men to distraction.

They found some relief at night. In the wafts of clean-smelling woodsmoke from their fire, the mosquitoes retreated. Now, when Berenger looked about the faces of his men, he saw how grey and gaunt they were. If they could not find food soon there would be problems. Some soldiers, he heard, had resorted to cooking their boots. His vintaine was not forced to that indignity yet, but they were half-starved. There were few difficulties more likely to raise the spectre of mutiny than hunger. If the French kept them restricted to this land, bounded by the sea and the river, they would be in real trouble. There were fewer and fewer farms and no obvious stores to plunder. They would have to scavenge as best they might.

Grandarse appeared in the middle watches, speaking softly. 'Frip, you need to get off and scout around north. There are rumours of men moving about.'

'Infantry?'

'Could be. Watch yourself.'

Berenger took Geoff, Clip and five more with him. Geoff was still sore from his wound, but he was more rested than the others after his rides in the wagon over the last days. Berenger's ankle was bad but he could hobble fast. Clip was brought partly because Berenger wanted to prevent his whining too much at the other men and disturbing them, and partly because of a growing conviction that no matter who else might be injured or killed, Clip would remain immune. In any case, he was the king of all the scroungers in the King's army. If there was any food within a ten-mile radius, Clip would sniff it out.

'With me, friends,' Berenger said, and they all walked off into the night.

It was an overcast evening, with the moon no more than a blur behind the clouds, which was all to the good so far as Berenger was concerned. But while they could move without being seen, so could the enemy. The marshiness of the land was a disadvantage: every five to ten steps took them into a bog. The puddles were cold and foul-smelling, and there were stifled grunts and gasps as the men tripped or tumbled into the belching mud.

Clip got the jitters when a flame came to life over to his left, flickering pale blue. 'What the . . .' he began. 'Is that a ghost?'

Jack laughed quietly. 'I hope so. It's our Will o' the Wisp come back to help us.'

They covered perhaps a mile or more, moving with great caution. They made slow progress, but when scouting in this kind of light, Berenger knew it was always hard to discover where the enemy was. Geoff walked without comment apart from an occasional hiss of pain: Clip muttered the whole way.

It was when they were within sight of a tiny copse that stood proud of the low-lying lands all about, that Clip stopped.

Berenger held up a hand. He knew the other man's every mood and movement, and this was not play-acting. Clip had sensed something in the woods ahead. When he hesitated like that, his eyes narrowed, his hook-like nose pointing and twitching like a greyhound's scenting game, a man was advised to take note.

Clip did not need to speak. He slowly brought up his arm, the hand flat like a blade, and pointed forward, then to the right. There was a narrow pathway there, and Berenger nodded. He motioned to Geoff to join him, and the two set off, stepping slowly so as not to make a sound. There were no twigs here, on this sodden ground, but Berenger was taking no risks. Geoff also stepped with exaggerated care.

They were almost around the trees when there came a squawk of fear. Suddenly the woods seemed alive, and Berenger and Geoff stood stock-still, wondering whether they should rush forward or remain where they were. Their task was to capture a local, ideally, or to find out where enemy movements were, but not to engage with stronger forces. There was no advantage in getting killed.

Berenger heard a bellow, and recognised the voices of his men. They were spread out in a screen to beat their prey forward. And then Berenger saw the figures: stalk-like shapes running towards him in the murk.

Geoff bent, hiding among the rushes, and Berenger copied him. Soon, there came a flurry of splashing and swearing, and Geoff sprang up. A scream of terror, and Geoff grabbed his man and threw him to the ground. At the same time Berenger saw a man appear in front of him, a tall, lanky fellow with a shock of thick hair and a beard. Berenger launched himself at the fellow.

'Ooh, Booger!' he heard, just as his shoulder connected with the man's waist and brought him down. 'Booger!'

Berenger and Geoff marched their two captives to the trees, where Clip and the others were enthusiastically rummaging through their belongings. 'Look at this, Frip!' Clip said. 'A basket of fish, most of it smoked.'

'Who are you?' Berenger demanded of the man he had caught.

'*Moi? Je ne . . .*'

'If you're French I'm a Saracen,' Berenger growled. 'Frenchmen don't cry "bugger" when they're caught.'

The man peered back at him in the gloom. Although there was no light to see his expression, Berenger was sure that there was a calculating gleam in his eyes. 'Who are you, then?' the man asked.

'You know who we are. Are you a deserter? The King has a quick way with deserters.'

'Booger that! I'm no soldier – I'm a fisherman. I married a maid from Oisemont and I live here.'

'Why are you out here, then?'

'Like I said, I'm a fisherman. We were out at sea yesterday, and couldn't get past you lot, so we decided to wait a bit. And while we were about it, we brought the spare fish from our store before you people stole the lot. I've a family to feed,' he added with a note of reproof.

'We've got an army to feed,' Berenger said without sympathy. 'You'll have to take us to your stores.'

'I can't do that.'

'You'll find you can,' Berenger told him. 'Once I start breaking your fingers and toes, for instance.'

The man tilted his head to one side. 'I could be more useful if you leave me in one piece.'

'How so?'

There was a flash of teeth.

'You want to cross the river, don't you? Well, I can show you where and how.'

CHAPTER FIFTY

Sir John eyed the fellow without enthusiasm. 'He could be leading us straight into a trap, my Lord.'

'He could,' the Prince agreed. Edward of Woodstock beckoned, and Berenger and Geoff brought the man nearer. 'What is your name?'

'Hugh of York.'

'You are a Yorkshireman?'

'Born and raised, as God's my witness,' Hugh said.

'Why are you here?'

'I've already said. I married a local maid, and I've been living here for nigh on ten years. I'm a fisherman, and I can ply my trade wherever I want. This land appealed to me.'

'You say you know a crossing place?'

'It's easily forded at low tide. Then the water is up to your knees, no higher. But leave it to high tide, and you'll drown.'

The Prince looked at the others. 'Well?'

The Earl of Warwick shrugged. 'I dare say it is worth the attempt.'

'Would we be able to cross in the dark?' the Prince asked.

Hugh shook his head. 'Not a good idea. Besides, the tide will go out with the dawn. The way would be difficult.'

'Is it guarded?' the Earl demanded.

'Yes. But so is everywhere else. At least at this ford the defence is not so strong.'

'How do you know?' Sir John said.

'I passed it tonight. There were maybe five hundred French guarding it, no more.'

'Five hundred?' Sir John repeated. 'Sweet Jesu! If they know their business, with that sort of force they could hold us for hours while we tried to storm the river. And then their army could fall on our rear.'

'What do you think, my Lord Warwick?' the Prince asked once more.

'I still believe it is worth testing this out. Your father must question him. Let us see what he thinks.'

'An excellent idea. Take him to my father,' the Prince said to Berenger and Geoff. 'And meantime, have the vanguard prepare to leave. If this man tells the truth, he may become the richest fisherman on the coast!'

24 August

Berenger was back with the vintaine shortly afterwards. When he found the men, they were all were chewing the dried, hard fish. It needed a day's soaking in water to make it softer, and the salt in it was enough to make a man want to drink for an hour, but for all that, it was food, and none of the men would turn their noses up at it. Berenger himself took a piece with gratitude.

The army was ready to move, and his vintaine was detailed to go with the Prince's men as they followed the directions of Hugh the Yorkshireman.

He took them northwards through the marshes, where the carts and wagons became bogged down, and the men grew adept at liberating their wagons. It was long after midnight when at last Berenger saw the black ribbon of the water before them.

Already there were shouts from the opposite bank as they approached. With the noise of their passage, it was no surprise that the French had been alerted, and the English troops stood with their weapons in their fists, eyeing the farther shore with misgivings. Crossing a river this broad while an enemy held the opposite bank and could keep up a steady fire was not a pleasant prospect.

'He said five hundred,' Jack grumbled to Clip. 'If there's only five hundred, *I'm* a fucking Yorkshireman too.'

Berenger grinned as he stared through the blackness. All he could see was the sparkle and flicker of hundreds of little fires.

'There're enough there for a hundred vintaines,' Jack went on. 'Maybe even more.'

Berenger grunted agreement. Christ's pain! This would prove a dark and bloody crossing if he was right.

'Did Hugh mean to trap us here, do you think, Frip?' Jack said in a low voice.

'No. But if we are trapped, what of it? We were trapped before, and the army is hot on our heels, so we're no worse off than before. We still have to cross that river.'

'Yes.' Jack was silent for a while, staring out over the turbulent waters. Then he said: 'If by fording here, we only win a few more days – so what? We may die trying – but we'll die here anyway if we don't. What the devil! I'm for it!'

Berenger felt a burst of hope flare in his heart. And then, he heard Clip's monotone.

'Aye, well, you know you'll all get killed?'

Berenger could have hugged him. The atmosphere lightened as though Clip's whining voice held a special magic all of its own.

They passed a miserable night at the side of the river, feeling their feet sinking into the cold, muddy soil. Berenger tried to sit down, but in moments his backside was sodden, and rather than sit there, he walked about to keep warm. His bad ankle seemed to have seized at first, and he limped painfully, but it grew less troublesome. For some reason the night had grown chillier, and all the men were shivering badly before the sun rose.

It was their good fortune that the tide was at its lowest in the morning. As soon as the light was clear enough, Berenger saw French warriors form into three lines. It was plain that this small section was where the ford stood. And here the success or failure of the English army would be decided.

To the clamour of drums and horns, a hundred English archers were ordered forward. Walking with their bows over their heads to keep their strings dry, the men stepped into the river, full quivers on their backs. One humorous fellow complained it was so cold that his cods had shrunk to acorns, but for the most part they waded silently, until the waters were above their thighs.

Behind them on foot came a hundred heavily armed fighters under Sir Reginald de Cobham and the Earl of Northampton and, as the fighters passed through the screen of archers, the bowmen began to loose their arrows. First one, then three, then more Frenchmen were struck as the arrows fell among them. Each bowman was firing as swiftly as only English archers could, and their bows were thrumming so loudly they almost drowned the shrieks and cries of the injured Frenchmen.

The Earl and Sir Reginald reached the other side unscathed and led their men up the bank, some floundering in the mud while others clambered on, only to be killed within yards of the shore by French crossbowmen. However, the Earl and the knight managed to reach the French, and a sharp fight began.

Meanwhile, more men were wading and splashing across the water. While the Earl and his fighters kept the French busy, the newcomers reinforced the bridgehead and began to push the French back.

There were over three thousand French fighters there to greet the English. Berenger could see them clearly from his vantage point on top of the archers' cart, but as a French fighter fell, there were no reserves. In comparison, the hundred English were soon two hundred, then three, and more and more were floundering through the water all the time. It was a fierce, bitter fight – but within an hour of the first men reaching the French bank, it was over. The last of the French were racing away towards Abbeville, while more English crossed and widened their bridgehead, and at last the wagons and carts could be sent to join them.

Berenger watched with frank astonishment. 'How did we do that?' he wondered.

'There's only one explanation,' Jack said. He snorted. 'We were a bloody sight more desperate than them.'

And so they were. Later, as Berenger stood on the north bank of the Somme and stared about him, he saw the last of the English forces cross the river, and then, a scant mile away to the south, he spotted a pennant. Beckoning Clip to him, he demanded, 'What is it? What can you see?'

'The French,' Clip droned. 'We're all going to get slaughtered now. It's the whole fucking French army, Frip.'

Berenger frowned at him. 'Are you serious? You're scared of them?'

Clip gawped at him. 'Aren't you?'

Berenger looked down at the river. It was already much deeper. 'The tide's in, Clip. No one's going to cross that today! We've been saved.'

'Are you sure?'

Berenger nodded, and then he began to laugh.

'You know what, Clip?' he chuckled. 'I reckon we really are going to win. I think we really do have God on our side.'

'God? Nah, it was Wisp!'

25 August

It was the day after their crossing, and Berenger stood with the rest of the vintaine, watching the French army assemble on the opposite bank.

'We've been on duty all night, Frip. Can't they find someone else to take over?' Clip whined. 'I need my sleep, me.'

'Shut up.'

'He's right,' Geoff said. Berenger hadn't expected him to support Clip, and looked at him with curiosity. 'Frip, they ought to have someone replace us by now. Look, most of the army's resting back there, isn't it? But we still get the bum jobs.'

They had cause for complaint. Since crossing, the vintaine had been told to remain on guard. But not alone. All along the bank, English lines stood waiting for the French to cross. Everyone was convinced that they would. Only the turn of the tide had prevented their immediate passage.

'How are you, Fripper?' Sir John had joined him.

Berenger nodded towards the farther bank. 'While they are over there, I'm happy.'

'We made it.'

'They can still cross the river, just as we did.'

'No. They fear attacking us on this kind of ground. We can hurry north and they won't hinder us.' He looked at Berenger. 'You reminded me of our journey here many years ago. I think you were right. The fields outside Crécy will serve us admirably well.'

'Provided they don't force their way over.'

'As you say. Do you not think it is a miracle?'

The priests had declared their escape to be a miracle, like that of the Jews' passage through the Red Sea when God held back the waters, only releasing the torrent when the Egyptians pursued them.

'Miracle?' Berenger chuckled. 'I see it more as making masterly use of that fisherman Hugh, and taking the opportunity that presented itself. If the advance guard had failed to push the French from the bank, the army would already be destroyed. All our skills at fighting would not have availed us against the French.'

'That is why the King has split our army.'

The main bulk was here to protect the crossing, but a large force under Hugh Despenser had been sent to the coast to seize all the provisions he could find. Bread, cattle, pigs – everything edible – must be gathered for the army. This while Berenger and the others were left behind, feet sinking into the mud and sand, bows unstrung, strings held next to the skin to keep them dry against the threatened drizzle from the dark skies.

'Keep a close eye on the enemy, Frip,' Sir John advised as he left. 'We don't want any surprises.'

Ed had returned to them, ready to bring them the arrows they would need if the French began to cross.

Now he asked. 'Do you think they'll come, Frip?'

The youth had grown in the last weeks. He was leaner, more

self-assured than the puny lad whom Berenger had found bleeding in the Portsmouth gutter. His eyes were more intent, as though they could see things that ordinary men could not. But the edge of lunacy that had characterised his appearance and manner in those early weeks was gone. In its place was a steadiness and reserve. Perhaps they would make something of the boy after all.

The vintener gave him an honest reply. 'They will have to try. If they don't attempt the river, they will have to travel miles eastwards, to cross by a bridge. And a bridge is a narrow passage at the best of times. We were able to cross with speed. On a bridge, they'll manage one cart or wagon abreast: we travelled two or three wagons abreast.'

'So they only wait for the tide?'

'I expect so. Then life will suddenly get very exciting.'

He didn't mention his greater fear: that French cavalry had already crossed the river by the bridge. That idea gnawed at him. The notion that at any moment a strong party of French cavalry might appear over the nearer horizon and charge into their flank, was one that brought him out in a cold sweat. If it were to happen before Despenser returned with his men, the English would be torn apart.

But for now, to his relief, there was no sign that the French had their main force on this side of the river.

'Berenger!'

His attention snapped to Jack, who stood warily staring over the waters. His hand was inside his chemise, and that was enough to put Berenger on the alert. Jack was gripping his bow-string, ready to assemble his bow again.

'What is it?'

'Those men over at the left: horsemen. They're riding back east.'

Berenger's eyes were not so farseeing as Jack's, but he could make out a strong party of men-at-arms riding away from the main French forces. 'I see them.'

'Is that what they are doing?' the Donkey asked. There was a slight quiver in his voice, as though he was assailed by sudden fear. 'They're riding round to the bridge to attack us?'

Berenger made a quick calculation. The tide was coming in again now, so soon the waters would be impassable once more. It wouldn't take the french forces that long to ride to the first bridge, cross it and return to the English camp, but no doubt they were being ordered to find additional men to bring with them. That would take about twelve hours clear, he estimated.

'Frip? There are more going. Look, over there!' Jack was pointing again, and now a smile was breaking out over his face.

Berenger stared, and as he did so, a sense of relief washed through his very soul.

'They're going!' he said happily. 'They're bloody going!'

CHAPTER FIFTY-ONE

26 August

The blare of trumpets woke Berenger with a start, and he muttered to himself as he threw off his blanket and stood stamping his feet in the cold air. There had been a time when he would always have woken before the dawn and before even the earliest heralds could draw breath to blow their horns. Not so now. Too many weeks of marching, fighting for survival, nights without sleep and the dread of being caught by the French had taken the edge off his early rising.

They had waited last afternoon until the French were all gone, and then only a small contingent was left to watch over the ford while the army packed and prepared. The King had them all moving as the tide rose and made a passage across impossible, and they had reached this wood late in the afternoon. With plentiful supplies of firewood and space for all to lie down, the men had spent their first comfortable night for some time. The wagons were lashed together to prevent a surprise attack from their enemy, with the horses and ponies herded inside, and then the men settled, seeing to their weapons and armour, and many taking Mass from the priests.

Berenger slapped his arms about his torso in an attempt to urge some blood into his fingers, and blew on them as he eyed his vintaine. Their losses had brought the originally under-manned unit to below half its strength. Although he now had Roger's men with his own, the addition of Tyler was not reas-suring. The man was untrustworthy.

As he kicked Clip, Berenger brought back to mind all those who had died. The smiling faces, the cheerful souls, the grim ones, the thoughtful, the angry. The man who screamed in rage when he ran to battle, the men who stood back, watching for a suitable target, those who grabbed the nearest woman, those who preferred to visit the church and bow their heads while outside their English comrades ran amok. So many had died in the last years of fighting. Too many to recall all their names, he realised to his shame. No, it was only that he was tired. Too tired.

He waited until the chuntering Clip had taken sticks and tinder and set about making a fire. Berenger had a little flour left, and he had bought some oats from a Welshman. The differ-ent teams were more than happy to swap or sell their provisions now that Despenser had returned with herds of cattle and swine and carts filled with other stores from le Crotoy, which he had sacked.

There was a lot of complaining as usual, but nothing serious. Compared with the concerns he had heard while they were stuck on the other bank of the river a few days ago, even Clip's nasally-voiced grumbles were a pleasure to hear. All was well in their world.

Berenger passed Jack the oats and flour and watched him mix and shape the rough patties into balls. There was a thick grey smoke rising from the fire now, and Clip blew on the embers until his face was purple, while the others supplied a running commentary.

'I could have been fed and watered by now, if I was at home. Up on the hills, if you don't get yoursel' out of your bed and ready, the foxes will have had all the lambs.'

'Don't blow it like that, man! You'll blow it out! Breathe on it *gently*.'

'Clip, if you stick your arse in the air like that, Geoff will be after you. He couldn't resist a backside like that.'

'You'd know, Grand*arse*!'

'Blow this side now, you lurdan! No! Round here!'

'You want to blow on it yourself, Jack – feel free,' Clip snapped, sitting up, his face black with soot and ash from a gust of wind. 'I'll put my feet up while you get the fire going.'

'Oh, aye. You go and rest, you lazy deofol,' Jack said without rancour. 'We'll get the fire going, and then, since I've made your cake, I'll eat that too. Yes, you laze around while we do all the work – as usual.'

'Work? You idle sods don't know the meaning of the word!'

'What does it matter? "Ye'll all be dead soon. They'll slaughter you."' There was a general guffaw.

Berenger sighed happily. While his men were taking the rise out of each other, he was content.

When the fire was burning well, Jack produced a griddle-iron from the cart and hung it from a tripod of sticks. Each man set his little patties on the hot surface and waited eagerly for them to cook.

Berenger took his and broke it open to release the steam before eating. It was good to feel the food in his belly, warming and filling at the same time. He took his sword and began to whet it with his stone, preparing for whatever the day should bring. He had a strong premonition that there would be a need for a good, sharp weapon soon.

The command to decamp came as the men were finishing their oaten cakes and gulping down beer liberated from a little farm Clip had found. Called to their feet, they moved in the slouching manner Berenger recognised so well. It was always the way of the English to pretend to a careless disobedience that they would never exhibit on the battlefield. Or not often, he amended.

For all their posturing, the men were quickly packed. While many esquires and heralds were still hurrying from tent to sumpter horse, Berenger's men were ready and waiting.

'Takes a lot longer for nobles to get their shit together, don't it?' Clip sniped. 'Why don't they wake those sods up first, and leave us to get our rest?'

'You need more beauty sleep, that's for certain,' Berenger grunted.

'At least my face isn't past improvement,' Clip countered. 'Not that it matters. We'll all be killed soon. All of us slaughtered.'

'Shut the fuck up!' came the general cry.

The delay had set some of the other men to fretting. 'When will we be moving?' Oliver asked.

'The French aren't here yet,' Jack told him.

'No, but they could be at any time. They're only a few miles away. I don't know – how far is it to Abbeville?'

Jack shrugged. 'Should have asked that Yorkshire git while we had him. He'd have known.'

'Maybe,' Berenger agreed.

'Why are you bothered? If they get here, we'll just use archers to keep them back while the army makes good its escape.' It was Tyler speaking. He was standing behind the remains of

Roger's men, a little apart. Berenger wondered whether that was his choice, or because he had been rejected by his companions.

'Do you think the King wants to run from them?' Oliver asked.

'Of course he does,' Jack said. 'He's no fool. He wants to stay a couple of steps ahead of them, doesn't he?'

'Then why are we still here? We could have set off earlier yesterday. What was the point of staying here all night, and having such a long sleep, Jack?'

Jack shrugged. 'I don't pretend to understand him and his plans. What are you getting so worked up about?'

'I like to know what someone's planned for me,' Oliver said.

Berenger shook his head. 'He's planning on giving us our battle, you lurdans! He kept us here to make sure we were rested, and now he'll take us to the place he reckons gives him the best chance of defeating the French army.'

'That won't be easy. They look like they have double the men we have,' Jack said

'Or more, yes,' Clip said.

'I thought nearer three times our force,' Berenger considered.

'Really? Christ's bones, I didn't realise there were that many.'

'Yes, Jack. So today you'd best keep your string dry and your arrows near to hand. And pray that we don't see the French before our King is ready to receive them. Because if they were to get here too soon and catch us in the open, we would be sitting targets.'

Clip nodded contentedly. 'Aye. We'll all be killed. There'll be a great slaughter.'

Berenger sniffed the air. There was a comforting odour of woodsmoke and toasting bread all about. It added to his sense of impending battle. He felt his face crack into a smile again. The waiting would be over, at last.

Oliver interrupted his thoughts. 'But you don't think that's going to happen?'

'Our King has brought us this far safe enough. I think he has something in his mind already,' Berenger said. Just as he spoke, there was a squeak and a rattle from the wagons ahead. A bellow, a blast on a horn, and the army began to trundle onward. 'Come, Jack. We've both been in enough wars to know how to fight. With luck, we'll soon have a chance to fight one last battle and stop this war with a good profit!'

Archibald rolled about on his wagon half-asleep, his head lolling with every jerk of the wheels over the uneven ground. His oxen team were well rested, but he wasn't. At one jolt, he almost fell from his perch, and was only saved by Ed and Béatrice, who each grabbed his jerkin and pulled him back.

'Thank you, thank you,' he mumbled.

Last night, in his mind, he had gone over all the miles of the journey to reach this place. He recalled the journey by sea, the many rivers and streams, the hurried flight from Paris, the troublesome crossing of the Somme, and now a thin mizzle began to spit at his face, reminding him of the Somme. In the middle of the night he had given up all attempts at sleep and instead made his way to the wagon park, where he sought out his barrels and weapons. To his relief all seemed well, but he was not content to leave them. Instead he wrapped himself in a blanket and lay down beneath his wagon, running through his mind the many things he must do in the morning.

And now it was morning, and he was behind with all his tasks. Still, he had food in his belly, for Béatrice was a helpful little filly about the camp. She was behind him now, sitting and staring out ahead. Without glancing at her, he knew what her expression would be. She would be glaring at the world, loathing France and all Frenchmen.

They had passed by the last of the trees, and now they clattered and rumbled past marching men. An uncountable number, he thought, stretching and towards the field. Ahead lay a road, which they must cross, and he could see a village on the left and a second on the right. Before them, the land rose slightly into a natural ridge, with a windmill on the right. The men were steadily trudging towards the left of the windmill, and he took his wagon lumbering and rumbling over to the right of it. Suddenly, a man bellowed, running up to him and pointing back the way he had come. When he was nearer, Archibald guessed he was a sergeant.

'Get this lump of shite away, you prick! This is where the men will be standing. Put the wagon back with the others!'

'Go and bully a loon who'll be scared by your bluster,' Archibald said calmly. 'This wagon's full of the King's favourites.'

'Favourites?' The sergeant strode to the wagon and lifted an edge of the waxed cloth protecting the contents. 'A metal pot? Don't play the fool with—'

'Sergeant, this toy is the King's favourite for today. And the barrels are meat and wine to them, so leave me in peace. When I've dropped them off, I will send the wagon back to you. But I am *not* carrying them all the way from here.'

The sergeant looked as though he was going to argue, but then there was a shout and two fellows in the line of men-at-arms marching to the front began jostling and fighting. After a sour look at Archibald, the sergeant spat a curse and then hurried to the squabbling men, bawling at them to stop.

'What's going on?' Béatrice asked, staring.

'Just soldiers having an argument,' Archibald chuckled. 'They aren't allowed to fight – at least, not with each other!'

They rumbled on until suddenly they were past the windmill and could take in the sweep of the land.

The ridge ran along in a curve, like an inverted 'U', with perhaps a half-mile between the two arms. A line of men was forming. Archibald aimed the wagon between them as he drove it to the field where the English troops hoped to join battle.

As they passed over the road, the wagon crashed over a stone, and the gynour swore as he was jolted to the side of his seat, throwing an anxious glance over his shoulder. Relieved, he blew out his cheeks.

'Perhaps our King will mend the roads, too, once he is undisputed ruler of this land,' he said under his breath as he used the reins to persuade the oxen to move.

'Why do we go here?' Béatrice asked.

'Hey? Oh, the King knows his business, I suppose,' he said, checking the position of the sun. 'If you have to have a battle, this isn't a bad place, is it?'

It was a shallow rise, perhaps only twenty yards above the road itself, but as Archibald gazed about him, he realised that this was a perfect ground for fighting. He hoisted himself up on the wagon's seat. At the top of the ridge the windmill made, a rallying point for the English. Before it, the land fell away in a shallow incline from the English ridge. On the right was the river, serving to protect that flank, and before them the land was clear and unobstructed all along the road. The road which would lead King Philippe to King Edward's trap. From here he could observe the men being led in to form three long battles, one behind the other, across the ridge. There was shouting and roaring from the vinteners and centeners as they bullied and pushed their men into lines. Flags appeared as nobles had their banners thrust into the ground, and already the Earl of Warwick's standard was held in place, and the positions of all the Lords were marked out by the time that the knights arrived, all on foot.

This was not to be a cavalry battle; this was to be a battle fought on a strong defensive position, tempting the enemy to attack and be riven by English arrows and Archibald's toys.

The men were in their positions, and now the gynour had to do the same. He must work out the best place for his little crackers.

CHAPTER FIFTY-TWO

Berenger swore as he marched up the hill towards the ridge. A series of greyish-yellow clouds had moved in, and a thick mizzle was in the air, blown with the wind.

The vintaine had already given up their ponies to the urchin who was detailed to take them to the rear of the army, and now they were squelching their way over the damp ground to their positions. After giving them instructions on where they were supposed to be standing, Grandarse had hurried off to discuss the plans with Sir John, leaving the men to find their own way.

When Berenger stopped and stared back the way they had come, he saw a thick straggle of men stretched all over the hill-side, with numbers gradually forming under their lords' banners, while more streamed towards the lines like iron filings inexorably drawn to a magnet.

He and the men were situated at the far left wing of the front battle. This was a line of foot-soldiers with, to the fore, the heaviest armoured men of all, the knights, mingled with the remaining Welsh pikemen. Berenger could see Erbin and his men in the midst of the first battle.

Behind this was a second battle, which could be thrown into the fight to support the front rank, and, held a little further back, a final reserve, with the wagons behind to form a solid defence against attack from the rear. Not that it would be easy for that to happen. Any assault would have to arrive from one of the two villages that stood at each side of the English lines, or come through the woods behind.

Today, the strength of the English would lie in the skill of the archers, that much was clear. For the English had learned that, while knights on horseback could serve a great purpose in fast, fluid campaigns, when it came to a purely defensive battle, it was better to have the heavily armoured men in the front line with the other foot.

The two vintaines were mingled with a thick group of archers, angled towards the field in front of them. On their right, the first battle of Englishmen stretched away into the distance, with the rest of the archers positioned on the opposite flank. Berenger could see them, all with their bows unstrung, just like himself and his own men. There was no point in letting the strings get wet: they would stretch and grow useless. Jack and the others had their strings tucked into their shirts or under their hats to keep them dry. Berenger had his wound up tightly and installed securely in his purse. The oiled leather would keep it dry for a long time.

Still the men kept coming. Some were walking through the English lines, having delivered wagons and carts to the wagon camp behind the lines, and were looking for their own sections, while others were toiling up the hill in the wake of Berenger and his men. He watched the wagons, led by Archibald, trundling over the grass and taking up a position down to their left, at the farthest point of the archers. Soon Archibald had other gynours helping him to erect a three-legged, makeshift crane beside his wagon, while their assistants unloaded little carts like wheelbarrows. When the tripod was ready, Archibald supervised the emptying of the wagon. First, a large wooden trestle was lifted and eased over the side to lie on the ground. Archibald and two helpers levered it around until they were happy with its position.

Next began the task of moving the cumbersome weight of his great gonne. Four assistants grabbed the ropes and began to haul. The tripod creaked and complained, but as they pulled, straining, the long tube appeared. Archibald gave directions for the massive tube to be set on the wooden frame.

Berenger was distracted by Jack, who frowned up at the clouds, saing, 'If there's more poxy rain, we'll be fucked this day, Berenger.'

'You think so? Perhaps. But at least there'll be a conclusion.' Berenger glanced about him. 'There'll be no running away today, that is certain.'

'Eh?'

'The men-at-arms and the knights, they're all standing together. No horses, they're all kept within the wagon park behind us. With the forest there, and the villages either side, it'll be hard to run anywhere. And we won't any of us make it to the sea, so, lads, here we are, and here we will stand.'

'Here we'll die, you mean,' Clip said immediately. 'Ye know, we'll all get—'

'Slaughtered – yeah, we know,' Geoff snapped. 'Now shut your gob and stop reminding us, you little git!'

'Only trying to cheer you up,' Clip beamed.

'What – by telling us we're all going to get killed?' Jack said scornfully. 'How's that going to cheer us up?'

'Well, could be worse,' Clip said.

417

'Shut up,' Geoff said.

'How exactly?' Jack demanded.

'We could be on board ship. Then we'd die feeling seasick and cold and wet. And get chucked overboard.'

'Oh, give me strength!' Geoff said. There was a spark of light in the distance. 'God's ballocks, what was that?'

'Don't blaspheme,' Jack reprimanded him. 'Not before a battle.'

Geoff opened his mouth to argue back, but then he nodded. 'You're right. My apologies. I'll say *Pater Noster* and ask for forgiveness.'

It began to spit with rain.

Geoff turned a face full of frustration to Clip. 'Now look what you've done!'

'Wasn't me!' said Clip. 'It was you bellyaching again. God thought to give you something to complain about for once.'

'You little . . .'

Berenger shoved Clip out of the way before Geoff could grab him. 'Enough! Clip, move to the left flank, Geoff, you to the right. No more bickering from either of you. I've had a bellyfull already.'

A loud rumble came across the plains: thunder.

'How long before it starts?' Ed asked. He had delivered the oxen and wagon at the park behind the men and hurried to help the archers. He stood on tiptoe, peering past them.

'Soon enough,' Jack muttered.

'Good to have you here, boy,' Geoff said.

Jack clapped him on the back as Berenger nodded. 'Just bring the arrows as fast as you can today, Donkey. We will have need of speed. The rest of you, keep your bowstrings dry!'

*   *   *

It was only when the entire army had been standing in their positions for two hours of the sun or more that the bannerets and barons rode to their men. Berenger watched as Grandarse and Sir John cantered down towards them from the windmill where the King had his command position. From there, the highest point of the whole area, he had an unrivalled view.

The cavalcade rode to the front of the archers, and Sir John trotted to the farthest extreme of the English lines. He remained astride his horse, pulling his bascinet from his head, and his hair shone grey as steel in the grim light. Shoving his helmet under his arm, he surveyed the men before him.

'Archers! This is your position for the fight to come! From here, you can see the dip in the ground clearly. The French will approach us from there, to the east, and we think it is likely that they will hurry towards us and meet us here today. We hope so. You have the day to prepare and take your ease; the French will arrive after marching for miles. Are you happy with your positions? Memorise your posts here, all of you. As soon as you hear the horns, you must be here, ready to throw yourselves into battle. You must hurry back here, no matter what you have been doing: no matter that you are standing with your hosen around your ankles, whether you are stirring a pottage or whoring with one of the army wives, you must return, grab your weapons and prepare to fight to the last.'

He cast an eye over the men before him. 'You are English archers. You have the skill and the weapons to put the fear of God and His Saints into the French. God willing, we shall win this battle. But God makes demands of all of us. You must all go to Mass and ask Him for His help during the battle to come, and then you must give Him all the help you can. Before then, and starting right now, I want to see the whole of the field in front of our lines pocked with holes: one foot square and one foot deep. Where there is a flat, clear space, I want you to savage it. If you can't measure that accurately – I mean you, Master Clip – just dig a short ditch. We must make the land intolerable for horses before they arrive. If the field has the same aspect as a paddock full of rabbit holes, they will not be able to charge us for risk of breaking their chargers' legs. Now, make sure you know where your rallying banners lie; make sure you know by whom you stand. Remember: this is where you must return when the French appear. And I say again: *you must return with all speed.*'

He looked at them again, this time shooting a glance at Berenger. Then he jerked his head in a gesture of beckoning, and trotted a short way down the grassy plain.

Berenger rode over to him as the men began to break out of their rigid lines and gather up mattocks and spades. 'Sir John?'

'Berenger, I have a task for you and your men.' The knight dismounted and passed the reins to a groom, who led Aeton back to the horse-lines. 'Bring the vintaine. Your friend Archibald is in need of aid.'

'Him?' Berenger asked. Looking to where Archibald had a number of gynours running around as he bellowed at them. 'Why?'

'It's his equipment – it's the Devil's fire, so far as I am concerned,' Sir John said, his lip twisted in distaste. 'I dislike the things. That damned powder burns so fiercely, it can ignite if you only strike it with a steel and flint. Damn it to hell, the odour afterwards makes you think you've been snatched away by the Devil. But it makes a crack so loud, it will put terror into the heart of the bravest destrier, or so they say.' His voice and his manner betrayed his doubts. 'Archibald needs more pairs of hands, and he has asked if you can give him assistance.'

'We will help him so far as we may,' Berenger promised.

'Good. I put you under his command for now. Keep your bows nearby, and remember: keep your bowstrings dry!'

Ed laboured like a slave that day. When he wasn't carrying Archibald's small but heavy barrels, or helping push carts into position, he was set to fetching food and water for the men.

It was ceaseless work, but it had the advantage that he was still at the front with her.

Béatrice was like a woman possessed. She almost ran as she carried the little bags filled with stone and metal balls, and tossed her head scorefully when Clip moaned about working too hard.

The whole vintaine, such as it now was, stayed there all morning while the English army dug their little pits all over the field, until there were only the holes with piles beside where the soil had been dumped. Men still wandered about, some sergeants and a knight or two, pointing to any areas where the ground could do with another assault. Some patches showed as little green islands, but they were few and far between. Mostly the ground was pitted as though a massive fork had been jabbed into the soil by an infuriated giant.

'What good will these things do?' Clip nagged as he rolled another barrel of powder up behind the great tube.

'You will be surprised,' Archibald said. He was squinting down the length of his gonne. 'You see this? When I set a spark to the hole at the back of the gonne here, it will stab flame and thunder at the victim. Those,' he went on, pointing to the three large tubes being set up nearby, 'those will hurl numbers of little balls of stone or steel darts straight at the enemy, and cut them down. Just you wait! You will see the first Christian battle making full use of this wonderful new invention. When these little crackers go off, the French will run for their lives!'

Ed pondered that as he helped dig trenches behind the other two gonnes. The latter were made of long steel bars that had been heated and hammered together. The individual staves were reinforced by more steel bands bound around them and holding them into their shape, like long steel barrels. Ed and the gynours had to dig deep to set three lengths of timber behind each barrel. Archibald kept talking about the barrels leaping into the air when they fired: these timbers were set to provide a firm support to stop them bucking and moving backwards. Ropes were laid over them and tethered to great metal spikes thrust into the ground on either side until Ed could not imagine how they could possibly move. They were too securely fastened. Even a kick from a destrier wouldn't shift them.

'Don't you believe it,' Archibald said contentedly. 'And *never* stand behind the gonnes when they launch their missiles or you will be crushed like a beetle. They leap like salmon!'

Ed had a ball in his hand, weighing it. It was enormously heavy, and at four inches in diameter, he wondered how it could be thrown with any great power. He would find it difficult to hurl it more than fifteen paces.

'And now,' Archibald concluded, 'we are ready. Any French whoreson who tries to come here and assail the archers in flank will wish he had never been born.'

CHAPTER FIFTY-THREE

The men were called back to their position at the braying of trumpets, and Berenger and the others hared back over the grass. Most of the other archers were already waiting, sitting on their shields against the damp of the grass, some gazing longingly to the west, thinking of their homes, while others stared at the ground as if wondering what it would feel like to be buried there.

Berenger stood bellowing at the others, urging them to greater speed. He fumbled and almost dropped his bowstring, slipping the noose over the top, fitting the knot to the bottom, then bending the bow and sliding the topmost noose into its grooves. The bow was ready.

'String your bows!' he yelled, looking up and down his line of men. They were already nocking arrows and gazing about them, alert for a target. On the opposite hill a trio of horsemen could be seen racing hell for leather towards the English lines.

'Archers! *Hold*!' Berenger roared. 'They're ours, men. Our scouts.'

MICHAEL JECKS

Now more figures appeared, pursuing the English scouts. There were five of them, and from the way their armour sparkled, they must have been men-at-arms. They reined in and stared at the army massed before them, two turning and haring away while the remaining three sat calmly observing the English dispositions.

Berenger relaxed. These were the forerunners of the French army, but the main force was not near enough for a sudden charge. Not yet.

But as he waited, their own scouts cantered back to the English lines.

'Are they far?' he cried as they raced past.

'One league, no more!' one man cried, and was gone.

'Three miles, men,' Berenger called unnecessarily. 'Give them another hour of the day and they'll be swarming all over that side of the field.'

'So long as they stay there!' Jack called.

Ed was nearby, and Berenger saw his pale features. 'Don't worry, boy. Stick to your duties and you'll be all right.'

There was a ripple of sound and then laughter. As Berenger turned and stared, he saw that a new banner had been unfurled in the English lines: a massive red flag with a golden dragon set upon it.

'What in God's name is that?' Geoff muttered.

'It looks as if the King's had a new flag made,' Berenger said.

Geoff sniffed. 'Very nice, I'm sure. But a silken dragon isn't going to win this battle for us. We need a couple of real ones.'

Berenger watched the shadows. It was closer to an hour and a half before the first of the vanguard of the French appeared over the ridge ahead.

424

But the time passed swiftly. While the men waited, some, like Berenger, unstringing their bows again and storing their strings safely, a roar went up from the main body of the English army, and Berenger made out a figure on a white palfrey, sitting calmly before the army and chatting. Something in the man's gestures caught his attention. And then, with a short, 'Aw, shite!' he recognised the fellow.

'Vintaine, stand straight. Clip, try to look like you're a brave, bold Englishman,' he hissed.

'Why?' Clip demanded. He was filthy to his armpits after shovelling soil all morning, and aching all over from lifting the heavy barrels of the gonnes into place.

'It's the King,' Berenger said.

'Archers, are you ready for this?' the King asked as he drew near the archers on the wing. 'Grandarse, is that you? In God's name, you will need a new belt soon! That one is too tight. Are your men eager? This will be a great day today, a glorious day. You know, I have ridden all over this land. It is my inheritance, and I always loved it. But this place I remembered, because I always felt it had a special significance for me. Here, I felt, I would prove that my country was as great as any – even France! We have been forced to bow the knee to France many times, but now it is we who are the stronger, and today we shall show it!

'Hold your courage! Remember that our cause is just. If we were hated by God, we would not have crossed the Seine or the Somme. We would have been held there, like rats waiting for the dogs to come and kill us. There we would have met the French hungry, thirsty, and without hope. It was God Who gave us our miracle and allowed us to cross the river so that Despenser could fetch us food and drink. And now look at us! We have made our way to this glorious field where we shall win renown for ever. Because I say this to you: in years to come, men will discuss your exploits here. They will say that they wished that they had been here at your side. For what happens here today will go down in history as the greatest battle of Christendom. You will defeat a French army. After today, no man will believe again that the French chivalry is superior to English.

'But remember: at all times, listen to your orders. Always remain in the ranks. Do not believe any feints by the enemy that are designed to tease you out from your positions in the battle. They will pretend to run in terror; do not give chase. They will fall back as though to retreat; let them. While we remain here, we are safe. Trust me: they cannot break us. Not here. So, friends, praise God, give Him your thanks, and eat a hearty meal. Before this day is out, we shall have won renown and glory, and in the future if any woman sees you, tell her you were here with me, and she will want to bed you immediately! Even *you*, Grandarse!'

There was a roar of delight at that, and several archers threw their hats in the air. As the handsome young King trotted back along the lines to chat to other soldiers, Berenger saw that the only archer not cheering was Geoff.

'Are you all right?' he asked.

'Aye, I'm fine,' he said. 'I just wish . . . oh, nothing.'

Berenger kept his eyes on the far hill. He stared at it as food arrived, thick stew that was slopped into their bowls and had to be scooped up with bread soaked in the gravy. He watched it as the food was taken away and women and boys with wineskins and jugs of ale wandered up and down the lines giving each man enough to keep them thirst-free. Many of them had to go and release their bladders afterwards, each receiving a curt, 'Don't leave the line again,' as they shamefacedly returned.

He watched the French line as the vanguard grew and swelled from a thin sprinkle of men into a thick carpet of colours and gleaming armour. Instead of a few figures, there was one mass, like a tide of men that moved and rippled in the failing light, broadening and becoming amorphous as the shape changed, suddenly developing into recognisable units, before they were washed away by a following wave of horsemen and additional foot-soldiers.

'Sweet Jesus, will you look at all that lot?' Walt said, aghast at the sight.

'Don't say it, Clip,' Jack growled.

'What? What d'you think I'd say at the sight of that army?' Clip's face had paled as he took in the view. 'By my faith, if the King's right, and God gave us a miracle when we crossed that river, do you think He has any more to spare for us now?'

'We could do with one,' Geoff muttered. 'What the devil does it matter though? Today is as good a day to die as any.'

They stared as the vast army formed into regular columns and the banners were brought forward. And then Berenger noticed a strange thing. None of the units and formations were stable. All were drifting forward like ships without anchors, as though they were impelled by an invisible tide. He frowned, patting his purse in brief reminder that there his bowstring lay, before peering more closely. 'They aren't stopping, are they?'

'I don't think they can, Frip.' Jack was gazing ahead raptly. 'The men behind are still marching, so those in front cannot halt. They're being pushed onward.'

Berenger nodded. Such a vast army of men would be impossible to direct. The English army itself was hard to command, and messages must be relayed at speed by riders to coordinate the army's march. The French army was many times larger, and seemed incapable of halting.

And their march seemed inexorable.

*　　*　　*

Sir John took a deep breath at the sight of the French troops rippling over the top of the ridge before him descending the slope towards the lower ground. To attack, they had to ride up the slope and into the teeth of the English archers. Yet still they kept coming. Men by the thousand, with the sun glinting from their spear-tips, making their helmets and mail glitter, and giving the red of their banners a demonic glow.

Dimly, on the afternoon air, the shouts of the French marshals could be heard, calling on their army to halt. The front rows of foot-soldiers and men-at-arms did stop, and some knights dismounted, but then they all rippled forward again, just as the waters of a river in flood would lap and then press on, reaching ever further.

'Richard, today we shall have our battle,' Sir John said, without looking at his esquire.

'God be with you, Sir John.'

'And you, Richard. Let us pray He will not look away from us this day.'

Sir John had been surprised to see the King's new banner. It was so unlike anything the English had seen before. Usually they fought under the King's own arms. And then Sir John saw that a vast banner was flying over the heads of the French, and understood: the Oriflamme of St Denis, the great crimson flag of the French kings since Charlemagne, was here. The two kings were setting their flags against each other as much as their armies. Their symbols of authority and confidence in God's support were there for all to see, fluttering gently in the breeze over their heads. Both claimed support from the same God and fought in His name, but only one could win today.

There were shouts along the English lines – defiance from some, jeers and insults from others – both intended to keep up their spirits, Sir John knew. He eyed the knights and men-at-arms who were near him: war-hardened men with the cold, indifferent eyes of professionals who knew themselves and their abilities. Behind them, the black-haired skirmishers and knife-men from Wales stood eagerly licking their lips and fiddling with their long daggers, gripping their pikes. There was an atmosphere of expectation now, not fear. Men ostentatiously took out their swords and studied the edges as if thinking they could have become blunted in the last few minutes, or adjusted thongs and strapping, tightening them in preparation.

Gradually a hush settled on the men. Sir John saw one man begin to convulse and then push through his companions to vomit on the grasses in front of them. He wasn't insulted or laughed at, however, but received encouraging comments and smiles. Two men patted him on the back as he returned to his post.

Sir John had none of that nausea. Only the old, familiar tension in his belly – and a slight feeling of doubt. In the lists he knew his position, he knew that the beast under him was reliable. He and Aeton together were an unstoppable force that could pass through any number of enemies, and to be waiting here without the reassuring bulk of Aeton beneath him, felt both strange and disquieting.

The French continued to advance.

'Sir John, do you see the people there on the roadway?'

Richard was pointing, and now Sir John saw a large number of people waving and egging the French on.

'So they have an audience for our defeat, do they?' Sir John said coolly. Somehow the sight of so many men and women determined to witness the destruction of the English was sufficient to calm him. His tension left him, and he eyed the approaching army with detached interest. 'They are proceeding in good order.'

'Crossbowmen to the fore. Genoese.'

'Yes, Richard. Soon they must stop and reorganise themselves into fighting formation. At present they are still in marching order.'

Even as he spoke, the first pattering of rain tinkled on the men's armour. A burst of lightning seared across the clouds, and a moment or two later the crackle of thunder was deafening. Sir John turned his face to the skies and closed his eyes, letting the cooling water strike his face and run down his cheeks. It was refreshing, and he wondered whether he would be one of those who would never again, after this day, feel the rain upon his face.

'They aren't stopping yet,' his esquire noted.

'They will,' Sir John said confidently, keeping his face to the sky.

A whim made him glance to the left, towards his archers. He saw them standing with their bows unstrung and nodded to himself. A good idea to keep their strings dry. But the crossbowmen in the plain before him were not so fortunate. This was more than a light shower, and their bows were all bent. It took a great effort to restring a heavy crossbow.

The rain was now falling in torrents, like a mass of grey pebbles smashing down on the field – and suddenly the field was hidden, as if a veil had been dropped over it. Sir John called to the men nearest: 'Be vigilant! The French may try to attack in the mists. Hold hard!'

He listened keenly, but there was nothing, only a clattering as drops as large as peas slammed against helmets, shields, armour. In moments the men-at-arms' tunics were soaked through. With the sides of his helmet giving him a strange sensation of being enclosed, imprisoned, it was hard for Sir John to make sense of the noises he could hear. A scream from the right made him turn, alarmed, but there was no other call. Later he heard that a man had been kicked by a destrier and had his leg shattered.

And then the rain was gone. The skies cleared again, and a warm, rich odour of damp soil rose to the aged knight's nostrils as the sun sprang out and illuminated the land. He took his sword's hilt and wiped it with a piece of tunic that was already so wet that it could achieve nothing, but he didn't notice. Gripping his sword again, he stared as the first of the men before him began once more to make their way forward.

'For God and Saint Boniface!' he shouted, and raised his sword high.

CHAPTER FIFTY-FOUR

Berenger and the men hunched their shoulders and peered through the thick rain, and then, when the downpour moved on, they saw the crossbowmen ahead of them.

'Archers! String your bows!' Berenger bellowed at the top of his voice, fumbling in his purse and grabbing his own cord. He snatched up an arrow and nocked it to the string, prepared to draw.

Watching, he felt his heart stop as the crossbowmen knelt and discharged their weapons. Most were aiming at the front rank of men-at-arms, but some were aiming at the archers, and Berenger had the feeling that a bolt there had been made for him and him alone. He felt the breath stop in his lungs, and saw the dark shadow rising against the sky as thousands of bolts flew. And then, to his astonishment, all the bolts fell harmlessly to earth many yards short of the English lines.

A roar came from behind him, and he heard '*Draw!*' Pulling the string and pushing away the bow, he leaned back, bending his right leg and lifting the arrow to the sky until the string touched his cheekbone and the arrow rested at the side of his face.

'*LOOSE!*'

It was a sound like no other: like a hundred thousand starlings flying past, like ten thousand whips whirling about a man's head. He felt the jolt of release in his left arm drawing him forward and rocking him on his broadly planted feet, but then there was the quick grab for the next arrow. Nock, draw, *loose*; nock, draw, *loose* – a constant, steady routine that dulled the senses. But it was essential work. Occasionally he glimpsed the battlefield, and when he did, he saw many corpses. The arrows the English sent up were so numerous that, when they fell, few could survive.

'*LOOSE!*'

As the arrows flew, a hundred and fifty thousand in every minute, they darkened the sky, as if another stormcloud was lying overhead and blotting out the sun. Surely those receiving this terrible tempest must feel that God had deserted them.

The crossbowmen still advanced, stolidly spanning and reloading their weapons, but more and more were felled. Already their numbers were reduced by a quarter, and as the next flight of arrows sheeted into them, Berenger felt a savage joy mingled with pity for the men who were out there, with no protection whatsoever.

'What the fuck are they playing at?' Grandarse snarled. He had come to join the men, and stood with a great bow clutched in his fist, staring down at the men struggling to cross the plain. 'Why don't they return our fire?'

'Their strings are wet and won't hold the tension. They can't reach us with their bolts,' Berenger said. He let fly, and watched his own and the other arrows rise, stoop – and plummet. Men were struck in the breast and the head. Two, he saw, ran screaming, with arrows in their bodies that they could not reach. Their shrieks of agony came clearly on the wind.

'So much the better,' Grandarse said with satisfaction. He took his own bow and sent an arrow hurtling towards them. 'I like being safe when the enemy approaches!'

Berenger nodded, but his own, unspoken sympathy lay with the hapless men out there. He had been on the receiving end of enemy bolts and arrows far too often not to feel some compassion.

'They're retreating! Sweet angels of mercy, they're pulling back!' Grandarse roared, and Berenger could see it too. The crossbowmen had taken enough. They were streaming back towards the bulk of the French cavalry, leaving in disorder, men taking out their knives and cutting their crossbows, throwing the expensive weapons away, already made useless, before the English could take them, and then running pell-mell for their own lines.

'Thanks be to God!' someone muttered, and when Berenger looked, he realised it was Ed. The Donkey was staring at them with tears in his eyes.

'They're bolting like bloody rabbits! They've had enough, and they're bolting!' a man shouted, and Sir John threw him a sour look.

'A few thousand crossbowmen leave the field, and you think that's a cause for celebration?' he said. 'There are plenty more waiting there in the wings.'

'We're going to win this battle,' another man said, and lifted his sword defiantly. 'Hey! We're here, France! If you think you can push us away, come and try it!'

Sir John gritted his teeth. It was fools like this who caused wars – fools like this who lost wars. 'Hold your tongues and hold your lines!' he commanded. 'That was only the first essay. Now will come the onslaught.'

'*Onslaught*, old man?' There was a rude laugh from behind him. 'They're already knocked back. One more little effort and we'll have the field.'

'Don't be a whore-swyving fool,' Sir John snarled. 'Look!'

The others turned and saw what Sir John had witnessed: as the crossbowmen fled, the horsemen in the first ranks spurred their mounts and charged down the farther hillside, straight into the running soldiers, and when they ran them down, it was no accident. As though blaming them for their inadequacy in bringing the English to their knees, the riders slashed and cut at the crossbowmen. Almost as many were hacked down as had been slain by the English arrows.

It was a bloodbath. The French knights had taken no more notice of the crossbowmen than they would of their enemies, slaying them with lance or sword or riding them down and trampling them. The poor fellows were caught between the hammer of their own knights, and the anvil of the English archers. To remain was to die, but to attempt to flee was to be killed by their own comrades. They fell in their hundreds, their bodies crushed into the mud by the knights on their huge destriers.

'Hold the line! Prepare to receive horses!' Sir John roared. He gripped his lance more tightly, setting the butt in the ground and gripping it tightly. 'Steady! *Steady!*'

Archibald darted from his gonne to those nearby, assessing the angles of fire and glancing up at the horses now thundering towards the English lines. He peered along the length of his barrel and as the horses began to come closer, closer. Grabbing his match, he blew on the smouldering cord until it glowed bright and white. And then, when the leading horse was almost in front of his barrel, he stood back and thrust the lighted match into the powder-hole of the gonne.

There was a vast belch of flame that engulfed the whole battlefield in stark horror. As the roar died away, all was obscured by a thick, grey-white smoke. The gynour's breath was sucked from him, and his ears felt as if water had been thrown into them: he had gone deaf. Choking fumes were blown into his face, and he shook his head, blinking, as he tried to see what his shot had achieved. As all cleared, he saw three horses thrashing, two riders stumbling towards the English lines, and one knight, dazed by the blast, walking in little circles that were leading him towards the archers. Three clothyard arrows found him.

Archibald moved to the next barrel while another man attacked the still-smoking barrel with a swab drenched in water. The next gonne sprang into the air as Archibald danced away, sending more flames to deal death to the French. His heart was also dancing, with excitement and – yes, with joy. There was nothing like this sensation, dealing death with the skill of a master-of-arms. He could kill and maim scores with his toys: this was the way to fight – with utter impunity.

A flash from the third gonne, and a gust of brimstone-filled smoke . . . and he saw two more horses rearing and thrashing in their agony. Archibald stopped for a moment, brought back to the present by their pain, but then he saw a fresh rank of knights thundering up the hill towards the English lines, and he ordered his men to reload their gonnes, while he leaned down and rammed and cleaned and dried, preparing the next charge, aiming as the beasts headed towards them.

Sir John waited, watching for the first of the French to reach the English lines, but none approached nearer than a few tens of yards. 'Hold your places!' he shouted as a couple of men-at-arms made as though to run at the wounded.

Now those same knights who had treated their own cross-bowmen with such cruelty were themselves slaughtered. Sir John saw the front row struck as though by an invisible rope: the foremost horses were killed at almost the same moment, plunging to the ground, while their riders were thrown or remained with their horses. Two men, he saw, lay trapped by their mounts' dead bodies, a leg caught beneath the steed. But as more and more arrows fell among them, these two were soon dead, stabbed by many arrows.

Another rank of horses and men were tumbled to the ground, then a third, and suddenly a mass of riders was making its way forward.

'Hold the wall! Shields and lances! For God and England!' he heard from all around, and he added his own, 'For Saint Boniface!' And then he added, 'For King Edward and for England!' And thrust the butt of his lance into the ground, pointing the tip at the enemy. He could hear the crackle of the banners overhead and feel the strange juddering in his legs. It was the ground, rebelling at the hoofbeats of thousands of horses. The very earth recoiled from the French attack.

There was no time to aim his lance. Suddenly the knights and destriers were all too close, and in the blink of an eye, they were on him.

It felt as though all those French lance-points were targeting his heart, his breast, his face. A matchless forest of steel-tipped lances were thrust towards him, but before any could reach him or the other men, the horses saw their danger. While many carried on, impaling themselves on the English weapons, many more reared or tried to run to one side or the other to avoid the bristling sharp steel points.

They crashed into each other, causing mayhem amongst the French chivalry. One beast ran along the English line, deflecting many lances, until a lucky stab brought him down.

Sir John felt his own lance pulled from his hand, and the butt was yanked from the soil and swiped at his legs, almost knocking him down. Before he could grab it again, three French men-at-arms appeared, their horses dead already, running at him.

Sir John pulled his sword free and hefted its weight with relief. This was the sort of fight he had trained for: the sort of fight he was born for.

CHAPTER FIFTY-FIVE

They charged and were repelled, charged and were repelled, and still they kept coming. Berenger had counted six charges already, but once more the men and horses were gathering at the other end of the field, and now they were charging again.

Archibald's gonnes roared and spat flames and missiles like an array of dragons, while from the other flank still more clouds of smoke were thrown at the French, and each time a few men were forced to the ground, a few more horses were slain.

There was an enormous cacophony of sound. Berenger felt a concussion at his ears, a searing flash of heat, and turned to see a bloom of flame. A figure was thrown high into the air, and the stench of brimstone was thick and cloying as wafts of greasy smoke rolled past them. Screams and shouts came from the edge of the archers' post, where Archibald stood with his gonnes.

Berenger let another arrow loose at the men approaching. More and more knights were thundering up the slope to the

English lines. He saw a strange group: knights, and a nobleman wearing three white feathers, riding together. Even when first one and then a second knight were hit and fell from their mounts, their horses remained with the rest, and he realised that they were all tied together as a group, as though their leader feared that one or more might attempt to flee the battle. All rode straight for the Prince's banner, and there was a moment when Berenger thought that they might succeed in punching through to him, but then there was a moment's blindness as the fog from Archibald's cannon rolled out, passing through them. They looked like wraiths in a mist, and then the smoke cleared and Berenger saw that the little party was dead. All had fallen before the English lines.

There was another massive charge building. It was the greatest collection of men he had ever seen, and his belly gave a lurch. Then three Frenchmen sprang forward, calling on their peers to ride with them. Suddenly, the whole line was moving: thousands of the noblest-born, best-trained warriors of Europe, mounted on the highest-quality destriers, first trotting, then beginning to canter, then lowering their heads and thundering at full gallop towards the centre of the English line. Berenger saw the English sergeants and vinteners rallying their men. He glimpsed the Earl of Warwick raising his massive sword over his head and shrieking his defiance, while nearby, Sir John de Sully was awaiting the enemy with a cool demeanour as though deciding which man he should aim his lance at first.

'ARCHERS! LOAD! ARCHERS LOOSE!' he heard, and aimed at a great black-armoured knight with a red surcoat. The arrow struck at the top of the man's shoulder and bounced away, and he rode on without injury.

There was a gathering rumble, a low roaring that came from thousands of French knights as each gave his battle cry from behind his visor. The noise rose as the knights came ever nearer, and Berenger could feel their charge through the soles of his feet. A crescendo of hoofbeats and screams, and the French slammed into them like a maul wielded by a giant. The English shields were up, and the array of spears did not waver. As the French came on, the horses were impaled and their riders thrown. Some lances penetrated, but only a small number of Englishmen were injured. Where Berenger stood, he could see the English lines rippling back and then springing forth again, their spears an impenetrable barrier.

A section of men was running up the slope now, more French men with armour and mail, coming to support their knights.

'*Archers!*' Grandarse's voice was hoarse from shouting, and now he directed the men's arrows to the enemy scurrying towards them. A fresh storm of arrows sleeted down, and the assault failed; many were killed. It was carnage. The sound of wailing and sobbing came up to him, but Berenger hardened his heart.

'Fripper! Fripper!'

He turned to find Ed pulling at his jack. 'What are you doing here, boy?' he snarled. 'Get back to your position!'

'A cannon blew up, and killed three men. Archibald needs help, or his gonnes will be overrun!'

Berenger turned back to the battlefield. He made a quick decision. 'Jack, Geoff, Clip – with me! *Now!*'

When the massed rank of French horsemen crashed into the English pikes and spears, Sir John was hurled backwards and his spear snapped. A blow struck his bascinet and, still clutching the broken shaft in his fist, he found himself on his back, staring up at the sky.

It was curiously peaceful. Men's legs hurried past, but he couldn't see any faces. A loud booming was in his ears, and he felt as though his body was floating, drifting, a few inches above the ground. It was calm there, as though he could merely close his eyes and doze off into sleep, and no one would bother him.

Then all rushed back into his consciousness. Blaring of horns and the screams and shouts. He was lying in a foul mud that had been drenched in the blood of the dead and thickened with faeces and flesh. His stomach lurched, and he rolled onto all fours, consumed by revulsion. Clambering to his feet, he discarded the stump of his lance with disgust and grabbed his sword.

The Prince was still standing beneath his banner, but Sir John could see that Edward of Woodstock was heavily pressed. French knights had seen his banner and were hacking at the knights about him. A knight fell even as he watched, and Sir John pulled down his visor and hefted his sword. Giving a shrill war cry, he threw himself into the fray, bringing his sword down heavily onto a man's forearm. There was a dull crack, and he was sure he had broken a bone beneath the mail. A blade struck his helmet, and his head was brought down by the blow, but then he span around, his sword at belly-height, and punched out with all his strength when it was level with the man's belt. His blade met the rings of the man's mail, and broke some, but didn't penetrate the thick leather coat beneath. He pulled his sword free and attacked the man's neck. A raised forearm blocked him, but he changed the direction of his weapon and thrust again, left hand gripping the blade. He felt the mail give again, and at the third stab he pierced it, and felt the steel slide greasily into the man's stomach. Giving the blade a twist and shove, he kicked the man away even as he began to collapse.

Another man, another sword aimed at his head. He ducked and heard the blade whistle over him like a bird of prey. Sir John rammed his head forward, feeling the top of his helmet crash into the man's face, then he jerked his head up, catching the front of the man's bascinet with the point of his own before shoving the tip of his sword up and beneath the man's helmet. It cut the man's chin but missed the soft, vulnerable base of his jaw. Sir John pulled it free and jabbed at the man's neck with the length of his blade, trying to cut away at it, but the mail was too strong.

The man fell away, but now another was before him, and Sir John was forced to retreat under the press of French men-at-arms. He found that he was being pushed back onto the Prince's group, with more lances and swords facing them than ever. He brought his blade down on one lance, but two more pointed at him, prodding his breast and belly. His armour was not the newest, but his coat of plates was strong, thank God, and he was safe enough. A horse reared above them all, and a sword slammed down on another man, but then the arm wielding the sword was grabbed by the man holding the Prince's banner. The horseman was dragged from his mount, still trying to fight, and died on the ground as three men hacked and bludgeoned at him. One man thrust his misericorde into the eye-slots of his visor, and the body jerked and twisted, then sagged.

The men about the Prince were exhausted, but they fought on like those possessed. There was no time to see who was who, only to glimpse the weapon being thrust towards them and to counter it: cut at them, grab them and pull the opponent off-guard, stab at them, thrust one's sword's pommel into their faces, smash gauntleted fists into them, batter them with the cross of one's sword – *anything* – to keep them at bay a little longer.

The hand-to-hand combat raged within the dwindling number of men about the Prince.

And then the Prince was no longer there.

Sir John was so weary from the battle that he had to blink. The Prince was gone! He had fallen! The French were cheering, and their attack redoubled – and even as Sir John felt the encroaching despair, he saw the Prince's banner fall, the material rippling as it was lowered to the ground like a kite in a feeble wind.

The sight gave him a fury that lent power to his arm. Shrieking like a demon of the moors, he fought with a renewed determination. If his Prince was dead, he would die on the same field. He hurled himself at his enemies, his sword now notched and dull, sending it crashing at faces and hands, at any limb or sign of weakness in mail or armour, and as he did so, he could hear the blood singing in his ears. A red fog enveloped him. All he saw was the man before him, then the next, and the next, and he fought like a berserker.

'For Saint Boniface!' he screamed.

A war hammer on a long pole slammed into his helmet with such force that the padded coif was crushed and he felt the metal crunch against his forehead. Blood washed into his eyes, and for a moment he could see nothing. He fell onto all fours and lifted his visor, wiping his face quickly, before trying to rise. A man's hand was on his back, and he felt a fresh blow that sent his senses reeling. It felt as though he was back aboard that damned ship when they landed from Portsmouth, the deck rolling beneath him and sending his gut into paroxysms. He waited for the next blow with fatalistic expectation.

'Sir John! Sir John – get up!' cried a voice. With a sudden recognition he realised it belonged to Richard, his esquire.

'Help me!' he grunted, and Richard put a hand under his armpit, hauling him upright once more.

The battle had ebbed, and Sir John had time to gaze about him as he got his breath back. So many bodies lay all about him, there was scarcely room to move. Many were Frenchmen, who had died in this undignified huddle while still more clambered over their bodies to fight.

'Sir John, I hope you are well, sir?' came another familiar voice.

'My Lord, I thought you were with the fallen!' Sir John said as the Prince grinned at him.

Edward of Woodstock was leaning on his sword, his long hair over his eyes. He had thrown aside his helmet for the nonce, while he panted for breath. Blood streaming from a gash in his forehead gave him a ferocious air. He looked like a Lyme pirate, Sir John thought, and felt his heart go out to the lad.

'Me? That is villeiny-saying, Sir John! You think I would dare desert the field by dying?' He laughed. 'I am about as dead as you are! And you look marvellously well, old friend.'

'I am, my lord,' Sir John said. The Prince's banner stood above them again, Sir Thomas Daniel clinging to it like a drowning sailor gripping a spar, as though it was all that kept him upright. 'I thought I saw your banner fall, too. Was that a dream?'

'No, Sir John. My foolish bearer considered that I was about to be bested by the enemy, and allowed the banner to slip while he drew steel to help me, but I have instructed him to hold it aloft once more. I don't wish my father to grow concerned for my health.'

He laughed again, wiping blood from his brow. 'I won't have any man running to demand help. This is *my* victory!'

Sir John nodded and stared ahead again. The French were reforming. Down at the far side of the rolling valley, their knights were shouting encouragement at the men-at-arms and horsemen, urging and cajoling them to return to the fray.

'Christ's blood, here they come again,' he said.

CHAPTER FIFTY-SIX

Berenger and the men ran to where Archibald was struggling, red-faced, with a massive iron spike, trying to roll his biggest gonne back onto the trestle where it had been set.

'Come on, you bastard, gutless lurdan! What, do you defy God's representative? In God's name, I command that you obey, in *nomine patris et . . .*'

'What in Christ's heaven happened here?' Berenger demanded.

There were shards of metal all about the place. A great splinter had embedded itself in the side of the nearest cart, and there were many smouldering remains that looked much like parts of men.

'They loaded it with too much powder, the bitch-clout deofols!' Archibald said with contempt. 'And then had the temerity to leave a powder keg open nearby, if you can believe it! Now are you going to help me get this damned lump of metal facing the enemy or not? I asked for your help, not for you to come and gawp!'

In a short time Berenger and the men were using great iron bars to roll the enormous bulk of the cannon back into the bed created for it. As it butted up to the timbers set in the ground, Archibald began bellowing at the bemused archers, pointing to a long rod with rags wrapped about one end sitting in a leather bucket. 'Fripper, grab that, man, bring it here! That's right,' he said, shoving the wet rags home into the barrel. He twisted and fiddled with it, then pulled it out again. Another rod with a blackened and filthy sheepskin wrapped about it lay on the grass nearby, and Archibald took it up and rammed that home. 'Ed!'

The Donkey was already at his side, his face red and sweaty, with streaks where perspiration had cut through the soot on his cheeks and brow. He held a long pole with a rounded copper shovel like a cylinder cut in half at the end, which was filled with coarse grains of Archibald's black powder. Archibald took it from him and gently inserted it into the barrel, turning the rod over so that the powder was all deposited in the barrel. He shoved a wooden plug after it, and poked it home with the back of the powder-scoop, before taking up a linen bag of stones and placing it in the tube. It too was pushed up to rest against the plug.

'Where are they, Donkey?' he rasped as he hurried to the opposite end of the gonne. He blew at the touch-hole's little dent, and took a small amount of powder from the flask under his shirt, tipping it into the dent and cupping his hand over it to stop it blowing away.

'They are coming now.'

'Very well. Stand back, the lot of you!' Archibald roared, and peered along the length of his barrel.

'Donkey, the match.'

Ed picked up the cord and blew on it carefully. Berenger saw the end begin to glow like coals in a fire, and when it was a brilliant red, Ed passed it to Archibald.

The gynour took it up, blew on it once more, and peered down the length of the barrel as he did so, aiming the tube at his enemy, his eyes narrowed. As the first of the enemy appeared through the mist, he held the match just above the touch-hole, waiting. When there were a hundred men visible, he touched the vent.

There was a deafening roar and a belch of smoke that almost, but not quite, concealed the vast purple and scarlet flames. An ochre-yellow tinge to the smoke made it look like poison, and then it was gone, and a thick, black fume washed past the men, carrying the unmistakable stench of brimstone.

Sir John irritably jerked away from the hands that tried to help him, and returned to his place in the line. 'I'm not a cripple! Leave me alone. There are men who need help, but I'm not one.'

His esquire returned with him and stood silently at his side as they stared down at the enemy. The French were running up the hill towards them again, many thousands, all on foot, and Sir John grasped a lance from the ground at his feet, sheathing his sword. 'One last push, men – one last push! For God and Saint Boniface!'

'For God and Saint Edward!' his esquire shouted beside him.

'Who?' Sir John demanded.

'Saint Edward,' Richard Bakere repeated calmly.

Sir John shook his head in disgust and turned back to the men coming to attack them. 'If you must . . . Form up! Hold the line, no matter what! *Hold the line!*'

Berenger coughed as the worst of the smoke curled lazily away. A swathe had been cut through the men racing towards them. While Archibald scurried with Ed to load another consignment of pebbles, Berenger bellowed at his men to return to the archers' stands where their arrows awaited them. They only had a paltry number with them, for Donkey was entirely involved with Archibald. Once back to their positions, they took up their bows in earnest. Each shot must count.

The men running up the hill were tired. They had marched for miles that day, encumbered with their heavy weapons, and now they were forced to charge uphill to attack the English in their impregnable position. Berenger nocked an arrow and drew back the string. The muscles in the back of his neck, his shoulder-blades, his upper arms, his belly – all were complaining at the fresh assault. He could still lift his bow and send arrows after his targets, but the strain of drawing a bow powerful enough to spear an arrow through an inch of oak was beginning to tell. It was a white-hot, searing agony that burned all his muscles without respite.

'Draw! Loose!'

The orders still came, and through the mists and smoke Berenger saw the French forces hurled to the ground as the arrows from around ten thousand archers took their toll. While their rate of fire had slowed from their peak, there were still four or five arrows rising into the air every minute from each of them: forty to fifty thousand arrows plunging down into the midst of the French army in an unremitting hail of death. The English stood safely distant, letting their arrows kill a hundred yards and more away.

There came a thunderous bark, and again the men were blinded as Archibald's great gonne fired. The sharper crackle of the smaller gonnes was almost a chattering compared with the vast bellow of that enormous maw. As it fired, Berenger saw French men before it slashed and dismembered before the smoke rolled thankfully before him and obliterated the sight.

There was a hideous sound now: an insane keening from men, horses, dogs, which verily grated on the soul. It was a terrible, horrible sound, and Berenger grabbed arrows and loosed still faster, trying to block it from his ears.

It was Jack who bellowed and pointed as the smoke cleared.

A group of the French had split away from the main body, and fifty or more were rushing at the gonnes and Archibald. Berenger shouted to the nearer men to have them redirect their arrows, but it was too late.

'With me!' he roared, and ran for the gonnes.

Archibald fired the charge and felt the ground shake as the great gonne leaped up in her bed.

He adored this beast. She was the largest of the big gonnes, and had the power to slaughter at a great distance. If treated with consideration, she would perform her duty with reliable, deadly effect.

Seeing Ed and Béatrice near the powder, he beckoned. They had to reload the gonne again. But the foolish boy was pointing and mouthing something. He could mouth all he liked, Archibald could hear only a dull ringing in his ears. 'Get over here, you Donkey,' he bawled. It was strange to be able to bellow at the top of his voice and hear almost nothing! He waved his arms to attract the boy's attention.

It was at the last moment that he finally realised Ed was shouting a warning about something behind him. He turned, the great iron pole in his fist still, and saw more than forty men rushing at him.

'*Christ's cods!*' he managed, before hefting his makeshift weapon and facing them with determination.

There was a contingent of archers near, and they loosed. Archibald saw three men flung aside as they caught the brunt of

451

it, one of them hit by four arrows together. Another man was left on his feet and running, but with an arrow in his shoulder. And still they came on.

'Come on, then, you whoreson deofols! I'm ready for you!' he shouted, and hefted the pole over his head.

Just then four more of the men fell, all with arrows in their chests. He turned to see Berenger and the vintaine, all sending arrows to the French, but it was too late, and soon the men were at them.

Archibald brought the pole down on the head of the nearest, and it entirely crushed his head and helmet with its massive weight. The next man caught the spike at his throat, where it mashed flesh against his spine. He fell, choking for air. Then Archibald was holding the pole half-staff, half the pole between his two fists. He sent one end into a man's face, used the bar between his hands to block a sword, and jabbed with the other end to knock senseless a man trying to grab for Ed.

Berenger was fighting nearby, coolly despatching men with a sword in one hand, his long-bladed dagger in the other, blocking and stabbing with the speed of an adder in the sun. Geoff was fighting with skill and vigour, but then something happened that made Archibald blink in astonishment.

A man had spotted Béatrice, and he rushed towards her, past Geoff. Archibald knew nothing of Geoff's murder of his family, but he saw the anguish in Geoff's face at that moment.

For Geoff, in that split second he saw before him again the face of his wife: Sarra's throat cut where he had killed her, the two boys dead beside her. A wave of revulsion washed through him, self-hatred at his actions that accursed night. He was nothing – a lustful, murderous brute at best. He remembered Gil, and the way he had stepped into the line ahead of the Donkey, and suddenly he saw why. Gil had been tired of this life, and more than ready for death.

And in that moment, Geoff made a decision. He cut wildly at the man heading for Béatrice. It was a lucky blow, and the man collapsed. Béatrice stood stock still, staring at her attacker in shock, while Geoff thrust at him until he was dead. And then Geoff stared at Béatrice, panting, and he smiled at her – a smile of great sweetness – before, with a roar of rage, he threw himself into the fray.

Hacking and slashing without elegance or care, he killed four and continued on into the midst of the men, his blade whirling with mad abandon in the fading light. His sword slammed into the face of one man, then came down dully on the helmet of a second, before piercing a man's visor, the blood spurting from the grille. As that man fell, Geoff put his head back and screamed in glee and fury before launching himself like an Angel of Death upon the rest of the French.

He was an awesome sight, but even as Archibald cast himself on the next man, he saw the three who closed in on Geoff. Two held his sword at bay while the third went behind him and stabbed at the back of his neck, between helmet and mail. The blade sank in deeply, and Geoff howled like a baited bear, turning to his adversary, but even as he lifted his sword to kill his assailant, the other two set about him. His fist was taken off at the wrist, a sword entered him from beneath the armpit, and Geoff fell to his knees, his head down, the blood scarring the grass all about him.

'No!' Archibald shouted and slammed his pole into another man, attempting to reach Geoff, but it was too late. The next time he saw the archer, Geoff's face was pressed into the bloody mud of the field.

That was when Archibald felt someone grip his shoulder, and he found Berenger at his side, staring before them at the field.

The French who were alive still were fleeing. There were no more attacks.

The space before Sir John and the other men was suddenly clear, and for a moment he thought his eyes had failed. He felt he could not trust his senses, and he stood panting for a while as the noise of battle receded all about him. Raising his visor once again, he took a deep breath as he stared about.

As the last men straggled or limped away, the field was a scene of unremitting carnage. Horses stood whimpering, while others thrashed about in agony on the grass. Horses with their rich caparisons smothered in gore, men in armour, in jerkins or mail, were all thrown hither and thither, as if a giant had stumbled upon them and had stamped and beaten them all to death. It was a vision of Hell. Here and there, an arm waved or a flag fluttered in the breeze, and on the still air coughs, sobs and cries for *Maman* could be heard. A horse floundered in the mess, trying to climb to his feet, but his hooves were entangled in his own intestines.

'*Horses!*' Sir John called, and through the ranks behind, he saw the reserves parting to allow the horses through. The first was that of a knight who lay at Sir John's feet, but a man-at-arms took it willingly and mounted before Sir John's horse had arrived.

'Sir John!' his esquire said, and presented him with Aeton.

'Very good,' Sir John said, and mounted stiffly. His muscles burned, but he would not miss the last episode of the battle, and as he sat on the tall saddle, he found some of his weariness falling away. His legs were gripping the beast beneath him as usual, and he felt the great muscles move, the enormous chest inflate and sink again, and it was as though his life-force was renewed by the sensation. When he gripped his sword, it felt entirely natural.

This was his destiny.

'After them!'

CHAPTER FIFTY-SEVEN

Berenger roared until he was hoarse as the English knights thundered past, the destriers' hooves throwing up massive clods of earth and grass. They could all see the French forces halt at the sight of the English racing down from both flanks. Suddenly, there was mayhem out there.

'Go on! Go on!' Jack was screaming excitedly at the top of his voice, waving his hands high over his head.

In the distance, Berenger could see the Oriflamme waving. Suddenly, he saw it dip and disappear. The French infantry were turning and fleeing the English knights. He could see Sir John's banner, and those of Warwick, Cobham, Burghersh and Dagworth, all galloping towards the terrified French.

'Their King's fled the field!' someone shouted. 'He's bolted!'

Berenger didn't know if that was true or not, but the Oriflamme was gone, and the collection of men about it had also disappeared.

Twilight was overwhelming the field as the English knights pounded after their foe. Screams came across the still evening air as they speared more of the enemy, and Berenger could see the line of English knights and men-at-arms breasting the far hill and then disappearing over the farther side in their pursuit.

With a blossoming of flame, the windmill behind the English lines caught fire. It would serve to mark the English army for returning soldiers.

Exhausted, the archers squatted or lay where they had fought. Berenger craved a cup or two of wine, but there was nothing here. He sat, his back to one of Archibald's gonnes and stared at the field, to where Geoff's body lay.

'Are you injured?'

He looked up to see Béatrice. 'No, maid. Are you?'

She shook her head.

'All this, does it help you?' he asked, tired to his very soul.

'All the men in France cannot bring back my father or my family,' she said. 'It's all gone. I have nothing.'

Berenger nodded. 'Nor have I,' he said. 'I lost my family long ago.'

She sat beside him, and they leaned together from mutual understanding. It was completely dark when he felt her sobbing gently.

Ed slumped on the ground as the battlefield began to empty. Only the bodies remained. So many bodies! Already men were walking about the dead and dying, giving a merciful killing stab where it was needed, and robbing the rest.

'Come on, lads,' Jack called. 'Ed, you too. There should be rich pickings here today!'

Ed was still walking as though in a trance as he followed slowly. A man lay at his feet, an older man with a grizzled beard and bright blue eyes set in a sun-browned face. In his breast was a trio of arrows, but there was no pain in his features, and no blood marred them. He might have been dozing in the sun. And next to him was a boy, perhaps only Ed's age, with his arm cut away and an expression of utter terror on his face.

'Could have been you, eh, brat?' Erbin said. He had come up behind Ed, and now stood watching him, his knife in his hand.

Ed had no words for him. He stood staring, too numbed to flee or fight.

'You bore yourself well. You've seen a great battle today,' Erbin said. He motioned to the bodies before them. 'A greater battle than most will see in their lives.'

'I have seen enough.'

'Really?' Erbin chuckled. 'I doubt it. War gets into a man's blood.'

'Like you, you mean? Well, I don't want to be like you! Robbing a boy who had bought me ale.'

'You bought us ale and we drank it, boy. But we thought you would clear off afterwards. It didn't occur to me that you'd come here. Nor that you'd invent stories about us.'

'What stories? You robbed me outside the tavern that night in Portsmouth. You broke my teeth.'

'That's what Tyler said you'd been saying about us,' Erbin spat. He grabbed Ed's jack and pulled him close. 'Listen here! I don't know who beat you, but we stayed in the tavern that night and embarked the following morning. We didn't follow you – we didn't attack you. Why you want to spread malicious stories about me and the men, I don't know, but you had better stop, if you don't want to be left dangling from a rope again.'

'What do you mean "Tyler said"?'

'He told us you'd been telling lies – blaming me and the boys for robberies and things. We aren't thieves, boy. And when someone calls us names like that, we'll give him something to complain about.'

'When did he tell you this?' Ed asked, a terrible suspicion forming.

'Ages ago. How should I know? Just stop spreading your lies.'

Ed didn't speak. In his mind, he was remembering that night in the alley, when a tall, dark figure had punched him in the face and taken his purse. And then he looked back at the short figure of Erbin.

Tyler was walking among the dead. He stopped at a body and started tugging at a ring. When he looked up and saw Ed staring at him, he smiled and waved. And Ed knew who had attacked him.

'I'll have my revenge,' he swore to himself. 'Oh yes, you churl. I'll have my revenge on you.'

Berenger walked about the field with a sense of awe. Men were picking trinkets from among the bodies, like so many carrion birds at a midden. It was no surprise that a man would never eat a crow after witnessing the result of a battle, but to see men robbing the dead and injured was to see them at their bestial worst.

Archibald stood bawling at some men to clear a path about his gonnes so that he could bring his wagon up to replenish his stores of powder and shot, but while guards and others tried to explain that the King wished for all the army to stand on the ground, Archibald could hear nothing said to him. His ears were ringing as though inside a church bell while the clapper struck.

Berenger left him to his argument, and stood a short way off, gazing over the field.

He had never seen so many bodies in one place. He saw one knight still sitting in his saddle on top of a second horse and rider. All four were pricked with a profusion of arrows. The stench of death was overpowering.

This, then, was the path he had chosen. To live and to die in dealing death. Berenger was transfixed, overwhelmed by the thought that so many souls could be snuffed out in a single afternoon.

'A grim sight, eh, Frip?' Grandarse had joined Berenger and now stood, hoicking his belt about his waist. From one shoulder dangled a wineskin. 'But I'll not deny that I'm glad it's them sprawled in the shit, and not us, eh?'

Berenger nodded.

'There'll be more all around here. The knights will have a merry hunt this night and tomorrow,' Grandarse added comfortably.

'What do we do now?' Berenger muttered.

'Now? Man, the King already knows where the worst pirates are, doesn't he? We'll be heading for Calais, to burn their ships and punish the populace for their behaviour. And then, when we've done that, we'll head for home. Aye, I'd reckon,' he added, pulling the stopper from his wineskin and drinking deeply, 'we'll be home by autumn – Christmas definitely. And then we'll be lauded from one end of the kingdom to the other for our glorious victory.'

He lowered the skin and passed it to Berenger. 'Sup this, Vintener,' he said, his mood sombre now. 'And in the future, when all the churls in a tavern are falling over themselves to buy you a drink to celebrate this glory, be grateful that you will never again have to see butchery on this scale. Never, ever again. Christ Jesus, I swear that the French King must accept our King's right! If ever God gave proof of His support, it was today. I doubt we'll ever see a victory like this again in our lifetimes.'

'In God's name, let us pray that you are right,' Berenger said, and he drank deeply of the wine.